"The Pola[r Treasure]"

M000025656

and
"Pirate of the Pacific"

TWO CLASSIC ADVENTURES OF

DOC SAVAGE

REG. U.S PAT. OFF.

by Lester Dent
writing as Kenneth Robeson

with a new historical essay
by Will Murray

Published by Sanctum Productions for
NOSTALGIA VENTURES, INC.
P.O. Box 231183; Encinitas, CA 92023-1183

Copyright © 1933 by Street & Smith Publications, Inc. Copyright © renewed 1960 by The Condé Nast Publications, Inc. All rights reserved.

This edition copyright © 2007 by Sanctum Productions/Nostalgia Ventures, Inc.

Doc Savage copyright © 2007 Advance Magazine Publishers Inc./The Condé Nast Publications. "Doc Savage" is a registered trademark of Advance Magazine Publishers Inc. d/b/a The Condé Nast Publications.

"Intermission" © 2007 by Will Murray.

This Nostalgia Ventures edition is an unabridged republication of the text and illustrations of two stories from *Doc Savage Magazine,* as originally published by Street & Smith Publications, Inc., N.Y.: *The Polar Treasure* from the June 1933 issue, and *Pirate of the Pacific* from the July 1933 issue. Typographical errors have been tacitly corrected in this edition. This is a work of its time. Consequently, the text is reprinted intact in its original historical form, including occasional out-of-date ethnic and cultural stereotyping.

ISBN: 1-932806-62-8   13 Digit: 978-1-932806-62-5

First printing: May 2007

Series editor: Anthony Tollin
P.O. Box 761474
San Antonio, TX 78245-1474
sanctumotr@earthlink.net

Consulting editor: Will Murray

Copy editor: Joseph Wrzos

Proofreader: Carl Gafford

The editors gratefully acknowledge the contributions of Tom Stephens, Scott Cranford and the Lester Dent Estate, in the preparation of this volume, and William T. Stolz of the Western Historical Manuscript Collection of the University of Missouri at Columbia for research assistance with the Lester Dent Collection.

Nostalgia Ventures, Inc.
P.O. Box 231183; Encinitas, CA 92023-1183

Visit Doc Savage at www.nostalgiatown.com

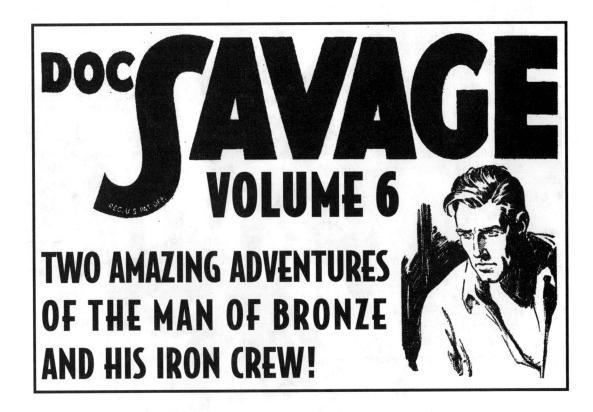

DOC SAVAGE VOLUME 6

REG. U S PAT. OFF.

TWO AMAZING ADVENTURES OF THE MAN OF BRONZE AND HIS IRON CREW!

Thrilling Tales and Features

**Cover paintings by Walter M. Baumhofer
Interior illustrations by Paul Orban**

Doc Savage fights against the devastating elements of the Northland, and against the cruel ruthlessness of a crooked mind staking all to gain

The Polar Treasure

By KENNETH ROBESON

Chapter I
THE BRONZE NEMESIS

SOMETHING terrible impended.

This was evident from the furtive manner of the small, flat-chested man who cowered in the shadows. He quaked like a terrified rabbit at each strange sound.

Once a cop came along the alley-like side street, slapping big feet heartily on the walk, twiddling his nightstick, and whistling "Yankee Doodle." The prowler crawled under a parked car, and lay there until the happy cop passed.

Nearby loomed the enormous bulk of the New York Concert Hall. From the stage door on the side street crept strains of a music so beautiful that each note seemed to grasp the heart with exquisite fingers.

A violin!

It was a Stradivarius violin, one of the most perfect in the world, and had cost the player sixty thousand dollars.

The player was a blind man!

He was Victor Vail. Many music lovers maintained him to be the greatest living master of the violin. He ordinarily got hundreds of dollars for rendering an hour of violin music before an audience. Tonight he played for charity, and got nothing.

The flat-chested man, cowering and fearful, knew little of Victor Vail. He only knew the music affected him strangely. Once it made him think of how his poor mother had sobbed that first time he went to jail, long years ago. He nearly burst into tears.

Then he got hold of his emotions.

"Yer gettin' goofy!" he sneered at himself. "Snap out of it! Ya got a job to do!"

SOON afterward, a taxi wheeled into the side street. It looked like any other New York taxi. But the driver had his coat collar turned up, and his cap yanked low. Little of his face could be seen.

The cab halted. The small man scuttled out to it.

"Ya ready for de job?" he whined.

"All set," replied the cab driver. He had a very coarse voice. It was as though a hoarse bullfrog sat in the taxi. "Go ahead with your part, matey."

The flat-chested man squirmed uneasily. "Is dis guy gonna be croaked?" he muttered anxiously.

"Don't worry about that end of it!" snarled the driver. "We're handlin' that. Keelhaul me, if we ain't!"

"Cripes! I know—but I ain't so hot about gettin' mixed up in a croakin'—"

A thumping growl came out of the cab.

"Pipe down! You've already shipped with this crew, matey! Lay to an' do your bit of the dirty work!"

Now that the man in the taxi spoke excitedly, one thing about his speech was even more noticeable. He had been a seafaring man in the past! His speech was sprinkled with sailor lingo.

The small man shuffled away from the cab. He entered the stage door of the concert auditorium.

Victor Vail had finished his violin playing. The audience was applauding. The hand-clapping was tremendous. It sounded like the roar of Niagara, transferred to the vast hall.

The flat-chested man loitered backstage. Applause from the delighted audience continued many minutes. It irked the man.

"De saps!" he sneered. "You'd t'ink Sharkey had just kayoed Schmeling, or somethin'!"

After a time, Victor Vail came to his dressing room. The blind maestro was surrounded by a worshipful group of great singers and musicians.

But the loitering man shouldered through them. His shoving hands, none too clean, soiled the costly gowns of operatic prima donnas, but he didn't care.

"Victor Vail!" he called loudly. "I got a message for yer from Ben O'Gard!"

The name of Ben O'Gard had a marked effect on Victor Vail. He brought up sharply. A smile lighted his artistic features.

Victor Vail was tall, distinguished. He had hair as white as cotton, and almost as fine. His formal dress was immaculate. His costly valet had seen to that.

His eyes did not seem like a blind man's—until an observer noticed it made no difference to Victor Vail whether they were open or shut.

"Yes!" he cried delightedly. "What is the message from Ben O'Gard?"

The intruder eyed the persons nearby.

"It's kinda private," he suggested.

"Then you shall speak to me alone." Victor Vail waved his admirers back. He led the way to his dressing room, only a hand thrust out before him showing he was blind.

THE flat-chested man entered first. Victor Vail followed, closing the door. He stood with his back to the panel a moment. His thoughts seemed delving into his past.

"Ben O'Gard!" he murmured reverently. "I have not heard that name for fifteen years! I have often sought to find him. I owe my life to Ben O'Gard. And now that worldly success has come to me, I should like to show my gratitude to my benefactor. Tell me, where is Ben O'Gard?"

"In de street outside." said the flat-chested man, trembling a little. "He wants ter chin with yer."

"Ben O'Gard is outside! And he wishes to talk to me!" Victor Vail whipped the dressing-room door open. "Take me to my friend! Quickly!"

The dirty man guided the blind master of the violin to the stage door.

Just before he reached the door, something happened which made the guide feel as if a bucket of ice water had been poured on him.

He saw the bronze man!

The bronze man presented a startling figure. He did not look like a giant—until it was noticed that some fairly husky men near him seemed puny, pale specimens in comparison. The big bronze man was so well put together that the impression was not of size, but of power. The bulk of his mighty form was forgotten in the smooth symmetry of a build incredibly powerful. His dress was quiet, immaculate, but expensive.

The bronze of this remarkable man's hair was a little darker than the bronze of his features. The hair was straight, and lay down tightly as a metal skullcap. A genius at sculpture might have made it.

Most striking of all were the eyes. They glittered like pools of flake gold as backstage lights played on them. They seemed to exert a hypnotic influence, a quality that would make the most rash individual hesitate.

So pronounced was the strange power of those golden eyes that the flat-chested rat shivered and looked away. Chill perspiration oozed out of his sallow skin. He glanced back uneasily, saw the weird golden eyes still upon him, and felt an overpowering impulse to run and hide in the darkest dive of the vast city.

He was very glad to get into the outer darkness.

"WHERE is Ben O'Gard?" Victor Vail asked eagerly.

"Aw, hold yer ponies!" snarled the flat-chested fellow. "I'm leadin' yer to 'im, ain't I?"

He was suddenly very worried—about the bronze man. The strange golden eyes seemed still boring into his back. He turned his head to make sure this wasn't so.

He wondered who the bronze giant was. He couldn't be a detective—no dick could ever wear dress clothes as immaculately as this astounding man had worn them.

"Cripes!" whimpered the rat. "Just lookin' at dem gold glims made me feel like I'd been kicked in de belt. What's de matter wit' me, anyhow?"

He didn't know it, but he wasn't the first man who had quailed before those weird golden eyes.

"Is it far to where Ben O'Gard waits?" Victor Vail inquired anxiously.

"Yer about dere."

They came abreast of a darkened doorway. Out in the street, a taxicab had been keeping even with them. This cab held the sinister seafaring man who had sent the small man into the concert hall after Victor Vail.

The musician's guide looked into the murky door. He made sure several men lurked there. He grasped Victor Vail's arm.

"Yer dere now!" he snarled.

Then he smashed a fist against Victor Vail's jaw.

Simultaneously, the gloomy doorway spouted the men it concealed. They pounced upon the famed blind violinist.

Victor Vail fell heavily from the traitorous guide's fist blow. But the sightless musician was more of a man than his assailants had expected. Though he could not get to his feet, he fought from his clumsy position on the sidewalk.

He broke the nose of one attacker with a lucky kick. His hands found the wrist of another. They were artistic hands, graceful and long and very powerful. He twisted the wrist in his grasp.

The man whose arm he held let out a shriek. It blared like a siren over the rumble of New York night traffic. The fellow spun madly to keep his arm from breaking.

The murk of the street aided the blind man, just as it hampered his assailants. The world he lived in was always black.

Blows whistled, thudded. Men hissed, cursed, yelped, groaned. Bodies fell noisily. Laboring feet scuffed the walk.

"Lay aboard 'im, mateys!" howled the seafaring man from his cab. "Make 'im fast with a line! And load 'im aboard this land-goin' scow! Sink 'im with a bullet if you gotta! Keelhaul 'im!"

A bullet wasn't necessary, though. A clubbed pistol reduced the fighting Victor Vail to quivering helplessness. A thin rope looped clumsily about his wrists and ankles. After the fashion of city dwellers, the men were slow with the knots.

"Throw 'im aboard!" shouted the seafarer in the cab. "Let a swab who knows knots make 'im ship-shape!"

The gang lifted Victor Vail, bore him toward the taxi.

And then the lightning struck them!

THE lightening was the mighty bronze man! His coming was so swift and soundless that it seemed magic. Not one of blind Victor Vail's attackers saw the giant metallic figure arrive. They knew nothing of its presence until they felt its terrible strength.

Then it was as though a tornado of hard steel had struck them. Chins collapsed like eggshells. Arms were plucked from sockets and left dangling like strings.

The men screamed and cursed. Two flew out of the mêlée, unconscious, not knowing what had vanquished them. A third dropped with his whole lower face awfully out of shape, and he, too, didn't know what had hit him.

Others struck feverishly at the Herculean bronze form, only to have their fists chop empty air. One man found his ankles trapped as in a monster vise of metal. He was lifted. His body swung in a terrific circle, mowing down his fellows like a scythe.

"Sink 'im, mateys!" shrilled the seafaring man in the cab. "Scuttle 'im! Use your guns—"

A piercing shriek from one of his hirelings drowned out the sailor's urgings. The unfortunate one had been inclosed in banding bronze arms. The fearsome arms tightened. The man's ribs breaking made a sound as of an apple crate run over by a truck. The fellow fell to the walk as though dead when released.

Incredible as it seemed, but two of Victor Vail's assailants remained who were capable of lifting as much as an arm. The sailorman in the taxi was unhurt, and one villain was upright on the walk. Even an onlooker who had seen that flashing battle with his own eyes would have doubted his senses, such superhuman strength and agility had the bronze giant displayed.

The man upright on the walk abruptly spun end over end for the taxi. He had been propelled by what for the bronze man was apparently but a gentle shove. Yet he caved in the rear door of the cab like a projectile would.

The seafaring hack driver got scared.

"Well, keelhaul me!" he choked.

He slammed the car in gear. He let out the clutch. The cab wrenched into motion.

The sailor saw the bronze man flash toward him. The metallic Nemesis of a figure suddenly looked as big as a battleship to the seafaring man. And twice as dangerous! He clawed out a spike-snouted pistol of foreign make. He fired.

The bullet did nothing but break the plate-glass window in a shoe shop. But the bronze giant was forced to whip into the shelter of a parked car.

The seafaring man kept on shooting, largely to prevent his vehicle being boarded. His lead gouged lone rips in the car behind which the bronze man had taken shelter, broke windows in a book store and a sea-food restaurant and scared a fat man far up the street so badly that he fainted.

The taxi skidded around a corner and was gone.

BLIND Victor Vail abruptly found himself being lifted to his feet by hands which were unbelievably powerful, yet which possessed a touch gentle as that of a mother fondling her babe. He felt a tug at his wrists.

Something was happening which he would not have thought possible. Bronze fingers were snapping the ropes off Victor Vail's wrists as effortlessly as though they were frail threads!

The sightless man had been dazed during the furious fight. But his ears, keener than an ordinary man's because of his affliction, had given him an idea of the momentous thing which had happened. Some manner of mighty fighter had come to his rescue. A fighter whose physical strength was almost beyond understanding!

"Thank you, sir," Victor Vail murmured simply.

"I hope you were not damaged seriously," said the bronze man.

It struck Victor Vail, as he heard his benefactor speak for the first time, that he was listening to the voice of a great singer. It had a volume of power and tone quality rarely attained by even the great operatic stars. A voice such as this should be known throughout the music world. Yet Victor Vail had never heard it before.

"I am only bruised a little," said the musician. "But who—"

The loud clatter of running feet interrupted him. Police were coming, drawn by the shots. A burly sergeant pounded from one direction. Two patrolmen galloped from the other. A radio squad car careened into the street with siren moaning in a way that stood one's hair on end.

Cops raced for the giant bronze man. Their guns were drawn. They couldn't see him any too well in the murk.

"Stick 'em up!" boomed the sergeant.

Then a surprising thing happened.

The policeman lowered his gun so hastily he nearly dropped it. His face became actually pale. He couldn't have looked more mortified had he accosted the mayor of the city by mistake.

"Begorra, I couldn't see it was you, sor," he apologized.

The bronze giant's strong lips quirked the faintest of smiles. But the sergeant saw the smile—and beamed as if he had just been promoted to a captaincy.

A roadster was parked nearby. It was a very powerful and efficient machine. The top was down. The color was a reserved gray.

Not another word was spoken. The bronze man escorted Victor Vail to the machine. The roadster pulled away from the curb. The police stood back respectfully. They watched the car out of sight.

"T'row these rats in a cell on a charge av disturbin' the peace," directed the sergeant. Then he looked more closely at the prisoners and grinned widely. "Begorra, 'tis in the hospital yez'd better t'row 'em. Sure, an' never in me born days did I see a bunch av lads so busted up!"

"But won't they be charged with somethin' besides disturbin' the peace?" questioned a rookie who had but lately joined the force.

The sergeant frowned severely. "Glory be, an' didn't yez see that big bronze feller?"

"Sure."

"Then button the lip av yez. If the bronze man had wanted these scuts charged wit' anyt'ing, he would av said so."

The rookie's eyes popped. "Gosh! Who was that guy?"

The sergeant chuckled mysteriously. "Me lad, yez know what they say about our new mayor—that nobody has any pull wit' him?"

"Sure," agreed the rookie. "Everyone knows our new mayor is the finest New York has ever had, and that he can't be influenced. But what's that got to do with the big bronze fellow?"

"Nothin'," grinned the sergeant. "Except that, begorra, our new mayor would gladly turn a handspring at a word from that bronze man!"

Chapter II
THE CLICKING DANGER

AS he was whipped along New York streets in the speedy gray roadster, it suddenly dawned on Victor Vail that he knew nothing about his rescuer. He didn't even understand why he had accompanied the strange man so readily.

The blind violinist was not in the habit of meekly permitting unknowns to lead him about. Yet he had gone with this mighty stranger as docilely as a lamb.

"Are you a messenger sent to take me to Ben O'Gard?" he asked.

"No," came the bronze giant's amazing voice. "I do not even know anyone by that name."

Victor Vail was so intrigued by the beauty of his unusual companion's vocal tones that he could not speak for a moment.

"May I ask who you are?" he inquired.

"Doc Savage," said the bronze man.

"Doc Savage," Victor Vail murmured. He seemed disappointed. "I am sorry, but I do not believe I have heard the name before."

The bronze giant's lips made a faint smile.

"That is possible," he said. "Perhaps I should

have been more formal in giving you my name. It is Clark Savage, Jr."

At this, Victor Vail gave a marked start.

"Clark Savage, Jr.!" he gasped in a tone of awe. "Why, among the violin selections I rendered in my concert tonight was a composition by Clark Savage, Jr. In my humble opinion, and to the notion of other artists, that composition is one of the most masterly of all time. Surely, you are not the composer?"

"Guilty!" Doc admitted "And it is not flattery when I say the selection was never rendered more beautifully than by your hand tonight. Indeed, your marvelous playing was one of two things which led me backstage. I wished to compliment you. I noted the furtive manner of the man leading you outside, and followed. That is how I happened to be on hand when they sought to seize you."

"What was the second thing which led you to seek me out?" Victor Vail asked curiously.

"That is something I shall explain later," Doc replied. "I hope you do not mind accompanying me."

"Mind!" Blind Victor Vail laughed. "It is a privilege!"

The sightless master of the violin, indeed, considered it such. He had many times wondered about the mysterious Clark Savage, Jr., who had composed that great violin selection. Strangely enough, the composer was listed as an unknown. He had claimed no credit for the marvelous piece of work.

This was astounding in itself, considering what money-mad beings the human race had become. The composer could have ridden to a fortune on the strength of that one selection.

Victor Vail could not help but wonder and marvel at the powers of this strange man who had rescued him.

THE roadster wended over into the region of great skyscrapers. It was the theater hour. Taxicabs swarmed the streets; for most New Yorkers go to the theater in taxis.

Hence it was that one cab attracted no particular notice as it followed Doc's roadster.

The seafaring man who had directed the ill-fated attempt to capture Victor Vail occupied the machine. However, he had stuffed his cheeks with gum, donned dark glasses, stuck a false mustache to his lip, thrust a cigar in his teeth, and changed his cap. He looked like a different man.

"Keelhaul me!" he snarled repeatedly to himself. "I gotta get that Victor Vail! I gotta!"

Doc's roadster halted finally before one of the largest buildings in New York. This was a gigantic white thorn of brick and steel which speared upward nearly a hundred stories.

Doc Savage led the blind violinist inside. They entered an elevator. The cage climbed with a low moan to the eighty-sixth floor. Noiselessly, the doors slid back.

They now entered a sumptuously furnished office. This held an inlaid table of great value, a steel safe so large it reached to the bronze giant's shoulder, and many comfortable chairs. A vast window gave an impressive view of a forest of other skyscrapers.

Doc ensconced Victor Vail in a luxurious chair. He gave the musician a cigar of such price and quality that it came in an individual vacuum container. Doc did not smoke, himself.

"If you do not mind telling, I should like to know what was behind that attack upon you tonight," Doc said.

The unusual voice of the bronze man held a strangely compelling quality. Victor Vail found himself answering without the slightest hesitancy.

"I am completely in the dark as to the reason," he said "I have no enemies. I do not know why they tried to seize me."

"Those who seized you had the earmarks of hired thugs. But there was a man in the cab, a sailor. He shouted at the others several times. Did you recognize his voice?"

Victor Vail shook his head slowly. "I did not hear it. I was too dazed."

Silence fell for a moment.

Then the office abruptly rang with the coarse tones of the seafaring man!

"Sink 'im, mateys!" it shrilled. "Scuttle 'im! Use your guns!"

Victor Vail sprang up with a startled cry.

"It's Keelhaul de Rosa!" he shouted. "Watch him closely, Mr. Savage! The devil once tried to kill me!"

"Keelhaul de Rosa is not here," Doc said gently.

"But his voice spoke just then!"

"What you heard was my imitation of the voice of the sailor in the taxi," Doc explained. "I repeated his words. Obviously, that man was Keelhaul de Rosa, as you call him."

Victor Vail sank back in his chair. He fumbled with the fine cigar. He mopped his forehead.

"I would have sworn it was Keelhaul de Rosa speaking," he muttered. "Why—why—holy smoke! What manner of man are you, anyhow?"

Doc passed the question up as though he hadn't heard it. He disliked to speak of his accomplishments, even though it might be but a few words that were well deserved.

A truly remarkable man, this golden-eyed giant of bronze!

"Suppose you tell me what you know of Keelhaul de Rosa," Doc said.

The blind man ran long fingers through his white hair. It was apparent he was becoming excited.

"Why, bless me!" he muttered. "Could this mystery go back to the destruction of the *Oceanic*? It must!"

WITH a pronounced effort, Victor Vail composed himself. He began speaking rapidly.

"The story goes back more than fifteen years," he said. "It was during the World War. My wife, my infant daughter, and myself sailed from Africa on the liner *Oceanic*. We were bound for England.

"But an enemy sea raider chased the liner northward. The U-boat could not overhaul us, but it pursued our craft for days. Indeed, the *Oceanic* sailed far within the Arctic ice pack before escaping.

"The liner was trapped in the ice. It drifted for months, and was carried by the ice far within the polar regions."

Victor Vail paused to puff his cigar.

"Trouble with the crew arose as food ran short," he continued. "A shell from the enemy raider had destroyed our wireless. We could not advise the outside world of our difficulty. The crew wanted to desert the liner although the master of the vessel assured them the ice pack was impassable."

Victor Vail touched his eyes. "You understand, I am telling this only as I heard it. I, of course, saw nothing. I only heard.

"The leaders of the crew were two men. Ben O'Gard was one. Keelhaul de Rosa was the other. They were persuaded not to desert the liner."

Victor Vail suddenly covered his face with his hands.

"Then came the disaster. The liner was crushed in the ice. Only Ben O'Gard, Keelhaul de Rosa, and about thirty of the *Oceanic's* crew escaped. I was also among the survivors, although that is a mystery I do not yet understand."

"What do you mean?"

"I was seized by members of the crew two days before the disaster, and made unconscious with an anaesthetic. I did not revive until the day following the destruction of the *Oceanic*. Then I awakened with a strange pain in my back."

"Describe the pain," suggested Doc.

"It was a sort of smarting, as though I had been burned."

"Any scars on your back now?"

"None. That is the mysterious part."

"Who saved you when the liner was lost?"

"Ben O'Gard," said the blind violinist. "He was hauling me across the ice on a crude sledge when I revived. I owe Ben O'Gard my life. Not only for that, but, some days later, Keelhaul de Rosa seized me and tried to carry me off by force. He and Ben O'Gard had a terrific fight, O'Gard rescuing me. After that, Keelhaul de Rosa fled with several of his followers. We never got trace of them again."

"Until tonight," Doc put in mildly.

"That is right—until tonight," Victor Vail agreed. "It was Keelhaul de Rosa who tried to seize me!"

The sightless musician now put his face in his hands again. His shoulders convulsed a little. He was sobbing!

"My poor wife," he choked. "And my darling little daughter, Roxey! Ben O'Gard told me he tried to save them, but they perished."

Doc Savage was silent. He knew Victor Vail's story must have brought back memories of his wife and infant daughter.

"Little Roxey, that was my daughter's name," murmured the musician.

DOC SAVAGE finally spoke.

"It strikes me as rather strange that the story about the fate of the liner *Oceanic* did not appear in the newspapers. Such a yarn would have made all the front pages."

Victor Vail gave a start of surprise. "But—didn't it?"

"No."

"That is strange! Ben O'Gard told me it had. Personally, I never mentioned the incident. The memory is too painful." The sightless violinist paused. He made a finger-snapping gesture of surprise.

"That is another mystery! Why should Ben O'Gard tell me falsely that everyone knew the story of the awful fate of the *Oceanic?*"

"Perhaps he desired to keep the fate of the liner a secret," Doc offered. "Did he suggest that you keep quiet?"

"Why—why—I recall that he did bring up the subject! And I told him I never wanted to hear of the ghastly affair again!"

Doc's great voice suddenly acquired a purr of interest.

"I should like very much to know what actually happened during that period you were unconscious!" he said.

Victor Vail stiffened slightly.

"I refuse to listen to anything against Ben O'Gard!" he snapped. "The man saved my life! He tried to save my wife and baby daughter!"

"You will hear nothing against him," Doc smiled. "I judge no one without proof."

Doc did not point out that Victor Vail only had Ben O'Gard's word about that life-saving business.

The blind man rubbed his jaw in a puzzled way.

"Perhaps I should mention another strange thing which may be connected with this," he said. "The mystery which I call the 'Clicking Danger'!"

"By all means! Leave out nothing."

"It has been nearly fifteen years since I last met Ben O'Gard," muttered Victor Vail. "With Ben O'Gard's faction of the survivors was a sailor with a nervous ailment of his jaws. This malady caused his teeth to chatter together at intervals, making a weird clicking noise. The sound used to get on my nerves.

"Here is the mystery: At frequent intervals during the last fifteen years, I have heard, or thought I heard, that clicking noise. I have gotten into the habit of playfully calling it the 'Clicking Danger.'

"Actually, nothing has ever come of it. In fact, I rather thought it was my imagination entirely, instead of the sailor. Why should the fellow follow me all over the world for fifteen years?"

"It is possible Ben O'Gard has been keeping track of you," Doc replied.

The sightless master of the violin considered this in a somewhat offended silence.

Doc Savage studied Victor Vail's eyes intently. After a bit, he came over to the musician. He led the man across an adjacent room. This was a vast library. It held hundreds of thousands of ponderous volumes concerning every conceivable branch of science. This was probably the second most complete scientific library in existence.

The one collection of such tomes greater than this was unknown to the world. No one but Doc Savage was aware of its existence. For that superb library was at the spot he called his Fortress of Solitude, a retreat in a corner of the globe so remote and inaccessible that only Doc knew its whereabouts.

To this Fortress of Solitude the giant man of bronze retired periodically. On such occasions, he seemed to vanish completely from the earth, for no living soul could find him. He worked and studied absolutely alone.

It was in these periods of terrific concentration and study that Doc Savage accomplished many of the marvelous things for which he was noted.

BEYOND the skyscraper library lay another room—a vast scientific laboratory. This, too, was of a completeness equaled by but one other—the laboratory at Doc's Fortress of Solitude.

"What are you going to do?" asked Victor Vail curiously.

"I came backstage tonight to see you for two reasons," Doc replied. "The first was to tell you how I enjoyed your rendition of my violin composition. The second was to examine your eyes."

"You mean—"

"I mean an artist as great as you, Victor Vail, should have the use of his eyes. I wish to examine them to see if vision cannot be returned."

Victor Vail choked. His sightless orbs filled with tears. For an instant, he seemed about to break down.

"It is impossible!" he gulped. "I have been to the greatest eye specialists in the world. They say nothing less than a magician can help me."

"Then we'll try some magic," Doc smiled.

"Please—don't joke about it!" moaned the blind man.

"I'm not joking," Doc said steadily. "I positively can give you sight of sorts. If conditions are as I think, I can give you perfect vision. That is why I wish to examine."

Victor Vail could only gulp and sag into a chair. It did not occur to him to doubt the ability of this mighty being beside him. There was something in the bronze man's voice which compelled belief.

An overpowering wonder seized Victor Vail. What, oh, what manner of person was this bronze master?

A lot of folks had wondered that.

Rapidly, Doc took numerous X-ray pictures of Victor Vail. He also got exposures using rays less familiar to the surgical profession. He continued his examination with ordinary instruments, as well as some the like of which could have been found nowhere else. They were of Doc's own invention.

"Now wait in the outer office while I consider what the examination shows," Doc directed.

Victor Vail went into the outside office. He did not comprehend why, but he had such confidence in the bronze giant's ability that he already felt as though he could see the wonders of a world he had never glimpsed.

For Victor Vail had been born blind.

The sightless violinist would have been even more happy had he known the true extent of Doc Savage's ability. For Doc was a greater master of the field of surgery than of any other.

Doc's composition of the violin selection marked him as one of the greatest in that field. He had done things equally marvelous in electricity, chemistry, botany, psychology, and other lines.

Yet these things were child's play to what he had done with medicine and surgery. For it was in medicine and surgery that Doc had specialized. His first training, and his hardest, had been in these.

Few persons understood the real scope of Doc's incredible knowledge. Even fewer knew how he had gained this knowledge.

Doc had undergone intensive training from the cradle. Never for a day during his lifetime had that training slackened.

There was really no magic about Doc's uncanny abilities. He had simply worked and studied harder than ever had a man before him.

Doc was developing the ray photos he had taken. The task quickly neared completion.

Suddenly Victor Vail, in the outer office, emitted a piercing howl.

A shot exploded deafeningly. Men cursed. Blows smashed.

Doc's bronze form flashed through the laboratory door. Across the library, he sped.

From the library door, a Tommy gun spewed lead almost into his face.

Chapter III
FIGHTING MEN

DOC had charged forward, expecting to meet danger. So he was alert. Twisting aside, he evaded the first torrent of bullets.

But nothing in the library offered shelter. He doubled back. His speed was blinding. His bronze figure snapped into the laboratory before the wielder of the machine gun could correct his aim.

The gunman swore loudly. He dashed across the book-filled room. Deadly weapon ready, he sprang into the laboratory. Murderous purpose was on his pinched face.

His eyes roved the lab. His jaw sagged.

"Cripes!" he choked. "Cripes!"

There was no bronze man in the lab!

To a window, the gunner leaped.

"Cripes!" he gulped again.

He flung it up, looked out.

No one was in sight. The white wall of the skyscraper lacked very little of being smooth as glass. Nobody could pull a human-fly stunt on that expanse. No rope was visible, above or below.

The gunman drew back. He panted. His pinched face threatened to rival in color the white shirt he wore.

The bronze giant had vanished!

Fearfully, the gunman sidled about on the polished bricks of the laboratory floor.

Two half circles of these bricks suddenly whipped upward. They were not unlike a monster bear trap. The gunman was caught.

His rapid-firer cackled a brief instant. Then pain made him drop the weapon. Madly, he tore at the awful thing which held him. It defied him. The bricks which had arisen were actually of hard steel, merely painted to resemble masonry.

Before the would-be killer's pain-blurred eyes, a section of the laboratory wall opened soundlessly. The mighty bronze man stepped out of the recess it had concealed.

The giant, metallic form approached, taking up a position before the captive.

"Lemme out of dis t'ing!" whined the gunman. "It's bustin' me ribs!"

The bronze man might not have heard, for all the sign he gave. One of his hands lifted. The hand was slender, perfectly shaped. It seemed made entirely of piano wires and steel rods.

The hand touched lightly to the gunman's face.

The gunman instantly slumped over.

He was unconscious!

He fell to the floor as the bronze giant released the mechanical trap which held him. The trap settled back into the floor—become a part of the other bricks.

Like an arrow off a bow, the bronze man whipped into the library, then to the outer office.

The gunman had never moved after striking the floor. Yet he breathed noisily, as though asleep.

In the outer office, the bronze man saw Victor Vail was gone!

A DRIBBLE of moist crimson across the floor showed the single shot which had sounded had damaged some one. The red leakage led to an elevator door. The panel was closed. The cage was gone.

Doc Savage glided down the battery of elevator doors. The last panel was shut. His finger found a secret button, and pressed it. The doors slid open. A ready cage was revealed.

This car always awaited Doc's needs at the eighty-sixth floor. Its hoisting mechanism was of a special nature. The cage went up and down at a speed far surpassing the other elevators.

Doc sent it dropping downward. For a moment or two he actually floated in the air some inches above the floor, so swift was the descent.

The cage seemed hardly to get going before it slowed. And with such an abruptness did it halt that only great leg muscles kept Doc from being flattened to the floor.

The doors opened automatically. Doc popped out into the first-floor lobby of the skyscraper.

An astounding sight met his gaze.

Directly before the elevator door stood an individual who could easily be mistaken for a giant gorilla. He weighed in excess of two hundred and sixty pounds. His arms were some inches longer than his legs—and actually as thick as his legs! He was literally furred with curly, rust-hued hair.

A more homely face than that possessed by this anthropoid fellow would be hard to find. His eyes were like little stars twinkling in their pits of gristle. His ears were cauliflowered; something had chewed the tip of one, and the other was perforated as though for an earring, except that the puncture was about the size of a rifle bullet. His mouth was so very big it looked like his Maker had made an accident.

This gigantic individual held three mean-eyed men in the hooplike clasp of his huge arms. The trio were helpless. Three guns, which they had no doubt held recently, lay on the floor.

The gorilla of a man saw Doc. His knot of a head seemed to open in halves as he laughed.

"Listen, Doc!" he said in a voice surprisingly mild for such a monster. "Listen to this!"

His enormous arms tightened on his three prisoners. As one man the three howled in agony. They sounded like a coyote pack.

"Don't they sing pretty, huh?" the anthropoid man chuckled. He squeezed the trio again, and listened to their pained howls like a singing teacher.

Across the lobby, two more mean-eyed men cowered in a corner. They had their arms wrapped tightly about their faces. Each was trying to crawl into the corner behind the other.

The cause of their terror was a slender, waspish man who danced lightly before them. This man was probably as immaculately clad a gentleman as ever twirled a cane on a New York street.

Indeed, it was with a sword cane that he now menaced the pair in the corner. A sword cane which ordinarily looked like an innocent black walking stick!

This man was "Ham." On the military records, he was Brigadier General Theodore Marley Brooks. He was one of the leading civil lawyers of the country. He had never been known to lose a case. But there was no sign of poor blind Victor Vail.

DOC SAVAGE addressed the grinning gorilla of a man.

"What happened, Monk?"

Monk! No other nickname would have quite fit the homely, long-armed and furry fellow. The highly technical articles he occasionally wrote on chemistry were signed by the full name of Lieutenant Colonel Andrew Blodgett Mayfair.

There apparently wasn't room back of his low brow for more brains than could be crammed into a cigarette. Actually, he was such a great chemist that other famous chemists often came from foreign countries to consult with him.

"We were coming in the door when we met our friends." Monk gave his three captives a squeeze to hear them howl. "They had guns. We didn't like their looks. So we glommed onto 'em."

Reaching forward, Doc Savage placed his bronze right hand lightly against the faces of each of Monk's three prisoners. Only Doc's fingertips touched the skin of the men.

Yet all three instantly became unconscious!

Hurrying over, Doc also touched lightly the pair Ham menaced with his sword cane.

Both fell senseless!

Ham sheathed his sword cane. He twirled the innocent black stick which resulted. He was quite a striking figure, sartorially.

Indeed, tailors often followed Ham down the street, just to watch clothes being worn as they should be worn!

"You didn't see more of these rats dragging a white-haired, blind man, did you?" Doc asked.

"We saw only these five." Ham had the penetrant voice of an orator.

Neither Ham nor Monk seemed the least surprised by the way in which their prisoners dropped unconscious at Doc's touch.

Ham and Monk were accustomed to the remarkable feats of this mighty bronze man, for they were two of a group of five men who worked with Doc Savage. Each of the other three was a master of some profession, just as Monk was a fine chemist and Ham a great lawyer.

The five men and Doc Savage formed an adventuresome group with a definite, although somewhat

strange, purpose in life. This purpose was to go here and there, from one end of the world to the other, looking for excitement and adventure, striving to help those in need of help, and punishing those who deserved it.

Doc suddenly went outside. He moved so effortlessly he seemed to glide. He had been seized by a suspicion. Either Victor Vail was still in the skyscraper, or he had been removed by way of the freight elevators.

Hardly was Doc on the walk when a bullet splashed chill air on his bronze face.

TWO sedans were parked down the street, near the freight entrance of the giant building.

One machine lurched into motion. It ran rapidly away. Doc did not get a chance to see whether Victor Vail was in it!

Doc flashed over into the shelter of a many-spouted fire hydrant. The hydrant had couplings for several hose lines. It was nearly as large as a barrel.

Down the street, the driver hopped out of the sedan which remained. He was a big man, very fat. He wore a white handkerchief mask.

"Git a hump on yer!" he howled.

The cry was obviously directed at some of his fellows who were still in the skyscraper.

Monk and Ham popped out on the walk. The shot had attracted them. Monk held a pistol which, in his hairy paw, looked small as a watch chain ornament.

The sedan driver leveled a revolver to fire again.

Monk's fist spat flame.

The driver jumped about wildly, like a beheaded chicken. His spasmodic actions carried him into the street. He caved down finally and rolled under the sedan.

Three or four evil heads poked out of the freight entrance. Another red spark jumped out of Monk's paw. The heads jerked back.

Suddenly, Doc's low voice reached Monk's ears. Doc spoke half a dozen staccato sentences. Silence followed.

When Monk glanced at the fire hydrant a moment later, Doc Savage was gone!

Several times in the next minute, guns roared in the gloomy street. The reports echoed from the man-made walls on either side like satanic laughter.

The driver of the sedan abruptly appeared! The fellow still wore his mask. He hauled himself laboriously to the sedan door. Getting it open, he fell limply into the machine.

This seemed to embolden the fellows in the freight entrance. They launched a volley of bullets at Monk and Ham. The pair were driven out of sight.

A tight group, the gunmen sprinted from the freight entrance to their sedan. They made it safely. They piled in, trampling the prone, white-masked form of the driver.

"T'row de stiff out!" snarled one man, seizing the driver.

The driver kicked the man who had grasped him.

"I ain't no stiff, damn yer!" he cursed. "Dey jest winged me!"

"Where'd they get yer, Honkey?" inquired another gunman in a more kindly tone.

"Right where I set down, damn 'em!" gritted Honkey. Somebody laughed unkindly.

"It's a lousy deal, us goin' off an' leavin' our pals in dat buildin'!" growled a gunster.

"What else could we do?" retorted another. "Dey was saps to go bargin' out wavin' der rods. If we hadn't heard 'em squawk, we'd have been caught, too."

"Dry up, you mugs!" snapped the man who had taken the wheel.

The sedan rolled down Broadway. It veered into a side street many blocks downtown.

The street became shabby. Smell of fish permeated the air. Ragged derelicts of men tottered along the thoroughfare. Men in seamen's clothing were plentiful. Raucous music blared out of cheap honkey-tonks.

It was the waterfront district—a region of sailor lodging houses, needled beer, and frequent fights.

"De others got here first!" growled a gunman. "Dere's de car dey was drivin'."

The machine the man indicated was the first sedan to pull away from the uptown skyscraper.

THE evil fellows left the two sedans parked close together. "Honkey," the former driver, staggered out, but nearly fell.

"Help 'im, you guys!" directed the man who seemed to be the straw boss.

Honkey was half carried across the walk. This side street was very dark. They did not bother to remove the white mask Honkey still wore.

"Damn, but he's heavy!" complained a man helping the driver.

They mounted a stairway. The rickety steps whined like dogs when they were stepped on. There was no light, except that from a match a man going ahead had struck.

Into a lighted room, the group went. Several other men waited here.

Still there was no sign of Victor Vail.

"Put Honkey on de bed in de nex' room!" commanded the straw boss.

The two thugs hauled Honkey into an adjacent chamber. It was a slatternly looking place. Wall paper draped from the walls in great scabs. The one bed was filthy.

The pair prepared to lower Honkey.

At this point, Honkey's hands came up with apparent aimlessness. The fingertips touched each man's face.

Instead of Honkey dropping upon the bed, both thugs collapsed upon it! They made no sound.

Honkey now stumbled back into the other room.

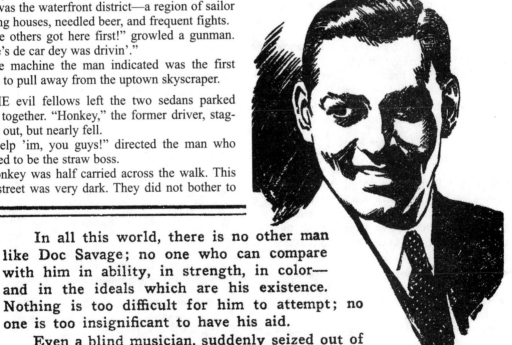

In all this world, there is no other man like Doc Savage; no one who can compare with him in ability, in strength, in color— and in the ideals which are his existence. Nothing is too difficult for him to attempt; no one is too insignificant to have his aid.

Even a blind musician, suddenly seized out of his sphere of activity, becomes the object of his interest and his remarkable ability. And the trail of treasure that leads to the frozen North is not too great a task for him to undertake at a moment's notice.

Astounding though he is, the man is entirely human. His ability is not for himself; his amazing exploits are not for personal gain. The welfare of all is his first consideration; to do good to everyone is his aim in life.

The gang assembled there eyed him in surprise.

"Yer'd better go ter bed, Honkey!" snarled the one who had been giving orders.

"Aw—I ain't feelin' so tough." Honkey muttered.

"Well, take dat crazy mask off, anyway!"

"In a minute," mumbled Honkey. "Soon's I find me a chair."

He weaved among the gangsters. He seemed very unsteady on his feet. To remain erect, he clutched the persons of such men as he passed. Always, his fingertips touched some portion of bare skin.

He came in contact with six men on his way across the room. The six sat in their chairs with a strange rigidity after he had passed.

The gangster who served as straw boss watched. Curiosity rippled over his face. Then came ugly suspicion.

He shucked two big automatics out of his clothing. He covered the reeling driver.

"Stick 'em up!" he snarled.

There was nothing the driver could do but obey. Up went his arms.

At this point, the six gangsters he had touched fell out of their chairs. They made a succession of thumps on the floor. They were unconscious.

"Whew!" gritted the gunman. "Keep dem hands up!"

He advanced gingerly. With a quick move, he plucked the mask off the driver.

"I t'ought so!" he hissed.

The features revealed were not those of Honkey, the driver.

They were the bronze lineaments of Doc Savage!

Chapter IV
THE BLIND-MAN HUNT

BEWILDERMENT gripped the assembled thugs. They could not comprehend that the bronze man had taken the place of Honkey, back at the uptown skyscraper. It was too much for them to believe that any one could be such a master of voice imitation as to fool them by emulating Honkey's hoarse growl.

They looked at the six of their comrades huddled senseless on the floor. A near-terror distorted their ugly faces.

The bronze man slowly pushed Honkey's cap off his head. The cap was none too clean. It was as though he didn't wish to wear it longer than was necessary.

For a brief instant his finger tips probed in the bronze hair that lay down like a metal skullcap.

"Keep clawin' fer the ceilin'!" snarled the gang chief.

Doc's arms lifted obediently. His hands nearly touched the ceiling, indicating what a really large man he was.

"Search 'im!" ordered the leader.

Gingerly, four of the thugs advanced. They frisked Doc with practiced fingers. They found some silver coins and a few bills which had belonged to Honkey. These they appropriated. But they unearthed no weapon.

"De umpcha ain't got a rod!" they muttered. The fact that Doc wasn't armed seemed to stun them.

Their leader eyed the six limp hulks on the floor. He moved to the bedroom door. He whitened perceptibly when he saw the two sprawled on the bed.

"I don't savvy dis!" he shivered. "What messed dem guys up like dat?"

Suddenly his mean eyes narrowed.

"Hunt in his sleeves!" he commanded his men.

They did so—and brought to light a small hypodermic needle.

The leader grasped the needle fearfully between thumb and forefinger. He inspected it.

"So dis is what laid 'em out!" he leered.

The other villains stirred uneasily. They didn't fancy weapons such as this. A gun was more their style.

"Croak 'im!" they suggested.

But their boss shook his head violently.

"Ixnay!" he snapped. "Dis guy is just de umpcha we need. We're gonna make 'im tell us where old Victor Vail is!"

A marked interest now registered on Doc Savage's bronze features. He was obviously surprised.

"You mean to say you haven't got Victor Vail?" he asked.

The remarkable power of his great voice held the gangsters speechless for a moment. Then their leader spoke sneeringly.

"D'you t'ink we'd be askin' where de guy is if we had 'im?" he demanded. He scowled blackly. "Say, whatcha drivin at—askin' us if we got 'im?"

"Victor Vail was seized," Doc replied. "I naturally supposed you fellows had him. That is why I am here."

The thugs exchanged angry glares.

"Dat damn Keelhaul de Rosa crowd got 'im first, after all!" one grated.

THIS morsel was very interesting to Doc Savage.

"You mean to say your outfit and Keelhaul de Rosa's outfit were both after Victor Vail?" he asked.

"Button de lip!" rasped the leader of the thugs. "I t'ink yer lyin' ter me about anybody gettin' Victor Vail!"

"Den why would he come here?" put in another fellow. "Don't be a nut! Dat's what the shootin' upstairs was. Yer remember we heard a typewriter turn loose. Dat's what scared us off."

Doc Savage gave the tiniest of nods. He understood now why the five captured by Monk and Ham had come dashing out of the elevators with their guns in hand. They had heard the machine-gun fire upstairs, and had become terrified.

"I wonder how Keelhaul de Rosa got ahead of us at de skyscraper?" mumbled the leader.

"He tried to grab de blind guy from under our snozzles at de concert hall, didn't he?" asked the other thug. "He drove off mighty fast in dat taxi, but he could've circled back an' followed de blind guy to dat skyscraper just de same as we did, couldn't he?"

Doc listened with interest to all this. These fellows must have arrived at the concert hall in time to witness the street fight. And they had been cunning enough to keep out of sight.

The leader swore loudly. "Cripes! Yer remember dat guy in a cab who had a trick mustache? De one dat was puffin' a cigar? He followed de roadster to de skyscraper, den went in right after dis bronze guy an' old Victor Vail. I'll bet dat was Keelhaul de Rosa!"

"Damn," growled a man. "What we gonna do?"

The leader shrugged. "Ben O'Gard will wanta know about dis. I'll go an' have a talk wit' 'im!"

This apprised Doc of another fact. These men were hirelings of Ben O'Gard!

Victor Vail had mentioned a strange feud between Ben O'Gard and "Keelhaul" de Rosa on the Arctic ice pack. It was evident that this old feud still continued.

But what was back of it? Did Victor Vail's unconsciousness at the time of the disaster to the liner *Oceanic,* and his awakening with a queer smarting in his back, have anything to do with this mystery?

The leader of the thugs came over and confronted Doc. He looked small and unhealthy before the mighty bronze man. He held up the hypodermic needle.

"What's in dis?" he questioned.

"Water," Doc said dryly.

"Yeah?" sneered the man. He eyed the unmoving forms of his fellows on the floor, shuddered violently, then got hold of himself. "Yer a liar!"

"There's really nothing but water in it," Doc persisted.

The thug leered. His hand darted like a striking serpent. The hypo needle was embedded in Doc's corded neck. The implement discharged its contents into his veins.

Without a sound, the giant bronze man caved down to the floor.

"So it was only water in dat t'ing!" snorted the gangster straw boss. "Dat needle is what got our pals!"

HE gave orders. The big bronze man was turned over, kicked a few times, and soundly belabored. He showed no signs of consciousness.

"Dat guy is harder'n brass!" muttered a thug, blowing feverishly on a fist with which he had taken an overly hard swing at the limp, metallic form.

"Watch 'im close!" commanded the leader. Then he pointed at a telephone on a stand against one wall. "I'm goin' to talk wit' Ben O'Gard in person. I'll either give you mugs a ring about what to do wit' the bronze guy, or come back myself an' tell yer."

The man now departed.

The other gangsters expended some minutes in seeking to revive their unconscious fellows. However, they had no luck.

They smoked. They muttered to each other, and one of their number took a post outside in the hallway as lookout.

Suddenly a shrill voice came from the room where the two thugs lay senseless on the bed.

"C'mere, quick!" it piped. "I got somethin' important!"

A number of gangsters rushed into the room. Others crowded about the door.

For a moment, not an eye watched the bronze figure of Doc Savage!

"Dat's funny!" declared a man, examining the pair on the bed. "He must've gone back to sleep! They're both out like a light now!"

"I never heard either one of dem guys talk in a shrill voice like dat," another fellow said wonderingly.

They came out of the bedroom, a puzzled group of villains.

Not one of them glanced at the telephone. So none noticed that a match had been jammed under the receiver hook, holding it in a lifted position!

The strong lips of Doc Savage began to writhe. Sounds came from them. Clucking, gobbling sounds, they were—absolutely meaningless to the listening thugs. The sounds were very loud.

"What kinda language is dat?" growled a man.

"Dat ain't no language!" snorted another. "De guy is jest delirious an' ravin'!"

The gangster was wrong. For Doc Savage was speaking one of the least-known languages in existence. The tongue of the ancient Mayan civilization which centuries ago flourished in Central America! And his words were going into the telephone!

When all the gangsters looked in the bedroom, they had given Doc sufficient time to call Monk at his skyscraper office. The thugs had been too excited to hear him whisper the phone number.

Doc was a ventriloquist of ability. He had thrown his voice into the bedroom to get the attention of his captors.

It would have surprised the absent leader of the thugs to know the hypodermic needle he had used on Doc had actually contained nothing more harmful than water! Doc had chanced to have the needle on his person. And he had slipped it up his sleeve for the purpose of deceiving the villains.

It was not the needle with which Doc made his enemies unconscious so mysteriously.

DOC SAVAGE continued to speak Mayan. The lingo sounded like gibberish to the listeners in the shabby room.

To homely Monk in the uptown skyscraper, however, it carried a lot of meaning. All of Doc's men could speak Mayan. They used it when they wanted to converse without being understood by bystanders.

"Renny, Long Tom, and Johnny should be there by now," Doc told Monk in the strange language.

The three men he had named were the remaining members of his group of five adventuresome aides!

"Tell Johnny to get the contents of Drawer No. 13 in the laboratory," Doc continued. "The contents will be a bottle of bilious-looking paint, a brush, and a mechanism like an overgrown field glass. Tell Johnny to bring the paint and brush here."

Doc gave the address of the dive where he was being held.

"There are two sedans parked outside," the bronze man went on in the gobbling dialect. "Tell Johnny to paint a cross on the top of each one. He is to bring his car which is equipped with radio. He is to wait in a street nearby when he has finished the painting.

"Long Tom and Renny are to take the overgrown field glasses and race to the airport. They're to circle over the city in my plane, Renny doing the flying, while Long Tom watches with the overgrown glasses. The glasses will make the paint Johnny will put on the sedan tops show up a distinctive luminous color. Long Tom is to radio the course of the sedans to Johnny, who will follow them."

The gangsters were listening to the clucking words. Evil grins wreathed their pinched faces. They didn't dream the gobble could have a meaning!

"You, Monk, will visit the police station where the thugs who attacked Victor Vail and myself outside the concert hall were taken." Doc said. "Question them and seek to learn where a sailor called Keelhaul de Rosa would be likely to take Victor Vail.

"Ham is to remain in the office and question the rat you found unconscious in the laboratory, also seeking to find Keelhaul de Rosa and Victor Vail.

"If you understand these instructions, snap your fingers twice in the telephone transmitter."

Two low snaps promptly came from the wedged-up telephone receiver. They were not loud. Not a thug in the room noticed them.

DOC SAVAGE now became silent. He lay as though life had departed from his giant form.

"Reckon he's kicked the pail?" a crook muttered.

Another man made a brief examination.

"Naw. His pump is still goin'."

After this, time dragged. The guard outside the door could be heard. Once he struck a match. Twice he coughed hackingly.

A gangster produced two red dice. The men made a pretense at a crap game, but they were too nervous to make a success of it. Seating themselves in the scant supply of chairs, or hunkering down on the filthy floor, they waited.

Doc Savage was giving his men time to get on the job. Johnny would have to daub the luminous paint on the sedans. Renny and Long Tom would have to arrive over the city in the plane. Twenty minutes should be sufficient time.

He gave them half an hour, to be sure. Indeed, his keen ears finally detected a series of low drones which meant the plane was above. Doc's plane had mufflers on the exhaust pipes. Renny was evidently cutting the mufflers off at short intervals to signal his presence to his pals.

Doc rolled over. He did it slowly, like a sleepy man. He now faced the hallway door.

The thugs tensed. They drew their pistols. They were as jittery as a flock of wild rabbits.

Doc imitated the raucous voice of the guard. He threw it against the hall door.

"Help!" the voice yelled. "Cripes! Help!"

The guard outside heard. He might have recognized his own tone. Maybe he didn't. He wrenched the door open, at any rate.

The instant his ugly face shoved inside, Doc threw words into his mouth. The guard was too astonished to say a word of his own.

"De cops!" were the words. "Dey're on de stairs! Lam, youse guys!"

Pandemonium fell upon the gangsters. They rasped excited orders. They actually squealed as though they were already caught.

One man saw the giant bronze figure of Doc Savage heave up from the floor. He fired his pistol. But he was a little slow. Doc evaded the bullets. He reached the light switch, punched it.

Darkness clapped down upon the room.

"De cops are inside!" Doc yelled in the guard's voice. "We gotta lam, quick!"

To make sure they fled in the right direction, Doc glided over and kicked the glass out of the window.

"Dis way out!" he barked.

A thug sprang through the window. Another followed. Then a succession of them.

Standing nearby, Doc darted his hands against such faces as he could find in the black void. Three men he touched in this manner. Each of the three instantly dropped unconscious.

The others escaped from the room in a surprisingly short space of time.

Doc listened. He heard both sedan engines roar into life. The cars streaked away like noisy comets.

INTO the room where Doc Savage stood there now penetrated a weird sound. It was low, mellow, trilling. It was exotic enough to be the song of some strange bird of the jungle, or the eerie note of wind filtering through a jungled forest. It was melodious, though it had no tune; it was inspiring, without being awesome.

This sound had the peculiar quality of seeming to arise from everywhere within the shabby room, rather than from a definite spot.

This trilling note was part of Doc—a small, unconscious thing which he did in moments of emotion. It would come from his lips as some plan of action was being arranged. Sometimes it precoursed a master stroke which made all things certain. Or it might sound to bring hope to some beleaguered member of Doc's adventuresome group.

Once in a while it came when Doc was a bit pleased with himself. That was the reason for it sounding now.

Doc turned on the lights. He lined up the thugs he had made unconscious.

Eleven of them! It was not a bad haul.

Doc used the phone to call Ham at the scraper aerie uptown.

"You might bring your sedan down here," Doc requested.

Ten minutes later, Ham came up the rickety stairs, twiddling his sword cane. Ham's perfection of attire was made more pronounced by the blowsy surroundings. He saw the pile of sleeping prisoners.

"I see you've been collecting!" he chuckled.

"Did you get anything out of Keelhaul de Rosa's man?" Doc asked.

"I scared him into talking," Ham said grimly, "but the fellow was just a hired gunman, Doc. He and his gang were hired to get Victor Vail. They were to deliver the blind violinist to Keelhaul de Rosa, right enough. But the delivery was to be made on the street. The man had no idea where Keelhaul de Rosa hangs out."

"That's too bad," Doc replied. "There's a chance one of the crew who attacked Victor Vail outside the concert hall will know where the sailorman hangs out. If they do, Monk'll make them cough up."

The unconscious thugs were now loaded into Ham's limousine. This car of Ham's was one of the most elaborate and costly in the city. Ham went in for the finest in automobiles, just as he did in clothes.

Ham did not ask Doc what they were going to do with the prisoners. He already knew. The senseless criminals would be taken to Doc's skyscraper office. In a day or so, men would call for them, and take them to a mysterious institution hidden away in the mountains of upstate New York. There they would undergo a treatment which would turn them into honest, upright citizens.

This treatment consisted of a delicate brain operation which wiped out all knowledge of their past. Then the men would be taught like children, with an emphasis on honesty and good citizenship. They would learn a trade. Turned out into the world again, they were highly desirable citizens—for they knew nothing of their own past, and had been taught to hate criminality.

The mysterious institution where this good, if somewhat unconventional, work went forward was supported by Doc Savage. The great surgeons and psychologists who ran it had been trained by Doc.

Ham drove his limousine to the skyscraper which held Doc's headquarters. The unconscious thugs were loaded in Doc's special elevator. The cage raced them up at terrific speed to the eighty-sixth floor.

Dragging along several of his unconscious prisoners, Ham behind him, Doc entered his office.

Surprise brought him up short.

Blind Victor Vail sat in the office!

Chapter V
GONE AGAIN!

DOC SAVAGE instantly noted a slight reek of chloroform about the sightless musician.

Otherwise, Victor Vail seemed undamaged.

"I am glad you are here, Mr. Savage," he said eagerly.

Like many blind men, it was obvious Victor Vail could identify individuals by their footsteps. Doc's firm tread was quite distinctive.

"What on earth happened to you?" Doc demanded.

"I was seized by thugs in the employ of Keelhaul de Rosa."

"I knew that," Doc explained. "What I mean is—how do you happen to be back here, alive and unharmed?"

Victor Vail touched his white hair with long, sensitive hands. His intelligent face registered great bewilderment.

"That is a mystery I do not understand myself," he murmured. "I was chloroformed. I must have been unconscious a considerable time. When I awakened, I was lying upon the sidewalk far uptown. I had a passerby hail a taxi, and came here."

"You don't know what happened to you beyond that?"

"No. Except that my undershirt was missing."

"What?"

"My undershirt was gone. Why anyone should want to steal it, I cannot imagine."

Doc considered.

"Possibly your captors removed your clothing to

get a look at your back, and forgot the undershirt when they dressed you again."

"But why would they look at my back?"

"I was thinking of the incident you mentioned as occurring more than fifteen years ago," Doc replied. "When you awakened after the alleged destruction of the liner *Oceanic* in the Arctic regions, you said there was a strange smarting in your back."

Victor Vail stirred his white hair with big fingers. "I must say I am baffled. But why do you say *alleged* destruction of the *Oceanic?*"

"Because there is no proof it was destroyed, beyond Ben O'Gard's unsupported word."

The blind violinist bristled slightly. "I trust Ben O'Gard! He saved my life!"

"I have nothing but admiration for your faith in O'Gard," Doc replied sincerely. "We will say no more about that angle. But I want to inspect your back."

Obediently, Victor Vail peeled off his upper garments.

Doc examined the blind man's well-muscled back intently. He even used a powerful magnifying glass. But he found nothing suspicious.

"This is very puzzling," he conceded, turning to Ham.

"You don't think, Doc, that Keelhaul de Rosa seized Mr. Vail just to get a look at his back?" Ham questioned.

"I think just that," Doc replied. "And another thing that puzzles me is why Keelhaul de Rosa turned Mr. Vail loose, once he had him."

"That mystifies me, also," Victor Vail put in. "The man is a murdering devil. I felt sure he would slay me."

SWINGING over to the window, Doc Savage stood looking out. The street was so far below that automobiles on it looked like chubby bugs. Street lamps were pinpoints of light.

There came soft sound of elevator doors opening out in the corridor.

Monk waddled in. He was smoking a cigarette he had rolled himself. The stub was no more than an inch long, and stuck to the end of his tongue.

Monk drew in his tongue, and the cigarette went with it, disappearing completely in his cavernous mouth. His mouth closed. Smoke dribbled out of his nostrils.

Throughout the performance, Monk's little eyes had remained fixed on the sartorially perfect Ham. This bit of foolishness was just Monk's latest method of annoying Ham.

For Monk was the one person alive who could get Ham's goat thoroughly. It had all started back in the War, when Ham was known only as Brigadier General Theodore Marley Brooks. He had been the moving spirit in a little scheme to teach Monk

certain French words which had a meaning entirely different than Monk thought. As a result, Monk had spent a session in the guardhouse for some things he had innocently called a French general.

A few days after that, though, Brigadier General Theodore Marley Brooks was suddenly haled up before a court-martial, accused of stealing hams. And convicted! Somebody had expertly planted plenty of evidence.

Ham got his nickname right there. And to this day he had not been able to prove it was the homely Monk who had framed him. This rankled Ham's lawyer soul.

"They're gonna clap you in the zoo one of these days!" Ham sneered waspishly at his tormentor.

The cigarette came out of Monk's mouth, together with a cloud of smoke. From his lips burst a *hoinck-hoinck* sound—a perfect imitation of a pig grunting.

The next instant he dodged with a speed astounding for one of his great bulk. Ham's whistling sword cane just missed delivering a resounding whack on his bullet head. Ham was touchy about any reference to pigs, especially when made by Monk.

Monk would probably have continued his goading of Ham for an hour, but Doc interrupted his fun.

"What did you learn from Keelhaul de Rosa's men being held at the police station?" Doc inquired.

"Nothin'," grinned Monk. "They was just a bunch of hired lice. They don't even know where Keelhaul de Rosa hangs out."

Doc nodded. He had half expected that.

"Ham," he said, "your legal work has given you connections with prominent government men in America and England. I want you to go at once and find out what you can about the liner *Oceanic*. Learn all possible of the crew, the cargo, and anything else of interest."

Ham nodded, sneered elaborately at Monk, and went out.

HE had hardly gone when the phone rang. It was Johnny.

Johnny's voice was that of a lecturer. He chose his words precisely, after the fashion of a college professor. As a matter of fact, Johnny had been both in his time. William Harper Littlejohn—for that was what his mother had named him—stood high on the roster of an international society of archaeologists. Few men knew more about the world and its inhabitants, past and present, than Johnny.

"I have your men located, Doc," said Johnny. "They halted their sedans before a low-class rooming house. Renny and Long Tom radioed me the location from the plane, where they were watching, and I arrived in time to see the men enter."

Johnny added an address on New York's Lower East Side, where the foreign element lived. It was not far from Chinatown.

"Be right with you!" Doc replied, and hung up.

Monk was already half through the door.

"Hey!" Doc called. "You're staying here."

"Aw!" Monk looked like a big, amiable pup who had been booted in the ribs. He was disappointed. He did love action!

"Someone has to guard Victor Vail," Doc pointed out.

Monk nodded meekly, pulled out his makings, and started a cigarette as Doc went out.

DOC SAVAGE'S gray roadster was equipped with a regulation police siren. He had authority to use it. His careening car touched eighty several times going down Broadway.

A dozen blocks from his destination, he slowed. The wailing siren died. Like a gray ghost, Doc's car slipped through the tenement district.

He pulled up around the corner from the address Johnny had given.

A tall man was selling newspapers on the corner. The fellow was very thin. His shoulders looked like a coat-hanger under his plain blue suit. The rest of him was in proportion, incredibly skinny.

He wore glasses. The left lens of these spectacles was much thicker than the right. A close observer might have noted that this left lens was in reality a powerful magnifying glass. For the wearer of the unusual spectacles had virtually lost the use of his left eye in the World War. He needed a powerful magnifier in his business, so he carried it in his glasses for handiness.

The newspaper vender saw Doc. He came over. As bony as he was, it was a wonder he didn't rattle when he walked.

"They're still in the room," he said. "Third floor, first door to your right."

"Good work, Johnny," Doc replied. "You armed?"

Johnny opened his bundle of papers like a book. This disclosed a small, pistollike weapon which had a large cartridge magazine affixed to the grip. A more compact and deadly killing machine than this instrument would be difficult to find. It was a special machine gun of Doc Savage's own invention.

"Fine," Doc breathed. "Wait on the street. I'm going up to that room."

THE steps whined under the giant bronze man's considerable weight. To avoid the noise, he leaped lightly to the banister. Like a tight-rope walker, he ran up the slanted railing.

He took the second flight in the same manner, not troubling to see if those steps squeaked also. By using the banister, he avoided any electrical alarms which might have been under the steps.

A white rod of light lying close to the floor marked the bottom of the door he was interested in. He listened. His keen ears detected men breathing. One grunted a demand for a cigarette. There was no other conversation.

Doc Savage lurked outside the door perhaps two minutes. His mighty bronze hands were busy. They dipped into his pockets often. Then he turned and started up another flight of steps in the fashion of the first two.

The structure had five floors. A creaking hatch let Doc out on a tarred roof. He moved over to a spot directly above the window of the room in which his quarry waited.

A silken line came out of his clothing. It was thin, strong. One end he looped securely about a chimney.

Like a spider on a string, Doc went down the cord. His sinewy hands gripped the line securely. He reached the window.

Hanging by one thewed fist, he dropped the other hand into a coat pocket. He boldly kicked the window inward. Through the aperture his foot made, he threw the objects he had taken from the pocket. A roar of excitement seized the room interior.

Back up the silken cord Doc climbed. He had no more trouble with the small line than he would have with a set of stairs. At the top, he replaced it inside his clothing. He seemed in no hurry.

Below him in the room, the excitement had died a mysterious death.

Doc ambled to the front of the building and seated himself on the parapet. Below, he could see the gaunt Johnny with his papers.

"Poi-p-e-r-s!" Johnny was bawling lustily. "W-u-xtra! Latest poi-p-e-r-s!"

No one would have dreamed Johnny was actually doing all the bellowing to cover any sounds from within the building.

Nearly ten minutes elapsed before Doc Savage went down to the third-floor room.

On the hallway carpet lay many colorless glass bulbs about the size of grapes. Doc had spread these there. Men charging out of the room had trampled many of them, crushing them. This had released the powerful anaesthetic they held. Anyone near, and not equipped with a gas mask, was certain to become unconscious.

The hallway floor, and the room itself, were littered with senseless men.

Doc stepped in, avoiding the unbroken bulbs of thin glass.

His bronze hand made a disgusted gesture.

Ben O'Gard was not among the vanquished!

DOC SAVAGE let his eyes range the room again, making sure. He noted that all the glass balls of anaesthetic which he had tossed through the broken window had been shattered. None of the

COLONEL RENWICK

John Renwick, or "Renny," is another of Doc Savage's loyal companions. His essential training is that of a civil engineer, but his knowledge extends far beyond that, and his ability covers a wide scope of things, including the smashing of doors with his giant fists. Renny is a man who is not built to hesitate. He plunges into things and has to be pulled out—but then, he also smashes out of things with equal ease, so that balances his failing.

gaslike stuff remained in the room or corridor—Doc had waited on the roof long enough for it to be dispelled.

Ben O'Gard was certainly not present. These were merely the gang Doc's men had trailed here.

"Bag anybody of any importance?" Johnny asked from the doorway. He had thrown his bundle of papers away.

"Not to us," Doc admitted. "We'll send these gentlemen upstate for our usual treatment, though. I imagine every one of them has a police record."

Johnny inspected the unconscious villains judiciously. "I'll at least bet our treatment can't hurt them any. But what about the chief devil, Ben O'Gard?"

"He simply wasn't among those present."

Doc and Johnny now loaded the prisoners aboard their cars. Doc's roadster held several.

Johnny's machine was a large touring car of a model at least ten years old. The thing looked like a wreck. A used-car dealer, if asked what he would give for it, would probably have taken one glance and said: "Twenty dollars! And I'm robbing myself at that!" Yet within less than a year, Johnny had paid three thousand dollars for the special engine in it. On a straightaway, the old wreck might do a hundred and fifty an hour without unduly straining itself.

They got their prizes in both cars and drove uptown. They parked before the white spike of a skyscraper housing Doc's office. Loading the captives into the elevators, they took them up to Doc's eighty-sixth floor aerie.

Gales of derisive laughter met them as they unloaded in the corridor. It was Ham laughing.

Doc stepped into the office.

Homely, hairy, gorillalike Monk sprawled in a chair. He held his bullet of a head in both furry hands. He rocked from side to side. His doleful groans made a somber orchestration for Ham's uproarious mirth.

A trickle of crimson wriggled through Monk's fingers.

Doc thought for an instant that Monk had been goading Ham again, and for once had been too slow in dodging the whack with the sword cane which Ham inevitably aimed at him.

Then Doc saw the implement which had struck Monk. This was a heavy metal paperweight. It lay on the rug. A twist or two of Monk's coarse, rust-colored hair still stuck to it.

Doc noted something else.

Victor Vail was gone!

Chapter VI
HANGING MEN

"WHAT happened?" Doc Savage demanded.

Ham tried twice before he choked down his mirth.

"I thought for a minute I'd die laughing!" he gulped hilariously. "The blind man said he wanted to feel the bumps on that wart Monk calls a head. Our fuzzy missing link of a pal let him—"

"He got a telephone call first," Monk put in sourly.

"Who did?" Doc inquired.

"Victor Vail," Monk grumbled. "The phone rang. Some guy asked to talk to Victor Vail. I put the blind man on the wire. He didn't say much to the guy who had called. But he listened a lot. Then he hung up. After a bit, we got to arguin' about tellin' fortunes by the knots on people's heads. He claimed there was somethin' to it, an' offered to feel my conk an' tell me plenty about myself."

"And you fell for it!" Ham screamed mirthfully. "And he kissed the top of your noggin with that paperweight! Then he beat it!"

"You weren't here?" Doc asked Ham.

"No," Ham laughed. "I came in just as Monk woke up talking to himself."

"Aw—how was I to know the blind guy was gonna hang one on my nob?" Monk demanded.

"You have no idea why he did it?" Doc questioned seriously.

"None a-tall," declared Monk. "Unless he got the notion from that telephone talk."

"You don't know who called?"

"He said his name was Smith. But it might've been a fake name that he gimmy."

Monk took his hands away from his head. A nesting goose would have been proud of such an egg as now decorated the top of his cranium.

"That's one bump it'd be easy to tell your fortune from!" Ham jeered, his hilarity unabated. "It shows you are an easy mark for blind guys with paperweights—"

Ham dodged just an instant too late. Monk's swinging toe caught him approximately where he sat down. Ham sailed across the office and landed heavily—on the part that had been kicked. He got up rubbing himself. He started to burst into jeering laughter again.

"Hoinck-hoinck!" said Monk, imitating a porker's grunt.

Ham's neatly barbered neck got red.

"It's too bad he didn't use an axe on you!" he told Monk waspishly.

Doc Savage swung into the laboratory. The prisoners were lined up there. Each man snored slightly. They would sleep thus until the administration of a chemical which was capable of reviving them from the thing which had made them unconscious.

Doc ignored them. He lifted from the heavily laden shelves of equipment an apparatus which resembled nothing so much as the portable sprayers used to treat apple trees.

He carried this into the outer office.

Monk and Ham eyed the contrivance with surprise. The thing was a new one on them.

Monk asked: "What is—"

He never finished the query. Sounds of distant shots came to their ears.

The noise was coming from the street below. Doc whipped to the window. He looked out and down.

An extremely flashy car, streamlined almost as beautifully as the world's record-holding racer, was canted up askew of the curb. Two machine guns stabbed red flame from the racer—flame that looked like licking snake tongues.

Across the street, other guns spat fire back at them.

"It's Long Tom and Renny!" Doc rapped.

THE giant bronze man was whipping into the corridor with the last word. Johnny, Monk, and

ANDREW BLODGETT MAYFAIR

That was the full, real name of the person directly above. In addition to that, he had the title of lieutenant colonel, with an enviable record in duty overseas. The name didn't fit the man, so his companions changed it for him. He was called "Monk" for short.

But, though he was physically a human gorilla, the man was one of the most intelligent chemists in existence. His knowledge of gases and explosives serves more than once to extricate his pals from perilous situations.

Ham followed. Monk had forgotten his cracked head with surprising suddenness.

The superspeed elevator sank them. Both Johnny and Ham, unable to withstand the force of the car halting, landed on the floor on their stomachs.

"Whee!" grinned Monk. "I always get a wallop out of ridin' this thing!"

Indeed, Monk had almost worn out the superspeed elevator the first week after Doc had it installed, riding it up and down for the kick it gave him.

Doc and his men surged for the street. A stream of lead clouted glass out of the doors.

Monk, Johnny, and Ham drew the compact little machine guns which were Doc's own invention.

The weapons released streams of reports so closely spaced they sounded like tough cloth ripping.

Doc himself doubled back through the skyscraper. He left by the freight entrance, furtively, almost before his friends realized he was not with them. He glided down the side street, haunting the deepest shadows.

Reaching the main thoroughfare, he saw the fight still waged about as he had seen it from above. A lot of lead was flying. But nobody had been hurt. Renny and Long Tom were sheltered by the flashy racer—it was Long Tom's car. Their opponents were barricaded behind the corner of a building across the street.

Somebody had shot out the street lights at either end of the block. The resulting gloom probably explained the lack of casualties.

Doc's bronze form flashed across the street. A bullet whizzed past, missing by ten feet. He was a nearly impossible target in the murk.

"It's de bronze swab!" howled one of the enemy. "Keelhaul me!"

The words were all that was needed to break up the fight. The gunmen fled. They had a car parked around the corner, engine running. Into this they leaped. It whisked them away.

A diminutive figure popped out from behind the racer. The small man sprinted wrathfully after the fleeing gunmen. His pistollike machine gun released spiteful gobbles of sound.

"Hey!" Doc called. "You're wasting your time, Long Tom!"

The small man came stamping back. Besides being short, he was slender. He had pale hair and pale eyes, and a complexion that looked none too healthy.

Only his extremely large head hinted that he was no ordinary man. "Long Tom," formally known as Major Thomas J. Roberts, was an electrical wizard who had worked with foremost men in the electrical world. Nor was he the physical weakling he appeared.

"The rats shot my car full of holes!" he howled irately.

The flashy racing car was the pride of Long Tom's heart. He had equipped it with about every conceivable electrical contrivance, from a television set to a newly perfected gadget projecting rays of an extremely short wavelength which were capable of killing mosquitoes and other insects that might annoy the driver.

This latter device, worked out with some aid from Doc Savage, was probably destined to bring Long Tom worldwide fame. Farmers could use it to destroy insect pests. It was worth billions to the cotton growers alone!

As they approached Long Tom's racer, a mountain heaved up from behind it.

THE mountain was Renny.

Six feet four would have been a close guess at his height. The fact that he looked nearly as wide was partially an optical illusion. He weighed only about two hundred and fifty pounds. On the ends of arms thick as telegraph poles, he carried a couple of kegs of bone and gristle which he called hands.

Renny was noted for two things. First, many countries knew him as an engineer little short of a genius. Second, there was no wooden door built with a panel so stout, Renny could not knock it out with one of his huge fists.

"How'd you birds start that fight?" Doc demanded.

Renny and Long Tom exchanged guilty looks.

"We drove up here as innocent as could be," Renny protested in a voice which resembled a very big bullfrog in a barrel. "Them guys ran out in the street and pointed a machine gun at us. Evidently we weren't the birds they were expecting, because they lowered their guns and turned back. But we figured if they was huntin' trouble, we'd accommodate 'em. So we started a little good-natured lead slingin'!"

Doc smiled slightly.

"If the fight did nothing else, it cleared up something that has been puzzling me," he said.

"Huh?" Renny and Long Tom chorused, while Doc's other pals came up to listen. No one of the group had been injured.

"Until a moment ago, it was a puzzle to me why Keelhaul de Rosa turned Victor Vail loose," Doc explained. "But now I see the reason. Keelhaul de Rosa and Ben O'Gard are fighting each other. Just why, is still a mystery. Both were after Victor Vail.

"The reason for that is another mystery. But Keelhaul de Rosa got Victor Vail, and I believe he got whatever he wanted from the blind man—something which required removal of the clothes from Vail's upper body. Then the violinist was turned loose as a bait to draw Ben O'Gard into the hands of Keelhaul de Rosa's gunmen. It was that crowd we just mixed with, because Keelhaul was along. They thought you birds were Ben O'Gard's men."

The moment he finished speaking, Doc beckoned Renny. The two of them entered the skyscraper.

The others, Monk, Ham, Long Tom, and Johnny, remained outside. They would have to explain the shooting to the police. Radio-squad cars laden with officers were hooting up from all directions.

There would be no trouble explaining. Each of Doc's five men bore the honorary rank of captain on the New York police force.

ENTERING his eighty-sixth-floor office, Doc secured the sprayerlike contraption which he had abandoned at the start of the fight down in the street.

"What's that doofunny?" Renny inquired. He, too, had never seen the sprayer of a contrivance before.

"I'll show you." Doc indicated a sticky material on the corridor floor outside his office door. This resembled extremely pale molasses. The color blended with the floor tiles so as to be hardly noticeable. "See that?"

"Sure," Renny replied. "But I wouldn't have, if you hadn't pointed it out."

"I chanced to have the foresight to spread that stuff outside the door when I left Monk here with Victor Vail," Doc explained.

"What is it?"

"I'm showing you. Take off your shoes."

Bewildered, Renny kicked off his footgear. Doc did likewise.

Doc now pointed the nozzle of his sprayer down the corridor—away from the pale molasses material. A shrill fizzing sounded. A cloud of pale vapor came out of the nozzle.

"Smell anything?"

"Not a thing," Renny declared.

Doc aimed a puff of the strange vapor at the molasses stuff.

"Smell anything now?"

"Ph-e-w!" choked Renny. "Holy cow! A whole regiment of skunks couldn't make a worse—"

Doc hauled Renny into the elevator.

"The stuff in this sprayer and the sticky material on the floor form a terrible odor when they come together, even in the tiniest quantities," Doc explained as the cage raced them down. "So powerful are these chemicals that anyone walking through the stuff in front of the door will leave a trail which can be detected for some hours. That's why we took off our shoes. We had walked through it."

"But I don't see—"

"We're going to trail Victor Vail," Doc explained. "But cross your fingers and hope he didn't take a taxi, Renny. If he did, we've got to think up another bright way of finding him."

But Victor Vail hadn't taken a taxi. He had walked to the nearest subway, and entered the side which admitted passengers to uptown trains, feeling his way along the building walls.

"We're sunk!" Renny muttered.

"Far from it," Doc retorted. "We merely drive uptown and throw our vapor in each subway exit until we find the odor which will result from its contact with Victor Vail's tracks."

Renny laughed noisily. "Ain't we the original bloodhounds, though!"

They tried the exits of seven stations. At the eighth, Doc's remarkable vapor, a chemical compound of his own making, combined with the other chemical left by Victor Vail's shoe soles, and gave them the nauseating odor.

"It goes down this side street!" declared Renny.

There were few pedestrians on the street at this late hour. Even these, however, promptly stopped to gawk at Doc and Renny. It might have been the fact that Doc and Renny were without shoes, and going through the apparently idiotic process of spraying an awful perfume on the sidewalk.

More likely, it was Doc's mighty bronze form which caught their eye. Doc was a sensation whenever he appeared in public.

"What puzzles me is how the blind guy got around like this," Renny offered.

"Simply by asking help of those near him," Doc retorted. "Everyone is glad to aid a blind man."

Renny got tired of the crowd of curious persons trailing them.

"Scat!" he told the rubberneckers violently. "Ain't you folks got a home you can go to?"

Renny had a most forbidding face. It was long, thin-lipped, serious, and grim. It looked like the face the cartoonists put on their drawings of old man Prohibition. Meekly, awed by that puritanical countenance, the crowd melted away.

Five minutes later, Doc and Renny halted before a door on which a plain gilt sign said:

DENTIST

"He went in there, Doc," said Renny.

LIKE two dark cotton balls before a breeze, Doc and Renny drifted into the shadows. This district was a moderate residential section. The buildings were neat, but rather old, and not showy.

"Wait here," Doc directed. Doc was always leaving his men behind while he went alone into danger. Long ago, they had become resigned to this, much as it irked them to stand back when excitement offered. They literally lived for adventure.

But no one could cope with danger quite as Doc could. He had an uncanny way of avoiding, or escaping from, what for another man would be a death trap.

Around to the rear of the brick building, Doc glided. He found the back door. It was not locked inside—it was bolted. Heavy iron bars crisscrossed it.

Doc leaped upward. The height of that tremendous spring would have astounded an onlooker. He clutched an extended ledge and worked his way to a window on a second-floor hallway, with hardly more sound than the noise of a prowling cat.

The hall was dark. Doc drew things from his pockets. Some sticky gum, he affixed to the windowpane. Then a faint, gritty hiss sounded.

Doc had cut the glass out of the window! He kept it from falling inward by the gum he had stuck to it. He eased inside.

Silence gripped the interior of the house. Doc

"LONG TOM"

"Long Tom" isn't long. He's built like the old cannons that went by that name. But where he isn't long on body, he is long on usefulness to Doc and his little following, for Thomas J. Roberts is the electrical wizard of the group. Under Doc's guidance, he constructs the electrical apparatus which proves to be the safeguard of the little company on more than one occasion.

prowled noiselessly. Only one room held a light. It was downstairs. The door was locked.

Doc let Renny in. They went to the fastened door.

"We might as well go in there all of a sudden!" Doc breathed.

"O. K., Doc," murmured Renny.

He lifted his gallon of iron-hard knuckles. He struck. With a rending crash, the door panel was driven inward by Renny's great fist.

They sprang into the room. Renny held a gun. Doc's powerful bronze hands were empty.

Horrified surprise halted them.

Only two men were in the room. One was Victor Vail. The other, as denoted by the sanitary smock he wore, was obviously the dentist who had his place of business here.

Both men hung suspended by ropes around their necks from a stout ceiling chandelier.

Chapter VII
THE MAP

THE sun was up. Doc's remarkable companions lounged in the skyscraper aerie. They had lost a night's sleep, but showed no effects of it.

Ham was honing the blade of his sword cane to a razor edge, looking ominously at Monk each time he tested its sharpness. Monk sat in an easy chair, reading a pocket manual of how to raise hogs. He took pains to hold the book so Ham could see the title. Monk often maintained—always within earshot of Ham—that some day he was going to retire and raise pork for a certain finely dressed lawyer he knew.

Johnny, the archaeologist, was penning a chapter in the book he was writing on the ancient Mayan civilization.

Long Tom, looking pale as an invalid, was in the laboratory, humped over an apparatus which for intricacy would have given Steinmetz a headache.

Truly an amazing crew, these men.

Doc Savage entered. With him was Victor Vail. Renny walked in after them.

The blind man's neck was swollen somewhat where the rope had nearly strangled him to death. For both Victor Vail and the unlucky dentist had not been so far gone but that Doc Savage had been able to revive them!

The explanation of Vail's situation was quickly made.

"The dentist don't know a thing about the gang that seized him," Doc concluded. "They called him to the door and cracked him over the head."

"It was Ben O'Gard!" Victor Vail put in, his voice thick with emotion. "Oh, Mr. Savage, I was so mistaken about that man! I thought he was my friend. I had every confidence in the world in him. When he called me here—"

"So it was Ben O'Gard who telephoned you!" Monk interposed.

At the sound of Monk's mild voice, Victor Vail registered great remorse. Obviously, he was terribly sorry for that crack he had taken at Monk's head with the paperweight.

"I do not know how I shall ever redeem myself for my horrible mistake," choked the blind man. "Ben O'Gard told me an awful story of how you men were holding me here to keep me from seeing him. I believed O'Gard. I know I was a fool to do that now, but at the time, I regarded O'Gard as a friend who had twice saved my life. He told me to escape and come to him. That is why I struck you."

"Forget it!" chuckled Monk. "Indirectly, it gave me the chance to do something I'd rather do than eat—kick the pants of my fashion-plate friend, here." And he leered pleasantly at Ham.

Renny spoke up. "What baffles me is why Ben O'Gard took over the dentist's office."

Doc's strong lips warped their faint smile.

"Simple," he said. "Ben O'Gard wanted to use the dentist's X-ray!"

THIS statement elicited surprised looks from everyone present.

"X-ray!" Renny grunted. "Why'd they want the X-ray?"

"I'll show you the reason in a minute," Doc replied. "First, though, I want to find out what Ham learned about the liner *Oceanic.*"

Ham now divulged the information which several transatlantic telephone calls to England had gathered.

"On the English records, the liner *Oceanic* is down as lost at sea—sunken without trace," Ham said. "There's no hint of this stuff about it being trapped in the polar ice pack."

"I'm not surprised," Doc Savage said dryly.

"I've got something that *will* surprise you," Ham smiled. "There was fifty million dollars in gold bullion and diamonds on the *Oceanic!*"

An electric shock seemed to sweep the room.

"Fifty million! Will you say that again!" Monk said mildly.

"Fifty million in gold and sparklers," repeated Ham impressively.

"That explains it!" Doc declared.

"Explains what?" Renny wanted to know.

"What's behind this whole mess," retorted Doc. "Come into the laboratory. I want to show you something, brothers."

It was an excited crowd of adventurers which surged into the vast laboratory room.

From a tray, Doc lifted several large photographic prints. These were X-ray pictures which he had taken of Victor Vail in his course of examining the violinist to determine his eye affliction. Until now, Doc had not had time to as much as examine the prints.

He held one up.

"Holy cow!" barked Renny.

"Exactly," Doc agreed. "More than fifteen years ago, while Victor Vail was under the influence of an anaesthetic, someone tattooed a map on his back with a chemical, the presence of which could only be detected by use of a certain tensity of X-ray."

"You mean I have carried the map on my back these many years without knowing it?" Victor Vail questioned wonderingly.

"You certainly have. You recall the man with the clicking teeth who seemed to haunt your trail through the years? Well, he was simply keeping track of you and the map."

"But what is the map?"

"It shows where the liner *Oceanic* is aground on a land far within the Arctic regions," Doc announced.

SOME minutes were expended examining the chart.

"But I cannot understand why I carried the map around unmolested for so many years!" Victor Vail murmured.

WILLIAM HARPER LITTLEJOHN

All of Doc's men have long, high-sounding names—when they give them in full. But they rarely do. The man with the glasses—one lens of which is a simple magnifying glass—is only "Johnny," and he is a geologist and archæologist of no mean proportions. When you are in this corner of the world today; in that tomorrow, then it is quite handy to have with you a man who knows sections and people from A to Z. That's what Johnny does.

"Possibly I can reconstruct a story which explains that," Doc told him. "The fifty millions in treasure aboard the *Oceanic* led Ben O'Gard, Keelhaul de Rosa, and the other members of the crew to mutiny. They probably disposed of all who did not join them!"

"The beasts!" Victor Vail covered his face with his hands. "My poor wife. My poor little daughter, Roxey! That devil, Ben O'Gard, murdered them! And I thought he was my friend!"

"It's merely guesswork about the murder part!" Doc put in hastily. "I said that simply because the eagerness of Ben O'Gard and Keelhaul de Rosa to get this map shows they think the *Oceanic* is where they left it, even now. This indicates there were no survivors but themselves."

Victor Vail recovered his control. "When Keelhaul

de Rosa tried to kidnap me from Ben O'Gard, he was really trying to steal the treasure map!"

"Of course," Doc agreed. "That explains why the two factions split. No doubt they have been waging unremitting war with each other since that day, each faction trying to slay the other so they would be free to secure the chart off your back, and go get the fifty millions."

"I'm surprised they left it behind in the first place!" Monk put in.

"We barely escaped with our lives as it was," Victor Vail assured him. "To carry more than food over the ice pack was impossible."

Ham made a quick gesture with his sword cane—and Monk ducked involuntarily.

"Both Ben O'Gard and Keelhaul de Rosa now have copies of this map," Ham said thoughtfully.

Doc Savage let his strange golden eyes rest on each of his friends in turn. The gilded orbs seemed to be asking a question—and receiving a highly satisfying answer.

"Brothers," Doc said softly, "these birds who are after that treasure are fellows who have no right to any man's gold. What say we get it ahead of them? We can use the money to enlarge our secret institution in upstate New York to which we send criminals to be made into useful citizens. The place is becoming a little crowded."

Pandemonium seized Doc's headquarters.

Renny swung over to the door. His enormous fist struck. The panel flew out of the door as though hit by a cannonball. No door was safe around Renny when he was happy.

Monk fled wildly about the place, each apelike leap barely taking him out of reach of the lusty whacks delivered by the pursuing Ham's sword cane.

Long Tom and Johnny got into a mock fight and promptly upset a stand of apparatus. In the ensuing crash, several hundred dollars' worth of equipment was ruined.

The horseplay was their way of saying they thought Doc's treasure-hunt scheme was the best idea they'd heard recently.

BEFORE that day was done, Doc Savage had operated on Victor Vail's eyes.

He performed the delicate bit of surgery in New York's finest hospital. Those who surrounded him as he worked were not ordinary nurses. They were some of the leading American eye specialists. One had flown from Boston to see the operation, another from Detroit, and two from Baltimore.

The ceiling of the operating room was of thick glass. To every square inch of this was pressed the face of an eye specialist. They used opera glasses so as not to miss the slightest move made by the rock-steady bronze hand of the master surgeon of them all.

They wanted to see this epochal piece of work, for Doc Savage was seeking to do something which every expert present had until this very day maintained was impossible.

And what the assembled specialists saw the mighty bronze man do that day in the New York hospital operating room was something they would talk about for a long time to come. The mastery of it held them breathless long after big Doc Savage had taken his departure.

Victor Vail would have his sight!

THE next morning, as Ham entered Doc's office, Doc was taking his exercises. Sometimes even the sharp-tongued Ham was awed by this remarkable bronze man who was probably the supreme adventurer of all time.

Ham was seized by one of these odd intervals as he sat down to wait. Doc took his exercises—a terrific two-hour routine—each day of his life, and nothing interfered.

Doc's ritual was similar to ordinary setting-up movements, but infinitely harder, more violent. He took them without the usual exercising apparatus. For instance, he would make certain muscles attempt to lift his arm, while other muscles strove to hold it down. That way he furthered not only muscular tissue, but control over individual muscles as well. Every ligament in his great, bronzed body he exercised in this fashion.

From a case which held his special equipment, Doc took a pad and pencil. He wrote a number of several figures. Eyes shut, he extracted the square and cube root in his head, carrying the figures to many decimal places.

Out of the case came a device which made sound waves of all tones, some of a wavelength so short or so long as to be inaudible to the normal ear. Years of straining to detect these waves had enabled Doc to make his ears sensitive enough to hear many sounds inaudible to ordinary people.

With his eyes closed, Doc rapidly catalogued by the sense of smell several score of different odors, all very vague, each contained in a small vial racked in the case.

There were other exercises, far more intricate.

Ham shook his head wonderingly. He knew that five minutes at the clip Doc was doing the routine would be more than he, himself, could stand. And Ham was husky enough to give most professional boxers a drubbing.

From the cradle, Doc had done these exercises each day. They accounted for his astounding physique, his ability to concentrate, and his super-keen senses.

"What's on your mind?" Doc asked suddenly. His routine was over!

Ham plucked a newspaper out of a pocket.

"What do you think of this?" He handed Doc the paper, indicating an item. It read:

WANT TO BUY A POLAR SUBMARINE EXPEDITION?

There is one for sale. Captain Chauncey McCluskey announced this morning that he is hunting a purchaser for a share of the projected trip of the submarine *Helldiver* under the polar ice.

Captain McCluskey has the submarine, fully equipped and ready to go. But it seems he has run out of money—

There was more of it, written up in typical tabloid style. But it told nothing more of importance—except that the submarine *Helldiver* was tied up at a local pier, and Captain Chauncey McCluskey could be found aboard.

"Who is Captain McCluskey?" Ham inquired.

Doc shook his head slowly. "Search me! I never heard of the man before. Nor have I heard of any other projected submarine trip under the pole— other than the rumor that Sir Hubert Wilkins intended to go up there again with a better under-seas boat than he had the last time."

"This sub may be just what we need," Ham declared. "But there's one point which has me guessing. It's darn queer the thing should pop up at just the time we're interested."

Doc smiled slightly. "It won't hurt to look into it, anyway."

The regular elevator—not the super-speed one—lowered them to the street level.

They took the first taxi which rolled up.

DOC gave their driver the address of the pier to which was moored the polar submarine, *Helldiver.*

Office workers were going to their daily tasks. The walks were crowded. Each subway kiosk vomited humanity like an opened anthill. The cab rolled down into a cheaper district, where merchants were setting a part of their wares out on the walks.

Ham toyed with his sword cane, and wondered what kind of a tub the *Helldiver* would be.

Suddenly he snapped rigid as an icicle.

In to the cab had permeated the low, mellow sound which was part of Doc. Weird, exotic, the note trilled up and down the musical scale. Looking directly at Doc's strong lips, Ham could not tell the sound was coming from them, such a quality of ventriloquism did the trilling note have. Indeed, Doc himself probably did not quite realize he was making it.

The sound could have but one meaning now. Danger!

"What is it?" Ham demanded.

"Listen!" Doc told him abruptly.

Silence lasted about a minute. Then Ham's high, intelligent forehead acquired a dubious pucker.

"I hear a clicking noise at intervals, I think," he said. "Sounds like somebody shaking a couple of dice!"

"Remember the clicking noise Victor Vail mentioned having heard often during the past years?"

Ham never got to say whether he recollected or not.

Their driver suddenly flicked several small objects back into the tonneau. He was careful to keep his face from being seen.

The objects he flung were the grape-like balls of anaesthetic Doc had used to overpower Ben O'Gard's hired gangsters. No doubt these had come from the scene of that affair, since Doc had neglected to retrieve such of them as had not been broken.

The globules shattered.

Doc and Ham were caught. With hardly a quiver, they tumbled over unconscious on the cushions.

They had not glimpsed the countenance of their driver.

Chapter VIII
STEEL WALLS OF DEATH

A BIG red cow was dancing.

She had bells on her neck, bells on her legs, bells on her tail. She even had a particularly big bell on a ring in her nose. The bells had a most particularly ear-splitting sound, somewhat like the noise a large plate glass window would make if dropped off the Woolworth building. Every time the cow danced, a lot of glass broke.

Ham sat up. He groaned loudly as all the bells on the big red cow exploded with a deafening roar that the bovine herself vanished amid a great display of colored lightning. She had been entirely imaginary.

"Holy cow!" moaned Ham, plagiarizing Renny's pet expression. "Am I blind, or in hell?"

"If you're complaining about the darkness," came Doc's steady, capable voice, "that's why you can't see anything. And as for where we are—we seem to be inside a steel vault."

"What a dream I had waking up!" Ham muttered.

"The anaesthetic sometimes has that effect. I judge we've been unconscious nearly two hours. One shot of the anaesthetic lays a man out for about that long."

Ham suddenly clutched at various parts of his person. His hands made loud slaps on his bare hide.

"Hey!" he yelled. "I'm naked as the day I was born!"

"So am I," Doc told him. "They took our clothing. They even combed our hair, from the way mine feels. And they swept the interior of the vault clean. There are no shelves, or anything else—except a candle and three matches which they kindly left us."

"Light the candle," Ham suggested. "This place is blacker than the inside of an African savage!"

"No, Ham," Doc replied. "They left the candle, hoping we'd light it."

"Huh?" Ham was puzzled.

"A flame will exhaust the oxygen in this place very quickly, and hasten our death by suffocation."

"You mean the vault is airtight?"

"Yes. And soundproof, too."

Ham now listened. He realized he could not hear a sound but the booming of his own heart. It was so quiet he could almost hear the blood gurgle through his arteries. He shivered. A heavy lead weight seemed to climb on his chest.

"The air in here must be pretty foul already," he muttered.

"Very," Doc agreed. "I have been thinking, Ham. You recall that some months ago a large chain of New York banks went out of business. Probably we are in the vault of one of those banks."

"Ugh!" Ham shuddered. "Can't you think of something cheerful?"

Doc Savage's low laugh vibrated through the awful steel cubicle. He rarely laughed.

"How's this for something cheerful?" he inquired. "As a matter of fact, I've only been waiting for you to regain consciousness before walking out of this place."

HAM emitted a howl of delight that was almost a sob. He sprang erect. They were two naked men inclosed in thick walls of hard steel. Their voices could not penetrate outside, just as no sounds could get in. The situation seemed hopeless.

But Doc Savage had a way! He never joked about matters as serious as this.

"How do we do it?" Ham demanded.

"Our captors probably looked in our mouths," Doc explained. "But they forgot to count my teeth. They didn't notice that in my upper jaw there is an extra wisdom tooth on each side. They're false, and they hold two chemical compounds of my own concoction. When combined, these form one of the most powerful explosives."

Doc now went to work on the vault door. He operated in darkness, guided only by his sensitive fingertips.

"Kind of them to leave us the candle," Doc said.

He used the candle wax to chink his explosive in the joint of the vault door, near the lock.

"Get in a corner!" he directed Ham.

"How you gonna explode it?" Ham questioned.

"It explodes itself, due to chemical reactions, about four minutes after the two compounds are mingled."

They huddled in the corner farthest from the vault door. Doc employed his mighty bronze form to shield Ham—although Ham did not realize it at the time, so great was his nervous tension.

"It's about time for the blast!" Doc breathed swiftly. "Open your mouth wide to equalize the pressure on either side of your eardrums, so there'll be less likelihood of them being ruptured."

Ham barely had time to comply.

Wh-a-a-m! Compressing air smashed them against the solid steel with stunning force. It crowded their eyeballs inward. It seemed to tear the flesh from their bones.

So terrific was the explosion that Ham was reduced to senselessness.

Doc Savage, huge and bronze and apparently affected not at all by the concussion, flashed to the heavy steel door. It was still shut. But the hard metal was ruptured about the lock. He shoved.

The door opened about a foot and stuck. But that was enough. Doc carried the unconscious Ham outside, thence through two vacant chambers.

Ham revived after several minutes in a large, bare room—the lobby of a former bank.

Pedestrians moved on the street outside the unwashed plate-glass windows. One of these chanced to look in. He was a portly man with spats and a cane, smoking a cigar. No doubt he had heard the blast.

When he saw two naked men, he nearly swallowed his cigar. Doc and Ham were bleeding profusely where the force of the explosion had broken their skin. They must have been a sight.

Doc Savage rushed Ham to a side door. It was locked. The lock came out of the hard wood like an ear of corn out of its shuck, when Doc exerted a little of his tremendous strength.

A taxi driver at a stand in the street heard the lock tear out. He glanced around. He was just in time to see two stark naked men climbing into his hack.

The driver bellowed for a cop.

The cop came. He did not know Doc Savage by sight. He pinched both Doc and Ham. Doc did not put up an argument. This was the quickest way of getting clothes. The cop was tough, and swore a lot.

At the police station, the captain in charge insisted on stripping to his underwear so that Doc would be properly clad.

And the cursing cop got a lecture from his captain that would make him remember the giant bronze man the rest of his life. He would also have gotten suspended a month without pay if Doc hadn't interceded.

"Anyway, begorra, yez had better learn to know some of the big men in this town by sight!" the captain warned his cop. "Sure, an' the next thing I know, you'll be cussin' out the president!"

TWENTY minutes later, Doc Savage stood on the wharf, appraising Captain Chauncey McClusky's under-the-polar-ice submarine.

The thing looked like a razor-backed cigar of steel. The hull was fitted with lengthwise runners resembling railway rails. As a matter of fact, these actually were such rails, converted to the purpose of ice runners. They were supposed to enable the underseas craft to slide along beneath the Arctic ice pack.

A wireless aerial, collapsible, was set up for action. There was a steel rod of a bowsprit ramming out in front, the size of a telegraph pole. The rudder and propellers were protected by a steel cage intended to keep out ice cakes.

Doc liked the looks of this latest of polar-exploring vehicles. He stepped aboard.

A man shoved his head out of the main hatch amidships. All this man needed to make him a walrus was a pair of two-foot tusks. Doc had always believed Monk the homeliest human creation. It was a toss-up between Monk and this man.

The man squeezed out of the hatch. He would tip a pair of scales at three hundred pounds, if he'd budge them at an ounce.

"What the blazes do you want aboard here, matey?" the man demanded.

His voice was a roar that frightened roosting gulls off floatsam in the middle of the bay.

"I'm hunting Captain Chauncey McCluskey," Doc announced.

"You've found him!" roared the walrus. "An' if yer a dinged landlubber just wantin' a look at this bloody hooker, you can take shore leave right now! I been pestered to death by cranks since that piece come out in the papers this mornin'!"

Doc didn't bat an eye. He rather liked to deal with a man who got down to business and said what he thought.

"Let's look your vessel over," he suggested.

The walrus blew noisily through his mustache. "Mean to say you're interested in buyin' a share in this expedition?"

"Exactly—if your craft meets my needs."

"Come below, matey," rumbled Captain McCluskey. "I'll show ye her innards."

They looked at her innards for an hour and a half. They came back on deck.

Doc was satisfied.

"It will take approximately two hundred and fifty thousand dollars to see you through," he said. "I will put up the sum—on one condition."

Captain McCluskey blew through his walrus mustache and eyed Doc as if wondering whether the bronze man had that much money.

The walrus would have been surprised if he had known the true extent of Doc's wealth. For Doc had at his command one of the most fabulous treasure troves in existence—a vast cavern stored with the wealth of the ancient Mayan nation. This was located in a lost canyon, the Valley of the Vanished, in the remote recesses of Central America. Survivors of the ancient Mayan civilization, living isolated from the rest of the world, kept Doc supplied with mule trains of gold whenever he needed it.

"What's the one condition?" McCluskey rumbled.

"The expedition must be entirely in my hands the first two months," Doc explained. "Within that length of time, I shall visit a certain remote spot in the Arctic regions, and secure the thing I am going after."

CAPTAIN MCCLUSKEY was surprised. "The thing you're goin' after—what d'you mean, matey?"

"I'm afraid you'll have to swallow your curiosity on that point, Captain. The object of our quest will be disclosed when we arrive, and not before. I can assure you, though, that it does not involve breaking the law in any way."

The walrus considered deeply. "All right, matey. I'll sail two months under your sealed orders. But, strike me pink, if yer breakin' the law, I'll throw ye into the brig the minute I finds ye out."

"Fair enough."

"Cap'n McCluskey is as honest a swab as ever sailed the ocean," the walrus continued his roaring. "I've saved me money many a long year to bank enough to build the *Helldiver*. The good lads in me crew have done the same. We want to do somethin' to leave our mark in the world, so we'll be remembered after we're in Davy Jones' locker.

"This explorin' v'yage under the pole is our bid for fame, matey. It means a lot to us. We ain't gonna be throwed off our course this late in the game. Maybe ye don't understand our feelin's, but that's the way it is."

"Naturally, my project will not interfere with your goal of sailing under the north pole," Doc replied. "And you may rest assured we shall make no effort to share in the glory of your accomplishment. I shall not permit my name to be mentioned, either as partial backer, or as having accompanied you."

The walrus man seemed deeply moved.

"Yer a generous man, matey," he mumbled. "But one other point, we'd better clar up."

"What's that?"

"The hearty lads in me crew," chuckled Captain McCluskey. "Them swabs ain't sissies, matey. They're good men. They've sailed in naval submarines aplenty in their time. But they're hard as iron an' a little rough in their ways. You said you'd bring five of your own mates along. That's all right. But if they ain't got hair on their chests, my crew is liable to haze 'em around some."

Doc smiled faintly. "I don't know about the hair, but I think my lads can hold their own."

"Blow me down!" grinned the walrus. "Then we'll get along like frogs on a log!"

"I wish to make a number of changes in this craft," Doc declared. "I shall pay for them, naturally."

The walrus frowned. "What kinda changes?"

"A special radio. Electrical apparatus for sounding and locating icebergs. A collapsible seaplane. Better diving suits than you have. And other things of that nature."

"Strike me pink," chuckled McCluskey. "Yer a swab that knows his business, I can see that. How long'll it take?"

"Two weeks."

Chapter IX
TOUGH CARGO

THE two weeks had passed.

"Helldiver is right!" Monk grumbled. "The name sure fits!"

The under-the-polar-ice submarine was off the Maine coast, sailing northward. The craft had run into a stiff blow. And nothing is quite as disturbing as the movement of a U-boat in heavy going.

As each gigantic sea approached the sharp bows of the sub, the steel cigar of a craft did a sort of devil dance of anticipation. It shimmied from side to side. It squirmed. It groaned like a thing in agony. Then it would sink in the wave as though going to its death.

They had to keep the hatches closed. To breathe the air inside was something like being shut up in a can of axle grease.

"It's an old-fashioned hell ship, if you ask me," Long Tom muttered.

Doc Savage glanced sharply at the frail, unhealthy-looking electrical wizard. This was Long Tom's way of telling important news.

"What do you mean by that, Long Tom?" Doc asked.

"Last night, I had a dream," Long Tom began.

"So did I," groaned Monk, who was slightly seasick. "I dreamed I was Jonah, and the whale had swallowed me."

"Shut up!" snapped Long Tom. "In my dream, I saw somebody bending over me as I slept. I heard a clicking noise, as though a pair of dice were being rattled in somebody's hand."

Strange lights flickered in Doc's golden eyes. "You're not trying to be funny, are you, Long Tom?"

"I never felt less funny. I grabbed at the man bending over me in the dream. I got this." Long Tom drew an object from his pocket. It was a black-haired wig.

"Did you get a look at his face?" Doc rapped.

"It was too dark. And he was gone before I could follow."

Doc considered in silence for perhaps a minute.

"This is serious, brothers," he said at length. "That killer of Ben O'Gard's is aboard this sub. And we don't know him by sight."

"It oughta be easy to find him now," snorted Monk, eyeing the black wig. "Just find the guy whose hair changed color during the night."

It was astounding, the way Monk's seasickness had vanished, now that danger threatened.

"No good," said Long Tom. "I looked everybody over this morning. And no hair had changed color. That means the man was wearing the wig as a disguise while he did his dirty work."

"What dirty work?" Doc inquired.

"I forgot to mention the fellow had a knife," Long Tom said dryly.

THE unhealthy-looking electrical wizard went below. Long Tom's looks were deceptive. Although the weakling of Doc's crowd, he was man enough to thrash a good nine out of ten of the men you pass on the street.

Long Tom was serving as radio operator. He had installed a radio set so powerful he could keep in touch with the remotest corners of the earth, even while resting on the bottom of the sea.

He had also equipped the *Helldiver* with the most sensitive devices for measuring underwater distances with sound waves. Simply by watching dials, Long Tom could tell how far below the sea bottom was, how far they were from the nearest iceberg, and how big the berg was. An alarm bell would even ring the instant they came within dangerous distance of any floating object big enough to harm the sub.

The only drawback about this last was—a whale swimming near the *Helldiver* was capable of ringing the alarm.

Monk left Doc considering the new danger which threatened them. Monk had confidence Doc would find a way to trap their enemy with the clicking teeth.

Monk retired to the cubicle where he kept his chemicals. Monk's contributions to the expedition were numerous. The most remarkable of these was a chemical concoction which, when released in quantities from the sub, would dissolve any ice which happened to be above it.

This removed any danger of the *Helldiver* being trapped under the ice!

Special apparatus for supplying oxygen within the sub, concentrated foods which were composed simply of the necessary chemical elements for nourishment in a form easily assimilated—these and other things were products of Monk's genius.

Renny was doing work which his experience as an engineer eminently fitted him. He was the navigator. At this, Renny had few equals. Moreover, he was making maps. The voyage of the *Helldiver* would lead through unexplored Arctic regions, and Renny's maps would be of great value to future generations.

The archaeologist and geologist, Johnny, possessed a fund of knowledge about the polar ice cap and ocean currents which would be invaluable. There were very few things about this old ball of mud we call the Earth which Johnny did not know.

As for Ham, he had taken care of the legal angles, such as securing the necessary permission to put in at Greenland seaports. The Danes run Greenland as a monopoly, and a hatful of permits are necessary before a foreign vessel can touch there.

Ham also furnished everybody aboard the *Helldiver* an example of what the well-dressed voyager under the polar ice should wear. His oilskins were impeccable. The fact that he always carried an innocent-looking black cane afforded Captain McCluskey's crew some chuckles. They didn't know this was a sword cane. If Ham ever drowned, he would still have that sword cane in one hand.

About noon, Ham searched Doc Savage out. Doc was on deck. It seemed a miracle that each terrific wave did not sweep him overboard. But the seas had no more effect upon Doc than upon a statue of tough bronze metal. There was a strange quality about Doc's bronze skin—it seemed to shed water like the proverbial duck's back, without becoming wet.

Ham was excited.

"Good news!" he yelled. "Radio message from New York, Long Tom just copied it!"

"What is it?" Doc asked.

"Victor Vail left the hospital this morning," Ham replied. "He is no longer blind. He can see as well as anybody!"

THE smashing waves soon drove the immaculate Ham into the greasy vitals of the submarine.

"I've inhaled so much oil already, it's oozing out of my hide," he told Monk.

But Monk was making a chemical concoction capable of giving off warmth for several hours at a stretch—something that would be very handy to tuck in a man's shoes and gloves when he took a stroll on the ice in the vicinity of the north pole. He didn't want to be bothered.

"G'wan off an' chew a bacon rind!" he sneered.

Ham bloated indignantly. Monk had been goading him for several days about pigs and pork, and Ham hadn't been able to devise a single way to get back at Monk. Ham wished mightily he dared take a swing at Monk, but he knew better. A grizzly bear with any sense would think twice before tackling Monk.

Muttering to himself, Ham ambled forward. He heard a sound which might have been an angry bull in a china shop. Ham quickened his pace. It sounded like a fight. He ducked gingerly through a slit of a door in a steel bulkhead.

One of the *Helldiver's* crew sprawled on the

grilled floor of the engine room. The man was an oiler. He was big—fully as big as Monk. He looked tough. Privately, Ham had considered getting this oiler and Monk embroiled in a fight, just for his own amusement.

But the fighting oiler now sprawled on his back. He whimpered. His lips had been smashed into a crimson pulp. One of his eyes was closed.

Over him towered walruslike Captain McCluskey.

"I kin lick any swab aboard this iron fish!" the captain bellowed. "Rust my anchor, but I'll wring the neck of the next scut I find shirkin' his work. Get up on yer feet, you! An' see that them engines is kept better oiled!"

Captain McCluskey evidently ran his craft like an old-time clipper master.

Ham mentally kissed the oiler goodbye as a prospective opponent for Monk. He addressed Captain McCluskey.

"I like your discipline methods," he said flatteringly.

"They'll do, pretty boy," bellowed the walrus.

Ham writhed under the appellation of pretty boy. But he kept the oily smile of admiration on his face.

"I'm afraid you're going to have trouble with one man aboard this vessel," he said in the air of imparting a warning to his hero.

"Who?" roared the giant captain.

"The hairy baboon they call Monk," said Ham blandly.

"I'll watch 'im!" boomed the walrus ominously. "If he bats an eye at me, I'll hit the swab so hard his fur will fall off!"

Ham had a foxy look in his eye as he ambled back to Monk's steel cubicle. He looked in at Monk.

Monk gave him an elaborate, pig-like grunt.

Ham ignored the insult.

"The captain says the next time you bat an eye at him, he's gonna hit you so hard you'll shed all that red fuzz," Ham advised.

"Yeah?" Monk heaved to his feet. "Yeah? Well, I'll just go tell 'im I don't like guys talkin' behind my back like that."

He waddled out. He was so big he barely got through the door of his cubicle.

Ham trailed along. He wouldn't have missed what was going to happen for a thousand dollars.

MONK found walruslike Captain McCluskey in the officers' quarters. The two giants promptly glowered at each other. Monk's little eyes sparkled with the prospect of a fight. The walrus blew noisily through his mustache, each hair of which was like a crooked black peg.

"Listen, guy!" Monk began in a sugary voice. "I don't like—"

The walrus hit Monk. It sounded like a gun going off.

Monk hadn't expected it so soon. He was caught off guard. The blow drove him backward as though he had accidentally stood in front of a twelve-inch coast-defense gun.

His bulk collided with Ham, who was standing behind him. That kept Monk from falling.

But Ham was tumbled end over end. His head cracked a valve wheel. He was promptly knocked senseless.

From Ham's point of view, nothing worse could have happened. He slept through the whole fight. He was cheated of enjoying the fruit of his devilment. It was the biggest disappointment Ham had suffered in years. For days afterward, he was wont to get off in a corner and swear to himself about it.

Monk emitted a series of deep bawling noises. He jumped up and down like an ape. This cleared his head. He rushed the walrus.

The walrus kicked him in the stomach.

Monk folded down to the floor. The walrus leaped high into the air, and came down—and his face collided forcibly with Monk's driving feet.

Captain McCluskey turned over completely in the air. He spat out three teeth. He got up, roaring. Monk knocked him down, loosening two more teeth in the process.

The walrus tried to bite off Monk's left ear with what teeth he had left.

Monk stopped this by grasping great folds of his opponent's ample stomach in monster fists and striving to tear the man open.

They stood toe to toe and traded haymakers. They hit each other. They spat in each other's eyes. They swapped indiscriminate kicks.

It was a battle of the giants. A fray primeval! A thing of pristine savagery! It would have drawn a million-dollar gate in the prize ring—except that the women's clubs would have stopped it.

And poor Ham, sleeping through it all, would have cut off an arm rather than miss it.

Captain McCluskey lunged unexpectedly. Monk was carried backward. His bullet of a head crashed against a hard steel bulkhead.

Monk fell senseless.

The walrus drew back a foot to kick him.

At this point, Renny dashed forward. He grasped McCluskey's huge arm.

"You whipped him!" Renny rumbled. "No need of crippling him!"

Renny only wanted to keep Monk from serious damage. He was a peacemaker. He got what peacemakers usually get.

The walrus knocked Renny flat on his back.

THE fight now started all over. Renny was nearly as heavy as Monk. He was also a fine boxer. And for years he had been smacking panels out of doors with his fists.

Renny got up from the floor and hung a left jab on McCluskey's nose. The way crimson splashed, it looked like someone had stepped on a sponge soaked with red ink.

The walrus emitted a sound that was a combination of Vesuvius and Niagara. By a marvelous feat of acrobatics, he managed to jump on Renny's midriff with both feet.

Air came from Renny's mouth so fast it almost blew out his teeth. He collapsed—largely to keep his middle from being jumped on again.

Captain McCluskey rushed in to the kill.

Renny hooked a fist. It hit McCluskey's ear. It smashed the ear flat as a well-ironed handkerchief.

A strange thing now happened.

McCluskey got to his feet as calmly as though he were arising from the mess table. He ambled toward the slit of a door. He was unsteady on his feet, it was true, and nearly walked a circle. But he seemed to have forgotten there was such a thing as a fight.

McCluskey was extremely punch drunk.

He sobered before he got out of the room, though. Whirling, he emitted a bellow and sprang upon Renny.

Renny roundhoused two good swings. The first folded McCluskey like a barlow knife. The second ruined the walrus' other ear and spun him like a top.

McCluskey staggered backward and fell into a bunk. An instant later, however, he came out of it.

He was a lot of man, that walrus.

The two bartered punches. Renny blocked one with his jaw. For an instant, he was dazed. That instant was his undoing. Another swing landed on top of the first.

Renny dropped, kayoed for one of the few times in his career.

Mountainous Captain McCluskey took two weaving steps for the narrow bulkhead door. Then he sighed loudly, and, turning around twice like a dog finding a place to lay down, slumped prone on the floor.

The casualties were dumped in assorted bunks.

Afterward, Ham awakened. The combatants had been attended to, and Ham was so disappointed that he crawled out on deck and actually mingled salty tears with the sea.

DOC SAVAGE now inaugurated a campaign of his own. He began to fraternize with the crew in a most diligent manner. It was only another evidence of his immense knowledge that he found something of interest to discuss with each man.

Doc was hunting for the fellow whose teeth clicked.

A strange thing became evident. None of the crew was willing to open up and talk frankly with him. Instead, half a dozen of them sought, none too adroitly, to worm from Doc his reasons for coming along on the under-the-polar-ice expedition.

The big oiler whom Captain McCluskey had chastised for neglecting the engines was most outspoken. His name was, not without reason, "Dynamite" Smith.

"Just where is this boodle yer goin' after, sir?" asked Dynamite Smith.

"What boodle?" queried Doc innocently.

Dynamite Smith shifted uneasily.

"Well, me an' my mates kinda got the idea yer was goin' after somethin' up in the bloody Arctic," he said. "Have yer got a map that shows where it is?"

"What put all this into your head?"

"Nothin'," muttered Dynamite Smith.

Then, unable to stand the searching gaze of Doc's strangely potent golden eyes, the big oiler turned away.

It was obvious the man knew more than he had divulged. It was also evident that some sinister devilment was breeding among the crew.

Doc didn't like it.

"I'll bet that bird with the clicking teeth is stirring up the crew," Doc decided.

An idea hit him. He went to make sure he still had the treasure map he had taken off the back of blind Victor Vail by X-ray.

The map was gone! Somebody had stolen it!

SEVERAL days passed. Nothing happened. The *Helldiver* now sailed off a barren section of northern Greenland. Great blue icebergs cocked nasty snouts out of the sea all about them. The sub sloughed through mile after mile of thin pan ice.

Occasionally, where the pan ice had joined with fields of growlers, or small bergs, to make a solid barrier, they submerged and passed under.

The submarine was behaving beautifully. Long Tom's wonderful apparatus kept them out of danger, with the double safeguard of Monk's special chemicals, should something go amiss.

Monk, Renny, and the walruslike Captain McCluskey had resumed relations. Indeed, they got along handsomely. They had a hearty respect for each other's fighting qualities.

Poor Ham! Monk made him lead a dog's life. For Monk realized now that Ham had been responsible for the beating he had received. Practically every morning, Ham woke up to find a clammy ham in bed with him. Pictures of fat hogs had appeared mysteriously in his quarters so often that he had given up erasing them. Worse yet, Monk had bribed fully half the crew to make piggy squealing noises whenever Ham was in earshot.

Doc hadn't found the man with the clicking teeth. He was mystified. He couldn't imagine who had his treasure map, but he did not worry greatly about it. His retentive brain held all details of the

chart. He could sit down and reproduce it perfectly from memory.

The only discovery of note he had made was that Dynamite Smith, the big oiler, used narcotics almost steadily. Doc consulted Captain McCluskey about this.

"Sure, I knowed the swab was a dope head," the walrus assured him. "Rust my anchor, but it don't seem to hurt him. He's been usin' the stuff for years. Let'm alone, matey. The stuff just keeps 'im harmless."

Doc was not so sure about that. But there was nothing to be gained by starting trouble.

Long Tom radioed their position daily to Victor Vail. The violinist showed a great interest in their progress, as well as the exact course they intended to follow.

Sometimes Doc wondered about Victor Vail's avid desire to know their whereabouts to the fraction of a mile.

They were in a zone of continuous daylight now. The sun shone the full clock around. It was never night.

"Confound such a region!" Ham complained. He had just found out that for the last three days, Monk had awakened him at midnight, and made him believe it was noon the next day. Consequently, Ham had been losing a lot of sleep, and couldn't understand what was making him feel so groggy.

A STRANGE, sinister tension was growing aboard the *Helldiver*.

The crew congregated in groups, whispering. They dispersed, or fell to speaking loudly of commonplaces when Captain McCluskey, Doc, or any of his five men came near.

"Rust my anchor, but I smells trouble!" Captain McCluskey confided to Doc.

Day after day, the submarine bored into the polar regions. Twice it traveled under the ice more than a score of hours. It made many shorter jaunts under the pack.

On one occasion, they would surely have been trapped under a vast field of ice more than thirty feet deep, had it not been for Monk's chemicals. Released from compartments in the skin of the underseas boat, the stuff let the craft reach the surface through a great self-made blow hole.

It was now but a matter of dozens of miles to the spot where the treasure map indicated the long-lost liner *Oceanic* lay.

Doc noted a perceptible increase in the sinister tension.

"We're in for a jam," he told his five men seriously. "The crew of this sub, part of them at least, know what we're after. And one of these surely must have my map."

Monk grinned with all his homely face, and popped his knuckles.

"Well, we ain't seen no signs of Keelhaul de Rosa or Ben O'Gard," he chuckled. "That's one consolation."

"It's my opinion that Ben O'Gard's man with the clicking teeth is behind this trouble brewing with the crew," Doc replied.

"Confound it," declared Ham. "The clicking of the teeth should make the man easy to find!"

"That's what I thought," Doc said wryly. "But, bless me, brothers, I do believe that fellow's teeth have stopped clicking. I've gone around, straining my ears day after day, and not a click have I heard."

"Maybe it was really a dream Long Tom had about the man with the noisy teeth bending over him that night?" Johnny suggested.

"I didn't dream the black wig!" Long Tom retorted.

There was nothing to be said to that. The conclave broke up. At a scant five miles an hour, the *Helldiver* nosed for the dab of unmapped land where the liner *Oceanic* supposedly lay.

This was virtually an unexplored region where they now cruised. Possibly a polar aviator had flown over it, but even that was highly unlikely.

Doc retired, confident another twenty-four hours would bring action of some sort.

It did.

Johnny's frantic plunge into Doc's quarters awakened the big bronze man. Johnny's breath was a procession of gulps. His spectacles with the magnifying lens on the left side, were askew his nose.

"Renny! Monk!" he shouted. "They are both gone! They vanished during their watch on deck!"

Chapter X
MAROONED

IN flash parts of seconds, Doc was in the control room.

"Put about!" His powerful voice volleyed through the monotonous complaint of the Diesel engines. It penetrated to every cranny of the submarine, from the "hard-nose" bow up front—loaded with steel and concrete in case of collision with the ice—to the little tunnel through the after trim tanks, which gave access to the rudder mechanism.

The helmsman spun his wheel.

"Full speed ahead!" Doc boomed into the engine-room speaking tube.

Captain McCluskey lurched in from the officers' quarters. He was sticky-eyed from sleep.

"What's goin' on here?" he roared. "Rust my anchor, what we puttin' about for?"

"My two men, Monk and Renny, have disappeared!" Doc told him. "We're going back to hunt for them!"

Captain McCluskey clambered up on deck. But he came down almost at once, his hairy shanks blue from the cold.

"No use!" he rumbled. "Stormin' up there! If them two swabs ain't aboard, they're in Davy Jones' locker."

McCluskey seized the speaking tube to the engine room, shouted into it: "Slow your engines to normal speed." Then, to the helmsman: "Hard over, me hearty. We're resumin' our course."

Cold and hard as a statue of bronze, Doc Savage was suddenly in front of McCluskey. Doc was big. The walrus was bigger. He outweighed Doc by nearly a hundred pounds.

"Countermand that order!" Doc directed.

Such a quality of compelling obedience did his remarkable voice have, that McCluskey made an involuntary gesture at compliance. Then he bristled.

"I'm skipper of this tin fish!" he bellowed. "We ain't wastin no time goin' back to look for them two swabs. Davy Jones has got 'em, I tell you!"

"Countermand that order!" Doc repeated. "We'll find Monk and Renny, or their bodies, if we have to winter in this ice pack!"

Captain McCluskey glowered. He had a lot of confidence in himself. He had whipped Monk and Renny in succession, and either one of them looked more dangerous than this strange bronze man.

"I'll show yer who's master of this hooker!" he snarled.

He reached for Doc's throat.

The walrus was now treated to the big surprise of his life.

His hand was trapped in mid-air by case-hardened bronze fingers. For an instant, McCluskey thought the hand had been cut off, so much did that grip hurt, and so numb did it make his arm.

He started a blow with his free fist.

It traveled hardly more than an inch. Then that hand was closed in a fearful clasp. The hard paw crushed like so much dough. Big blisters of blood popped out on the fingertips, and burst with fine sprays of crimson.

The walrus screamed like a hurt child.

He stared at his hands. His eyes nearly fell out. Both his monster claws were now being held easily by one hard hand of bronze. Strain as he would, he could not budge them. The largest vise could not have held them tighter—or more painfully.

The walrus screamed again. He had thought himself a mighty fighter. Not in the scope of his memory had he met a scrapper who could stand before him.

But in the hands of this strange bronze man, he was like a fat sheep in the jaws of a hungry tiger. Then a Big Bertha shell seemed to go off in the captain's head. He slumped senseless.

Doc had kayoed him with one punch!

THE submarine rooted through growlers and pan ice. Back and forth, right and left, lunged and wallowed. Sometimes sheets of pan ice crowded up on the deck until Doc, Long Tom, Ham, and Johnny had to dive hastily down the hatch to avoid being crushed or swept overboard.

They had been searching for five hours.

No sign of Monk or Renny had they found.

A bitter wind was swooping off the distant wastes of ice-capped Greenland. It froze spray on the steel runners affixed to the hull of the under-the-ice sub. But the chemicals on the sides of the U-boat flushed the frigid coating away at intervals.

"The gale was worse during the night," Johnny muttered. "Poor Monk! Poor Renny!" He blinked his eyes back of his spectacle lenses.

Although Monk and Renny had indeed vanished during the night, it was night only by their watches. The sun hung well above the horizon—where it had lingered for some days. It was wan, almost lost in a pale, nasty haze.

Ice which had piled up on deck abruptly slid off with a grinding roar.

Doc went outside. He carried powerful binoculars. But once more, a search through them disclosed nothing.

However, the sub now surged across a comparatively open lead in the ice pack. This was what Doc had been hoping for.

"Stand by to put out the seaplane!" he ordered.

The crew crowded the deck. They were surly. The air of sinister trouble still hung about them. But they obeyed Doc's orders with alacrity. Some of them had seen what had happened to Captain McCluskey. They had told the others. It was something they would never forget.

A deck plate was lifted. A folding boom was jacked into position.

Out came an all-metal, collapsible seaplane. Doc himself got the tiny hornet of a craft ready for the air.

Captain McCluskey came on deck while the work was under way. Doc Savage rested his golden eyes intently upon the walrus of a man.

McCluskey scowled for a second or two. Then he grinned sheepishly.

"Ye won't have anymore trouble from me, matey," he mumbled. Then he winced and moved his hands.

Each paw was bundled in bandages until it resembled the foot of a man with the gout.

Doc drew his three remaining companions aside.

"Keep your hands on your guns," he warned them. "I don't think McCluskey will make more trouble immediately. But watch his crew!"

It seemed a miracle when the cockpit of the diminutive seaplane held Doc's mighty bronze form. The little radial engine was fitted with a starter. Doc turned it over. The cold made it stubborn. It fired at last.

The exhaust stacks smoked for a while. Then they lipped blue flame. The engine was warm.

The plane floats left a ribbon of foam as they scudded across the open lead in the ice pack. Doc backed the control stick. The ship vaulted off the water.

He banked in circle after circle, each one wider than the last.

The pale haze hadn't looked so thick from the surface. But it hampered vision amazingly from the air. The gloom was increasing, too.

No sign of Monk or Renny could he discern.

He flew back at last and alighted beside the submarine. The frozen rigidity of his bronze face told Long Tom, Ham, and Johnny the worst.

"Monk and Renny are—finished," Long Tom said thickly.

"Monk—how I'm gonna miss that guy!" Ham mumbled. He was near tears.

The crew hoisted the seaplane aboard, collapsed it, and stowed it under the deck plates.

TWO hours later, walruslike Captain McCluskey was pointing with a thick arm.

"Rust my anchor—look!" he boomed. "Two points off the starboard bow!"

Doc Savage, coming up from below, was a bronze flash. He thought Monk and Renny might have been sighted. There was always the possibility they had been washed overboard, and had reached one of the many icebergs.

This, however, was only a herd of walrus asleep on an enormous pan of ice.

"We need fresh meat," explained Captain McCluskey. "It's unusual to sight 'em this far north. I'm goin' after some of the critters. Want to go along, matey?"

Doc nodded. He advised Ham, Johnny, and Long Tom to go also. It would get their minds off the loss of Monk and Renny.

Several of the crew were also going, big Dynamite Smith included in them. Doc made sure a number of the surly faction amid the crew, the suspected plotters, were among the hunters. There seemed nothing to be lost in deserting the sub for a time.

Two folding kayaks—long and narrow boats with a covering of sealskin—were set up. They also assembled a umiak, overgrown brother of the kayak.

Doc went below. He was gone about ten minutes. During that time, he was alone below decks, everyone being outside to witness the departure of the hunters.

Doc came up, bearing a sizable bundle. This was done in waterproof silk.

"What's that, matey?" Captain McCluskey wanted to know.

Big bronze Doc Savage seemed not to hear the query.

They put off.

Bullets dug into the ice hammock, showering Doc and his friends with fragments of ice.

The edge of the iceberg, near where the walrus herd slept, arose almost vertically. It was too sheer for a landing. The hunters decided to stalk the animals from the berg. They paddled directly to the floe, alighted, and drew the folding boats well out of the cold water.

Captain McCluskey and the rest of the *Helldiver* crew led the stalk. Doc, with his strange bundle, kept warily in the rear. Ham, Long Tom, and Johnny trod his heels.

The bitter cold bothered them at first, but became less noticeable in a few minutes. They wore regulation Eskimo garb—moccasins reaching to their knees, and lined with reindeer skin, bearskin trousers, shirts of auk skins with the feathers inside, and shirts of sealskin, with a hood which covered their heads.

The surface of the ice pack was rough. Progress became laborious. The need for silence made it harder. Their speed was hardly half a mile an hour.

Captain McCluskey and his men drew a little ahead.

Suddenly they whirled. They aimed rifles at Doc and his friends.

"Kill the swabs!" shrieked Captain McCluskey.

DOC had been alert. He was not taken off guard. Hardly had the *Helldiver* men started their show of hostilities when a mighty bronze arm rushed Johnny, Long Tom, and Ham to cover behind an ice hummock.

The move was executed so quickly they were sheltered before the first rifle volley spattered out noisily.

Bullets dug into the ice hummock, showering Doc and his friends with fragments of ice. The pieces tinkled down the hard flanks of the ice mound with a sound like tiny bells.

"Retreat!" Doc commanded his friends. "We're between the gang and their boats. We'll try to keep them from reaching the craft."

They were extremely thankful for the rugged surface of the iceberg, now that the situation had changed.

Doc found a small crevice in the ice. Into this he lowered his bundle. With a single rap of his tempered fist, he shattered enough brittle ice to conceal the bundle.

Captain McCluskey's booming voice reached them.

"The deck swipes!" thundered the walrus. "Put the lot of 'em in Davy Jones' locker!"

"They don't seem to be trying to beat us back to the boats!" Doc said in a tight voice of wonder.

A storm of lead scored the ice all about. The *Helldiver* gang had caught sight of them.

Ham whirled. He secured a glimpse of a fur-swathed head. His rifle jarred. A man slouched out from behind an ice spike and lay down as though tired. Steam curled up from the scarlet pool that gathered around his feebly squirming body.

"I haven't lost my shooting eye!" Ham said with grim mirth. "Did you see who I winged?"

"Dynamite Smith, the oiler," Doc retorted. "Let's veer over to the right here. It looks like better footing."

There ensued a frightful couple of minutes before they reached the spot Doc had indicated. The more frantic the effort they put forth, the more they slithered around on the terrifically rough and slippery ice.

"Seas have been breaking over this berg recently," Doc explained. "That's why it's so infernally slick."

Bullets gouged ice around them like hard-driven, invisible picks. Ricocheting, the lead squawled like unseen wild cats.

Doc, Long Tom, Ham, and Johnny finally reached the smooth footing which Doc had indicated. This was a great crack which had opened in the berg, filled with water, then frozen. They glided down it.

"We're gonna beat 'em to the boats, anyhow!" said the bony Johnny. He had taken off his glasses with the magnifying lens on the left side. His breath steam had been fogging the spectacles. Johnny really did not have much need of glasses on his good right eye, anyway.

"It's funny they're not putting up more of a race to keep us from reaching the boats!" Long Tom snapped. "I don't understand it!"

But they did understand it a moment later.

They came in sight of the boats—more properly, the spot where the boats should have been, for the craft were gone.

And the submarine was not where they had left it!

"THEY'RE clever rats!" Doc Savage said grimly. "The men who remained aboard the *Helldiver* put another folding boat in the water the instant we were out of sight. They secured the craft we left on the ice. And look—there's why McCluskey's gang were not so ambitious in pursuing us." A bronze arm pointed.

Long Tom, Johnny and Ham stared. Their hearts sank.

The *Helldiver* had cruised down the edge of the iceberg. Standing by, the submarine was picking up members of the villainous crew as they slid off the sheer edge of the vast pan of ice.

Doc's pals opened fire with their rifles. The range was considerable. A high tribute to their shooting was the fact that they put two of the *Helldiver* crew out of commission.

The rest of the sailors reached the submarine safely. The craft sped down an open lead in the pack ice, headed northward. It was making for the spot where, according to the map, the liner *Oceanic* lay. The dense mist swallowed the sub completely.

The last thing they saw was the gigantic figure of Captain McCluskey standing on deck, shaking both his fists in their direction.

"Brothers," Doc said mildly, "we have been guilty of an unforgivable mistake."

"What's that?" Ham wanted to know.

"We underestimated the intelligence of friend McCluskey," Doc replied. "Some days ago, McCluskey commented on the furtive actions of his own crew, giving the impression, he, himself, feared trouble from them. The clever fellow must have been aware I had noticed the attitude of the crew, and he expressed himself thus to allay my suspicions of him."

"They've got the treasure map, of course," Ham clipped waspishly. "They've set out to grab the treasure."

"And they've left us in a pretty serious position," Johnny muttered. "Marooned on this Arctic ice pack is tantamount to a sentence of death."

Johnny's words carried awful portent. Johnny knew the polar regions. It was a part of his profession. And if he said their situation was bad—it was really bad!

"We might as well realize we're up against it," Doc told them, "and stop talking about it."

"The racket scared the walrus off the floe," Long Tom grumbled, his unhealthy-looking features drawing deeper into the hood of his fur parka, like the head of a turtle into its shell. "We're without grub!"

Ham whipped his bearskin trousers vigorously with his sword cane. "I've heard of Eskimos living quite a while by eating their clothes," he said.

"We won't need to start on our wardrobe for a while," Doc smiled. "We have concentrated rations for about a month."

"Where?" the others yelled in chorus.

"In the bundle I brought along," Doc replied.

THE party retraced their steps to secure the all-important bundle Doc had cached in the ice crevice.

There was no excitement now. They had leisure to realize the full peril of their predicament.

The deathlike quiet of the polar wastes had enveloped them. The stillness was as of a tomb.

From time to time, the awful silence was shattered by a crashing roll of sound like thunder. These noises would start with a report sharp and loud as a cannon crack, and there would follow an increasing volley until the very ice under their feet seemed to quake.

This was the awesome voice of the ice waste—it was simply cracks opening in the floes.

"Nice music!" Ham shuddered.

Thoughts came to them of Renny and Monk, of the death both giants seemed certain to have suffered. This depressed them.

There was a quality of horror in the grisly spells of silence. It was as though they existed in some weird, frozen habitat of lost souls. They found themselves listening with an eagerness near pathetic for the sporadic cannonade of the ice—then shivering when the sound did come.

Only big bronze Doc Savage showed no emotion. He swung along easily, keeping his feet on the slick iceberg under foot as surely as though his mukluks were arms with steel spikes. Often, he waited for his three friends to overhaul him.

The mighty bronze man seemed to sense that his very presence offered a bolster to the courage of Long Tom, Ham, and Johnny. So he remained near them, although the best pace they could manage was but the speed of a snail compared to the swiftness with which Doc could have reached the cache.

They secured the bundle from the crevice in the ice.

Doc let his men squat around it. They went to work on the wrappings with cold-stiffened fingers. The more they kept busy, the less they would brood over their fearsome predicament.

Suddenly, Ham gave a start—stopped fiddling with the knots.

To his ears had come the low, exotic trilling sound which was part of Doc. So low, so nearly unreal was the mellow note that it was almost lost in the fearful silences about them. It might have been the voice of some fantastic sprite of this domain of cold.

Ham grasped his sword cane. Johnny and Long Tom became rigid as the ice hummocks about them.

Doc's trilling slipped away into nothingness in a manner as intangible as its coming.

For a long minute, silence fairly reeked. It was the kind of a quiet, this dead apathy of the Arctic, which you momentarily expected to explode, as Ham was wont to remark.

Came a new sound! Doc had heard it before. That was what had surprised him into setting up his trilling note. Now Johnny, Long Tom, and Ham also heard it distinctly.

A clicking! A clicking as of dice rattled together in a palm!

The noise which had haunted Victor Vail down through the years! The noise which marked the presence of Ben O'Gard's man!

"That, brothers," Doc Savage said softly, "is one of the last things I expected to hear at this spot!"

WITH the final word, Doc glided forward. The others raced after him. But they were left behind as though their feet were frozen in the ice pack.

Doc Savage was lost to their sight.

When they overhauled him, Doc was standing over a human figure that sprawled in a steaming lake of scarlet.

"Dynamite Smith!" Ham clipped. "The bird I shot."

Doc and his three friends now exchanged understanding glances.

An uncontrollable palsy had seized Dynamite Smith's jaws. They rattled together—made the distinctive clicking.

Dynamite Smith was the one of Ben O'Gard's villains who had kept track of Victor Vail down through the years.

"I don't understand it!" Long Tom muttered.

"When he bent over me that night in my bunk, his teeth clicked. But we have talked with him many times since then, aboard the submarine, and his teeth made no sound."

"I see the explanation of that—now," Doc replied. "Dynamite Smith has been using narcotics almost steadily throughout the submarine voyage."

"You mean—"

"That the dope quiets his jaws." Doc explained. "In other words, every addict gets the heebie-jee-bies when deprived of his narcotic. When Dynamite Smith is without it, his jaws shake. When he has it, they don't."

The wounded man was conscious. He rolled his eyes.

Doc Savage now examined the man's wound. But Ham had made an accurate shot.

"You're doomed," Doc told Dynamite Smith without emotion.

The dying man's lips moved. Doc was forced to bend close before even his keen ears could decipher the fellow's gaspings.

"Ben O'Gard an' my mateys went off an' left me here, huh?" Dynamite Smith said.

Emotion rarely showed on Doc Savage's hand-some bronze face. But it was in evidence now.

"Was Ben O'Gard on the *Helldiver?*" he demanded.

Dynamite Smith did not answer the question. His glazing eyes rolled slowly until they focused upon Long Tom.

"I was huntin' the map when yer grabbed the black wig offn my head that night," he whispered feebly, "After I come near gettin' caught, Ben O'Gard hisself done the huntin'. It was him found the map an' swiped it from yer."

"Which one of the *Helldiver* crew is Ben O'Gard?" Doc demanded.

An evil, vicious sneer distorted the blue lips of the dying man. His whisper gurgled in his throat.

"We fooled the crew of ye plenty neat," he labored.

It seemed he would never get the next words past his stiffening throat muscles. The villainous sneer spread upon his lips.

"Ben O'Gard is Cap'n McCluskey!" he coughed.

ONE startled glance Doc and his three friends exchanged. When they looked back at Dynamite Smith, the man was dead.

"Ben O'Gard and Captain McCluskey—the same person!" Ham muttered. "For cryin' out loud!"

Doc Savage's strong lips warped slightly.

"It seems, brothers, that we kindly financed the expedition of our enemies to get the treasure," he said dryly. "No doubt Ben O'Gard—we'll call him that from now on, instead of Captain McCluskey—no doubt Ben O'Gard did take some of the treasure

from the *Oceanic* when he left the liner more than fifteen years ago. He used that money to fit up the *Helldiver.* But his funds were not sufficient. He advertised for a sucker to back him. Imagine his pleasure when we presented ourselves!"

Ham groaned loudly.

"It was me called your attention to that newspaper story about the under-the-ice submarine," he berated himself. "What a mess I got us into!"

Doc's low laughter danced merrily among the ice hummocks.

"Forget it, Ham. If the fault belongs anywhere, it's on my shoulders. Let us go back and open that bundle of mine."

They retraced their steps to the bundle. The seal-skin thong was untied. The waterproof covering was removed.

"Hey!" barked Johnny in surprise. "This wrapper is a small silk tent!"

"It's more than a tent, also," Doc informed him. "With it in the package is a collapsible frame of alloy metal. Expanded, and with that silk tent stretched over it, the frame becomes a boat. There are web paddles which can be attached to our rifle barrels for propulsion."

They all now dived into the rest of the bundle. They were anxious to see what fresh wonders it held.

Long Tom released a howl of delight.

"A radio set!" he squawled. "Transmitter and receiver, complete!"

Swiftly, Long Tom drew aside with the wireless equipment. He proceeded to put it in operation. The apparatus was of Doc's own devising, marvelously compact. It had no bulky batteries which might be rendered useless by moisture or cold, or exhausted by use. Current was supplied by a generator operated by a powerful spring and clockwork. The set operated on very short wavelengths.

In fifteen minutes, Long Tom had it ready for a test. Eagerly, the electrical wizard cocked an ear at the tiny built-in loudspeaker, and twirled the tuning dials.

Suddenly a voice purred out of the speaker.

The astonishment of Doc and his friends at hearing that voice was unbounded. It was as though they had tuned in on the other world.

They jumped up and down. They bellowed at each other in a near hysteria of delight. They danced circles on the iceberg.

"I tell you we're tuned in on hell!" Ham howled.

Ham was back in his old form.

For it was Monk's voice coming out of the loud-speaker!

Chapter XI
POLAR PERIL

ONE hour had passed. In the haze-soaked sky

hung a dark spot. This spot emitted a loud droning. The droning increased in volume.

The spot became a seaplane.

It was a two-motored job, not the latest and speediest type of plane, and somewhat shabby. But an angel would not have looked better to the four men watching it from the iceberg.

The ship sloped down in the fog. It circled. It lowered. The floats scraped a long white chalk mark of foam on the open lead in the ice pack. Then they settled. The plane taxied in to the rim of the berg.

Monk and Renny stood on the floats. With acrobatic leaps, they bounded to the ice.

Probably no more hearty reunion ever occurred than took place there in the cold shadow of the north pole.

Unnoticed at first, a man clambered out and sat on the cabin of the plane.

Doc Savage was the first to glimpse him.

"Victor Vail!" he called in surprise.

The famous violinist smiled at Doc. He tried to speak, but could find no words to express the depth of his feeling.

Finally, Victor Vail pointed at his own eyes. It was a simple gesture. But its meaning was unbounded.

Victor Vail now had eyes which were entirely normal. So deep was his gratitude to this giant bronze man that he could not put his emotion into coherent sentences.

"I sure thought I was rid of the sight of your ugly mug," Ham told Monk happily. "What happened?"

"The dang submarine submerged while we were keeping watch on deck," Monk explained in his mild way. "We were washed off. We swam like polar bears. I'll bet we swam ten miles. Talk about cold! We happened to have some of that chemical concoction I fixed up to keep a man warm, or we'd have frozen stiff. Anyway, we finally found an iceberg big enough to roost on."

"And we roosted on it until Victor Vail came along and took us off," Renny put in, his vast voice rumbling over the ice pack like thunder.

Doc Savage eyed Victor Vail. The violinist was alone in the plane. Surely, he had not flown into the Arctic wastes alone?

Victor Vail sensed his puzzlement.

"I hired this plane and a pilot to overhaul you," he explained. "You may have wondered why I have been so interested in your exact position, and the course you intended to follow. The reason was because I intended to join you."

"But why?" Doc questioned.

"My wife and my infant daughter, Roxey," Victor Vail said quietly. "I wanted to satisfy myself as to their—fate."

LONG TOM now busied himself taking down the portable radio outfit. It had served its purpose well, for it had guided the plane to this iceberg.

"Where is the pilot Victor Vail hired to fly him?" Doc asked.

"The monkey got cold feet!" Renny grinned. "Looking at all these icebergs got his goat. He refused to go on. So we took him back south to a little settlement on the coast of Greenland, bought his plane for twice what it is worth, and left him."

"That accounts for our not finding you," Doc decided.

Long Tom stored the last of the radio equipment into its container.

"Ham" Brooks, whose mind, whetted by careful legal training, was clever enough to save a whole division in the War, was not able to overcome the weighty evidence piled up against him in a case of stealing hams from the commissary. "Monk" still reminds Ham of that incident, which is about the only thing that can upset the impeccable, waspish Theodore Marley Brooks and his great legal mind. Ham's wit is as sharp as the point of the sword cane he invariably carries.

"You haven't told us how you happened to be marooned here," Monk grunted.

So Doc explained. "Captain McCluskey is Ben O'Gard," he concluded.

Victor Vail made a gesture of regret.

"I could not describe Ben O'Gard to you," he murmured. "I had no eyes to see him at the time I was in contact with him."

The famous violinist was now seized again with emotion. In halting words, he sought to express his gratitude to big bronze Doc Savage for the return of his vision.

"Any debt of gratitude you owed me is already paid in full!" Doc assured him. "You have saved me and my friends from almost certain death. In the winter, when the ice pack is frozen solid, we might have reached civilization. But as it was, we were in a death trap."

"McCluskey and Ben O'Gard are the same guy!" Renny ruminated. He popped his enormous fists together. They were so hard it was a wonder sparks did not fly. "I'd like to have another chance at that walrus! I'll bet the chump wouldn't lick me the second time!"

"You an' me both, pal!" Monk said with deceptive gentleness. "Dibs on first whack at 'im when we meet again!"

Long Tom had been delving in Doc's bundle. Now he gave a bark of surprise.

"Hey, what's this jigger?" he demanded.

He held up an oddly shaped blob of metal. It weighed quite a number of pounds.

"That," Doc explained softly, "is something I took off the submarine before we came away on our walrus hunt. It's a valve from one of the submerging tanks."

Long Tom grinned widely. He sensed that Doc had pulled a fast one.

"Furthermore," Doc continued, "Monk's chemical which melts the ice is all exhausted from the containers in the hull of the sub. There's material for more of the stuff aboard, but the *Helldiver* crew don't know how to mix it."

"You mean the gang can't take the submarine beneath the surface without this valve?" Long Tom demanded.

"Exactly," Doc replied. "They will realize they'd never come up if they did. The craft would be flooded. Too, they haven't the chemical to melt themselves out of a jam. The *Helldiver* cannot escape from this Arctic ice pack without submerging to pass under solidly frozen floes."

"Then we've still got the upper hand on the gang!" Monk chortled.

THE spirits of the adventurous group now soared. They boarded the seaplane. Old though the craft might be, it was amply large to accommodate all of them. Doc himself handled the controls.

The shabby buzzard of a plane seemed to take a drink out of the Fountain of Youth, or whatever rejuvenates decrepit seaplanes. It wiggled its tail like a fledgling. With a skipping lunge, it took the air.

"The *Helldiver* cannot have sailed far," Doc remarked.

Long Tom, Ham, and Johnny were taking stock of the plane fittings. There was an emergency outfit for Arctic travel, including pemmican and concentrated fruit juices intended to combat scurvy.

There were also parachutes.

"They may come in handy," Long Tom grinned. "From what I've seen of this ice pack, a man sometimes can go many a mile without finding enough open water to land a plane."

"Suppose you birds use binoculars on what's below us," Doc suggested mildly. "Finding the submarine in this fog is going to be a job."

"You said it," agreed Renny. "We'd never have found you on that iceberg if it hadn't been for the radio compass with which this plane is equipped."

Long Tom hastily seated himself before the radio compass. He twirled the dials, and cranked the gear which turned the loop aerial of the compass. Then he growled disgustedly.

"They're not operating the radio on the submarine," he declared. "Finding them would be a pipe if they were."

It was much colder in the air. They shivered in spite of their fur garments. Such warmth as there was in this frigid waste seemed to come from the water.

Doc's great voice suddenly reached every ear in the plane. He spoke but one word.

"Land!"

Several intent looks were required before the others saw what Doc's sharp gaze had discerned.

Land it was, right enough. But it looked more like a vast iceberg. Only occasional rocky peaks projecting from the glacial mass identified it as land.

"No map shows this land!" declared Johnny. "It can't be very great in area."

"What we're interested in is the fact that the liner *Oceanic* is aground on it somewhere," Doc informed him.

Victor Vail peered eagerly through the cabin windows. He had spent terrible weeks somewhere on that bleak terrain below. It held the secret of the fate of his wife and daughter, Roxey. Yet this was the first time he had ever actually seen it. The sight seemed to depress him. He shuddered.

"No one could live down there—more than fifteen years," he choked.

In Victor Vail's heart had reposed a desperate

hope that he might find his loved ones alive. This now faded.

"There's the *Helldiver!*" Doc said abruptly.

The others discovered it a moment later.

"Holy cow!" exploded Renny. "The ice is about to crush the submarine!"

BEN O'GARD and his villains were trapped! They had nosed the *Helldiver* into an open lead in the ice pack, close inshore. Excitement over the nearness of their objective must have made them reckless.

The ice floe had closed behind them. Slowly, inexorably, it now squeezed toward the sub. The bergs, a pale and revolting blue in the haze, crept in like the frozen fangs of a vast monster. No more than a score of feet of water lay open on either side of the sharp-backed steel cigar of an underseas boat.

Ben O'Gard and his thugs crowded the deck. They saw the seaplane. They waved frantically.

"I do believe they're glad to see us!" Monk snorted grimly. "We oughta sail around up here and watch 'em get squashed."

"There might be some pleasure in that," Doc admitted. "But we need that submarine to take the treasure home. There's too much of it to fly back by plane."

Monk shrugged. "How can we help 'em? There's not enough open water to land the plane."

"Take the controls," Doc Savage told Renny.

Renny remonstrated: "Hey—what on—"

Then he made a leap for the controls. Doc had deserted them. Renny banked the plane in a circle. Like all of Doc's five friends, he was an excellent pilot. Doc's teaching had made accomplished airmen out of them. Doc seemed able to impart a share of his own genius to those whom he taught.

Doc now snugged a parachute harness about his powerful frame. He grasped the valve which was all-important to the safety of the submarine.

Before the others could voice an objection, Doc shoved open the cabin door. He dived through.

The white silk of the parachute came out of the back pack like a puff of pale smoke. Doc was lowered to the ice near the distressed *Helldiver.*

Ben O'Gard and his crew held guns. They made threatening gestures. Doc displayed the valve. This was the magic wand that quieted the villains.

"Throw your weapons overboard!" Doc commanded.

For this order, he was roundly cursed. Ben O'Gard waxed especially eloquent. He must have gathered swear words from most of the dives of the world. He swore in six distinct languages, not counting pidgin English.

But the guns went overboard!

DOC SAVAGE now sprinted forward. The ice had closed in perceptibly. But more than a score of feet still separated the *Helldiver* from the remorseless blue jaws.

The surface of the floe was slippery. The leap to the submarine was prodigious. But from the ease with which Doc made it, he might have been gifted with invisible wings.

More than one gasp of awe escaped from the gullets of the *Helldiver* villains as they witnessed the great leap. They recoiled from the mighty bronze man. They still remembered what a child their huge walrus of a leader had been in those bronze hands.

One thug even backed away so hastily he fell overboard. He squealed like a rat in the icy water until he was hauled back on deck.

Not a minute could be wasted. Doc hardly touched the steel deck before he was gliding through the intricate insides of the submarine.

Doc worked swiftly at replacing the valve.

Ben O'Gard's men flocked around him like children. They already had the deck hatches closed in readiness.

Even Ben O'Gard himself came fawning up with a wrench to assist in the work. But Doc waved him aside. His bronze fingers were more speedy than any wrench—and they could tighten a tap just about as snugly.

"All clear!" Doc called at last. "Fill the main tanks!"

The crew flocked to station. The electric motors started.

With a windy gurgle that was nothing if not joyful, the *Helldiver* eased down out of the fearsome blue jaws of ice.

Doc watched the valve for a moment. Satisfied it was not going to leak, he turned away.

At that instant, the steel door of the compartment in which he crouched clanged shut. The dogs which secured it rattled fast.

He was imprisoned!

Chapter XII
ICE TRAP

DOC shrugged. He sat down on a convenient pipe. He was not worried. He was armed.

True, Ben O'Gard and his crew probably had guns themselves, by now. The weapons they had thrown overboard so profanely at Doc's request had hardly comprised their entire armament. They were too wily for that.

But Doc had the explosive he always carried in his pair of extra molars. With it, he could speedily blast open the bulkhead.

And once the sub came to the surface, he had simply to unscrew the valve—and he would have the gang at his mercy again.

THE POLAR TREASURE 43

The electric motors set up a musical vibration. The *Helldiver* had slanted down steeply in its hurried dive. Now it trimmed level. After a time, it sloped upward perceptibly. There came a jar as it touched the underside of the ice pack.

Other crunching shocks ensued. They were of lesser violence. The submarine was feeling blindly for another spot free of ice. This continued interminably. Open leads seemed to be very scarce.

Doc got up and rapped tentatively on the thick steel bulkhead.

He was cursed. He was told he would be killed if he didn't behave. He was promised all kinds of dire fates.

This didn't worry him much. Danger seldom worried Doc. A telegraph operator in a great relay office becomes accustomed to the uproar of instruments about him. A structural-steel worker comes to think nothing of the fact that a single misstep means sudden death.

By the same token, Doc Savage had haunted the trails of those who sought his violent end for so long that he took danger as a matter of course.

The interior of the submarine was fitted with a shell of thin metal some inches from the pressure plates. Over this was a coat of composition board intended to insulate the cold out. But it was frigid inside the *Helldiver*, for all that.

More than an hour passed. Doc became impatient.

Finally, the submarine arose to the surface. The stopping of the electric motors and the starting of the oil-burning Diesel engines showed that.

Doc promptly removed the all-important valve.

Through the steel bulkhead, he informed Ben O'Gard what he had done.

He got a surprise. Ben O'Gard gave him the horse laugh.

DOC was puzzled. He had thought he held an ace. But the missing valve seemed to worry his enemies not at all. There was but one explanation.

They had found a snug harbor on the uncharted coast!

Doc settled down to await developments. They came twenty minutes later.

There reached his ears a sound like six or seven hard hailstones tapping the submarine hull.

Doc knew what it was.

Machine-gun bullets!

Were his friends starting hostilities? He hoped not. They'd fool around and get themselves shot out of the air. The old seaplane was no battle wagon.

With a jarring bedlam, the Diesel engine sped up. The mad race of the vertical-trunk pistons vibrated the whole submarine. The *Helldiver* lunged away soggily.

Next instant came a shock which, catching Doc by surprise, piled him against a bulkhead.

The *Helldiver* had gone aground.

Men yelled. They sounded like chicks cheeping in an incubator. A machine gun cut loose on deck. Another joined it. Their clamor was hollow, like crickets shut up in a can.

This continued for the space of time it would take a man to count to several hundred.

Wham! The sub all but rolled completely over. The plates shrieked. Loose tools jumped about as beans in a shaken box.

Doc picked himself up.

"I'd better hold onto something," he remarked to no one in particular.

A bomb had just exploded in the water near the submarine.

Doc shook his head slowly. His friends had no bombs!

Ben O'Gard's bellow penetrated the bulkhead. "Come out!" he boomed. "You gotta help us!"

"Go take an ice bath!" Doc suggested.

Ben O'Gard spewed profanity hot enough to melt the steel bulkhead.

"Rust my anchor, matey!" he yelled at last. "You've got the upper hand on us again. We'll do anything you say, only you gotta help us."

"It sounds like you're aground," Doc told him. "My replacing the valve won't help any now."

"T'hell wit' the valve!" roared Ben O'Gard. "Ain't none of us swabs can fly the foldin' seaplane. You gotta take the sky hooker up an' fight off them buzzards that's bombin' us!"

"Who's bombing you?" Doc questioned.

"Keelhaul de Rosa's gang—the dirty deck lice."

DOC digested this. It was an entirely new development.

Since the *Helldiver* had left New York, there had been nothing to show Keelhaul de Rosa still existed upon the earth. Now the explanation for that was plain.

Keelhaul de Rosa had one of the treasure maps. He had secured a plane and flown to the wreck of the liner *Oceanic*. And now he was seeking to wipe out his rivals.

"Stand away from the door," Doc ordered. "I'll come out."

The dogs securing the steel panel clanked free. Doc swung the panel open. Several of Ben O'Gard's villains faced him. But not a gun was turned in his direction. They were a scared lot.

"Four of me hearties was swept overboard an' drowned by that bomb." Ben O'Gard roared. "The swabs are in Davy Jones' locker."

The thugs split like butter before a hot knife as Doc went through them. A vault, and he was out on deck. He had his valve along.

Ben O'Gard's men were frantically assembling the folding seaplane.

Doc scanned the skies.

"Where's the plane?" he demanded.

"Figure it went back after another load of bombs," boomed Ben O'Gard. "Rust my anchor, matey. We gotta shake a mean leg, or it'll be back 'fore you set sail in the air."

The *Helldiver* was indeed aground. The bow canted half out of the water. The stern portion of the deck slanted down beneath the surface.

Around about was a glacier-walled cove. Ordinarily, it would have been a snug-enough harbor. But the attack from the air had turned it into a trap.

Doc scrutinized the heavens once more. His strange golden eyes sought everywhere for the shabby plane flown by his friends. There was no sign of it.

Doc juggled the all-important valve. Some of Ben O'Gard's men eyed it enviously. Doc had no idea of surrendering it, though.

"What became of my friends?" he questioned.

Ben O'Gard shrugged his walrus shoulders.

"The last of 'em I saw, they was fightin' Keelhaul de Rosa's sky tub." He leveled an arm which was a cone of beef. "The fracas wandered off down that way."

He was pointing down the glacial coast of the uncharted land.

No line changed on Doc Savage's firm bronze features. But inside, his feelings were far from pleasant. The shabby old seaplane flown by his friends was no fighting craft. An Immelman or a tight loop would pull her wings off.

The tiny folding seaplane was now ready for the air.

"Take 'er off, matey," howled Ben O'Gard. "Rust my—"

He fell silent. The drone of a plane had come to their ears.

"That's Keelhaul de Rosa comin' back," bawled the walrus. "Hurry, matey. Our lives is in your hands."

"I wish they were," Doc said under his breath. Then, aloud: "Give me the best machine gun. And throw every other weapon overboard."

"Aw, don't worry about us keepin' our hands offn you from now on," fawned the walrus. "Why, we'll cut you in on a share of the boodle—"

"Over with the guns," Doc rapped.

There was more squawking. But the motor sound of the approaching plane was like the howl of doom. No argument could have been more persuasive. Falling pistols, rifles, knives, and machine guns whipped the surrounding water into a foam.

Doc waited until the last arm vanished.

Then his mighty bronze form plugged into the tiny seaplane cockpit. The motor purred like a big cat.

He took the air. The all-important valve went with him.

HE was none too soon. With a bawl like a banshee spawned by the foul gray haze overhead, Keelhaul de Rosa's plane dived. It opened with a machine gun. The craft had come into the Arctic spurred for war. It had a pair of cowl guns, synchronized through the prop.

Every fourth or fifth slug it fired was a phosphorus-burning tracer. The bullets scuffed the water below Doc's fleet little flivver craft. In the green sea, before they were extinguished, the tracers glowed like a streak of scattered sparks.

Cobwebby, gruesome, tracer strings waved before Doc's golden eyes. Phosphorus fumes reeked in his nostrils. Lead gashed a hole in the right-wing bank. The flivver wouldn't stand much of that.

Doc banked quickly. The tiny seaplane was agile as a fly in his master hand.

Twice more, Keelhaul de Rosa's killer craft dived angrily. Its lead missed both times.

Ben O'Gard and his gang now gathered the fruit of all that squawking about giving up their guns. They had delayed Doc almost too long.

Keelhaul de Rosa's plane swooped upon the *Helldiver*. It released an elongated metal egg. This hatched a choice lump of hell alongside the submarine. Water geysered two hundred feet in the air. A huge wave sprang outward in a circle.

Over heeled the sub, over—over. It writhed. It skewered like a tadpole out of water.

Then it slipped free of the ledge upon which it had been hung.

For a long minute, the *Helldiver* was lost under the water. Then it came up—and floated.

The bomb had been a blessing.

Doc flung his flivver for the other plane. If size of the craft had been important, the scrap would have been ridiculous. Doc's steed was to the other like a sparrow to a hawk. But size counts little in an air battle.

Doc, however, was handicapped by having to fly his plane and shoot his submachine gun by hand at the same time.

He jockeyed in above the enemy. His rapid-firer burred noisily, the breech mechanism spewing a string of smoking empty cartridges.

The other plane jumped in the sky like a thing bitten.

NO serious damage had been inflicted, however. The two craft sparred wanly. At this, they were about evenly matched.

Keelhaul de Rosa's seaplane was a low-wing, all-metal job of late production. Its two motors were huge and speed-cowled for efficiency. Even the pontoon floats were streamlined in a fashion which made them virtually another pair of small wings.

Only two men occupied the craft.

Neither of these was Keelhaul de Rosa. They had, rather, the wind-burned look of professional airmen of the northland. Probably Keelhaul de Rosa had picked them up to do his flying.

The jockeying for position ended suddenly. A quick flip of Doc's bronze wrist, a gentle pressure from one foot, and the tiny seaplane pounced like a bull pup. It was doubtful if the pair in the big plane understood quite how the maneuver had been managed. But Doc was upon them while the pilot still goggled through the empty sight rings of his cowl rapid-firers.

Doc's small machine gun shimmied and lipped flame. His bullets pushed cabin windows out of the other ship. They tore the goggles off the other pilot. Then they went to work on the fellow's brains.

The big plane did half a wingover, eased into a dizzy slip, and would have collided with Doc's little bus. He evaded it by zooming sharply.

The second man in Keelhaul de Rosa's craft took over the controls. Callously, he boosted the lifeless body of his companion through a shattered cabin window. The cadaver fell, warm and floppy, still spilling crimson.

Once again, the man-made birds skulked each other's sky trails warily. The motors panted and steamed. The evil gray mist squirmed and boiled in the prop wakes.

Doc got in a burst. His lead started colorless streams of liquid stringing from the wings of the other plane. He had opened the fuel tanks in the wings.

In return, he took a lead-whipping that gnawed a ragged area in the fuselage of his little flivver. After that, the craft flew with a strangely broken-backed feel.

Then fresh trouble loomed. Doc's fuel gauge needle had retreated a lot. It already covered the first two letters of the word "empty." There had been no time to charge the fuel tanks before he took off.

Doc calculated. Fifteen minutes more, and he would have to come down. He'd better finish this sky brawl quickly.

For the second time, Doc's small craft pulled its bewildering pounce of a maneuver. His gun hammered. Lead went home to vital points of the opposing plane.

Keelhaul De Rosa's pilot hardly moved a face muscle. But his plane climbed up on its tail and hung hooting at the borealis. It slipped off on a wing tip. It rocked into a tailspin.

It hit a floe hard enough to knock a hole through four feet of pan ice. After that, nothing was left but a wad of tin and wire sticking out of the ice.

Doc slammed his bus back for the cove. He found it in the gray haze.

A disquieting sight met his gaze.

The *Helldiver* was steaming straight for the open sea—or, rather, the ice-covered sea. All hatches were battened.

Doc's powerful bronze hand closed over the tank valve. He had it in the plane cockpit. If the submarine dived with the tank open, it would never come up.

The sub dived!

TWO minutes—three—Doc circled the spot where the Helldiver had gone under the ice pack. Green water boiled. A lot of bubbles came up. Small growlers of ice cavorted like filthy blue animals. And that was all.

Doc's bronze features, remarkably handsome in their rugged masculine way, did not alter expression. He banked away. The tiny folding seaplane climbed. It boomed along at the speed most economical on the fuel.

Doc was hunting his friends.

The outlook was not pleasant. The plane his friends had flown was no match for Keelhaul de Rosa's killer ship. This tiny collapsible crate of Doc's was far more efficient, and Keelhaul de Rosa's bus would have sky-scalped it easily except for Doc's master hand at the controls.

The fog wrapped him around like an odious, ash-colored death shroud. The small engine moaned defiantly. But its life blood, the high-test gas in the tank, ran lower and lower.

Suddenly Doc sighted a human figure below. It was a tiny form. It crawled on all fours, like a white ant in its light-hued fur garments.

Doc dropped his plane to within a score of feet of the ice. The jagged hummocks fanged hungrily at the floats. They seemed to miss them by scant inches.

The crawling human being flashed beneath.

It was Victor Vail. He carried a bundle of white silk.

Doc's bronze head gave the barest of nods. He could guess why Victor Vail was down there, carrying the folds of a parachute.

Monk, Renny, Long Tom, Ham and Johnny—Doc's five iron-nerved, capable friends—had given battle to the sky killer of Keelhaul de Rosa. They had dumped Victor Vail overboard by chute. They had wanted him clear of danger. That meant they knew they were fighting hopeless odds.

It boded ill for Doc's five pals, did that crawling figure of Victor Vail. It meant the five had felt they were going to their death.

Doc flew on. He aimed the noisy snout of his little plane in the direction Victor Vail was crawling. For the violinist had been headed, not for land, but out into the grisly waste of the polar ice pack.

This indicated he had some goal out there.

Doc found that goal in slightly more than a

minute—about two miles from where Victor Vail crept.

It was a horrible sight. The mighty bronze man had seen few more ghastly. None that tore at the insides of him like this one did!

A ruptured seaplane float lay on the ice. It was a mass of splinters. Forty yards farther on was the second. Then the ice bore a sprinkling of airplane fragments.

A section of a wing still poured off gruesome yellow smoke.

Gaping, sinister, an open lead in the ice yawned just beyond. Into this had plainly gone engine, fuselage, and the heavier parts of the plane.

To Doc's golden eyes, the whole sickening story was clearly written. Tracer bullets had fired the fuel tanks of the shabby seaplane. It had crashed in flames.

The odious green depths of the polar sea was the grave of whatever and whoever had been in the fuselage when the old crate cracked up.

Doc circled slowly.

The engine of his plane gurgled loudly. It coughed.

Then it stopped dead.

Chapter XIII
ICE GHOSTS

THE fuel had run out! Doc realized this—and slammed the nose down.

Practically no height for maneuvering lay below. The little flivver, due to small wingspread and not inconsiderable weight, would glide about as well as a brickbat.

The only landing place was the lead which had swallowed the remains of the shabby seaplane flown by Doc's friends. And that had hardly the width of a city street. It was about half a block long.

Had Doc Savage's hand on the controls been a whit less masterful than it was, the rent in the Arctic ice would have claimed his life. Nothing short of a miracle was the landing Doc made in the cramped space.

Above one end of the lead—smaller than many a private swimming pool—the plane abruptly turned broadside in the air. As swiftly, it turned to the other side. This fishtail maneuver lowered air speed to near the stalling point. With a sizable splash, the floats dug in the icy water. They plunged so deep the plane wetted its belly.

Doc had known from the first he was due for a crack-up. He was not wrong. The plane sloughed for the wall of ice. Doc vaulted out of the cockpit.

Only fractional seconds elapsed between the time the plane plumped into the water and the instant it smashed into the icy bank of the lead. It taxed even Doc's blinding speed to get out of the control

bucket in time. He leaped. His feet landed on the ice. He slid a dozen yards as though on skates.

The plane hit. There was a jangling crash remindful of an armload of tin cans dumped on a concrete walk. Metal rent, crumpled. The plane sank like a monkey wrench.

By the time Doc had ceased sliding and wheeled back, the craft was gone. The repellent water boiled as in a hideous cauldron. Big bubbles climbed to the surface with ghastly *glub-glubs*. It was as though a living thing was drowning in the depths.

Doc Savage turned away. The valve from the submarine had gone down with the plane. So had the machine gun.

Doc stood on the menacing Arctic ice pack armed only with his tremendous muscles and his keen brain. He had no food. He had no tent, no bedding, no boat to cross leads in the ice.

Probably no one could have understood more fully than Doc the meaning of this. He was in a region so rugged, so bleak, that out of countless expeditions traveling on the ice and equipped with the finest of dog teams and food, but one has ever succeeded in reaching the North Pole—Admiral Peary.

Yet one beholding the quiet composure of the bronze man's features would have thought he didn't realize what he was up against. Doc's giant figure was striking, even swathed as it was in fur garments.

He roamed the vicinity of the wrecked planes for an hour. Nothing did he find to indicate his five friends still lived. So Doc went to meet Victor Vail.

VICTOR VAIL was above the average physically. In an ordinary group of men, he would have stood out as being rather athletic.

He had progressed a scant half mile from where Doc had sighted him from the plane. His breath sobbed through his teeth. He tottered, near exhaustion. He was indeed glad to see the bronze man.

Doc Savage had covered thrice the distance negotiated by Victor Vail. Yet Doc's bronze sinews were unstrained. He breathed normally. He might have been taking a stroll down Park Avenue.

"Your friends!" gasped Victor Vail. "Did you find them safe?"

Doc Savage shook a slow negative. "I found where their plane sank through a hole in the ice. That was all."

Victor Vail sagged down wearily, disconsolately.

"I heard the plane crash," he murmured. "I was making for the spot. I could not see the crash, because of the haze. But Keelhaul de Rosa's hired killers shot them down."

Doc made no sound. Victor Vail nipped his lips, then continued.

"Your five friends forced me to leave the plane by parachute—to save my life," he murmured.

"Others of the five could have escaped. Yet they chose to fight together, to the end. They were brave men."

Doc still made no sound. The moment was too pregnant with sorrow to be shattered by cold words.

"What do we do now?" Victor Vail queried at length.

"We'll find the lost liner *Oceanic*," Doc replied. "And we will find Keelhaul de Rosa."

The chill ferocity in the bronze giant's expressive voice made Victor Vail shiver. At that instant, he wouldn't have traded places with Keelhaul de Rosa for all the wealth in the world, with a safe return to New York City thrown in.

Keelhaul de Rosa was going to feel the kind of justice this mighty bronze man dealt.

THEY set a course for the uncharted land.

"What about Ben O'Gard?" questioned Victor Vail. "Do we still have him and his crew of devils to fight?"

"The *Helldiver* submerged with all aboard," Doc replied. "I had that valve off the tanks with me."

Victor Vail gestured as if tossing something away. "We're rid of them, then. Water will flood the submarine through the hole left by the missing valve."

A vast quaking and rumbling seized the ice pack. They became aware that a wind had sprung up. This gave signs of increasing to a gale. The ice was beginning to shift. It was as though they strode the white, heaving, crusted paunch of a great monster of cold.

A crevice opened unexpectedly. Victor Vail toppled on the brink. He slipped into space. But strong bronze fingers snatched him back as if he were a morsel from the jaws of a ravenous beast.

The crevice closed as swiftly as it had opened. It made a ghastly crunching. Chunks of ice flew high in the air. The frozen monster might have been angry at being cheated of a victim, and was spitting its teeth out in a rage.

It was several minutes before Victor Vail could still the trembling of his knees.

"What a ghastly region!" he muttered.

"There must be a hard storm to the southward," Doc explained. "It is causing a movement of the ice field."

The going was incredibly rough. Sheer blocks of bergs jutted up everywhere. Many were as large as houses. Occasionally these toppled over. Sometimes they piled one atop the other after the fashion of cards shuffled together. These occurrences were without warning.

Twice more, Victor Vail was saved by his giant bronze companion.

"I shall never be able to pay my debt of gratitude to you," the violinist said feelingly.

Doc had a two-word reply to all such protestations.

"Forget it," he said.

As they neared land, the seemingly impossible happened—the going became harder. The Arctic ice pack was at its worst. Summer, such as it was, was in full swing. The sun had been shining steadily for two months. This had rotted the ice enough that it broke up under a brisk blow.

Doc now virtually carried Victor Vail. Time after time, ice pinnacles crashed upon the very spot where they stood. But in some magic manner, the mighty bronze man always managed to get himself and the violinist in the clear.

The air was filled with a cracking and rumbling so loud as to almost produce deafness. They might have been in the midst of a raging battle.

"You can tell your grandchildren you went through about the worst danger nature can offer," Doc said grimly. "For sheer, terrifying menace, nothing quite equals a storm with the Arctic ice pack breaking up under foot."

Victor Vail made no reply. Doc glanced at him sharply.

Tears stood in Victor Vail's eyes.

Doc's chance remark about grandchildren had made Victor Vail think of his long-lost daughter, Roxey.

THEY braved an inferno for the next few minutes; an inferno of ice and wind. Pressure was forcing the pack ice high on the shore of the uncharted land. Frozen death crashed and lurched everywhere.

Doc Savage made it through in safety. He carried Victor Vail under one thewed arm, seeming not to feel the burden at all.

"We licked it," Doc said dryly. "The storm accounts for the thick haze we've had the last few days."

They hurried inland. Their mukluks still trod ice. It lay below to a depth of many feet. Occasional ridges of dark, impermeable stone rammed unlovely fangs out of the white waste.

The wind hooted and shrieked. Sometimes it whirled the two men along like crumpled balls of paper.

They mounted higher. The glacier thinned. The dark stone reared in greater profusion.

Doc Savage halted suddenly. He poised, motionless, metallic. No breath steam came from his strong lips.

"What is it?" breathed Victor Vail.

Doc released breath from his mighty lungs. It made a spurting plume that frosted on the fur of his parka. The air was turning colder.

"Something is stalking us!" Doc said dryly.

Victor Vail was astounded. His own senses were very keen—made so by the years when he had been blind, and depended upon them. But he had heard nothing.

"I caught the odor of it," Doc explained.

Amazement gripped Victor Vail. He had not known this strange bronze man, through unremitting exercise, had developed the olfactory keenness of a wild thing.

Doc Savage pressed Victor Vail into a convenient crevasse.

"Stay here!" Doc commanded. "Don't leave the spot. You might become lost!"

The void of shrieking wind swallowed Doc's bronze form. He glided to the right. His speed was amazing.

A few flakes of snow came sizzling through the gale. More followed. They were hard as fine hailstones. When Doc flattened close to a rock spine to listen, the snow sounded like sand on the stone. He heard nothing.

He crept on. The snow shut out visions beyond a few yards. It stuck to his bearskin trousers. It rattled off his metallic face like shot.

Suddenly he caught blurred movement in the whistling abyss. He flashed for it. His hands—

hands in which steel bars became plastic as tin strips—were open and ready. His charge was that of a mighty hunter of the wild.

The next instant, Doc became quarry instead of hunter.

It was a polar bear he had rushed!

Bruin was a granddaddy of his species, judging from his size. The animal bounded to meet Doc. It

Doc had fastened himself to the back of the animal. He struck the bear just back of the head.

seemed clumsy. The awkwardness was only in its looks, however. It weighed more than a thousand pounds! Its speed was as tremendous as its size. It was the most terrible killer of the Arctic!

Doc sought to veer aside. The footing was too slippery. Straight into the embrace of the polar monster, he skidded!

SOME men acquainted with the Arctic regions maintain the polar bear will flee from a human being, rather than attack. Others cite instances when the bruins were known to have taken the aggressive.

The truth of the matter is probably covered by the words of a certain famous Arctic explorer.

"It depends on the bear," he said.

The bear Doc had met was the attacking type.

It erected on its rear legs. It was far taller than Doc. It flung monster forepaws out to inclose Doc's bronze form. A blow from one of those paws would have crushed down a bull buffalo.

Twisting, half ducking, Doc evaded the paws. His sinewy fingers buried in the fur of the polar monster. A jerk, a lightening flip, put him behind the bear.

Doc's fist swung with explosive force. It seemed to sink inches in the fat flesh of the animal. Doc had struck at a nerve center where his vast knowledge told him there was a chance of stunning the monster.

Bruin was not accustomed to this style of fighting. This small man-thing had looked like an easy quarry. The bear snarled, showing hideous fangs. With a speed that was astounding, considering the animal was nine feet long and weighed in excess of half a ton, it whirled.

Doc had fastened himself to the back of the animal. He clung there solely by the pinching power of his great leg muscles. Both his arms were free.

He struck the polar bear just back of the small head. He slugged again, hitting a more vulnerable spot.

Snarling horribly, the terror of the northern wastes sank to the glacier. The animal had met more than its match.

Doc could have escaped easily. But he did not. They needed food and a sleeping robe. Here were both. Doc's metallic fists pistoned a half dozen more stunning blows. Slavering and snarling, the bear stretched out.

Doc's mighty right arm slipped over the bear's head, just back of the ears. It jerked. A dull pop sounded. A great trembling seized all the great, white monster. The fight was over.

Silence fell, except for the moan of the blizzard.

Was it a low, mellow, trilling sound, remindful of the song of some exotic bird, which mingled with the whine of the wind? Or was it but the melodious note of the gale rushing through the neighboring pinnacles of rock and ice?

A listener could not have told.

Doc's strange sound sometimes came when he had accomplished some tremendous feat. Certainly, there was ample cause for it now.

No man, bare handed, had ever vanquished a more frightful foe.

Doc skidded the huge, hairy animal to a nearby pock in the bleak stone. He searched until he had found boulders enough to cover the cache of potential food and bedding. He did not want other bears to rob him.

He now hurried to get Victor Vail.

He reached the crevasse where he had left the violinist.

Ten feet from it, a gruesome red sprinkling rouged the ice. Blood! It no longer steamed. It was frozen solid, crusted with flakes of snow.

Scoring in the ice, already inlaid with snow, denoted a furious fight.

No sign was to be seen of Victor Vail!

Chapter XIV
CORPSE BOAT

LIKE a hound in search of a scent, Doc set off. He ran in widening circles. He found faint marks that might have been a trail. They led inland. They were lost beyond the following within two rods.

Doc positioned himself in the lee of a boulder the size of a box car. Standing there, sheltered a little from the blizzard, he considered.

An animal would have devoured Victor Vail on the spot! There had been no bits of cloth scattered about, no gory patches on the ice, such as certainly would have accompanied such a cannibalistic feast.

Something else loomed large in Doc's mind, too. The odor his supersensitive nostrils had detected at first!

Doc's mighty bronze form came as near a shiver as it ever came.

There had been a bestial quality about that scent. Yet it had hardly been that of an animal! Nor was it human, either. It had been a revolting tang, reminiscent of carrion.

One thing he began to realize with certainty. It had not been the polar bear!

Doc shrugged. He stepped out into the squealing blizzard. Inland, he journeyed.

The terrain sloped upward. The glacier became but scattered smears of ice. Even the snow did not linger, so great was the wind velocity.

Doc crossed a ridge.

From now on, the way led down. Progress was largely a matter of defying the propulsion of the gale.

Snow was drifting here. This was a menace, for it covered crevasses, a fall into which meant death. Doc trod cautiously.

In a day or two, perhaps in a week, when the blizzard had blown itself out, the haze above would disperse, and let the everlasting sun of the Arctic summer beat down upon the snow. This would become slush. Cold would freeze it. A little more would be added to the thickness of the glacier. For thus are glaciers made.

Warily, Doc sidled along. He let the wind skid him ahead when he dared. Had he been a man addicted to profanity, he would have been consigning all glaciers to a place where their coolness probably would be a welcome change.

A hideous cracking and rumbling began to reach his ears. He could hear it plainly when he laid his head to the ice under foot.

It was the noise of the icepack piling on the shore. This uncharted land must be but a narrow ridge projecting from the polar seas.

Doc neared the shore.

An awesome sound brought him up sharp. It split through the banshee howl of the blizzard. It put the hairs on Doc's nape on edge.

A woman's shrieking!

DOC sped for the sound. The snow collapsed under him unexpectedly. Only a flip of his Herculean body kept him from dropping to death on the snaggled icy bottom of the wide crevasse far below.

He ran on as though he had not just shaken the clammy claw of the Reaper.

A white mass hulked up before his searching golden eyes. It looked like a gigantic iceberg cast upon the shore. But it had a strangely man-made look.

A ship!

The ice-crusted hulk of the lost liner *Oceanic!*

Doc raced along the hull. It canted over his head, for the liner was obviously heeled slightly. A hundred feet, he ran. Another!

He came to an object which might have been a long icicle hanging down from the rail of the liner. But he knew it was an ice-coated chain. The links were a procession of knobs.

These knobs enabled Doc to climb. But the mounting was not easy. A greased pole would have been a stairway in comparison. The blizzard moaned and hooted and sought to pick him bodily from his handhold.

The woman was no longer shrieking.

Doc topped the rail. A scene of indescribable confusion met his eyes. Capstans, hatches, bitts, all were knots of ice. The rigging had long ago been torn down by the polar elements. Masts and wire-rope stays and cargo booms made a tangle on the deck. Ice had formed on these.

The forward deck, it was. A frozen, hideous wilderness! The gale whined in it like a host of ravenous beasts.

Doc reached a hatch. It defied even his terrific strength. The years had cemented it solidly.

The deck did not slope as much as he had thought. It was not quite level, though. He glided for the stern.

An open companion lured him. Snow was pouring in. Half inside, he saw the floor was seven feet deep in ice—snow which had formed a glacial mass through the years.

Doc tried another companion. The door was closed. It resisted his shove. His fist whipped a blow which traveled a scant foot. The door caved as though dynamite had let loose against it.

Doc pitched inside.

A wave of pungent aroma met his nostrils.

It was the smell of the *things* which had stalked them on the glacier! It was horrible—yet there was a flowerlike quality to it.

Gloom lurked in the recesses of the cabin where he stood. Formerly, it had been a lounge. But the once luxuriant furniture was now but a rubble on the floor. Some fantastic monster might have torn it to bits, as though to line a nest.

Bones lay in the litter. Bones of polar bear, of seal. Flesh still clung to some. Others were half-eaten carcasses.

Doc sped ahead. He shoved through a door.

Something whipped at him out of the darkness. A bestial hiss sounded simultaneously.

With an instinctive gesture, Doc caught the thing flying at his head. He looked at it. His hair stood on end.

It was a human head!

Doc Savage's iron nerve was jarred for an instant. He dropped the head. The long, fine hair attached to it tangled in his fingers. The grisly thing swung to and fro after the manner of a pendulum. It touched the leg of his bearskin trousers with gruesome, soft pattings.

At that instant, mighty Doc Savage came as near running from danger as he ever had.

Then understanding dawned. The head was frozen. It was the remain of a former passenger on the *Oceanic!*

He lowered it.

A SHUFFLING movement came from across the room. Doc charged the sound.

There was a squealing noise, ratlike, eerie. A door slammed.

Doc hit the panel. It was metal. It smashed him back. His fists could not knock down an inch of steel. He wrenched at the lock. That defied him, too.

Doc sought another route for pursuit. A companionway deposited him on a lower deck. He went forward.

It was more gloomy here. Doc's capable bronze fingers searched inside his parka. They brought out a flashlight of a type Doc himself had perfected.

This flash had no battery. A tiny, powerful generator, built into the handle and driven by a stout spring, supplied the current. One twist of the flash handle would wind the spring and furnish light current for some minutes. A special receptacle held spare bulbs in felt beds. There was not much chance of this light going out of commission.

The flash sprayed a slender, white-hot rod. Doc twisted the lens adjustment to widen the beam.

His elbow brushed something. It toppled against him. Then he wrenched his hand away. Involuntarily, he jumped back.

With a stony clank, the gruesome object hit the floor.

It was the body of a British soldier. It was frozen hard as iron. The soldier's throat had been cut.

"A derelict liner laden with corpses!" Doc said tightly. His own powerful voice seemed to quiet the upended hair on his nape. "And strange living creatures of some sort!"

He thought of the bones and the half-eaten carcasses in the lounge.

Doc went on. His flashlight cast a funnel of white. He stopped often to listen.

The derelict liner seemed alive with sinister shufflings and draggings. Once a bulkhead door banged. Again, there came another of the ratlike squeals.

Even Doc's sensitive ears could not tell whether that squeal was human! The flowerlike odor was stronger.

He came to a long passage. It was painted white. It might have been used but yesterday. For wood does not decay in the bitter cold of the Arctic.

A pipe, evidently a steam line, ran down the center of the passage ceiling.

Nine men and women hung from this pipe by their necks. Doc counted them. They must have hung there more than fifteen years. Yet the bodies were in a perfect state of preservation.

Doc sidled past the awful array.

He reached the third-class dining room.

Another scene of butchery met his eyes there. Many of these were colored soldiers. Men going from Africa to fight in France! The others were steerage passengers, judging from the quality of their clothing.

The bodies reposed in grotesque shapes. There was a quality of added frightfulness in the way the polar cold had preserved the tableau of carnage through this more than fifteen years. They might have been murdered but yesterday.

Machine-guns had done the bloody work.

Doc thought of Victor Vail.

So this was what had happened during the time the blind man was unconscious!

Pirates, human fiends, had taken over the *Oceanic.*

They were as bloodthirsty a gang as ever swung a cutlass or dangled a victim from a yardarm on the Spanish Main. Wholesale murder, they had committed.

Keelhaul de Rosa, Ben O'Gard, Dynamite Smith—greater villains never trod a deck. And, like the corsairs they were, they had fallen out over the loot.

The whole thing might have been lifted from the parchment chronicles of another century and transplanted to this summer of 1933.

Doc quitted the hall of murder.

The door of a bath gaped open. His flashlight picked up a couple of bodies huddled there.

Uncanny whisperings and shufflings still crept through the lost liner. Yet Doc saw nothing. It was as though the tormented souls of those butchered here were holding spectral conclave.

Like that—except for the flowery odor of living things. It was present everywhere.

Doc stepped out into another lounge.

His light picked up movement!

What it was, his sharp eyes failed to detect. The thing dropped behind the massive furniture before more than the backglow of Doc's light found it.

Warily, Doc sidled along the lounge wall. This was no animal confronting him. Animals would have devoured the frozen bodies which lay everywhere about the lost liner.

What happened next came without the slightest sound.

Something touched Doc's bronze neck. It was warm. It was soft, yet it possessed a corded strength.

It encircled Doc's throat!

DOC made one of the quickest moves of his career. He ducked and whirled. But he did not get the beam of his flashlight lifted in time. All he saw was the blank panel of a tightly shut door.

He wrenched at it.

Chug! A hard object hit him in the back with terrific force. Only the sprung steel of cushioning muscles kept his spine from being snapped. He was knocked to all fours. But he did not drop his flashlight.

He sprayed the beam on the lounge. A dozen frothing, hideous figures were leaping toward him.

It was seldom that Doc felt an impulse to hug an enemy. But he could have hugged these.

For their appearance dispelled the sinister air of supernatural foes which hung over the lost liner.

These were but Eskimos!

Doc doused his light. This was something he could cope with. He glided sidewise.

An avalanche of bodies piled onto the spot he had vacated. Clubs—it was a thrown club which had hit Doc's back—beat vigorously. An Innuit or two squealed painfully as he was belabored by a fellow. They seemed to use the squeals to express both excitement and pain.

Silence fell.

The Eskimos were puzzled. Their breathing was gusty, wheezing.

"Tarnuk!" whined one of the cowering Innuits. This gave Doc a clew to the dialect they spoke. Roughly translated, the word meant "the soul of a man." So swiftly had Doc evaded their charge that one of the Eskimos had remarked he must be but a ghost!

"Chimo!" Doc told them in their own lingo. "Welcome! You are my friends! But you have a strange way of greeting me."

This friendship business was undoubtedly news to everybody concerned. But Doc figured it wouldn't hurt to try that angle on them.

He spoke several variations of Eskimo dialect, among scores of other lingos he had mastered in his years of intensive study.

He might as well have saved his breath.

In a squealing knot, the Innuits bore down upon him. Again, they found themselves beating empty space, or whacking each other by accident.

From a position thirty feet away, Doc planted his flash beam on them. They were in a nice, tight bunch. A great chair stood at Doc's elbow. No doubt it would have been a load for any single steward who had long ago sailed on the ill-fated *Oceanic.*

It lifted in Doc's mighty hand as lightly as though it were a folding camp stool. It slammed into the midst of the Eskimos. They were bowled over, practically to a man.

Those able to, raised a terrific squawling.

They were calling upon more of their fellows outside for help.

Doc saw no object in standing up and fighting an army. If there had been some reason for it, that would be different.

He made swiftly for the forward staircase out of the lounge.

His thoughts flickered for an instant to the strange thing which had touched his neck. It had been none of these queer-smelling Innuits.

He forgot that puzzle speedily.

The staircase he was making for erupted warlike, greasy Eskimos. His retreat was cut off!

There was nothing to do now but make a fight of it.

FOUR of the five Innuits carried lighted blubber lamps. Doc wondered where they had conjured them from. They illuminated the lounge.

"You are making a mistake, my children," Doc told them in their lingo. "I come in peace!"

"You are a *tongak,* an evil spirit sent to harm us by the chief of all evil spirits!" an oily fellow clucked at him.

Doc sneezed. He had never smelled an Eskimo as aromatic as these fellows—and Eskimos are notoriously malodorous.

"You are wrong!" he argued with them. "I come only to do you good."

They threw gutturals back and forth at each other. All the while, they kept closing in on the giant bronze man.

"Where you come from?" demanded one.

"From a land to the south, where it is always warm."

Doc could see they didn't believe this.

One waved an arm expressively.

"There is no such land," he said with all the certainty of a very ignorant man. "The only land besides this is *nakroom,* the great space beyond the sky."

They had never heard of Greenland, or any country to the south, Doc gathered.

"Very well, I come from *nakroom,"* Doc persisted. "And I come to do good."

"You speak with a split tongue," he was informed. "Only *tongaks,* evil spirits, come from *nakroom."*

Doc decided to drop the subject. He didn't have time to convert their religious beliefs.

Doc took stock of their weapons. They carried harpoons with lines of hair seal thong bent in the detachable tips. Some held *oonapiks,* short hunting spears. Quite a few bayonets were in evidence. These had evidently been garnered from the *Oceanic.* No firearms were to be seen.

Not the least dangerous were ordinary dog whips. These had lashes fully eighteen feet long. From his vast knowledge, Doc knew an Eskimo could take one of these whips and cut a man's throat at five paces. Flicking at distant objects with the dog whips bordered on being the Eskimo national pastime.

"Kill him!" clucked the Eskimo leader. "He is only one man! It will be easy!"

The Innuit was underestimating, a mistake Doc's enemies quite often made.

DOC picked up a round-topped table. This would serve as a shield against any weapon his foes had.

He seized a chair, flung it as though it were a chip. Three Innuits were bowled over. They hadn't had time to dodge.

A flight of harpoons and short hunting spears chugged into the table. Doc threw two more chairs. He retreated to a spot far from the nearest flickering blubber lamp. He lowered the table, making sure they all saw he was behind it. Then he flattened to the lounge floor and glided away, unnoticed.

The Eskimos rushed the table, bent on murder. They howled in dismay when they found no one there. The howls turned to pain as hunters in the rear began dropping from bronze fists that exploded like nitro on their jaws.

An Innuit lunged at Doc with a harpoon. Doc picked the harpoon out of the fellow's hands and broke it over his head. A tough walrus lash on a dog whip slit the hood of Doc's parka like a knife stroke.

The bronze giant retreated. Thrown spears and bayonets seemed to whizz through his very body, so quickly did he dodge.

A bayonet flashed at his chest. He half turned to let it miss, then picked it out of the air with a lightning gesture. The next instant the long blade had fastened the most beligerant of the Eskimos to a bulkhead.

His uncanny skill began to have its effect. The greasy fellows rolled their little eyes at each other. Fear distorted their pudgy faces.

"Truly, he is a *tongak,* an evil one!" they muttered. "None other could be so hard to kill."

"All gather together!" commanded their leader. "We will rush him in a group!"

The words were hardly off the leader's lips when he dropped, his blank and senseless face looking foolishly through the rungs of the chair which had hit him.

The harm had been done. The Innuits grouped. They took fresh holds on their weapons.

They charged.

They had hit upon the only chance they had of coping with Doc. There were nearly fifty of them. Despite their short stature and fat, they were stout, fierce fighters.

With mad, bloodthirsty squeals, they closed upon the mighty bronze man. For a moment, they covered him completely. A filthy tidal wave of killers!

Then a bronze arrow of a figure shot upward from the squirming pile.

The ceiling of the lounge was criss-crossed with elaborately decorated beams. Hardly a handhold could the naked eye detect, yet Doc clung easily. Moreover, he ran rapidly along the beam, hanging only by his casehardened fingers.

He dropped to the floor, clear of the fight, before he was hardly missed.

But the Eskimos still had him cut off from the exits. They closed in again. They threw spears and knives and an occasional club, all of which Doc dodged. They shrieked maledictions, largely to renew their own faltering nerve.

The situation was getting desperate. Doc put his back to a bulkhead.

He did not pay particular attention to the fact that he was near the spot where the strange, warm, soft object had touched his neck.

With hideous yells, the killing horde of Innuits charged.

A door opened beside Doc. A soft, strong hand came out. It clutched Doc's arm.

It was a woman's hand.

Chapter XV
THE ARCTIC GODDESS

DOC SAVAGE whipped through the door. He caught a brief glimpse of the girl.

She was tall. Nothing more than that could be told about her form, since she was muffled in the garb of the Arctic—moccasins reaching above her knees, and with the tops decorated with the long hair of the polar bear, trousers of the skin of the Arctic hare, a shirt-like garment of auk skins, and an outer parka of a coat fitted with a hood.

But her face! That was different. He could see enough of that to tell she was a creature of gorgeous beauty. Enthralling eyes, an exquisite little upturned nose, lips as inviting as the petals of a red rose—they would have made most men forget all about the fight.

Had there been light to disclose Doc's features, however, an onlooker would have been surprised to note how little the giant bronze man was affected by this entrancing beauty.

Doc worked at the prosaic, but by no means unimportant, task of securing the door. He got it fast.

He turned his flashlight on the girl. He had noted something he wanted to verify. The gaze he bent upon her was the same sort he would give any stranger he might be curious about.

Her hair was white! It was a strange, warm sort of white, like old ivory. The girl was a perfect blonde.

Doc thought of Victor Vail. The violinist had this same sort of hair—a little more white, perhaps.

"You did me a great favor, Miss Vail," Doc told the girl.

She started. She put her hands over her lips. She wore no mittens. Her hands were long, shapely, velvety of skin.

"How did—?"

"Did I know you were Roxey Vail?" Doc picked up her question. "You could be no one else. You are the image of your father."

"My father!" She said the word softly, as if it were something sacred. "Did you know him?"

Doc thought of that smear of scarlet on the ice near the spot where Victor Vail had disappeared. He changed the subject.

"Did anyone besides you escape the massacre aboard this liner?"

The girl hesitated.

Doc turned his flash on his own face. He knew she was uncertain whether to trust him. Doc was not flattering himself when he felt that a look at his strong features would reassure her. He had seen it work before.

"My mother survived," said the girl.

"Is she alive?"

"She is."

Enraged Eskimos beat on the bulkhead door. They hacked at the stout panel with bayonets. They yelled like Indians.

BEAUTIFUL Roxey Vail suddenly pressed close to Doc Savage. He could feel the trembling in her rounded, firm body.

"You won't let them—kill me?" she choked.

Doc slipped a corded bronze arm around her—and he didn't often put his arm around young women.

"What a question!" he chided her. "Haven't you any faith in men?"

She shivered. "Not the ones I've seen—lately."

"What do you mean?"

"Do you know why those Eskimos attacked you?" she countered.

"No," Doc admitted. "It surprised me. Eskimos are noted as an unwarlike people. When they get through fighting the north for a living, they've had enough scrapping."

"They attacked you because of—"

A slab breaking out of the door stopped her. The Innuits were smashing the panel!

"We'd better move!" Doc murmured.

He swept the girl up in one arm. She struck at him, thinking he meant her harm. Then, realizing he was only carrying her because he could make more speed in that fashion, she desisted.

Doc glided sternward. They passed a cluster of the horrible, frozen bodies. Doc noted that the girl shuddered at sight of these and closed her eyes tightly.

"You haven't visited this death ship often in the passing years, have you?" he hazarded.

She shook her head. "No. You could count the number of times on the fingers of one hand."

They reached a large, rather barren room amidships. Doc knew much of the construction of ships. He veered abruptly to the left, descended a companion, wheeled down a passage.

He was now face to face with the liner's strong room.

He took one look at the great vault. He dropped the girl.

The treasure trove was empty!

THE young woman picked herself up from the floor.

"I'm sorry," Doc apologized. He pointed at the strong room. "Has that been empty long?"

"Ever since I can remember."

"Who got the gold, and the diamonds?"

She was plainly surprised. "What gold and diamonds?"

Doc smiled dryly. "You've got me! But fifty mil-lions dollars' worth of gold and diamonds is at the bottom of this mess. If it was carried aboard this liner, it would have been stored in the strong room. It's not there. So that means—Hm-m-m!" He shifted his great shoulders. "I'm not sure what it means."

He glanced about. Here seemed to be as good a spot as any to linger. It would take the Eskimos some minutes to find them.

"You started to tell me why the Innuits attacked me," he prompted the girl. "What was the reason?"

"I'll tell you my story from the first—I think there's time," she said swiftly. Her voice was pleasant to listen to. "My mother and myself escaped the wholesale slaughter of the others aboard the *Oceanic,* because we slid overboard by a rope. We were apart from the other passengers, hunting father—he had disappeared mysteriously the day before.

"We hid on land. We saw the mutineers depart over the ice, hauling the fur-wrapped figure of a man on a sledge. We did not realize until it was too late that the man they hauled was my father."

She stopped. She bit her lips. Her eyes swam in moisture. They were very big, enthralling blue eyes.

Doc made an impatient gesture for her to go on.

"Oh—I'm neglecting to tell you it was the crew who murdered those aboard the liner. Men named Ben O'Gard, Dynamite Smith, and Keelhaul de Rosa, were ring leaders—"

"I know all that," Doc interposed. "Tell your side of it."

"My mother and I got food from the liner after the mutineers had gone," she continued. "We built a crude hut inland. We didn't—we couldn't stay on the liner, although it was solidly aground. The mutineers might return. And all those murdered bodies—it was too horrible. We couldn't have borne the sight—"

"When did the Eskimos come?" Doc urged her along.

"Within a month after the mutineers had departed. This spit of land was their home. They had been away on a hunting trip."

She managed a faint, trembling smile. "The Eskimos treated us wonderfully. They thought we were good white spirits who had brought them a great supply of wood and iron, in the shape of the liner. They looked upon myself and my mother as white goddesses, and treated us as such—but refused to let us leave. In a way, we were prisoners. Then, a few days ago—the white men came!"

"Oh, oh!" Doc interjected. "I begin to see the light."

"These men were part of the mutineer crew," Roxey Vail said. "Keelhaul de Rosa was in command. They came in a plane. They visited this wrecked liner. After that, they seemed very angry."

"Imagine their mortification"—Doc chuckled—"when they found the treasure gone!"

"They gave the Eskimos liquor," Roxey Vail went on. "And they gave them worse stuff, something that made them madmen—a white powder!"

"Dope—the rats!" Doc growled.

"My mother and I became frightened," said the girl. "We retreated to a tiny hideaway we had prepared against just such an emergency. None of the Eskimos know where it is.

"An hour or so ago, I came to the liner. We needed food. There are supplies still aboard, stuff preserved by the intense cold.

"I heard the Eskimos come aboard. I spied on them. They had a white man prisoner. A white man with hair like cotton. There was something strange about this man. It was as though I had seen him before."

"You were very small when you were marooned here, weren't you?" Doc inquired softly.

"Yes. Only a few years old. Anyway, the Eskimos talked of killing this white-haired man. I do not quite understand why, but it filled me with such horror I went completely mad. I screamed. Then you—you came."

"I heard your scream." Doc eyed her steadily. Then he spoke again.

"The white-haired man was your father," he said.

Without a sound, Roxey Vail passed out. Doc caught her.

AS he stood there, with the soft, limp form of the exquisitely beautiful girl in his arm, Doc wondered if it could have been the fact that white-haired Victor Vail had been murdered which had caused her swoon. She was not the type of young woman, from what he had seen of her, who fainted easily.

He heard the search of the Eskimos drawing near. They did not have sense enough to hunt quietly. Or perhaps they wanted to flush him out like a wild animal, so he wouldn't be in their midst before they knew it.

Doc quitted the strong room. He sped down a passage, bearing the unconscious girl in his arms. He was soundless as a wraith. He came to a large clothes hamper. It was in perfect shape. It still held some crumpled garments.

Doc dumped the clothes out. The hamper held Roxey Vail nicely as the big bronze man lowered her into it. He closed the lid. The hamper was of open wickerwood. It would conceal her, yet she could breathe through it.

Directly toward the oncoming Innuits, Doc strode.

His hand drew a small case from inside his parka. With the contents of this, he made his preparations.

He stepped into a cabin and waited.

The first Eskimo passed. Like a striking serpent, Doc's bronze hand darted from the cabin door. His fingertips barely stroked the greasy cheek of the Innuit. Yet the man instantly fell on his face!

Doc flashed out of the cabin. His fingers touched the bare skin of a second Eskimo, another—another. He got five of them before the fat fellows could show anything like action.

All five men who felt Doc's eerie touch seemed to go suddenly to sleep on their feet.

It was the same brand of magic Doc had used on the gangsters in New York City.

Murderous Eskimo with his harpoon, or pasty-cheeked New York rat, with his fists full of high-power automatics—both are the same breed. Doc's magic worked in the same fashion.

The Innuits saw their fellows toppling mysteriously. They realized the very touch of this mighty bronze man was disastrous. They forgot all about fighting. They fled.

Ignominiously, they piled out on deck. Rigging tripped them. After the fashion of superstitious souls, the instant they turned their back on danger, their peril seemed to grow indescribably greater. They were like scared boys running from a graveyard at night—each jump made them want to go faster.

Two even committed unwilling suicide by leaping over the rail of the lost liner to the hard glacier far below.

In a matter of minutes, the last Innuit was sucked away into the screaming blizzard.

Chapter XVI
THE REALM OF COLD

THE lost liner *Oceanic* lay like something that had died.

Wind still boomed and squealed in the forest of ice-coated, collapsed rigging, it was true. The sand-hard snow still made a billion tiny tinklings as the gale shotted it against the derelict hulk. But gone were the uncanny whisperings and shufflings which had been so unnerving.

Doc Savage went below, moving silently, as had become his habit when he trod the trails of danger. His flashlight beam dabbed everywhere. Sharp, missing nothing, his golden eye took stock of his surroundings. He was seeing everything, yet speeding along at a pace that for another man would have been a lung-tearing sprint.

A squarish, thick-walled little bottle chanced to meet his gaze. He did not pick it up. Yet the printing on the label yielded to his near-telescopic scrutiny.

It was a perfume bottle. Two more like it reposed a bit farther down the passage.

Here was the explanation of the flowery odor of the Eskimos which had so baffled description. To the characteristic stench of blubber, perspiration and plain filth which accompanied them, they had added perfume. The whole had been an effluvium which was unique.

Doc opened the clothes hamper where he had left unconscious Roxey Vail.

Emptiness stared at him.

Doc dropped to a knee. His flashlight beam narrowed, becoming intensely brilliant. The luminance spurted across the carpet on the passage floor. This looked as though it had been laid down yesterday. But the years had taken the springiness out of the nap, so that it would retain footprints.

The girl had gone forward—alone. This told Doc some of the Eskimos had not remained behind and seized her.

"Roxey!" he called.

Doc's shout penetrated the caterwauling of the blizzard in surprising fashion. A sound expert could have explained why. It is well known that certain horn tones, not especially loud, will carry through the noise of a factory better than any others. Doc, because of the perfect control he exercised over his vocal cords, could pitch his voice so as to waft through the blizzard in a manner nearly uncanny.

"Here!" came the girl's faint voice. "I'm hunting my father!"

Doc hurried to her. She was pale. Terror lay like a garish mask on her exquisite features.

"My father—they took him with them!" she said in a small, tight voice.

"They didn't have him when they fled a moment ago," Doc assured her. "I watched closely."

Her terror gave way to amazement.

"They fled?" she murmured wonderingly. "Why?"

Doc neglected to answer. How he produced that mysterious unconsciousness with his mere touch was a secret known only to himself and his five friends.

But no! Doc shivered. His five friends had met their end in the burning plane. So the secret was now known to but one living man—Doc Savage himself.

"The Eskimos must have removed your father before they attacked me," Doc told Roxey Vail.

He wheeled quickly away. The glow of his flashlight reflected off the paneling of the lost liner, and made his bronze form seem even more gigantic than it was. Fierce little lights played in his golden eyes.

"Where are you going?" questioned his entrancing companion.

"To get Victor Vail," Doc replied grimly. "They took him away, and that shows he was alive. No doubt they took him to Keelhaul de Rosa."

ROXEY VAIL hurried at his side. She was forced to run to keep abreast.

"You haven't told me how you happen to be here," she reminded.

In a few sentences, as they climbed upward to the ice-basted deck of the lost liner, Doc told her of the map on her father's back which could only be brought out with X-rays, of the efforts of Keelhaul de Rosa and Ben O'Gard to kill each other off so one could hog the fifty-million-dollar treasure, and the rest.

"But where is the treasure?" asked the girl.

"I have no idea what became of it," Doc replied. "Keelhaul de Rosa expected to find it in the strong room, judging from his actions as you described them to me. Too, it looks like he suspects the Eskimos of moving it. That's why he gave them liquor. He wanted to get them pie-eyed enough to tell him where they hid it."

"They didn't get it!" Roxey Vail said with certainty. "It was removed before the mutineers ever left the liner, more than fifteen years ago."

They were on deck now. Doc moved along the rail, hunting a dangling, ice-clad cable. He could drop the many feet to the glacial ice without damage, but such a drop would bring serious injury or death to the girl.

Roxey Vail was studying Doc curiously. A faint blush suffused her superb features. To someone who had been with Doc a lot, and watched the effect his presence had on the fair sex, this blush would have been an infallible sign.

The blond young goddess of the Arctic was going to fall hard for big, handsome Doc.

"Why are *you* here?" Roxey Vail asked abruptly. "You do not seem to be stricken with the gold madness which has gripped everyone else."

Doc let a shrug suffice for an answer.

Probably it was a brand of natural modesty, but Doc did not feel like explaining he was a sort of supreme avenger for the wrongs of the world—the Great Nemesis of evildoers in the far corners of the globe.

They found a hanging cable. It terminated about ten feet from the ice. With Roxey Vail clinging to his back like a papoose, Doc carefully went down the cable.

Into the teeth of the moaning blizzard, they strode.

An instant later, Doc's alertness of eye undoubtedly saved their lives. He whipped to one side—carrying Roxey Vail with him.

A volley of rifle bullets spiked through the space they vacated.

The Eskimos had returned, accompanied by Keelhaul de Rosa and four or five riflemen and machine gunners.

AFTER the flashing movement which had saved their lives, Doc kept going. He jerked the white hood of the girl's parka over her face to camouflage the warm color of her cheeks. He shrugged deep in his own parka for the same reason.

He wanted to get the girl to safety. Then he was going to hold grim carnival on the glacier with Keelhaul de Rosa and his killer group.

For his share in those hideous murders aboard the *Oceanic*, Keelhaul de Rosa would pay, as certainly as a breath of life remained in Doc Savage's mighty bronze body.

Another fusillade of shots clattered. The reports were almost puny in the clamor of the blizzard. Lead hissed entirely too close to Doc and his companion.

Doc's fingers slipped inside his capacious parka, came out with an object hardly larger than a high-power rifle cartridge—and shaped somewhat similarly. He flipped a tiny lever on this article, then hurled it at the attackers. The object was heavy enough to be thrown some distance.

Came a blinding flash! The glacier seemed to jump six feet straight up. A terrific, slamming roar blasted against eardrums. Then a rush of air slapped them skidding across the ice like an unseen fist.

There had been a powerful explosive in the little cylinder Doc hurled at his enemies.

Awful quiet followed the blast. The very blizzard seemed to recoil like a beaten beast.

A chorus of agonized squealings and bleatings erupted. Some of the enemy had been incapacitated. They were all shocked. The Eskimos felt a vague, unaccountable terror.

"Up an' at 'em, mateys!" shrilled a coarse tone. "Keelhaul me, but we ain't gonna let 'em get away from us now!"

It was Keelhaul de Rosa's voice. He, at least, had not been damaged.

More lead searched the knobby glacier surface. None of it came dangerously near Doc and his fair companion. They had gotten far away in the confusion.

Doc suddenly jammed the young lady in a handy snowdrift. He wasn't exactly rough about it, but he certainly didn't try to fondle her, as a man of more ordinary caliber might have been tempted to do. And it wasn't because the ravishing young woman would have objected to the caresses. All signs pointed to the contrary.

The big bronze man had long ago decided a life of domestication was not for him. It would not go with the perils and terrors which haunted his every step. It would mean the surrendering of his goal in life—the shunning of adventure, the abandoning of his righting of wrongs, and punishing of evildoers wherever he found them.

So Doc had schooled himself never to sway the least bit to the seductions of the fairest of the fair sex.

"Stay here," he directed the entrancing young lady impassionately. "And what I mean—*stay here!* You can breathe under the snow. You won't be discovered."

"Whatever you say," she said in a voice in which adoration was but thinly veiled.

She was certainly losing no time in falling for Doc.

The giant bronze man smiled faintly. Then the storm swallowed him.

KEELHAUL DE ROSA was in a rage. He was burning up. He filled the blizzard around about with salty expletives.

"Ye blasted swabs!" he railed at the Eskimos, forgetting they did not understand English. "Keelhaul me. The bronze scut was right in yer hands, an' ye didn't wreck 'im!"

"I tell ya, dat guy is poison!" muttered a white gunman. "He ain't human! From de night he tied into us outside de concert hall in de big burg, we ain't been able ter lay a hand on 'im!"

Another white man shivered. He was fatter than Keelhaul de Rosa or the other gunmen. It was to be suspected he had some Eskimo blood in his veins.

As a matter of fact, this fellow was a crook recruited in Greenland. He knew the Arctic. It was he who served as interpreter in all discussions with the Eskimos.

"Dat bane awful explosion a minute ago," this man whined. "Aye sure hope we bane get dat feller damn quick."

"Scatter!" rasped Keelhaul de Rosa. "We'll get the swab!"

The Eskimos spread out widely. The white men kept in a group for mutual protection.

One Eskimo in particular rambled a short distance from the others. He floundered through a snowdrift.

He did not see a portion of the drift seemingly rise behind him. No suspicion of danger assailed him until hard, chill bronze fingers stroked his greasy cheek with a caress like the fingers of a ghost. Then it was too late.

The Innuit collapsed without a sound.

Doc pounced upon the inert Eskimo. From his lips came a loud shout—words couched in the tongue of the native.

Excitement seized the white man who understood the Eskimo lingo, and he listened intently to the distant voice.

"Dat Eskimo bane kill the bronze feller!" he shrieked. "He bane say come an' look!"

Three men sprinted for the voice they had heard.

The interpreter glimpsed two figures. One was prone, motionless. The second crouched on the first. That was about all Doc Savage could see in the flying gale.

"There they bane!" he howled.

They charged up. Two of them prepared to empty their guns into the prone form just to make sure.

The crouching man heaved up. Strikingly enough, he seemed to grow to the proportions of a mountain. Two Herculean bronze fists drove accurate blows. Both gunmen described perfect flip-flops in mid-air—unconscious before their feet left the glacier.

The interpreter whirled and ran. He knew death when he saw it. And big Doc Savage was nothing less.

Doc did not follow him. For to the bronze man's sensitive ears came a stifled cry.

Roxey Vail was being seized!

EVEN as he raced toward where he had left her, Doc fathomed what had occurred. She had disobeyed his injunction to stay hidden. The reason—she had heard the shouted information that Doc was dead. She had started out with some desperate idea of avenging him.

Doc appreciated her good intentions. But at the moment, he could have gotten a lot of satisfaction out of turning her over his knee and paddling her.

A bullet squeaked in Doc's ear. He folded aside and down. A machine gun picked savagely at the ice near him. He traveled twenty feet on his stomach, with a speed that would have shamed a desert lizard.

"Take the hussy to the boat!" Keelhaul de Rosa's coarse voice rang. "Step lively, me lads!"

Doc tried to get to the hideous voice. Murderous lead drove him back.

He was forced to skulk, dodging bullets while Roxey Vail was taken aboard the ice-coated hulk of the lost liner.

More Eskimos soon arrived. Keelhaul de Rosa was arming some of them with guns. The interpreter instructed the Innuits on how to operate the unfamiliar firearms.

The natives were far from effective marksmen. More than one greasy eater of blubber dropped a big pistol after it exploded in his hand and ran as though the worst *tongak*, or evil spirit, were hot on his trail. But the guns made them more dangerous, for wild shots were almost as liable to hit the elusive figure of Doc Savage as well-aimed ones. In fact, they were worse. Doc couldn't tell which way to dodge.

The heat of the hunt finally drove Doc to the remote reaches of the glacier and rock crest of the land.

There he replenished his vast reservoir of strength by dining on frozen, raw steaks he wrenched with his bare, steel-thewed fingers, from the polar bear he had slain.

The mighty bronze man might have been a terrible hunter of the wild as he crouched there at his primeval repast. But no such hunter ever possessed cunning and knowledge such as Doc Savage was bringing to bear upon the problem confronting him.

But caution remained uppermost in his mind. He had been crouching with an ear pressed to a pinnacle of rock. The stone acted as a sounding board for any footsteps on the surrounding glacier.

Noise of men passing in the blizzard reached Doc. There seemed to be four or five in the group.

Doc fell in behind them. He followed as close as was possible without discovery. Growled words told him they were white men.

"De skipper says for us to take de stern of de liner, mateys," one said. "Our pals will join us dere. We're to string out an' see dat not a swab gets away! Everybody's helpin' in dis party, even de cook."

"We'd better throw out an anchor," another grunted. "Keelhaul an' his whole bloody crew, together wit' de Eskimos, is movin' bag an' baggage onto de liner. We wanta give 'em time to get settled."

Doc Savage sought to get even closer. He was not three yards away as the group of men came to a stop in the shelter of a rock spire. There were five of them.

What he was hearing was most interesting!

ONE of the five men laughed nastily.

"De bronze guy has just about got Keelhaul de Rosa's goat!" he chuckled. "To say nothin' of de panic de Eskimos are in. Dat's why they're all movin' onto de liner. Dey figure dey can fight 'im off better."

Another man swore.

"Don't forget, pal, dat we gotta smear de bronze guy ourselves before we leave here!" he growled.

"Time to begin worryin' about dat after we got Keelhaul an' all de others croaked!" another informed him.

"Yer sure Keelhaul an' his gang don't suspect we're around?"

"Dey sure don't. I crawled up close an' listened to 'em gabbin'. Here's what happened, pal—de bronze guy got de idea we had croaked. He tol' de skoit dat. De broad, she up an' told it to Keelhaul when they caught her. An' he believes her."

Once more, an evil laugh gurgled in the blizzard.

"Well, Keelhaul is sure due to change his mind!" sneered the one who had laughed.

"Yeah—only he won't have the time to change 'is mind before we boin 'is insides out wit' Tommy lead."

"How long yer figure we'd better wait here?"

"About an hour."

A brief silence ensued.

"I don't like dis ting much," muttered one of the five uneasily. "We could light out wit'out all dis killin'."

"Yah—an' have somebody from dis place show up in a few years an' spill de woiks to de law," was the snarled reply. "We gotta clean up de loose ends, pal. We ain't leavin' nothin' behind but stiffs. We're playin' safe."

Once more there was quiet. One of the evil gang broke it with a startled ejaculation.

"What was dat?"

They peered at each other, turtling their vicious faces forward to see in the blizzard.

"I didn't hear nothin'!" muttered one.

"Sounded like de wind," suggested another.

They got up and circled their shelter. They saw nothing. They heard only the hoot of the gale. They gathered behind the outthrust of stone once more, huddling close for warmth.

They had dismissed what they heard as a child of the storm.

Indeed, it almost could have been some vagrant creation of the wind—that strange, low, trilling note which had come into being for a moment, then trailed away into nothingness. However, it was Doc's sound which they had heard.

Doc was now scores of yards away. He had much to do for he had learned a great deal.

The five were Ben O'Gard's thugs. And Doc's listening ears had detected enough to tell him the submarine had not met disaster, as he had thought. Yet he had carried the all-important valve with him in the folding seaplane!

The survival of the *Helldiver* without the valve could be explained, though. Ben O'Gard's crew had simply fashioned a substitute valve. There was a small machine shop aboard the underseas craft which they could use for this purpose. No doubt they had started work on the substitute shortly after they marooned Doc on the iceberg during the walrus hunt. It had not been finished in time to use when they were so nearly trapped in the ice. But they had completed it while Doc was locked in the compartment aboard the *Helldiver.*

This, Doc believed, was the true explanation of their presence on land.

Ben O'Gard was preparing to slay everyone on this forlorn spot!

No blood-bathed Jolly Roger ever held more frightful ambitions.

Doc's great bronze form traveled like the wind. He had much to do—not much time in which to accomplish it.

Doc had formulated a plan of action which boded ill for his enemies.

Chapter XVII
THE CAPTIVES

IT was midnight, but the sun shone brightly. The storm had abated as swiftly as it had arisen. Snow no longer swirled. Such drifts as had gathered glittered like tiny, ridged diamonds in the solar rays.

Around the uncharted Arctic land, the short, terrific gale had made a startling change. It had pushed the ice pack away. For miles in every direction, comparatively open water could be seen. This was spotted with a few vicious-looking blue growlers, but no ice floes of any size.

In the main lounge of the lost liner *Oceanic,* Keelhaul de Rosa walked angry circles, kicking chairs out of his path.

"Keelhaul me!" he bellowed. "The bloody treasure has gotta be somewhere!"

He came over and planted himself in front of pretty Roxey Vail. He glowered at the young woman. He had a face that mirrored indescribable evil.

Two rat-faced thugs held Roxey Vail. Their bony claws dug painfully into her shapely arms.

"Where's the swag?" Keelhaul de Rosa roared at her.

"I don't know anything about any treasure!" the girl replied scornfully.

It was perhaps the fiftieth time she had told her captors that.

"You an' your maw swiped the gold an' diamonds!" snarled Keelhaul de Rosa.

Roxey Vail made no answer.

"The Eskimos told me all about you an' your maw," the hulking pirate chief informed her. "Where's she hidin'?"

The young woman gave him a look of scorn. If she had practiced all her life squashing mashers on New York streets, she couldn't have done it better.

"C'mon—cough up!" the man hissed in her face. "Where's your old lady hangin' out? I'll bet she's sittin' right slap-dab on the bloomin' treasure! Keelhaul me if I don't think that!"

"You're wrong!" the girl snapped.

"Then where is she?"

Roxey Vail tightened her lips. That was something she would never tell. No horror they could inflict upon her would bring the information from her lips.

"You'll spill the dope, sister, or I'll cut that swab of an ol' man of yorn to pieces right here in front of you!" gritted Keelhaul de Rosa. "I'll start by puttin' out the ol' geezer's bloody eyes again!"

Roxey Vail said nothing to this. What could she say? Her cheeks became pale as damask, though.

Keelhaul de Rosa kicked over a couple of additional chairs. He picked up a book that had lain on a table for more than fifteen years, saw it was a Bible and threw it at a greasy Eskimo.

Coming back, the pirate chief tried softer arguments.

"Listen, sister," he purred, "gimme the swag an' I'll see that you an' yer ol' man gets safe passage back with me an' my crew."

"How can you escape?" Roxey Vail questioned curiously. "Your plane is destroyed. You have no submarine."

"I'm makin' the Eskimos haul the swag to Greenland for me."

"Then you'll kill them, I suppose," the young woman said coldly.

The way Keelhaul de Rosa gave a guilty start showed the young woman's guess had been close to the truth.

"Will you spare the life of the bronze man, also?" Roxey Vail asked tentatively.

Keelhaul de Rosa scowled.

"That swab is already dead," he lied, hoping it would help break the nerve of the beautiful girl.

THE statement had an effect exactly opposite. Roxey Vail sprang forward so suddenly that she eluded the pair holding her. She clawed Keelhaul de Rosa's villainous face. She handed him a haymaker that completely closed his left eye.

"Lay aboard her!" he howled in agony. "Pull her off, you swabs! Keelhaul me, but she's a bloody wildcat!"

His two men secured fresh hold on Roxey Vail, but not before one of them collected a flattened nose. Her Arctic life had made a very hard young woman out of Roxey Vail.

The pretty girl now broke into sobs. The reason for her grief was easily understood—she believed Doc Savage was dead. It was incredible that the bronze man, mighty as he was, could cope with such odds as confronted him now.

Suddenly a bellowing voice filled the lounge.

"Boarders!" it roared. "Ben O'Gard and his swabs! They're comin' aboard by the stern!"

Every eye in the lounge went toward the source of that roaring voice. It seemed to come from a small companionway which led off in the direction of the purser's office.

"It's Ben O'Gard, I tell yer!" crashed the voice. "They're crawlin' up some lines danglin' near the stern!"

Any doubt which might have been arising was dispelled by the loud clatter of a machine gun on deck. The sound came from the stern!

Another rapid-firer joined it. A white man—one of Keelhaul de Rosa's small gang—shrieked a warning.

"Ben O'Gard—" The howling of Eskimos drowned out the rest.

Ben O'Gard was indeed making his attack.

"One of you hold her!" rasped Keelhaul de Rosa. "Keelhaul me—I gotta look into this!"

He sprinted out of the room. One of the pair who had been holding the young woman followed him.

Roxey Vail promptly engaged in combat with the single rat who now pinioned her arms. She stamped his toes through his soft mukluks. She did her best to bite him.

Although strong and agile for a woman, Roxey Vail would have been overpowered by the man.

But from the spot where that great voice had first roared a warning, there glided a form that might have been liquid bronze. Nearing the struggling man and girl, this became a giant, Herculean man of hard metal. Hands floated out.

They were hands which could have plucked the very head from the rat now belaboring the poor girl with his fists. Yet those hands barely stroked the man's face.

The thug fell senseless.

ROXEY VAIL stared at her rescuer. It was apparent she could hardly believe her eyes.

"You—oh, thank—"

"Listen—here's what you're to do!" Doc interrupted. He didn't like the tearful business of receiving thanks from young women whether they were pretty or not.

The girl became attentive.

"You are to go and get your mother!" Doc told her. "You know where the finger of land juts into the sea half a mile to the north of this spot?"

"Yes."

"Take your mother there. The storm left a floe of ice attached to the point. It is long and narrow. It protrudes out into the sea fully half a mile. The tip is rather rough where ice cakes were piled upon it by the force of the gale. You are to hide, with your mother, among those ice cakes."

Roxey Vail nodded. But she wanted to know more. "What—"

"No time to explain!" Doc waved an arm in the general direction of the stern. A bloody fight was going on back there, judging from the bedlam.

Doc now grasped the girl. He shook her like a child—but not very hard.

"Now get this!" he said sharply. "I don't want any more disobeying my orders just because you think something has happened to me!"

She smiled at him. Tears were in her eyes.

"I won't," she said. "But my father is—"

"I'll attend to him." Doc gave her a shove. "Scoot, Roxey. And be on the end of that ice neck with your mother as soon as possible. Things are going to happen fast around here."

Obediently, the young woman raced for the bows. These were deserted, due to the fight at the stern. She should have no trouble escaping.

Doc disappeared down a companionway as though in the grip of a great suction. He knew where he was going. He had overheard a chance remark, while skulking aboard the lost liner a few minutes ago, which told him where to look.

He shoved a stateroom door inward. A long leap—and he was working over tough walrus-hide thongs which bound Victor Vail.

"They told me you were dead!" Victor Vail choked.

"Have you seen your daughter yet?" Doc grinned.

Victor Vail's long, handsome face now became a study in emotions. His lips trembled. Big tears skidded down his cheeks. His throat worked convulsively.

"Isn't she—a wonderful girl" he gulped proudly.

He had seen her, all right.

"She's swell," Doc chuckled. "She's gone to get her mother. They'll meet us."

At this, Victor Vail could not restrain himself. He broke into open sobs of delight and gratitude and eagerness.

It would be a strange reunion, this of father and mother and daughter, after more than fifteen years. It would be something, in itself alone, worth all the perils and hardships Doc Savage had undergone.

The fight astern was coming closer. Automatics hammered fiercely. Machine guns tore off long strings of reports. Men shrieked in the frenzy of combat. Not a few of them were screaming from their wounds, too.

"We'd better drift away from here!" Doc declared.

They ran down a passage.

An amazing thing happened to a stateroom door ahead of them.

The panel jumped out of the door, literally exploding into splinters. An object came through which resembled a rusty keg affixed crosswise to the end of a telephone pole.

Such a hand and fist could belong to only one man on earth.

"Renny!" Doc yelled.

Big Renny leaped out, somber face alight.

A GREASY Eskimo now popped through the shattered door. His eyes were wells of terror, and his mouth was a frightened hole. He headed down the passage. He made two jumps.

Through the door after him came two hundred and sixty pounds of red-fuzzed man-gorilla.

Monk! He overhauled the Innuit as though the greasy bag of fright were standing still. Both his hands grasped the Eskimo and yanked backward. Simultaneously, his knee came up. The Innuit landed on his back across that knee. He all but broke in halves.

Doc looked into the stateroom.

Ham, not quite the fashion plate he usually presented, was grimacing and wiping the steaming red life fluid of another eskimo off his sword cane.

Long Tom was astride another Eskimo. The oily native was twice the size of the pale electrical wizard. But he was getting the beating of his life.

Johnny, the gaunt archaeologist, was dancing around with his glasses, which had the magnifying lens on the left side, askew on his bony face.

Doc groped for something that would express his happiness, for he had given these five friends of his up as dead men. The proper words refused to come. His throat was cramped with emotion.

"What a bunch of bums!" he managed to chuckle at last.

"We've been praying for the sun to come out," said Ham waspishly. He pointed at a porthole. A strong beam of sunlight slanted through it. "Johnny used that magnifying lens to burn his bonds apart. It's lucky for us our captors stink like they do—they can't smell anything but themselves. They couldn't smell the smoke from the thongs as Johnny burned them through."

The group ran for the stern. Renny secured an automatic pistol from the Eskimo whom Ham had skewered with his sword cane. Long Tom carried another he had seized from his opponent. Monk had obtained a third from his own victim.

"I had written you guys off my books," Doc's expressive voice rumbled pleasantly. "How'd you escape from that burning plane?"

"What d'you think we had parachutes for?" Monk inquired in his tiny murmur.

"But I flew over the ice, and saw no sign of you," Doc pointed out.

Monk grinned widely. "I'm tellin' you, Doc, we didn't linger after we landed. We come down in the middle of a gang of wild and woolly Eskimos. They started throwin' things at us—harpoons mostly. Our ammunition was gone. We'd wasted it all on the plane that shot us down. So we made tracks. We thought the Eskimos was cannibals, or somethin'—"

Ham scowled blackly at Monk.

"And you, you missing link, suggested leaving me behind as a sort of pot offering!" he said angrily.

Ham wasn't mad, though. It was just the old feud starting again. Things were back to normal.

"Listen, you overdressed little shyster!" Monk rumbled. "You were knocked cold when your parachute popped you against an iceberg, and I had to carry you. Next time, I'll sure-enough leave you!"

"The Eskimos set a trap for us," Renny finished the story for Doc. "They were too many for us. They finally got us."

THE bow of the lost liner *Oceanic* was deserted. The fight at the stern had drawn everybody. And a bloody fray that was, for the noise of it had become more violent.

Doc halted near an ice-crusted, dangling cable which offered safe, if somewhat slippery, transit to the ice below.

"Half a mile north of here, an ice finger juts out into the sea," Doc said rapidly. "Go there, all of you! Roxey Vail and her mother should be there already. Wait for me."

"What are you going to do?" Ham questioned.

"I'm staying behind for a short time," Doc replied. "Over the side with you, brothers!"

Rapidly, they slid over the rail.

Monk was last. His homely face showed concern over Doc's safety. He tried to put up an argument.

"Now listen, Doc," he began. "You better—"

Doc smiled faintly. He picked up the argumentative two hundred and sixty pounds of man-gorilla by the slack of the pants and the coat collar, and sent him whizzing down the icy cable.

"Beat it!" he called down at them, then sank behind a capstan.

They ran away across the ice.

One of the battlers on the derelict liner saw the group. He threw up a rifle and fired. He missed. He ran forward to get a better aim.

The man was one of Ben O'Gard's thugs. He crouched in the shelter of a bitt and aimed deliberately. He could hardly have missed. Squinting, he prepared to squeeze the trigger.

Then, instinctively, he brushed at something which had touched his cheek. It felt like a fly. It was no fly—although the rifleman toppled over senseless before he realized it.

Doc retreated as soundlessly as he had reached the man's side.

Rapidly, Doc removed metal caps from the ends of his fingers. These were of bronze. They exactly matched the hue of Doc's skin, and they were so cleverly constructed as to escape detection with the naked eye. However, one might have noticed Doc's fingers were a trifle longer when the caps were in place.

These caps each held a tiny, very sharp needle. A potent chemical of Doc's own concoction fed through glands in those needles. One prick from them meant instant unconsciousness.

This was the secret of Doc's magic touch.

Doc now saw men gathering astern. They were Ben O'Gard's thugs. Victory had evidently fallen to them.

A captive was hauled up from below. He squealed and whimpered and blubbered for mercy.

Two pirates held him. An automatic in Ben O'Gard's hand cracked thunder. The prisoner fell dead.

The man they had murdered was Keelhaul de Rosa.

His proper deserts had at last reached the fellow. As an unmitigated villain, he had been equaled only by the devil who now slew him so cold-bloodedly—Ben O'Gard.

Doc Savage suddenly yelled loudly. His great voice tumbled along the ice-coated deck.

Ben O'Gard saw him, shrieked: "Get the bronze guy, mateys!"

Doc whipped over the rail.

This was what he had remained behind for. He wanted Ben O'Gard and the rest to follow him!

Chapter XVIII
THE THAWING DEATH

DOC SAVAGE sped away from the lost liner *Oceanic*. Bullets jarred showers of ice flakes from hummocks behind which he dodged. Other slugs ran about in the snow like little moles that traveled too fast for the eye.

Doc was careful not to offer too good a target. But he showed himself often enough to lure his pursuers on.

Yelling excitedly, huge Ben O'Gard led the pack. The walrus of a pirate was careful not to get too far ahead of his men, though. Once, Doc saw him stumble deliberately so as to permit the others to catch up with him.

The man was cautious. He had felt the frightful strength of Doc Savage once. In fact, he still wore bandages on his hands from that occasion.

Doc's golden eyes ranged ahead. They held anxiety. Had his friends reached the neck of ice?

They had. Doc could see Monk jumping up and down like the gorilla he resembled as he watched the exciting chase. Monk's yells even reached Doc's ears. They sounded like the noise two fighting bulls would make. For a man with such a mild voice, Monk could emit the most blood-curdling howls.

Doc quickened his pace. No doubt the pirates thought he had been going at full speed—for a chorus of surprised shouts arose as they saw the bronze man was leaving them as though they stood still.

"Shake out your sails, mateys!" Ben O'Gard bellowed. He waddled out ahead of his killer gang like an elephant. Then, seized with caution, he was careful to let them catch up.

Doc reached the headland. The ice pack had piled up here. Passing through it was laborious business. It was as though the houses of a great white city had been shoved into one huge pile.

Rifle and submachine-gun bullets swarmed like unseen hornets through the ice hummocks.

Doc finally gained the finger of ice. He sprinted. The footing was only moderately rough here—offering correspondingly less shelter.

There was one point where the ice neck narrowed. Thirty or so steps would have spanned it from one side to the other.

In the middle of this narrow place stood a slightly unnatural-looking drift of snow.

Doc sped past this snow pile without giving it a glance.

A rifle slug made such a noise in his ear that he thought he was hit. But the hood of his parka had only been torn.

He doubled low, zigzagged a little—and reached cover.

Here, the ice finger widened again. Doc joined his friends.

Victor Vail stood to one side. He was doing his best to hug both his wife and pretty daughter simultaneously.

"I hope you got a deck of aces up your sleeve, Doc," Monk said, his voice again mild. "If you ain't, we're in a pretty pickle."

AS Monk hinted, they were indeed trapped. For it seemed Doc had led them to a spot from which there was no escape. Ben O'Gard and his bloodthirsty pirates had already passed the narrow part of the ice finger. Regaining the shore was now impossible.

To continue their flight in boats, even should Doc have a craft concealed in the rugged ice nearby, was also unfeasible. The pirates would have a perfect chance to riddle them with their machine guns.

Doc Savage showed no concern.

"Keep your shirt on, Monk," he suggested. Then, as a burst of rapid-firer slugs all but parted Monk's bristling red hair, he added: "And your head down!"

"Let the missing link get a lead haircut if he wants it!" Ham clipped. "He needs barbering."

Monk leered at Ham as if he was trying to think of something—got it, and made his inevitable *"Hoinck! Hoinck!"* of a porker grunting.

Ham subsided.

Doc was now introduced to Victor Vail's long-lost wife. The introduction lacked something in courtliness, considering that it was made with all of them lying as flat as they could, with flocks of bullets passing but a few inches over their backs.

Mrs. Vail was a tall woman, fully as beautiful as her entrancing blond daughter, although in a more mature way. She showed little effects of her long years of isolation on this barren Arctic spot.

Victor Vail might have been blind, but he knew how to pick a peach for a wife.

Doc turned hastily to his men to avoid the heart-felt gratitude Victor Vail's wife sought to express, as well as the adoring look in pretty Roxey's eyes.

"Let me have a pistol!" Doc requested.

His friends were surprised. It was rarely that Doc used firearms on his human foes.

Renny handed over an automatic he had taken from one of his Eskimo guards.

Doc left them. In an instant he was lost completely to their sight, so expertly did he conceal himself.

They heard his automatic crack once—then four times more.

They stared at the oncoming pirates. Not a man dropped. This was little short of astounding to the five who knew Doc well. Doc was one of the finest marksmen they had ever seen, even if it was seldom that he fired a shot. They had seen him toss up twelve pennies in a single handful, and using two pistols, touch every one with lead before it fell to earth.

Yet he seemed to have missed the easy targets the pirates offered.

"Hey—look!" Monk howled suddenly.

Behind the pirates, where the finger of ice narrowed, a surprising phenomena was in progress.

The ice was melting at great speed!

MONK was first to comprehend. "My chemical mixture for dissolving ice!" he chuckled. "Doc put a supply of it under that snow drift. He simply punctured the containers!"

Ben O'Gard and his pirates came to a stop. They had discovered the melting ice. That worried them. But their thirst for blood got the better of them. They resumed their charge.

"Come!" Doc called. "And keep down low!"

He led them for the end of the ice finger.

It became noticeable that the whole formation of ice was now in motion. Enough of the narrow neck had dissolved to permit the rest to break free. The whole thing was now an ordinary floe, plaything of the currents of the polar sea.

Doc reached his objective. He pointed.

"How does that look?" he questioned.

Monk grinned from ear to ear. "Heaven will never look any better to this sinful soul!"

The under-the-ice submarine, *Helldiver,* lay before them. It was moored to deadman anchors which had obviously been sunken in the ice by depositing a bit of Monk's remarkable chemical concoction.

They threw off the moorings, then dived down the main hatch.

Doc started the electric motors—there was no time to get the Diesels going. The *Helldiver* surged away from the floe.

"How'd it happen to be here?" Monk questioned.

Doc smiled faintly.

"I'm afraid I stole it," he explained. "Ben O'Gard kindly helped me out by leaving no one aboard. But I must say I never put in a busier twenty minutes than I did running the tin whale here single-handed."

A sporadic burst or two of bullets rattled on the submarine hull. They did not have sufficient power to penetrate the steel plates, however.

The shooting stopped abruptly.

Renny took a chance and thrust his head out. He was not shot at.

"If any of you guys are interested in stark drama, come here and watch," he suggested.

Doc, Long Tom, Monk, Ham, and Johnny crowded up beside him, along with Victor Vail.

Roxey Vail and her mother, after one glance, could not bear the horror of the sight.

GRIM fate had at last grasped Ben O'Gard and his pirates.

They knew that to drift on the floe would of a certainty mean slow starvation. So they were making desperate tries to reach shore. Some had already plunged into the frigid water, and were battling the strong current.

Others, who could not swim, were fighting those who could, trying to make them serve as unwilling pack horses. A few faint shots rang out.

Those swimming began to go down, overcome by the deadly chill of the water, for some distance now separated the floe from land. Their fur garments handicapped them, yet to remove them was to freeze.

After a while, the last man sprang wildly, hopelessly, into the numbingly cold sea.

Two actually reached the ice-rimmed shore. One of these was the walruslike Ben O'Gard. But they could not climb upon the ice, so depleted was their strength.

Ben O'Gard was last to slip back to his death.

Monk let a long breath swish from his cavernous lungs.

"He'd better get plenty chilled, because it's mighty hot where he's goin'!" muttered the gorilla of a chemist. "He paid a mighty high price tryin' to get the—"

Monk swallowed twice. His eyes stuck out. He whirled on Doc.

"Hey—what about the treasure?" he howled. "Now we're in a nice fix! Everybody's dead who knows anything about it!"

DOC SAVAGE was forced to postpone his answer for a time. Handling the under-the-ice submarine occupied his attention. The tanks had to be trimmed, the Diesels had to be started. He and his five men would have only moderate difficulty piloting the *Helldiver* southward, although they would be very short-handed.

Long Tom had gone to the radio room. It was hard to keep him away from any electrical equipment that might be handy.

Now Long Tom bounded excitedly into the control room.

"Listen!" he barked. "I just gave the radio dials a whirl. And I counted no less than fourteen stations calling us continuously."

The others eyed him, puzzled.

"Practically every high-power station north of the equator was trying to raise us!" Long Tom snapped. "They'd sidetracked their other business to do that. What I mean, it takes something important to cause them to do that! Furthermore,

they all seemed to be trying to reach us with the same message!"

"Well—why not copy the message from one of them?" Ham asked sarcastically.

"I did."

Long Tom passed a slip of paper to Doc Savage.

Doc read the radiogram. The others watched his face. Ordinarily, Doc's bronze features reflected no feeling. Not even one of his five friends could, as a usual thing, decipher what was going on behind those sphinxlike, metallic lineaments.

This moment was an exception.

Expression came to Doc's features. It was a look hard to define, but something cold and terrible and grim. His five friends saw. They seemed to feel small things crawling along their spines. For it was ghastly news indeed which could effect Doc like that.

"What is it, Doc?" Monk asked softly.

"The Orient," Doc said in a voice strangely drawn. "I've got to find out more about this before we discuss it. It's a thing so horrible that—well, I've got to know more about it before I can believe it."

The others fell silent. But they felt a strange sort of warmth suffuse their hard muscles. Here was something that promised fresh adventure and peril—the things which were spice of life to this unusual group of men. And it was coming almost before they had extricated themselves from this polar treasure quest.

That the new adventure promised excitement and danger aplenty, they could tell from the cold grimness in Doc's manner. Doc didn't get that way often.

The Orient held something ominous, horrible. They wondered what it was.

Rather, they all wondered but Monk.

Monk got his mind back on fifty millions in gold and diamonds.

"Say, Doc, we ain't goin' off an' leave all that money layin' around on that bleak land somewhere, are we?" he asked plaintively.

Doc awakened from his perusal of the radiogram. He thrust it in a pocket as though to get the ghastly secret it held out of his sight.

"Ben O'Gard and his gang moved the treasure from the strong room of the *Oceanic* when they mutinied more than fifteen years ago," Doc said dryly. "In other words, they filched it from their pals, headed by Keelhaul de Rosa, and cached it in a hiding place of their own."

"Holy cow!" groaned Renny. "Then we have no way of finding that hiding place! Ben O'Gard and his men are all dead."

"We don't care about the hiding pace," Doc assured him. "Ben O'Gard and his gang had recovered the loot before they set out a few hours ago to commit wholesale slaughter on the lost liner."

Monk emitted one of his best howls. "You mean it's—"

"The whole business is aboard this submarine," Doc told him. "To be exact, it's piled some feet deep on the floor of your cabin, Monk!"

It was startling information to Monk. At the end of a most startling adventure. Out of the frozen grip of the North came a fortune in gold and diamonds, saved from the lost liner. But more than that—out of this thrilling adventure came the rescue of two precious lives, and the reunion of a family lost for many years.

To the blind violinist and his reunited family, this was the greatest thing that could have happened, and the battles of Doc and his companions were most marvelous.

But they did not know of the past of Doc and his friends; of the many narrow escapes, the thrilling exploits that were part of their lives.

Neither did they know of the future—the immediate future which held forth adventure and thrills some way connected with the Orient.

Doc himself did not know, and did not care. Somewhere someone else was in danger, some other person needed help. Whatever it was, wherever Doc was needed, there he would go, heedless of danger, conquering all obstacles. And his five companions, adventurers-in-arms, would follow their leader to still greater exploits.

THE END

RESTORATIONS IN BRONZE

Selecting the front cover image for this volume wasn't easy, since both stories featured exceptional covers by Doc Savage's premier cover artist, Walter M. Baumhofer. However, the cover art for *Pirate of the Pacific* so impressed Lester Dent (a.k.a. Kenneth Robeson) that he requested the original painting, which hung for decades in his Missouri home. This volume's cover is reproduced from that original painting, thanks to the generosity of its current owner, Robert Lesser. (And if you'd like to see more classic paintings from the golden age of illustration, check out Lesser's wonderful *Pulp Art* book. It's available at many fine bookstores, and also through Nostalgia Ventures' www.nostalgiatown.com website.)

The Polar Treasure and *Pirate of the Pacific* were Lester Dent's fourth and fifth Doc Savage novels. Lester Dent Estate literary agent Will Murray observes: "As Doc Savage evolved during 1933, Street & Smith exerted pressure on Lester Dent to tone down the more grisly aspects of his imagination, while burnishing the Man of Bronze into an unalloyed hero who refused to kill, even in self-defense." Because of these changes, editor John L. Nanovic trimmed some of *The Polar Treasure*'s more violent scenes. With the kind permission of the Norma Dent Estate and through the considerable efforts of Murray and William T. Stolz of the Western Historical Manuscript Collection of the University of Missouri at Columbia, we have restored more than a thousand words of previously-unpublished material from Dent's original manuscript.

More than two dozen of Lester Dent's Doc Savage novels suffered significant deletions, usually at the hands of Nanovic's assistant editor, Morris Ogden Jones. For example, two-and-a-half chapters were cut from *Mystery Under the Sea,* including never-revealed information on Doc's 86th floor headquarters' many secret entrances, exits and pneumatic escape system. These were occasionally alluded to in later novels, but never fully explained except in these lost passages. In future volumes, we hope to restore this missing material and publish special "manuscript editions" of many of Dent's best Doc Savage novels.

Speaking of restorations, I'd like to officially welcome Michael Piper, the newest contributor to our *Doc Savage* and *The Shadow* reprints. If you've recently noticed an improvement in our cover images, it's due to Piper's Photoshop and graphics wizardry. Nowhere are his contributions better illustrated than on the second printing of the Bama variant of *Doc Savage Volume One: Fortress of Solitude & The Devil Genghis.* There's a considerable improvement over the cover image on the first edition, and it's solely due to Michael's expertise. Piper joins our regular Sanctum Productions team that includes copy editor Joseph Wrzos (who edited *Amazing Stories* and *Fantastic* during the mid-1960s) and proofreader Carl Gafford (a veteran comics professional who has worked for DC, Marvel, Disney and Hanna-Barbera during his long career).

Next time, we'll return with two more classics from Doc Savage's debut year: *The Lost Oasis* and *The Sargasso Ogre.* —Anthony Tollin, series editor

INTERMISSION by Will Murray

The Polar Treasure was Lester Dent's fourth Doc Savage novel, and a fabulous example of the brand of story through which the young writer from Tulsa broke into the pulp magazine field. It's also an example of pulpeteer persistence.

In March 1930, with only four fiction sales under his belt, Dent tore a page out of newspaper headlines of the day and wrote "Time's Domain" for Street & Smith's *The Popular Magazine.* It was based on a risky plan to explore the North Pole by submarine being floated by Sir George Hubert Wilkins. In Dent's story, the imaginary explorers discover a steamy lost valley inhabited by surviving dinosaurs.

The Popular asked for a rewrite, but still rejected the final version. So Dent attempted to market it elsewhere. Several more magazines bounced it.

Early in 1931, Dent had landed in New York City as a contract writer for Dell Publications. Editor Richard E. Martinsen kept him busy filling the pages of *Scotland Yard* and *Sky Riders,* but Dent had his eye on Dell's new *All-Fiction Stories,* edited by Carson W. Mowre.

In April, Dent recorded the sale of "Under the Pole" to *All-Fiction.* Was this a revision of one of the earlier manuscripts, or an entirely fresh story devised under Mowre's guidance? No one knows.

The story was announced as forthcoming with the title changed to "Underwater Ice." Dent's bubble collapsed when the worsening Depression forced Dell to cancel most of their pulps. The August 1931 issue of *All-Fiction Stories* was never published. As far as anyone knows, "Underwater Ice" never saw print anywhere. Out of work and fighting resistant markets, Lester Dent and wife Norma retreated to Missouri to lick their psychic wounds.

That summer, the Wilkins-Ellsworth Arctic expedition finally got underway. This dangerous venture is today a forgotten chapter in Polar exploration. In 1930, Australian explorer Sir Hubert Wilkins leased a decommissioned U. S. naval submarine, and began refitting her for operating under the North Polar icecap as the Arctic Submarine *Nautilus.* The venture was abandoned in August.

When it came time to plot the fourth Doc Savage tale, Dent clearly saw his chance to exploit all the research and hard work he had put to fictionalizing the ill-fated Arctic expedition. And no doubt he took satisfaction in the irony that after rejecting the idea so many times, Street & Smith finally printed it.

The *Helldiver* depicted in *The Polar Treasure* was clearly inspired by the *Nautilus.* Many of her special features were lifted directly from that unique design, although the sub Dent imagined is much larger and more advanced than Wilkins' vessel.

The Polar Treasure came close to revealing one of Doc Savage's greatest secrets. In Dent's outline, Chapter XIX was originally entitled "The Fortress of Solitude." Here is how he described the unwritten sequence:

Doc swam to the ice pack, a feat only one of his vast strength and hardihood could accomplish in the intense cold. He struck out—away from his enemies. For a number of days, he journeyed, living off the bleak waste. He neared his 'fortress of solitude,' the secret retreat which he had long maintained here in the Arctic; the spot to which he came to do his experimenting and studying. He secured a plane, arms and ammunition.

The Polar Treasure is one of the great formative Doc Savage exploits. And well it should be. By the time Dent got around to writing this yarn, he was as well-prepared as if he had conquered the North Pole himself. Lester thought so highly of it that he adapted it for a 1938 *Doc Savage* radio pilot. Four serial chapters were completed, but the show never aired.

In later years, Dent joked, "I've never been north of southern Alaska, but I write wonderful stories about the North Pole." This was the story he meant.

An accidental theme of this Doc Savage volume reflects Lester Dent's lifelong fascination with pirate lore, a common interest of boys of his generation. Early in his Doc writing, Dent liked to segue from one adventure to the next. *Pirate of the Pacific* picks up immediately upon the bronze man's triumphant return from the North Pole. With one brand of buccaneer vanquished, Doc and his two-fisted crew are called upon to tackle another. Like the previous novel, *Pirate of the Pacific* is torn from the headlines. Then as now, the Far East was one of the last remaining outposts for modern piracy.

Here, the fictitious "Luzon Union" is simply a thinly-disguised Philippines. In 1933, the Philippines was a U. S. protectorate seeking its independence. Street & Smith magazines were available there. Thus the setting was calculated to woo faraway Filipino readers.

Within a week of completing *Pirate of the Pacific,* Lester Dent and his wife took a cruise of South America and the West Indies on the Cunard liner *Mauretania.* It was there during these rounds that he became interested in coming back to the area in a boat of his own, to search for buccaneer gold.

These stories depict the formative Doc Savage. He's rough, slangy, is still learning to be an effective superhero. After three bloodthirsty adventures, mindful of the Hippocratic Oath he took as a physician, Doc has devised non-lethal methods of defeating his adversaries, and will create more.

For more on these stories, visit http://www.nostalgiatown.com/articles/docsavage1.html

PIRATE of the PACIFIC

Not ships, but nations, were the prize this modern buccaneer sought. And Doc Savage and his companions give him a run that's worth reading!

A complete book-length novel of the exploits of Doc Savage, by

KENNETH ROBESON

Chapter I
THE YELLOW KILLERS

THREE laundry trucks stopped in the moonlight near a large commercial airport on Long Island. They made little noise. The machines bore the name of a New York City laundry firm.

The drivers peered furtively up and down the road. They seemed relieved that no one was in sight. Getting out, they walked slowly around the trucks, eyes probing everywhere, ears straining.

They were stocky, yellow-skinned, slant-eyed men. Their faces were broad and flat, their hair black and coarse. They looked like half-castes.

Satisfied, the three exchanged glances. They could see each other distinctly in the moonlight. No word was spoken. One driver lifted an arm—a silent signal.

Each Mongol dragged a dead man from the cab of his truck. All three victims had been stabbed expertly through the heart. They wore the white uniforms of laundry drivers, and on each uniform was embroidered the same name the trucks bore.

A roadside ditch received the three bodies.

Rear doors of the trucks were now opened. Fully a dozen Mongols and half-castes crawled out of the vehicles. They clustered beside the road.

Their faces were inscrutable; no muscle twitched, not a slant eye wavered. They were like a collection of placid, evil yellow images.

No weapons were in sight. But their clothing bulged suspiciously.

The first driver's arm elevated in another noiseless signal. The fellow seemed to be in charge.

The whole crowd glided quietly down the side road that led to the airport.

Plane hangars were an orderly row of fat, drab humps ahead. Faint strains of radio music came from one of them. A high fence of heavy woven wire encircled both hangars and plane runways.

Near the main gate in the fence, a guard lounged. His only movement was an occasional lusty swing at a night insect.

"These blasted mosquitoes are bigger'n hawks!" he grumbled, speaking aloud for his own company. "They must be flyin' over from the Jersey marshes."

The guard discerned a man approaching. He forgot his mosquitoes as he peered into the darkness to see who was approaching. When the man came within a few yards, the guard was able to distinguish his features.

"Hy'ah, yellow boy!" he grinned. "You can't poke around here at night. This is private property."

The Mongol replied with a gibberish that was unintelligible to the watchman.

"No savvy!" said the guard. "Splickee English!"

The Oriental came closer, gesturing earnestly with his hands.

The unfortunate guard never saw another figure glide up in the moonlight behind him. Moonlight flickered on a thick, heavy object. The weapon struck with a vicious, sidewise swipe.

The sound, as it hit, was like a loud, heavy *thump*. The guard piled down on the ground, out in a second.

THE other Mongols and half-castes now came up. They strode past the unconscious guard as though they hadn't seen him, passed through the gate in the high fence, and continued purposefully for the hangars.

No commands had been spoken. They were functioning like a deadly machine, following a deliberate plan.

Music from the radio was thumping a more rapid tempo—the musicians were working up to one of those grand slam endings. The radio instrument itself was a midget set, no larger than a shoe box.

Another night worker of the airport had plugged it into a power outlet on a workbench in a corner of the hangar. He lolled in the cockpit of a plane and listened to the music.

"Get hot!" he exhorted the radio, and beat time on the taut fuselage fabric with his palms.

Night traffic at this airport was negligible, and two men were the extent of the airport staff—this man, and the one at the gate.

The radio music came to an end. The station announcer introduced the next feature—a regular fifteen-minute news broadcast.

The man scowled and slouched more lazily in the plane cockpit. He was not enthusiastic about this particular news broadcaster. The fellow handled the news in too dignified and conservative a fashion. He didn't set things afire.

"Good evening," said the radio commentator. "Tonight, somewhere out on Long Island Sound, the under-the-polar-ice submarine, *Helldiver*, is coming. The craft was sighted by an airplane pilot shortly before darkness. She was headed toward New York.

"Arrival of the *Helldiver* in New York will bring to a close one of the most weird and mystifying adventures of modern days. The submarine left the United States many weeks ago, and vanished into the Arctic regions. Approximately forty persons started the trip. Yet the craft is returning tonight with but six living men aboard, the others having perished in the polar wastes."

The man listened with more attention. This was quite a change from the news broadcaster's usual routine of foreign and political stuff.

Another fact made the news interesting and surprising to the listener. This was the first he had heard of the submarine *Helldiver*, on an expedition into the Arctic regions. About forty had started out. And six were coming back!

Here was something worth listening to! Strange the papers had not carried a lot of ballyhoo about the start of the expedition! Explorers were usually anxious to get their pictures on the front pages.

The next words from the radio clarified this mystery.

"From the beginning, this polar submarine expedition has been a strangely secret affair," continued the commentator. "Not a newspaper carried a word of the sailing. Indeed, the world might still know nothing of the amazing feat, had several radio operators not tipped newspaper reporters that messages were being sent and received which disclosed the submarine was in the vicinity of the north pole. This information was something of a shock to the newspapermen. It meant they were losing out on one of the big news stories of the year. They had not even known the expedition was underway.

"During the last few days, there has been a great rush among newspapers striving to be first to carry a story of the expedition. They seem to be up against a blank wall. The men aboard the underseas boat sent word by radio that they wanted no publicity and that no story of the trip would be given out.

"Only two facts have been learned. The first is that but six men out of approximately forty are returning. The second bit of information was that the expedition is commanded by one of the most mysterious and remarkable men living in this day.

"That man is Doc Savage!"

THE news broadcaster paused to give emphasis to the name he had just pronounced.

The listening man was leaning over the cockpit edge, all interest. He did not see the yellow murder mask of a face framed in a small, open side door of the hangar. Nor did he see hands like bundles of yellowed bones as they silently lifted a strange death instrument and trained it on him.

"Doc Savage!" grunted the man. "Never heard of the guy!"

The voice from the radio continued. "Doc Savage is a man practically unknown to the public. Yet in scientific circles, he has a fame that is priceless. His name is something to conjure with.

"Last night, I was fortunate enough to attend a banquet given by scientific men here in New York. Many learned men attended. In the course of the evening, I heard references to important discoveries made by Doc Savage. The really bewildering thing about these discoveries was that they were made in widely different fields, ranging from surgery, chemistry, and electricity to the perfecting of a new, quick-growing species of lumber tree.

"Amazement seized me as I listened to eminent scientists discuss Doc Savage, the man of mystery, in the most glowing words. It seemed impossible they could speak in such terms of one man without exaggerating. Yet these were men certainly not given to exaggeration. I am going to give you a word picture of this man of mystery of whom they talked.

"Doc Savage is, despite his amazing accomplishments, a young man. He is a striking bronze giant of a figure. His physical strength, my informants assured me, is on a par with his mental ability. That means he is a marvel of muscular development. One of the scientists at the banquet told me in entire seriousness that, were Savage to enter athletic competition, his name would leap to the headlines of every paper in the country.

"This man of mystery has been trained from the cradle, until now he is almost a super being. This training, given by his father, was to fit Doc Savage for a definite purpose in life.

"That purpose is to travel from one end of the world to the other, striving to help those who need help, punishing those who deserve punishment.

"Associated with Doc Savage are five men who love excitement and adventure, and who have dedicated themselves to their leader's creed of benefiting humanity.

"A strange and mysterious group of men, this! So unusual that the bare facts I am telling you now cannot but sound unreal and far-fetched. Yet I can assure you my information came from the most conservative and reliable sources."

The listening man blinked as he digested the words that came to his ears. "This Doc Savage must be quite a guy," he grunted.

Then the sneaking face was near. As unknowing as the watchman's companion at the gate, the man in the plane fell before the blow of the weapon, crumpled in his seat, unconscious or dead—the attacker did not look to see.

SLANT-EYED men poured into the hangar. No orders were uttered. The half-caste Orientals were still following their plan. Their efficiency was terrible, deadly. The whole group worked as one unit, an expert killing machine.

Two opened the hangar doors. Others busied themselves making four pursuit planes ready for the air. These ships were the most modern craft, yet the sinister men showed familiarity with the mechanism.

Three yellow raiders rushed up to the planes carrying guns and bombs. The guns were quickly attached; the bombs were racked in clips on the undersides of the planes.

More men secured four parachutes from a locker room.

No time was wasted in scampering about the airport hunting for things. They knew exactly where everything was located.

The planes were strong-armed out of the hangars. Four Orientals dug goggles and helmets out of their clothing. The helmets were a brilliant red color.

The men cinched on the parachutes, then plugged into the cockpits. The scarlet helmets made them resemble a quartet of red-headed woodpeckers.

Exhaust thunder galloped across the tarmac as the motors started. Prop-streams tore dust from under the ships and pushed it away in squirming masses.

The planes flung along the runway, vaulted off, and slanted up into the now moon-whitened sky.

The Orientals who had been left behind lost no time in quitting the airport. Racing to the three laundry trucks, they entered, and drove hastily away.

Three or four minutes after the planes departed, no one was left at the airport. The two watchmen lay where they had dropped, still unconscious. In the ditch beside the road sprawled the three slain drivers of the laundry trucks.

The adjacent countryside slept on peacefully. The four planes booming overhead attracted no attention, since night flying was not unusual even at this quiet port.

Within ten minutes, Long Island Sound was crawling under the craft. The surface of the Sound was like a faintly pitted silver plate, shimmering in the brilliant moonlight.

The planes spread out widely and flew low. Each Oriental pilot had high-magnification binoculars jammed to his eyes. With the same machine thoroughness which had stamped their bloody actions at the airport, they searched the Sound surface.

It was not long before they found what they sought—a narrow craft trailing across the Sound at the head of a long wedge of foaming wake.

The planes headed purposefully for this vessel.

Chapter II
SEA PHANTOM

THE quarry came rapidly closer. More details of the craft were discernible. The half-caste Mongol pilots continued to use their binoculars. They tilted their planes down in steep dives toward the unusual vessel below.

It was a submarine. It resembled a lean-flanked, razorback whale several hundred feet long. Big steel runners extended from bow to stern, sled fashion. Amidships, a sort of collapsible conning tower reared.

The underseas craft floated high. On the bows, a lettered name was readable:

HELLDIVER

It was this submarine which had been the subject of the radio news commentator's broadcast.

With deadly precision, the four planes roared down at the submersible. The Orientals had discarded their binoculars, and had their eyes pasted to the bomb sights. Yellow hands were poised, muscles drawn wire-hard, on bomb trips.

A naval bombing expert, knowing all the facts, would have sworn the submarine didn't have a chance of escaping. It would be blown out of the water by the bombs.

The Mongol pilots were hot-eyed, snarling—yellow faces no longer inscrutable. They were about to accomplish the purpose of their bloody plot—the death of everyone aboard the under-the-polar-ice submarine.

They got a shock.

From a dozen spots, the sub hull spewed smoke as black as drawing ink. Heaving, squirming, the dense smudge spread. It blotted the underseas boat from view, and blanketed the surface of the Sound for hundreds of feet in every direction.

With desperate haste, the Orientals deposited bombs in the center of the smoke mushroom. These explosions drove up treelike columns from the black body of the smoke mass. It was impossible to tell whether the sub had been damaged.

The four planes might have been angry, metallic bees droning over some gigantic, strange, black blossom, as they hovered watchfully. They did not waste more bombs, since the smoke cloud was now half a mile across. In it, the sub was like a needle in a haystack.

Several minutes passed. Suddenly, as one unit, the four planes dived for the western edge of the heavy smoke screen.

Their sharp eyes had detected a long, slender mass moving some feet beneath the surface. This was leaving a creamy wake.

In quick succession, the war planes struck downward at the object under the water. Four bombs dropped. The half-caste Mongols knew their business. Each bomb scored an almost perfect hit.

Water rushed high. The sea heaved and boiled. The concussions tossed the planes about like leaves.

Swinging in a wide circle, the planes came back. The commotion in the water had subsided. The pilots made hissing sounds of delight.

The long, slender mass was no longer to be seen. Oil filmed the surface. Oil such as would come from the ruptured entrails of a submarine.

THE pursuit planes whirled a half dozen lazy spirals. Convinced the deadly work was done, the leader of the quartet angled for the shore, four or five miles distant. Once over land, he dived out of the cockpit, fell a hundred feet, and opened his parachute. The plane boomed away. Eventually, it would crash somewhere.

Two other pilots followed their leader's example.

The third lingered a bit above the grisly smear of oil on the Sound surface.

He chanced to notice a small object near the cloud of black smoke. This seemed nothing more than a floating box. It bobbed lightly on the choppy waves.

The flyer ignored the box. It looked harmless— a piece of wreckage. A few moments later, he winged to shore and quitted his plane by parachute, as the others had done.

The man might have saved himself a lot of trouble had he taken time to investigate the floating box he had noted. Close scrutiny would have shown the top and sides of the box were fitted with what resembled large camera lenses.

Inside the box were other lenses, spinning disks perforated with small holes, sensitive photo-electric cells—a compact television transmitter. Waterproofed electric wires led from this down into the water.

Long Island Sound was not deep at this point. The under-the-polar-ice submarine, *Helldiver*, rested on the bottom. The wires from the television box entered the undersea boat.

Before the scanning disk of the television receiver in the sub, six men stood. They were a remarkable group. Six more unusual men than these probably had never assembled. Each possessed a world-wide reputation in his chosen profession.

There was "Renny," a hulking six feet four and two hundred and fifty pounds of him—with possibly fifty pounds of that weight concentrated in a pair of monster fists. Renny had a sober, puritanical face. About the only entertainment he permitted himself was knocking panels out of doors with his huge fists—a stunt he pulled at the most unexpected moments. As Colonel John Renwick, the engineer, Renny was known in many nations, and drew down fabulous fees when he worked.

There was "Long Tom," pale and none too healthy-looking, the weakling of the crowd in appearance. His looks were deceptive, though, as more than one big man had discovered. As Major Thomas J. Roberts, the electrical wizard, he had worked with the greatest electrical minds of his day.

"Johnny"—William Harper Littlejohn—was tall, gaunt, studious and bespectacled. He seemed half starved, with shoulders as bony as a coat hanger. Once he had headed the Natural Science department of a famous university. His knowledge of geology and archaeology was profound. His books on these subjects were in every worthwhile library.

Two individuals stood on the edge of the group and scowled at each other like a cat and dog. They were "Monk" and "Ham." They always seemed on the point of flying at each other's throats. They swapped insults at every opportunity. Yet Ham had several times risked his life to save Monk, and Monk had done the same for Ham.

They were as unlike as men could be. Monk was a hairy monster of two hundred and sixty pounds, with arms some inches longer than his short legs, and a face incredibly homely. He was a human gorilla. The world of chemistry knew him as Lieutenant Colonel Andrew Blodgett Mayfair, one of the most learned chemists alive. But he looked dumb as an ox.

Ham was slender, lean-waisted. His clothing was sartorial perfection—tailors had been known to follow Ham down streets, just to see clothes being worn as they should be. His business cards read: "Brigadier General Theodore Marley Brooks," and he was possibly the most astute lawyer Harvard ever turned out. Ham carried a black cane of innocent aspect—a sword cane, in reality. He was never to be found without it.

The sixth member of the group was a mighty man of bronze—Doc Savage.

MAN OF MYSTERY, the radio commentator had labeled Doc Savage. Wizard of science! Muscular marvel!

The radio speaker had not exaggerated. Doc Savage was all of these things. His mental powers and strength were almost fantastic. He was the product of intensive expert, scientific training that had started the moment he was born.

Each day of his life, he had performed a two-hour routine of unusual exercise. Doc's powers might seem unbelievable, but there was really no magic about them. Rigid adherence to his exercise, coupled with profound study, was responsible.

Doc was a big man, almost two hundred pounds—but the bulk of his great form was forgotten in the smooth symmetry of a build incredibly powerful.

The bronze of his hair was a little darker than that of his features, and the hair lay down tightly as a metal skullcap.

Most striking of all were the bronze man's eyes. They glittered like pools of flake gold when little lights from the television scanning disk played on them. They seemed to exert a hypnotic influence.

The lines of Doc's features, the unusually high forehead, the mobile and muscular and not-too-full mouth, the lean cheeks, denoted a power of character seldom seen.

"There goes the last of the flyers!" Doc said.

Doc's voice, although low, held a remarkable quality of latent power. It was an intensively trained voice—everything about Doc had been trained by his exercise routine.

"They sure enough thought it was the sub they had bombed," grinned Johnny, the bony archaeologist. He adjusted the glasses he wore. These spectacles had an extremely thick left lens which was actually a powerful magnifying glass. Johnny, having practically lost the use of his left eye in the War, carried the magnifier there for handiness.

"Our contraption fooled them," Doc admitted. "But it might not have worked so well in daytime. A close look would have shown the thing was only a strip of canvas painted the color of steel, and some oil barrels, pulled along under the surface by a torpedo mechanism."

At the rear of the group, Monk stopped scowling at Ham long enough to ask: "You made that torpedo mechanism a couple of days ago—but how'd you know that early that something like this would happen?"

"I didn't know," Doc smiled faintly. "I only knew we were barging into trouble—and made preparations to meet it."

"If you was to ask me, we didn't have to barge into it," Monk grinned. "It came right out and grabbed us around the neck. Who were them guys who just tried to lay eggs on us?"

For answer, Doc Savage drew two radio messages from a pocket.

"You all saw the first one of these when it came," he said.

THE FIVE men nodded. They had been far within the Arctic regions when the first message had reached them by radio. It was very short, reading:

IN DESPERATE NEED OF YOUR HELP.
                          JUAN MINDORO.

Doc Savage had promptly turned the submarine southward. There was no need of lingering in the Arctic, anyway. They had just completed the mission which had sent them into the polar regions—a desperate, adventurous quest for a fifty-million-dollar treasure aboard a derelict liner.

That treasure now reposed in the submarine—a hoard of wealth that had threatened to cost its weight in the blood of men.

Doc had not told his five men what meaning Juan Mindoro's mysterious message might have. They had not asked questions, knowing he would tell them in good time. Doc was sometimes as much of a mystery to his five friends as he was to the rest of the world.

They had guessed there was danger ahead, however. Several days ago, Doc had hailed a liner they chanced to pass, and had put aboard the vessel three persons who were passengers on the submarine. These three people—a famous violinist and his wife and daughter—were, with Doc and his five men, the only survivors of the grisly episode in the Arctic through which they had just passed.

The radio commentator had not mentioned these three. He had not known of them. Nor would he ever know, for the polar episode was now a closed book.

The fact that Doc had transferred the three passengers to the safety of a liner showed he wanted them out of danger—and told Doc's men they were headed for more trouble. They didn't mind. It was the thing they lived for. They went to the far corners of the earth to find it.

But they had not known Doc had received a second message from the same source.

Doc extended the missive. "I copied this myself a few days ago. Read it."

Crowding about, the five men read:

> I HAVE BEEN FORCED TO GO INTO HIDING AT THE HOME OF THE MAN WHO WAS WITH ME WHEN I LAST SAW YOU. MEET ME THERE UPON YOUR ARRIVAL. AND BE PREPARED FOR ATTACKS ON YOUR LIFE.
> JUAN MINDORO.

"Huh!" ejaculated Monk, wrinkling his flat, apish nose. "That don't tell us any more than the first one."

"Exactly," Doc replied. "And that explains why I have not informed you fellows what we're headed for. I don't know myself—except that it has something to do with the Orient.

"Juan Mindoro is a political power in the Pacific island group known as the Luzon Union. He is the most influential man in the islands. And you know what recently happened to the Luzon Union."

"They were given their independence," said Ham. "I remember now. Juan Mindoro had a big hand in electing the first president after the island group became self-governing. But what could that have to do with this?"

Doc shrugged. "It is too early to say."

He glanced at the television scanning disk. "The men who tried to bomb us are gone. We might as well get underway."

The submarine arose to the surface. The pall of black smoke still hung over the Sound.

Doc pulled in the television box which had been trailing the boat. Then the sub put on speed. It ran low in the water to escape attention from passing boats.

Once it dived to pass a launch loaded with newspaper reporters.

Chapter III
MONGOL PERIL

PRACTICALLY every wharf in New York City was watched by newspaper reporters that night. The return of a submarine which had ventured under the polar ice was big news. The fact that those aboard the submarine wished no publicity made the story bigger. Each paper wanted to be the first to carry it.

Forty or so men had gone into the Arctic—only six were coming back. A whale of a yarn! City editors swore over telephones at reporters. Photographers dashed about, answering false alarms turned in by news hawks who had mistaken rowboats and mud scows for the sub. Everybody lost a lot of sleep.

In a remote corner of the harbor, a rusty old tramp steamer swung at anchor. The captain of the ancient hulk, who was also the owner, happened to be an acquaintance of Doc Savage.

Shortly after midnight, this captain turned all of his crew out of their bunks. They fell to and made the submarine *Helldiver* fast alongside the tramp steamer. No one from land noted this incident.

A launch now sped ashore. It bore a small fortune in gold and diamonds—a load of the treasure Doc had brought back from the Arctic. An armored car and a dozen guards with drawn guns met the launch and received the wealth. This also escaped the notice of the reporters.

The launch made more trips—until the whole treasure was on its way to an all-night bank.

Doc and his five men came ashore with the last load. Newspaper reporters would discover the submarine tied alongside the tramp steamer in the morning, but the tramp captain would profess mystification as to how it got there.

The whole Arctic submarine expedition business was destined to be a mystery the news hawks would never solve.

A taxicab took Doc and his five men uptown. Doc rode outside, barehead, standing on the running board. He habitually did that when danger threatened. From this position, Doc's weird golden eyes missed very little—a sniper had hardly a chance of getting a shot at them before he was discovered.

The cab halted before the most impressive building in the city. This skyscraper stabbed upward, a great white thorn of brick and steel, nearly a hundred stories.

Few people were on the sidewalk at this hour. But those who were, stopped and openly stared, such a striking figure did Doc Savage present. The big bronze man was a sensation wherever he went.

Doc and his five men rode an express elevator to the eighty-sixth floor of the skyscraper. Here Doc had his New York headquarters—a richly furnished office, one of the most complete libraries of technical and scientific tomes in existence, and an elaborately equipped chemical and electrical laboratory.

Doc had a second headquarters, fitted with another library and laboratory which were the most complete in existence. This, however, was at a spot he called his "Fortress of Solitude." No one knew its whereabouts. To this retreat Doc went at frequent intervals for the periods of intense study to which he devoted himself. At such times he vanished as completely as though he had dropped from the earth. No one could get in touch with him.

It was these periodic disappearances, as much as anything else, which had given Doc repute as a man of mystery.

MONK planted his furry bulk on a costly inlaid table in the office and began rolling himself a cigarette.

"Did you make arrangements by radio about the treasure?" he asked Doc. "I mean—about what the money is to be used for."

"That's all taken care of," the bronze man assured him.

They knew what that meant. The money was to be spent enlarging a weird institution which Doc maintained in upstate New York—a place where Doc sent all the criminals he captured. There, the lawbreakers underwent an amazing treatment in which their brains were operated upon and all memory of their past wiped out. Then they received training which turned them into useful citizens.

This unusual institution was Doc's own idea. He never sent a criminal to prison. They all went to the institution, to be operated upon by specialists whom Doc had trained. They were turned loose entirely reformed men—they didn't know they had ever been crooks.

"It's a little stuffy in here," complained Ham.

He crossed over and threw up the window. He stood there for a moment, staring at the impressive panorama of New York City spread out below. Then he turned away.

A moment later, a slate-colored pigeon fluttered up and landed on the window ledge. Doc and his men paid no particular heed. Pigeons were plentiful around the skyscrapers.

"What's our next move?" Ham wanted to know.

"You fellows scatter and attend to such of your private business as needs it," Doc suggested.

"We've been gone several weeks, and no telling what we're headed for now. It may last longer."

"I got a secretary who takes care of my business," homely Monk grinned. "Better let me go with you, Doc."

Monk was proud of his secretary, maintaining she was the prettiest in New York.

"Nothing doing," said Doc. "There's no need of any army of us interviewing Juan Mindoro."

The slate-hued pigeon on the window ledge had not moved.

"You know where to find Juan Mindoro?" questioned Monk.

"His wireless message said he had gone into hiding at the home of the man who was with him when I saw him last," Doc replied. "I last met Juan Mindoro in Mantilla, the capital city of the Luzon Union. The man with him at the time was Scott S. Osborn, who is a sugar importer doing a large business in the Luzon Union trade. Osborn has a home near the north edge of the city. I'll go there."

Johnny had been squinting owlishly through his glasses which had the thick left lens—studying the pigeon. He took off his spectacles. As a matter of fact, he saw very well without them.

"That's what I call a sleepy pigeon!" he grunted. "It hasn't moved."

Doc glanced at the pigeon—his gaze became fixed.

Suddenly, a weird sound permeated the interior of the office; a trilling, mellow, subdued sound. It might have been the dulcet note of some exotic jungle bird, or the sylvan song of wind filtering through a leafless forest.

The strange trilling had the weird quality of seeming to come from everywhere within the office.

Electric tension seized Doc's five men. They knew what that sound meant. Danger!

For the sound was part of Doc—a small, unconscious thing that he did in moments of mental stress, or when he had made some astounding discovery, or when death threatened.

The pigeon abruptly flipped backward off the window sill.

Doc reached the window with flashing speed. The bird was some yards away, flying sluggishly. Doc watched until it was lost in the moonlight.

"That pigeon was where every word we spoke could reach it!" he said dryly.

"What if it was?" Monk snorted. "Pigeons can't tell what they hear."

"That one could."

"Huh?"

"It had a small microphone attached to its tail feathers."

MONK gaped after the departing pigeon. "For

the love of Mike! But the thing flew away as though no wires were attached!"

"The wires were very small, about like silk threads," Doc declared. "They had to be small, or we would have seen them. A sharp jerk broke them, and left the bird free."

Leaning out of the window, Doc glanced up the sheer side of the skyscraper, then down. Only darkened windows met his gaze.

He examined the window ledge, noting bits of grayish powder. In a crack, he discovered a particle of cracked corn.

"The bird has been fed on the ledge!" he declared. "Either the office door was forced, or the grain was lowered from above. That was how it was taught to fly here."

He spun from the window, crossed the office. The speed with which his big bronze form moved was startling. He entered the corridor, glided down it to the end elevator. At his touch upon a secret button, the elevator door leafed back.

So quickly had Doc moved that his five men were still in the office. They piled out, big-fisted Renny in the lead, and joined Doc in the lift.

The cage sank them. It was a special installation, used only by Doc Savage, and geared at terrific speed. Such was the pace of descent that their feet were off the floor for the first sixty stories. Monk, Johnny, and Long Tom were wrenched to their knees by the shock of stopping.

"What I mean, that thing brings you down!" Monk grinned, getting up from all fours.

Monk had nearly worn out the high-speed elevator the first week after Doc had it installed, riding it up and down for the wallop he got out of it.

A cop was twiddling his nightstick out in front.

"See anyone leave this neighborhood in a hurry within the last few minutes?" Doc demanded.

"No, sor," said the cop. "Sure, an' the only lads I've seen come out 'av a buildin' around here was two slant-eyed fellers. 'Twas in no hurry they were."

"Where'd they go?"

"Took a taxi."

Doc eyed his five friends.

"They must have been the men who sent us the pigeon," he told them. "They knew we'd discovered their trick, and fled. We'd be wasting time to hunt them."

Doc whirled back into the skyscraper.

His five men milled uncertainly, then trailed Doc. But the speed elevator was already gone. They rode a slower lift lip to the eighty-sixth floor aerie, only to discover Doc had gotten whatever he had wanted from his laboratory, and had departed.

THE home of Scott S. Osborn, sugar importer, was a castlelike stone building perched atop a low hill in a wooded section of Pelham, one of the northern residential suburbs of New York City. The medieval castle architecture was carried out in a water-filled stone moat which surrounded the walls. A replica of a drawbridge, large enough for heavy automobiles to be driven across, spanned the moat.

Doc Savage arrived alone, driving a roadster which had the top entirely removed. The car was a reserved gray in color, but expensive, sixteen-cylindered. On a straight road, the machine could better a hundred and fifty an hour.

Doc alighted, crossed the drawbridge, and rang the bell.

No answer. An electric fixture cast pale light on the drawbridge.

He thumbed the bell again, received no response. The vast castle of a building was quiet as a tomb. The gatelike door was locked.

Doc returned to his roadster, got a black box somewhat larger than a good-sized suitcase, and carried it into the shrubbery near the drawbridge. On one end the mysterious box had a cameralike lens. He pointed this at the drawbridge entrance, then silently plucked enough branches from nearby hushes to cover the box, hiding it thoroughly.

The moon shadows in the shrubbery swallowed his big bronze form. He made practically no sound, no stirring of leaves.

He reappeared again near one wall of the castle. The masonry was rough. He climbed to the top as easily as an ordinary man would walk a flat surface, although only the narrowest of ledges offered purchase to his tempered fingers.

For a moment, he poised at the top and reconnoitered. The same deathly silence gripped the mansion.

On either side were long, two-story buildings, their outer walls formed by the castle walls. In the center was a tiled court, a fountain, shrubbery, flowers. None of the windows were lighted.

Directly below Doc was a sheer drop of perhaps twenty-five feet. He sprang down—and so tremendously powerful were his leg muscles that the great leap hardly jarred him.

Moving swiftly, Doc tried a door. Locked. He sought another, then the rest, in quick succession.

Every door facing the court was secured.

Doc glided noiselessly into the shadows of the fountain. His fingers touched a box of an affair strapped under his coat. This was a bit greater in size than a cigar box. A switch on it clicked at his touch.

Doc plucked back his left coat sleeve. The object thus revealed looked at first glance like an enormous wrist watch. Closer scrutiny would have revealed a startling fact about the crystal of this watch.

It mirrored a very pale moving picture!

The scene was the drawbridge outside the castlelike dwelling of Scott S. Osborn, friend of Juan Mindoro. A shadowy figure stood on the drawbridge. His arms windmilled, gesturing orders to other vague forms.

The castle was being surrounded!

The oversize edition of a wrist watch on Doc's wrist, together with the box inside his coat, was a television receiver of marvelous compactness. It was tuned to the wavelength of a transmitter in the black box he had hidden under the brush outside the drawbridge.

Doc continued to watch the apparatus on his wrist. More slant-eyed men joined the one on the drawbridge. They carried revolvers, swords, knives. Two had deadly submachine guns.

One fitted a key in the lock of the gatelike door.

The faint click of the lock operating reached Doc's sensitive ears.

They must know he was inside. Probably they had seen him atop the wall. They were coming in, the murderous horde of them.

Chapter IV
THE DRIPPING SWORD

DOC SAVAGE quitted the murky vicinity of the fountain. He ran six light, springy paces. His bronze form shot upward in a tremendous leap. His corded fingers grasped the sill of a window which was open several inches. The window slid up. Doc slipped inside.

The whole thing had taken no more than a dozen ticks of the clock.

The drawbridge door opened. A group of half-caste Mongols skulked into the court, weapons bared for action.

The slant-eyed men poked about in the shrubbery until convinced Doc was not there. They tried the courtyard doors, and discovered them all locked.

"The bronze devil has gotten away!" one singsonged in his native tongue.

"That is impossible," replied the leader gravely. "Our lowly eyes beheld him upon the wall even as we arrived. He dropped inside." The man scowled at the high rear wall. "I marvel that the neck of the troublemaker was not broken."

"Then, oh mighty Liang-Sun Chi, he must have entered the house."

Liang-Sun Chi bent a bilious stare on the two sections of the residence.

"Is the bronze demon a magician, that he can go through locked doors and windows—for we left them all locked when we departed this afternoon."

"Only on the ground floor were they left locked, oh lord," answered the other. He pointed. "See! There is one second floor window open."

The aperture the Mongol indicated was the identical window through which Doc Savage had entered. And Doc now stood in the darkened room behind, listening to the talk. He understood the language—it was one of scores he could handle as fluently as he spoke English.

"No kangaroo could leap that high, much less a man!" snorted Liang-Sun Chi. "But we will search this place well. It is said that the greatest mysteries have the simplest explanations. Perhaps we left a door open this afternoon."

He produced keys, unlocked one of the doors, and waved his men in. They entered cautiously, jabbing flashlight beams ahead.

Doc retreated from the window out of which he had been watching. He passed soundlessly through a door into a corridor. At the second step, his toe was stopped by a heavy object.

A flashlight came out of his pocket. It tossed a beam that was hardly more than a white thread.

The body of a man lay on the corridor floor. A sword slash had cleaved into his heart.

THE flash ray disclosed other details about the murder victim. He was an elderly man, at least sixty. He wore plum-colored knee breeches, white stockings, a braided coat with long tails, a powdered white wig—a very flashy butler's livery.

Doc examined more closely. The flunky had been dead several hours at least.

The Orientals were making considerable noise downstairs. Draperies ripped as they were torn down. Moving furniture grated on waxed floors.

"My sons, it is a wise man who gets all his troubles in front of him," called their leader, Liang-Sun Chi. "Search the basement."

Liang-Sun seemed to be something of a philosopher.

Working with silence and speed, Doc searched the upper floors. He found this side of the castle contained only servant quarters, gymnasium, indoor swimming pool, billiard rooms, and a few guest chambers.

Back at the open window. he glanced down. One of the guards left in the court stood directly below.

Doc returned to the second-floor corridor. At one end of this he had noted a suit of armor. The metal plates of the gear were supported on an iron framework. Inside the helmet was mounted a papier-mâché cast of a face. This did not differ greatly in color from Doc's tanned features.

There was no sound as Doc dislodged the armor from its pedestal. He carried it to the open window. It weighed fully a hundred pounds.

He tossed it down on the Mongol guard. The fellow was knocked cold and battered to the ground. The armor clanked loudly on the court tiles.

Men poured into the court. Yelling excitedly, they pounced on the armor. They thought Doc was inside.

None of them heard the window at the opposite end of the building lift, or saw a mighty bronze figure that flitted, silent as a great bat, across the court to the other house.

They speared swords into cracks in the armor. Chopping furiously, one half-caste got the helmet severed.

They saw they had been fooled.

"We are but dumb dogs!" Liang-Sun squawked. "We have brought shame to our ancestors! Continue the search!"

WHILE the Mongols pushed the murderous hunt a few yards away, Doc Savage scrutinized the other half of the vast mansion.

He found no traces of Juan Mindoro, or Scott S. Osborn. In the library, however, he noted the floor cords had been wrenched from some of the reading lamps. Evidently these had served to bind prisoners.

Doc was now certain the Orientals had visited the castle some hours earlier. They had slain the butler. Probably they had made off with Juan Mindoro and Scott S. Osborn.

The Mongols finished with the other side of the house. They entered the room below Doc.

"It is said the lowly fly is never caught napping because he has eyes that see in all directions," Liang-Sun singsonged. "You will do well to imitate the fly, my sons. Should this bronze devil escape, some of us may lose our heads."

The flowery speech enlightened Doc on an important point. These Mongols and half-castes were serving some master—a master who wielded the power of life and death over them.

Their chief might be one of the pair who had listened in on the talk in Doc's office with the microphone-carrying pigeon, or the gist of the conversation might have been relayed to him. It was certain the talk the Mongols had overheard had brought them to Scott S. Osborn's home—for Doc had said he was coming here.

Two slant-eyed men mounted the stairs.

Doc located a light switch, clicked it. The fixtures remained dark. Doc recalled the wires torn from the reading lamps—fuses must have been blown when that was done.

The pair coming up the stairs exchanged whining whispers.

"Cold worms of fear are crawling up and down the spine of this insignificant person," one complained. "We have made many inquiries about Doc Savage, since we were so fortunate as to learn Juan Mindoro had appealed to him for help. We heard everywhere that Doc Savage was a mighty fighter. *Aie!* But no one told us he was a ghost. He must be lurking in this place, yet we have heard no sound and saw no one—"

"Swallow thy tongue, fool!" growled the other. "Only cowards talk of fear!"

"You are wrong. Only an idiot thinks not of danger—"

The Orientals had reached the top of the stairs. Now, without another word, one slowly lowered to his hands and knees. A moment later, he slouched prone on the hall carpet.

The second man eyed him foolishly. His lips writhed apart, showing teeth stained black from chewing betel nut. He seemed to be trying to cry out. Then he piled in a silent heap on the floor.

A giant, ghostly bronze figure, Doc Savage loomed over the pair. His fingers explored their clothing. He found nothing to indicate who their leader might be.

Both men snored as though asleep.

Doc retreated noiselessly down the second-floor corridor.

Liang-Sun droned words up from below. Receiving no answer from his two men, he mounted the stairs, flanked by three guardsmen and a machine gunner.

The outburst of cries as the two unconscious men were found sounded like the clamor that comes when a hawk flies into a flock of guineas.

A whispered consultation followed. Doc could not catch the words. The Orientals retreated to the lower floor, apparently to consider the situation.

"What manner of thing could have overcome our brothers?" Liang-Sun repeated over and over.

Suddenly, at the opposite end of the house, came a terrific uproar. Furniture overturned. Men gasped, cackled profanity.

"The bronze devil! He is here!" a man sang excitedly.

There was a loud clatter as the Mongols made for the noise.

Doc was puzzled. But it was too good a chance to pass up. He eased down a rear stairway, intent on quitting the place.

The stairs he chose let him into the lower floor library, a room walled with bookcases and floored with rich rugs.

The moment he stepped into it, he knew he had made a mistake. A dozen shadowy, slant-eyed men flung upon him.

THE noise at the other end of the house had been a trick to draw him down from upstairs.

The first leaping Mongol seemed to meet a bronze wall in mid-air. He was hurled back, and was impaled on the blunt sword of one who followed.

A second slant-eyed man got an open-handed slap that turned him over in the air like a Fourth-of-July pinwheel. Another found himself grasped about the chest. He shrieked, and the piercing shrillness of his voice was punctuated with the dull crack of breaking ribs.

The Mongols had not expected an easy fight. But they had not dreamed it would be like this. The giant bronze man moved with a speed that defied the eye. Sword slashes, delivered point-blank, sliced thin air. And when they did lay their hands on him, it was as if they had grasped living steel.

"He is not human!" wailed the man who had had his ribs broken.

More Orientals joined the fray. They blocked the doors. Flashlights came on. Time after time, light beams found the bronze giant, only to lose him.

A machine gun opened up, making a deafening gobble of sound in the room.

"Idiot!" Liang-Sun howled at the gunner. "Stop shooting! Do you want to kill us all?"

It was Liang-Sun who put a finish to the fray. He caught a momentary glimpse of Doc. The bronze man stood in the center of a large rug. Dropping swiftly, Liang-Sun seized the rug and yanked. Doc was brought down.

Liang-Sun flung the rug over Doc in a big fold.

"Are you snails that you cannot help me!" he squawled at his men.

A brisk twenty seconds followed—and they got Doc rolled up like a mummy in the rug. They brought tire chains from the garage and tied them securely about the rug.

Liang-Sun was proud of himself. He beat his chest with a fist.

"Single-handed, I did more than the rest of you dogs!" he boasted.

He plucked open one end of the rug roll and threw his flash beam inside.

He could see Doc's face. The bronze features bore absolutely no expression. But the cold fierceness in the strange golden eyes made Liang-Sun drop the rug folds and stand up hastily.

"Half of you go outside, my sons," he commanded. "Should anyone be drawn here by sounds of the fighting, kill them. This house stands alone, and probably the sounds were not heard. But if anyone comes, show them that curiosity is indeed a fatal disease."

A part of the Orientals hurried out into the moon-bathed court.

"Watch the prisoner closely!" Liang-Sun directed the others. "If he should escape, I can promise there will be heads lopped off. I am going to call the master to see what he wants to do with the bronze devil."

LIANG-SUN strode through rooms, playing his flash beam about, until he located a telephone. He swept the instrument up with a flourish.

When the phone operator's voice came, Liang-Sun spoke in English. He handled the language well enough, except that, Chinese fashion, he turned all the "R's" into "L's."

"Give me numbel Ocean 0117," he requested.

It was almost a minute before he got his party.

He recognized the singsong voice at the other end of the wire. Without delay, he launched rapid words in his native tongue.

"We have secured the merchandise after which we came, oh lord," he said. "We now have it rolled in a rug and bound securely. This lowly person wishes to know how you want it delivered."

"In two pieces, dumb one!" rasped the voice in the receiver. "Cut the merchandise in two in the middle. Then you may leave it there. I have other work for you to do."

"My understanding of your wishes is perfect. What is this other work?"

"The sugar importer, Scott S. Osborn, has a brother who lives up on Park Avenue. We are holding merchandise which this brother might be greatly interested in buying."

"I understand, oh lord. No doubt, Scott S. Osborn's brother will indeed want to purchase our merchandise."

The two were speaking in vague terms, lest a phone operator be listening. But they understood each other perfectly. They had Scott S. Osborn prisoner, and were going to try to ransom him to his brother.

"This sale of merchandise is not extremely important," continued the voice over the wire. "But since we are holding the goods, we might as well take a profit. You will visit the brother and seek the best price you can obtain."

"I comprehend most clearly, oh lord. Exactly where does Scott S. Osborn's brother live, that I may find him without trouble?"

"Get the address from the phone book, dumb one!"

"I shall do that."

"Returning to the subject of the merchandise you have wrapped in the rug—you are perhaps aware there are five others of a similar pattern, although of lesser importance. We may find it desirable to seek them also. But I shall discuss that with you at a later time. Cut the goods you have in two pieces. Do so at once."

Liang-Sun singsonged that he understood. He hung up the receiver, drew his sword, and swung into the room where Doc Savage had been captured.

The rolled rug had not moved. The slant-eyed guards sat about the room, lost in the shadows. But their flash beams blazed upon the rug.

Liang-Sun sprang forward, sword uplifted.

"Behold, dogs!" he shouted. "I will show you how a master swings his blade."

The sword hissed down.

Rolled rug—the body within it—were chopped neatly in halves.

A ghastly crimson flood spurted from the rug and washed over the floor.

LIANG-SUN callously wiped his blade. "Never, my sons, will you see a man cut in halves in more expert fashion!" he addressed his men.

He got no answer.

The half-caste leader stared about. He seemed to lose inches in height. His eyes bloated out from behind their sloping lids.

"Have your tongues been eaten, that you do not answer?" he gulped.

Leaping to the nearest Mongol, Liang-Sun shook him. The man toppled out of his chair. Liang-Sun jumped to another, a third, a fourth.

All were unconscious!

With mad haste, Liang-Sun shucked the rug off the head and shoulders of the man he had cut in two.

Liang-Sun's squawl of horrified surprise was like that of a cat with its tail stepped on.

The body in the rug was one of his own men!

Terror laid hold of Liang-Sun, a fright such as he had never before experienced. He dashed headlong out into the court.

"The bronze man is a devil!" he shrilled. "Flee, my sons!"

The Orientals who had been on guard outside needed no urging. They battled each other to be first across the drawbridge and into their cars. They had their fill of fighting the bronze giant.

They departed without knowing what had made their fellows unconscious. A close inspection of the room where the men slept would have shown the remains of many thin-walled glass balls. Perhaps they might have guessed these had originally contained an anaesthetic gas which made men unconscious the instant they breathed it, yet which became harmless after it had been in the air two or three minutes.

These anaesthetic globes were Doc's invention. He always carried a supply with him.

Cars bearing the fleeing Mongols were not out of earshot when Doc arose from the concealment of a divan not six feet from the phone over which Liang-Sun had talked to his chief.

Doc had heard that conversation.

Doc's escape from the tightly-chained rug, so mystifying to Liang-Sun, had not been difficult. Doc had employed a simple trick used by escape artists. He had tensed all his muscles when the rug was being tied. Relaxing later, he had plenty of room to crawl out after he had reduced the guards to unconsciousness with the anaesthetic.

Doc had not been affected by the anaesthetic for the simple reason that he could hold his breath during the two or three minutes it was effective.

He sped out of the castle, with the idea of following Liang-Sun and the others. But they had stolen his gray roadster.

Doc ran for the nearest boulevard. It was a quarter of a mile distant. Had official timers held stop watches on that quarter, the time Doc did it in would have been good for a headline on any sport page in the country. But the only observer was a stray dog which sought to overhaul the bronze man.

On the boulevard, Doc hailed a taxi.

Chapter V
THE DRAGON TRAIL

THE cab let Doc Savage out before an uptown New York police station. He entered. The marked deference of the cops, the celerity with which they sprang to grant his wishes, showed they knew him as a person of power. The police commissioner himself would not have gotten better service.

A "back number" telephone directory was produced. This listed the phone numbers, and the names to which they belonged, rather than the name followed by a number, as in an ordinary directory.

Doc looked up the number Liang-Sun had called—Ocean 0117. It was listed as the:

DRAGON ORIENTAL GOODS CO.

The address was on Broadway, far south of the theatrical portion of the street known as the Great White Way.

Doc took a cab downtown. The hack driver wondered all the way why his passenger rode the running board of the taxi, rather than inside. The hackman had never before had a thing like that happen.

The building, housing the Dragon Oriental Goods Company, was a shabby, ten-story structure. It was decorated in the ornate fashion popular thirty years ago. "The Far East Building," a sign said.

Chinatown lay only a few blocks away.

Directly across the street, a new forty-story skyscraper was going up. The steel framework of this was nearing completion. A night force of men was pushing construction. Noise of riveting machines banged hollowly against nearby structures and throbbed in the street.

A dusty directory told Doc the Dragon concern occupied a tenth-floor office.

An elevator, driven by a man in greasy tan coveralls, was in operation. The fellow's round moon of a face and eyes sloping slightly upward at the outer ends advertised that some of his recent ancestors had come from the Far East.

This man never saw Doc enter. The bronze giant walked up. He did not want to advertise his presence—the elevator operator might get word to whoever was leading the Mongol horde.

The office of the Dragon Oriental Goods Company faced the front of the building. The door lock yielded readily to a thin steel hook of an implement from Doc's pocket. He entered.

No one was there.

For furniture, the place had a couple of desks, worn chairs, filing cabinets. Desk drawers and filing cabinets were empty. There was not a sheet of paper in the place. No fingerprints were on the telephone, desk, window shade, or doorknob.

The window was dirty. Across the street, the girders of the building under construction made a pile like naked brush. The *drum-drum* of riveters was a somber song.

The elevator operator did not see Doc quit the building.

HALF an hour later, Doc entered his eighty-sixth-floor skyscraper office uptown.

He was surprised to find none of his five friends there. He consulted one of the elevator boys.

"They all five went out a few minutes ago to get something to eat," explained the youth.

"When they come back, tell them I was here," Doc directed.

He did not depart immediately, though. His next actions were unusual.

From a pocket, he took a bit of colorless substance shaped like a crayon. He wrote rapidly on his office window with this—putting down a lengthy message.

Yet when he finished, there was no trace of what he had written. Even a magnifying glass would not have disclosed the presence of the writing.

The elevator carried him down to the street. He walked away rapidly.

Some ten minutes later, his five men returned. Their faces mirrored the satisfaction of men who had just eaten a hearty shore dinner after some weeks of dining in the grease-soaked interior of a submarine.

"I missed the pint of grease I've had to take with my meals recently," Monk grunted contentedly. Then he leered at Ham. "Them pigs' knuckles and sauerkraut was swell!"

The distinguished, snappily-clad Ham scowled at hairy Monk. Any mention of pigs that Monk made was sure to aggravate Ham. This hearkened back to a couple of incidents in the War.

Ham had taught Monk certain highly insulting French words, and told him they were just the thing to flatter a French general with. Monk had used them—and landed in the guardhouse.

Monk had barely been released when there occurred one of the most embarrassing incidents of Ham's career. He was haled up on a charge of stealing hams, somebody had framed him!

To this day, Ham hadn't been able to prove the framing was Monk's work. That rankled. Especially since Ham had received his nickname from the incident; a nickname he didn't care for in the least.

"After the way you stuffed yourself, I have hopes!" Ham snapped.

"Hopes of what?" Monk queried.

"That you'll croak of indigestion!"

The elevator operator spoke up eagerly when he saw them.

"Mr. Savage was here, and has gone," he said.

Doc's five men exchanged sharp glances. They lost no time getting up to the eighty-sixth floor.

LONG TOM, the scrawny-looking electrical wizard, hurried into the laboratory. He came out with an apparatus which might easily be mistaken for an old-time magic lantern.

The lights were switched off. Long Tom flicked a switch on his machine. He pointed at the window on which Doc had written.

Doc's message sprang out on the darkened windowpane. Glowing with a dazzling electric blue, its appearance was uncanny.

Long Tom's apparatus was simply a lamp which projected strong ultraviolet light rays. The substance with which Doc had written on the window, although invisible to the naked eye, would glow in eerie fashion in the ultraviolet light.

It was by this method that Doc habitually left messages for his men.

The five read the communication. Doc's handwriting, machinelike in its perfection, was as easy to read as newsprint:

Here is your job, Ham: The Mongols are holding Juan Mindoro and his friend, Scott S. Osborne. A messenger will visit Osborn's brother, to demand a ransom.

Your work as a lawyer has probably brought you in contact with the family attorney of Osborn's brother, so you should be able to work through him and persuade them to pay the ransom demanded. We will then follow the man to whom it is paid.

But do not follow the messenger who demands it.

"This will be a cinch," Ham declared, spinning his sword cane adroitly. "I happen to be quite well acquainted with that attorney. Incidentally, he is the lawyer of both Scott S. Osborn and his brother."

"Shut up!" Monk grunted insultingly. "Don't you think we want to read the rest?"

They deciphered the remainder of the instructions in silence:

Monk, Renny, Long Tom, and Johnny will go to Scott S. Osborn's home north of town. The place is built like a medieval castle. Inside are perhaps a dozen Mongols and half-castes. You will ship them to our institution, then come back here and wait.

"Holy cow!" Renny was bewailing. "There won't be any excitement in our part of it!"

Monk's big grin was crowding his ears.

"I got hopes, though!" he chuckled. "If Doc has bagged that many men this early in the game, it shows we've tackled something that is plenty big. We may get our feet wet yet!"

Monk was no prophet. His feet wet! He'd be deep enough in trouble to drown, before long. But he had no way of knowing that.

HAM watched the others depart to ship the Orientals Doc had captured to the upstate institution, where they would receive the effective, if unusual, treatment that would turn them into honest men.

A telephone call put Ham in touch with the elderly lawyer who served Scott S. Osborn and his brother. Ham explained what he desired.

"The family might hesitate about complying with the wishes of a stranger," he finished. "It would help greatly if you would sort of put the O.K. on me. I am, of course, working for the interest of your clients."

"I'll do better than that!" declared the other attorney. "I shall be at the home of Osborn's brother when you arrive. When I advise them of the situation, I am sure they will do as you desire."

"That will be great," Ham assured him.

Ham hurried to his bachelor quarters, in a club which was one of the most luxurious in the city, although not widely known. The members were all wealthy men who wished to live quietly.

A change of clothing was the object of Ham's visit. He donned formal evening garb, secured a more natty-looking sword cane from a collection he kept on hand, and took a taxi to the home of Scott S. Osborn's brother.

The dwelling was large. It might have been mistaken for a small apartment building.

Dismissing his taxi, Ham mounted the steps. He was about to ring the bell when his hand froze.

A stream of scarlet was crawling slowly from under the door.

Ham listened. He could hear nothing. He tried the knob. It turned, but the door, after opening about two inches, would go no farther. Ham shoved. He could tell that he was pushing against a body lying on the floor inside.

He got the panel half open, put his head in cautiously.

The vestibule was brilliantly lighted. No living person was in sight.

The body of the old lawyer whom Ham had called not many minutes ago, had been blocking the door. The elderly man had been stabbed at least fifteen times.

Ham, his sword cane ready, stepped inside. The weight of the dead man against the door shoved it shut. The lock clicked loudly.

As though that were a signal, a man hurtled from a nearby door.

The fellow was chunky, lemon-complected, sloping of eye. His face was a killer mask. He waved a sword.

It was Liang-Sun, although Ham didn't know that, not having seen him before.

Liang-Sun got a shock when Ham unsheathed the slender, rippling steel blade of his sword cane. Ham's blade leaped out hungrily.

With desperate haste, Liang-Sun parried. He was surprised, but still confident. Among the fighting men of Mongolia and China, he had been considered quite a swordsman.

Ten seconds later, Liang-Sun's confidence leaked out like water from a gunnysack. The air before his face had apparently turned into a whistling hell of sharp steel. A chunk of his hat brim was sliced off and fluttered away.

Liang-Sun felt like a man clubbing a swarm of hornets with a stick. Backing up, he sought to haul a revolver from his coat pocket with his left hand. He hadn't wanted to use the gun before, because of the noise. But he would be glad to do so now.

A dazzling slash of Ham's sword cut the whole skirt and pocket from Liang-Sun's coat, and the revolver bounced away.

STEEL whined, clashed, rasped. Both fighters sought to get to the revolver. Neither could quite do it.

Liang-Sun felt a tickling sensation across his stomach. He looked down and saw his clothing had been slit wide. Another inch would have finished him.

He backed away swiftly, passing through the door from which he had leaped. Ham followed, cutting and parrying briskly.

A man was sprawled across a table in the room. He had white hair, ruddy features. He, too, had been stabbed to death.

Ham had seen the man once before, perhaps a year ago. It was the brother of Scott S. Osborn.

A wall safe gaped open.

On the table with the dead man lay a heap of jewels, rings, currency.

This explained the situation to Ham.

The Mongol messenger had come to demand ransom, had seen the money, and decided a bird in hand was better than one in the bush. He had slain and robbed Osborn's brother, rather than bother with ransom.

The poor old lawyer out by the door had been murdered when he arrived.

White with rage, Ham redoubled his sword play.

Liang-Sun fairly ran backward. A sudden spring put him through a door. He slammed it. Ham pitched against the panel. It resisted.

Seizing a chair, Ham battered the door down. He ran across a dining room, then a kitchen. A rear door gaped open beyond. It let him into an alleylike court. There was only one exit from this, a yawning space between two buildings, to the right.

An indistinct, rapidly moving figure dived into this opening.

Ham pursued. He pitched headlong between the buildings, came out on the walk, and saw his quarry scuttle under a street lamp at the corner.

Ham set out after him—only to bring up sharp as a powerful voice came to him from a nearby door recess.

"I'll follow him, Ham!" the voice said.

It was Doc Savage.

Ham understood, then, why Doc had directed, in the message on the skyscraper window, that the ransom-demanding courier was not to be followed. Doc intended to do the trailing, hoping to be led to the mastermind who was behind all this callous, inhuman bloodletting.

In order not to make the fleeing Oriental suspicious, Ham continued his chase. But at the first corner, he deliberately took the wrong turn.

When he came back, there was no sign of Doc or the half-caste Mongol.

Chapter VI
THE STOLEN GLASS

AT the precise moment Ham was wondering about them, Doc and Liang-Sun were five blocks distant. Liang-Sun was just climbing the steps of a Third Avenue elevated station.

The Mongol had lived much of his life in violence, and knew enough to watch his back trail. He saw nothing suspicious. He kept wary eyes on the stairway until a train came in. Even after he boarded the almost deserted train, he watched the platform he had just quitted, as well as the one on the other side of the tracks. He saw no one—not a single other passenger got aboard.

He should have watched the rear platform. Doc was already ensconced there. He had climbed a pillar of the elevated a short distance above the station and run down the tracks.

The train clanked away southward, disgorging a few passengers at each stop.

At Chatham Square, very close to Chinatown, Liang-Sun alighted. To make sure no one got off the train after him who seemed in the least suspicious, he waited on the platform until the cars pulled out. Greatly relieved, he finally descended.

Doc Savage, having slid down a pillar of the elevated, was waiting for him, seated in someone's parked car.

Liang-Sun walked rapidly toward the Oriental section. He passed two sidewalk peddlers who, even at this late hour, were offering for sale filthy trays of melon seeds and other celestial dainties.

A moment later, Doc Savage also sauntered past the peddlers.

Both venders of melon seeds and dainties shoved their trays of merchandise in the handiest waste can and followed Doc. Their hands, folded across their stomachs, fingered large knives in their sleeves. Their faces, the color of old straw, were determined.

Doc did not look back. Several times, he glanced down at his hands swinging at his sides. In the palm of each hand was a small mirror.

The mirror showed him the two who haunted his trail.

Doc's bronze features held no feeling as he watched. This master of the Mongols was clever in having men follow Liang-Sun to see that no one dogged his tracks.

Gone were any hopes Doc had of locating the mastermind through Liang-Sun—unless he could be induced to talk by force.

Doc's left hand wandered casually into his pocket, drew out four of the glass balls filled with anaesthetic. Holding his breath, Doc dropped them. They shattered, releasing the colorless, odorless vapor.

Doc strode on.

Behind him, the two peddlers walked into the anaesthetic. They fell forward on their faces, nearly together.

LIANG-SUN chanced to turn around at this moment. He saw Doc, saw what had happened. His piping yell of fright sounded like a rat squeal in the dingy Chinatown street. He fled.

A bronze blur of speed, Doc raced after him.

Liang-Sun was fumbling inside the waistband of his trousers. He brought out his sword. Evidently he carried it in a sheath strapped next to his leg.

Doc overhauled him rapidly. The Mongol was only a hundred feet away—seventy-five—fifty.

Then a big policeman, attracted by Liang-Sun's yell of fear, popped around a corner. He stood directly in Liang-Sun's path, revolver in hand.

The Mongol was desperate. He slashed his sword at the cop—and the cop shot him, killing him instantly.

The policeman had acted instinctively in defense of his life. He watched Doc come up.

"Sure, an' this is the first man I ever killed. I hope he needed it," the cop spoke.

He eyed Doc suspiciously. He did not know the bronze giant.

"Was ye chasin' this bird?" he demanded.

"I was," Doc admitted. "And don't let the fact that you killed him bother you. He is a murderer, probably several times over. He killed a man at the home of Scott S. Osborn tonight. And I think he must have committed other crimes at the residence of Scott S. Osborn's brother not very many minutes ago."

Doc did not know what had happened in the dwelling of Scott S. Osborn's brother. But the fact that Ham had chased Liang-Sun out showed something had gone wrong.

The cop was suspicious of Doc.

"Yez jest stick around here, me b'y!" he directed. "We'll want to ask yez a lot av questions."

Doc shrugged.

The officer slapped big hands over Doc's person in search of a gun. The fact that he did that was unfortunate. He broke one of the anaesthetic balls in Doc's pockets.

A minute afterward, he was stretched on his back on the walk, snoring loudly.

Doc left the cop where he lay. The fellow would revive after a time, none the worse for his slumber.

From a nearby call box, Doc turned in an alarm to the police station. He did not give his name.

He hurried back to get the two peddlers who had been following him. They should be asleep on the walk.

But they weren't! Some denizen of Chinatown had moved them. Doc knew it must have been the work of some of the Mongol horde.

Chinatown, despite all the fiction written about it, was actually one of the quietest sections in the city. No legitimate resident of the district would court trouble by assisting the unconscious pair.

A brief but intensive search disclosed no sign of the vanished two.

HALF an hour later, Doc was in his skyscraper office uptown. None of his five men had returned.

With a chemical concoction from the laboratory, Doc erased the invisible writing off the window. Then he inscribed a fresh message there.

Swinging out into the corridor, he rode the button until an elevator came up. The cage doors opened noiselessly, let him in, and closed. There was a windy sigh of a sound as the lift sank.

Adjoining Doc's office was a suite which had been empty some months. Rents were high up here in the clouds, and times were tough, so many of the more costly offices were without tenants.

It would have taken a close examination to show the door of this adjoining suite had been forced open.

Inside, a man was just straightening from a large hole which had been painstakingly cut in the wall of Doc's office. The actual aperture into Doc's sanctum was no larger than a pin head. But by pressing an eye close, an excellent view could be obtained.

The watcher was a round-faced, lemon-skinned Oriental. He hurried out and tried to force the door of Doc's office. The lock defied him. The door was of heavy steel—Doc had put that steel in to discourage Renny's joyful habit of knocking the panels out with his huge fists.

Returning to the vacant suite, the Oriental set to work enlarging his peep-hole. He used an ordinary pick. In ten minutes, he had opened an aperture in the plaster and building tile which would admit his squat frame.

He crawled in. First, he made sure the corridor door could be locked from the inside. He left it slightly ajar.

The window next received his attention. He had watched Doc write upon it. Yet he could discern no trace of an inscription.

Working with great care, the Mongol removed the pane of glass. He carried it outside. He was going to take it to a place where someone with an understanding of invisible inks could examine it. He rang for the elevator.

The elevator operator eyed him doubtfully as they rode down.

"You work here?" he demanded.

"Wolk this place allee time now," singsonged the Mongol. He grinned, wiped his forehead. "Allee same wolk velly much and get velly little money."

The operator was satisfied. He hadn't seen this man before. But who would go to the trouble of stealing a sheet of plate glass?

The cage stopped at the ground floor. The Mongol bent over to pick up his glass.

What felt like a steel trap suddenly got his neck.

THE slant-eyed man struggled desperately. The hands on his throat looked bigger than gallon buckets.

They were Renny's hands—paws that could knock the panel out of the heaviest wooden door.

Monk, Long Tom and Johnny danced about excitedly outside the elevator. They all had just come in.

"Hey!" Monk barked. "How d'you know he's one of the gang?"

They were nearly as surprised as the Mongol at Renny's sudden act.

"He's got the window out of Doc's office, you homely goat!" Ham snapped, after a glance into the elevator.

"Yeah!" Monk bristled. "How can you tell one hunk of glass from another?"

"That is bullet-proof glass," Ham retorted. "So far as I know, Doc has the only office in this building with bullet-proof windows."

Monk subsided. Ham was right.

Renny and the Oriental were still fighting. The Oriental launched frenzied blows, but he might as well have battered a bull elephant, for all the effect they had.

Desperate, the Mongol clawed a knife out of a hidden sheath.

"Look out, Renny!" Monk roared.

But Renny had seen the knife menace. He hurled the slant-eyed man away. The fellow spun across the tiled floor. He kept a grip on his blade.

Bounding to his feet, he drew back his arm to throw the knife.

Wham! A gun had appeared magically in Long Tom's pale hand, and loosed a clap of a report.

The bullet caught the Mongol between the eyes and knocked him over backward. His knife flew upward, point-first, and embedded in the ceiling.

A cop, drawn by the shot, ran in, tweeting excitedly on his whistle.

There was no trouble over the killing, though. Long Tom, as well as Monk, Renny, Ham and Johnny, held high honorary commissions in the New York police force.

Within a quarter of an hour, the five were up in the eighty-sixth floor office examining the pane of glass with ultraviolet light.

The message Doc had written upon it flickered in weird bluish curves and lines. They read:

> To RENNY: The chief of this Mongol gang sometimes uses an office listed under the name of the Dragon Oriental Goods Co. It is the center, front office on the tenth floor of the Far East building on lower Broadway. A new skyscraper is going up across the street.
>
> Your engineering training will enable you to get a structural steelworker's job on the new building, Renny. Watch the office of the Dragon Oriental Goods Co., and trail anyone you see using it.

With the chemical eraser, Monk carefully cleaned the glass plate. They were taking no chances on the leader of the Mongols getting hold of it. Such a misfortune might mean Renny's finish.

"We'll drop around sometime and watch you doing a little useful labor on that building," Monk grinned at Renny.

Chapter VII
DEATH TRAIL

RENNY had been working as a structural steel man for half a day. He was operating a riveting gun on what would eventually be the tenth floor of the new building. In his monster hands the pneumatic gun was a toy.

None of the other workers knew why he was here, not even the job foreman. Renny had come with such excellent references that he had been given a job instantly. The quality of his work had already attracted favorable attention. The crew foreman was proud of his new recruit.

"Stick with us, buddy, and you'll get ahead," the foreman had told Renny confidentially. "We can use men like you. I'll see that you get a better job at the end of the week."

"That'll be fine!" Renny replied.

Not a muscle of Renny's sober, puritanical face changed during this conversation. The crew foreman would probably have fallen off the girder on which he was standing, had he known Renny had handled engineering jobs for which he had been paid a sum sufficient to buy a building such as this would be when finished.

At lunch hour, most of the workers went to nearby restaurants to eat. But Renny consumed a sandwich, remaining near where he had been working.

Renny didn't want to lose sight, even for a short time, of the office of the Dragon Oriental Goods Company. And it was during the lunch hour that his watch produced results.

A lemon-skinned fellow entered the tenth-floor office. His actions were unusual. Producing a rag from his clothing, the Oriental went over every object in the room which might have been handled, polishing it briskly.

"Making doubly sure no fingerprints were left behind!" Renny told himself. "I'll just trail that bird."

Throwing away the wrapper of the sandwich he had consumed, Renny stretched lazily and remarked to another steel worker smoking nearby: "Think I'll go get some hot coffee."

He descended.

Within ten minutes, the man who had been in the Dragon Oriental Goods Company office put in his appearance. A close look showed Renny he was one of the half-castes, an admixture of Mongol and some other race.

The fellow boarded one of the open street cars which ran down Broadway. This vehicle had no sides, only a roof. Passengers simply stepped aboard wherever was handiest.

Renny followed in a taxi. He slouched low in his seat, hoping his work-stained clothing and greasy cap would help him escape detection. Renny had wiped off the motor of his automobile with the garments, before going to his new job. This gave them the proper coating of grime.

The quarry alighted near Chinatown. He soon passed a shabby Celestial walking up and down the street with a sign on his chest and another on his back, advertising a chop-suey restaurant.

No sign of recognition did Renny's quarry and the sandwich man exchange, yet the sandwich man studied Renny most intently—and was very careful Renny did not notice.

The fellow then scuttled down a side street.

Renny continued his shadowing, unaware of this incident.

THE half-caste Mongol turned into a little shop which seemed to sell everything from edible bamboo shoots to cloisonné vases. He purchased a small package of something, then came out. He began to chew some of the package contents.

He might have given a message to the shop proprietor, or received one. Renny could not tell.

The Mongol breed's next move was to enter—of all things—a radio store.

Renny sauntered past the front. No one was visible within the store; not even the proprietor. Renny hesitated, decided to take a chance, and entered.

There was a door in the back. Listening, Renny heard nothing. He opened and shut his enormous hands uneasily. Finally, he shucked an unusual pistol from under one armpit.

This gun was only slightly larger than an ordinary automatic, but it was one of the most efficient killing machines ever invented. Doc had perfected the deadly weapon—an extremely compact machine gun. It fired sixty shots so rapidly it sounded like the bawl of a great bull fiddle, and it could be reloaded in the time required to snap a finger.

Renny shoved the rear door open. A gloomy passage yawned beyond. He stepped in.

The door wrenched out of his hand and shut with a bang, actuated by strong levers. The inner side of the door was plated with sheet steel.

Renny darted his machine gun at the panel, locked the trigger back, and flipped the muzzle in a quick circle. The gun made a deafening moan; empty cartridge cases rained to the floor by scores.

Renny snarled hoarsely. The bullets were barely burying themselves in the steel. It was armor plate.

Whirling, he plunged down the passage. Black murk lay before him. He shoved out the machine gun, threw a brief spray of lead. He was taking no chances.

Into another door, he crashed. It, too, had a skin of armor plate.

Renny carried a small waterproof cigarette lighter, although he did not smoke. It was handier than matches. He brushed this aflame with his thumb and held it high.

Walls and floor were solid timbers. The ceiling was pierced with slits. They were about two inches wide, and ran the entire passage length.

An iron rod, more than an inch in diameter, delivered a terrific slashing blow through one of these cracks. Dodging, Renny barely got clear.

Crouched to one side, he heard the rod strike again and again. He changed his position, thinking furiously. He hosed bullets into the cracks.

A jeering cackle of laughter rattled through the slits.

"You allee same waste plenty bullet, do no good!" intoned an Oriental voice.

With silence and speed, Renny slid out of his coat. He bundled it about his right fist, making a thick pad. Guessing where the iron rod would strike next, he held out his fist to catch the blow. Three times, he failed. Then—*thud!*

The impact was terrific. He was slammed to the passage end. The coat pad saved bones in his enormous fist from breakage.

Slumping to the floor, Renny lay perfectly motionless.

REDDISH light spurted down through the cracks.

"The tiger sleeps," a man singsonged. "Seize him, my sons."

The rear passage door opened with little noise. A band of Mongols flung through and pounced upon Renny.

With an angry roar, Renny heaved up. He spun a complete circle, the machine-gun muzzle blowing a red flame from his big fist.

Yells, screams, gasps made a grisly bedlam. Bodies fell. Wounded men pitched about like beheaded chickens.

Renny hurtled out of the passage—and received a blow over the head from one of the iron rods. He sagged like a man stricken with deathly illness. He lost his gun.

He was buried by an avalanche of slant-eyed men. His wrists and ankles received numberless turns of wire-strong silk cord. A huge sponge was tamped between his jaws and cinched there with more silken line.

One man drove a toe into Renny's ribs.

"The tiger devil has slain three of our brothers!" he snarled. "For that, he should die slowly and in great pain. Perhaps with the death of a thousand cuts."

"You have not forgotten, oh lord, that the master wants this white man alive?" queried another.

"I have not forgotten. The master is wise. This man is friend to our great enemy, the bronze devil. Perhaps we can persuade the bronze one to bother us no more, lest we slay this friend."

These words were exchanged in their cackling lingo. Renny understood the language, and could speak it after a fashion. He was no little relieved. He had expected to be killed on the spot, probably with fiendish torture.

A large wooden packing case was now tumbled into the room. It was a shipping crate for a radio, and was marked with the name of an advertised set.

They shoved Renny into the box, packing excelsior around him tightly, so he could hardly stir. The lid was nailed on. Thin cracks admitted air enough for breathing.

At this point, a commotion arose out in front. A neighbor had heard the shots and screams of dying men, and had called a cop.

"Velly solly!" a half-caste Celestial told the officer smugly. "Ladio, him makee noises."

"A radio, huh?" grunted the policeman, not satisfied. "Reckon I'll take a look around, anyway."

In the rear of the establishment, Orientals worked swiftly. They removed the dead and wounded. They threw rugs over the bloodstained floor and hung draperies over the bullet-marked armor plate on the doors.

"Ladio makee noise," repeated the Oriental. "If you want takee look-see, all lightee."

The cop was conducted into the rear. He noted nothing peculiar about the passage—the slits in the ceiling had been closed. He saw two bland-looking, moonfaced men loading a large radio case onto a truck behind the store. The truck already bore other crates.

"Me show how ladio makee lacket," said the Celestial.

He turned on one of several radio sets which stood about. Obviously, it was not working properly. Loud scratchings and roarings poured from it. The voice of a woman reading cooking recipes was a procession of deafening squawks.

The cop was satisfied.

"Reckon that's what the party who called me heard," he grunted. "After this, don't turn that thing on so loud, see! I ain't got no time to go chasin' down false alarms."

The officer departed.

The proprietor of the radio store made sure the policeman was out of sight, then he padded back to the truck.

"Take our prisoner to the master, my sons," he commanded.

THE truck rumbled away. It mingled with traffic that jammed the narrow streets of Chinatown. The two Orientals sat stolidly in the cab. They did not look back once.

Eventually, the truck rolled into a large warehouse. The packing cases were all unloaded and shoved on a freight elevator. The cage lifted several floors.

Renny was having difficulty breathing. The excelsior had worked up around his nostrils. It scratched his eyes.

He felt himself being tumbled end over end across the floor. He could barely hear his captors talking.

"Go and tell the master we are here," one said, speaking their native tongue.

An Oriental padded off. In three or four minutes, he was back.

With swift rendings, the lid was torn off Renny's prison. They hauled him out and plucked the excelsior away.

He was in a large storeroom. A few boxes of merchandise were scattered about. Judging from the tags, most of it was from the Orient. In addition to the elevator and a stairway door, there was an opening to the right.

A man grunting under the weight of Renny's shoulders, another bearing his feet, they passed through the opening. A flight of creaking stairs was ascended. A trapdoor lifted, letting them out on a tarred roof.

An unusually high wall concealed them from other buildings near by. Renny was carried over and flung across a narrow gap to the roof of the adjacent building. Next, he was carried to a large chimney.

Reaching into the flue, an Oriental brought out a rope. This was tied under Renny's arms. They lowered him. He saw the interior of the chimney was quite clean, fitted with a steel ladder.

He was handed down all of a hundred feet. Then half a dozen clawlike hands seized him and yanked him through an aperture in the chimney.

Renny gazed about in surprise.

His surroundings were luxurious. Expensive tapestries draped the walls; rugs, many more than an inch thick, strewed the floor. A low tabouret near one wall bore a steaming teapot, tiny cups and containers of melon seeds and other delicacies of the Far East.

Mongols and half-caste Chinese stood about. Each one was dressed neatly and might have been an American business man, except for their inscrutable faces and the hate blazing in their dark eyes. Renny counted seven of them.

Suddenly an eighth man appeared. He made a startling announcement.

"The master has received important news!" he singsonged. "News which makes it no longer necessary that we refrain from taking the life of this one who has hands the size of four ordinary men. He is to pay for slaying our fellows."

RENNY felt as if he had been shoved into a refrigerator. The Oriental's statement amounted to a pronouncement of death.

But it was more than that. It told Renny something terrible had happened. They had intended to hold him as a hostage to force Doc Savage to leave them alone. Now they no longer needed him for that. Had they succeeded in slaying Doc?

"This man is to be administered the death of many cuts," continued the slant-eyed man. "Four of you bring the other two prisoners here."

Obeying the order, four men departed. They came back almost at once bearing two bound and gagged figures.

Renny had no trouble guessing who they were.

Juan Mindoro and Scott S. Osborn!

Juan Mindoro was a slender, dynamic man. His high forehead and clear eyes gave him a distinctive look. Gray peppered his dark hair. A gray mustache bristled over his gag.

Scott S. Osborn, the sugar importer, was a guinea-pig fat man. Ordinarily, his hair was stuck down with grease, but now it was disarrayed and hung in thin strings. His eyes were bubbly and running tears.

The spokesman of the yellow horde slanted an arm at Scott S. Osborn. He spoke in snarling English.

"This one is also to leceive the death of many cuts!"

Scott S. Osborn's fat body convulsed. Tears fairly squirted from his little, fat-encircled eyes. His scream of terror was a shrill whinny through his nostrils.

The Mongol wheeled on Mindoro.

"You will watch!" he grated. "As you watch, you will do well to think deeply, my fliend!"

Juan Mindoro only glowered back at his tormentor. No quiver of fear rippled his distinctive features.

"You have lefused to give us the names of the men in the seclet political society of the Luzon Union, which you head," continued the Mongol, only a few "R's" turned into "L's" marring his pronunciation of the English words. "We need those names."

Dropping to a knee, the slant-eyed man hastily removed Juan Mindoro's gag. "Maybe so, you give us the names now. In such case, we would see fit not to halm these two men."

"I am not fool enough to trust you!" Juan Mindoro said fiercely, speaking crisp, Americanized English. "You want the names of my friends in the secret political society so you can slay them and get them out of the way. They would all be assassinated."

"But, no," smirked the Mongol. "We would only lemove them fol a sholt time. Kidnap them, pelhaps."

"Kill them, you mean!" snapped Mindoro. "You won't get their names from me. That's final!" Then, looking at Renny, he added, as though to explain his action, "The information they want would mean the death of hundreds of innocent men. The decision I must make is a horrible one, for it means my death as well as your own. I think they will kill me within a few hours."

Renny shrugged—the only reply he could make.

Snarling, the Mongol pointed at Renny. "Begin! Cut out his eyes to stalt!"

A yellow man flashed a needle-bladed knife. He dropped on Renny, put his knee on Renny's chest, grasped the big man's hair with his left fist.

The knife lifted. Every eye in the room watched it.

A Mongol over by the entrance to the chimney shrieked. He shot like a living cannon ball across the room. He struck the knifeman with a shock that knocked them both unconscious.

Wild stares centered on the chimney entrance.

A giant man of bronze stood there!

Chapter VIII
A PIRATE OF TODAY

FOR once, the yellow faces of the Mongols were not inscrutable. They goggled like small boys seeing their first lion.

"Fools!" ripped their leader. "Kill this bronze devil!"

A man darted a hand to his sleeve and forked out a kris with a foot-long serpentine blade. He drew back his arm and flung the knife.

What happened next was almost black magic. The kris was suddenly protruding from the chest of the man who had thrown it! It was as though he had stabbed himself.

Not one present could believe the mighty bronze man had plucked the flashing blade out of mid-air and returned it so accurately and with such blinding speed. No one, except Renny, who had seen Doc perform such amazing feats before!

Even while the dead man sloped backward to the floor like a falling tree, Doc seized another Mongol. The fellow seemed to become light as a rag doll, and as helpless. His clubbed body bowled over a fifth Oriental.

Only three were now left. One of these drew a revolver, flung it up, fired rapidly. But he did nothing, except drive bullets into the body of his fellow as it came hurtling toward him. The next instant, he was smashed down, to lose his senses when his head smacked the wall.

The surviving pair spun and fled with grotesque leaps. They squawked in terror at each jump.

They dived through a door, but retained presence of mind enough to slam and lock the panel.

Doc struck it, found it was of armor plate, and did not waste more time.

Whirling back, he scooped up a knife and cut through the bonds of the captives.

Renny was hardly on his feet before Doc had entered the chimney.

The hundred feet to the top, Doc climbed in almost no time. He ran across the roof.

Down in the street, the Orientals were piling into a sedan. The machine hooted up the thoroughfare, skidded around a corner, and was gone.

Doc knew any attempt to follow would be fruitless. He descended the chimney, joining the others.

"How'd you find us?" Renny wanted to know.

"Through the police," Doc explained. "They had been telephoning me news of every suspicious incident, however unimportant, in this part of town. I got word of the reported screams and shots in the radio store, and came to investigate. I heard the two truck drivers receive orders to take their prisoner to their boss. It was a simple matter to follow them here."

Doc now shook hands with Juan Mindoro.

DOC SAVAGE had once visited a number of islands in the Pacific, studying tropical fevers and their cures. It was on this trip that he had first met Juan Mindoro. The meeting had come about through a medical clinic which Mindoro maintained. Mindoro was extremely wealthy, expended tremendous sums on projects for the general benefit of humanity. The medical clinic, treating poor people without charge, was only one of the many philanthropies he indulged in.

Doc had been impressed with the high character of Juan Mindoro. So much so, indeed, that he had offered his services to Mindoro, should they ever be needed.

"It is hopeless for me to try to express my thanks to you with mere words," Juan Mindoro said, his orator's voice husky with emotion. "They would surely have killed me, those Mongol fiends."

Doc now turned to Scott S. Osborn. He was surprised when Osborn shrank away as if expecting a blow.

"You can't do anything to me!" Osborn shrieked hysterically. "I've got money! I'll fight you through every court in the land!"

Puzzled, Doc turned to Juan Mindoro. "What does he mean?"

Mindoro gave Osborn a scowl of scathing contempt.

"I came to this man, thinking he was my friend," he said. "He offered to hide me, and took me to his home. Then he went to my enemies. They paid him money to tell them where I was."

"But they captured him at the same time they took you," Doc pointed out. "And a moment ago, they were going to kill him."

Juan Mindoro's laugh was a dry rattle. "They double-crossed him. He was a fool. He thought they could be trusted."

Osborn wiped his bubbly eyes. His weak mouth made a trembling sneer.

"You can't do anything to me for selling you out!" he said shrilly. "My money will see to that! I've still got the dough they paid me for telling where you were, Mindoro! Fifty thousand dollars! I'll spend every cent of it to fight you in court!"

Mindoro suddenly picked up a gun one of the Mongols had dropped. He fingered it slowly, gazing all the while at Osborn.

"I wish I were less of a civilized man!" he said coldly. "I would shoot this dog!"

Doc reached up and got the gun. Mindoro gave it up readily.

"Osborn has been punished," Doc said grimly. "He became involved with the Mongols through his own greed. They murdered his brother last night. Had he not gone to them, that would never have happened."

Osborn's fat little face went starkly white. "What's this—this about my brother?"

"He was murdered last night."

This was obviously Osborn's first knowledge of his brother's slaughter. It hit him hard. He turned whiter and whiter until his repulsive little head became like a thing of bleached marble. He seemed hardly to breathe. Tears oozed from his small eyes, chased each other down his puffy cheeks, and wetted his shirt front and necktie.

"My own brother—I just the same as murdered him!" he choked in a voice so low the others hardly heard.

Ignoring him, Doc indicated the doorway into the chimney. "I suggest we get out of here."

They turned toward the chimney. Then Renny yelped excitedly and sprang for Osborn.

He was too late. Osborn, crazed by the grief of his brother's death, crumpled to the floor, his body falling upon the upturned blade held by one of the dead Mongols.

THE body of the fat little man executed a few spasmodic jerks before it became a spongy pile upon the floor.

Mindoro, gazing at the body religiously, said in solemn tones: "May I be forgiven for speaking to him so harshly. I did not know of his brother's murder."

"He had it coming!" grunted Renny, who was about as hard-boiled as they came.

Doc Savage made no comment.

They climbed the chimney, crossed the roof tops, and descended to the street by the same route Renny had been carried into the room.

Doc telephoned the police a brief report of what had happened. He ended with the request: "Keep my connection with the affair secret from the newspapers."

"Of course, Mr. Savage!" said the police captain who was receiving the news. "But can you give us a description of the leader of this herd of Mongols and half-castes?"

Doc turned to Juan Mindoro. "Who is behind this mess?"

"A man known as Tom Too," replied Mindoro.

"Can you describe him?"

Mindoro shook his head. "I have never seen the man. He did not show himself to me, even when I was held prisoner."

"No description," Doc told the police official.

They rode uptown in a taxi. Doc remained outside on the running board for the first few blocks. Then, as the machine slowed for a traffic light, he dropped off.

Even as Renny and Mindoro started to bark excited questions, the giant bronze man vanished—lost himself in the crowd that swarmed the walks of Broadway.

Mindoro wiped his high forehead in some bewilderment.

"A remarkable man," he muttered.

Renny grinned. "That ain't saying the half of it!"

A couple of blocks farther on, Renny sobered abruptly.

"Holy cow!" he ejaculated. "I forgot to tell Doc something! And I dang well know it's important!"

"What!"

"When the Mongols first got me, they were going to keep me alive as a hostage to make Doc behave. Then they suddenly decided to kill me, remarking that something had occurred which made it no longer necessary to keep me alive. I thought at the time that maybe they had gotten Doc. But that couldn't have been it."

"Well?"

Renny knotted his enormous hands. "I wonder what made them decide to kill me!"

IT was fully an hour later when Doc Savage appeared at his eighty-sixth-floor skyscraper retreat.

Ham, Renny, and Mindoro were waiting for him. They were perspiring and excited.

Waving his sword cane, Ham yelled: "Doc! They've got Monk, Johnny, and Long Tom!"

A stranger watching Doc would not have dreamed the shock this news conveyed. The bronze face remained as devoid of expression as metal. No change came into his eyes that were like pools of flake gold.

"When?" he asked. His strange voice, although not lifted to speak the single word, carried with the quality of a great drum beat.

"We were all going to meet here about noon," Ham explained. "I stopped for a manicure and was late. When I arrived, there was a lot of excitement. Several of the Mongols had just herded Long Tom, Johnny, and Monk out at the point of guns. They rode off in waiting cars. Nobody as much as got the license number of the cars."

Renny beat his big fists together savagely—the sound they made was like steel blocks colliding.

"Blast it, Doc!" he said sorrowfully. "I knew something was wrong when the devils decided so suddenly to croak me. But I forgot to tell you—"

"I heard their sudden change of intention," Doc replied.

Renny looked vastly relieved. He had thought that his forgetfulness was responsible for half an hour's delay in Doc getting on the trail of the captors of the trio.

"Did you guess they had captured our three pals?"

"The suspicion occurred to me," Doc admitted. "It became certain when I dropped off the taxi and called the manager of this building."

"Then you've been on their trail!" Renny grinned. "Find anything?"

"Nothing."

Renny's sober face set in disconsolate lines. With the others, he followed Doc back into the office.

From a drawer, Doc took a box containing cigars—cigars so expensive and carefully made that each was in an individual vacuum container. He offered these to the others, then held a light—Doc never smoked himself.

There was tranquility in the giant bronze man's manner, a sphinxlike calmness that had the effect of quieting Ham and Renny. Even Juan Mindoro was noticeably eased.

Doc's weird golden eyes came to rest on Juan Mindoro.

"The master of the Mongol horde is a man named Tom Too, and they are seeking to wipe out your secret political society in the Luzon Union," he said. "That is substantially all I know of this affair. Can you enlighten me further?"

"I certainly can!" Juan Mindoro clipped grimly. "This Tom Too is a plain pirate!"

"Pirate?"

"Exactly! A buccaneer compared to whom Captain Kidd, Blackbeard, and Sir Henry Morgan were petty thieves!"

DOC, Renny and Ham digested this. Renny had taken one of the cigars, although he rarely smoked. The weed looked like a brown toothpick in his enormous fist. Ham was leaning forward in an attitude of intense concentration, the sword cane supporting his hands under his jaw, his eyes staring at Mindoro.

"Tom Too got his start with the pirates of the China seaboard," Mindoro continued. "As you know, the China coast is the only part of the world where piracy still flourishes to any extent."

"Sure," Renny put in. "The steamers along the coast and on the rivers carry soldiers and machine guns. Even then, two to three hundred craft a year are looted."

"Tom Too became a power among the corsairs," Mindoro went on. "A year or two ago, he moved inland. He intended to set up an empire in the interior of China. He established himself as a warlord.

"But the armies of the Chinese republic drove him out. He moved into Manchuria and sought to seize territory and cities. But the Japanese were too much for him."

Renny twirled the cigar absently in his gigantic fingers. "This sounds a little fantastic."

"It is not fantastic—for the Orient," Doc Savage put in. "Many of the so-called warlords of the Far East are little better than pirates."

"Tom Too is the worst of the lot!" Mindoro interjected. "He is considered a devil incarnate, even in the Orient, where human life is held so very cheaply."

"You said you had never seen Tom Too," Doc suggested. "Yet you know a great deal concerning his career."

"What I am telling you is merely the talk of the cafés. It is common knowledge. Concrete facts about Tom Too are scarce. He keeps himself in the background. Yet his followers number into the hundreds of thousands."

"Huh?" Renny ejaculated.

"I told you the pirates of the Spanish Main were

petty crooks compared to Tom Too!" Mindoro rapped. "It is certain no buccaneer of history ever contemplated a coup such as Tom Too plans. He is moving to seize the entire Luzon Union!"

"How much has he accomplished?" Doc asked sharply.

"A great deal. He has moved thousands of his men into the Luzon Union."

At this, Renny grunted explosively. "The newspapers have carried no word of such an invasion!"

"It has not been an armed invasion," Mindoro said grimly. "Tom Too is too smart for that. He knows foreign warships would take a hand.

"Tom Too's plan is much more subtle. He is placing his followers in the army and navy of the Luzon Union, in the police force, and elsewhere. Thousands of them are masquerading as merchants and laborers. When the time comes, they will seize power suddenly. There will be what the newspapers call a bloodless revolution.

"Tom Too will establish what will seem to the rest of the world to be a legitimate government. But every governmental position will be held by his men. Systematic looting will follow. They will take over the banks of the Union, the sugar plantations—the entire wealth of the republic."

"Where do you come in on this?" Renny wanted to know.

Mindoro made a savage gesture. "Myself and my secret political organization are all that stands in the way of Tom Too!"

Chapter IX
HIS ARM FELL OFF

HAM had said nothing throughout the discussion. He maintained his attitude of intense concentration. Ham was a good listener on occasions such as this. His keen brain had a remarkable capacity for grasping details and formulating courses of action.

"Have you taken this matter up with the larger nations?" Ham asked now.

Mindoro nodded. "That was my first move."

"Didn't you get any action?"

"A lot of vague diplomatic talk was all!" Mindoro replied. "They told me in so many words that they thought I exaggerated the situation."

"Then no one will interfere, even if Tom Too seizes power with this bloodless revolution he plans," Doc said. His words were a statement of fact.

Tilting back in his chair, Doc drew his sleeve off his left wrist.

Mindoro stared curiously at the contrivance that looked like an overgrown wrist watch. He did not know the thing was the scanning lens of Doc's amazingly compact television receiver. He seemed about to ask what it was, but the gravity of his own troubles dissuaded him temporarily.

"I will describe my secret political organization briefly, and show how we are fighting Tom Too," Mindoro stated. "In the secret group are most of the prominent men of the Luzon Union, including the president, his cabinet and the more important officials. We have money and power. We control the newspapers. We have the confidence of the people.

"Most important of all, we are sufficient in number to take up arms and offer Tom Too very stiff opposition. We already have the very latest in machine guns and airplanes. We stand ready to fight the instant Tom Too comes into the open.

"Tom Too has learned this. That alone is forcing him to postpone his coup. He is seeking to learn our identity. He captured me here in New York and tried to force me to reveal the names of the secret society members. Once in possession of those names, he will remove every man. Then he will seize power."

Doc put a hand inside his coat, where he wore the receiving apparatus of his television receptor. A faint click sounded. He glanced at his wrist.

A molten glow came into his golden eyes, a strange, hot luminance.

"Isn't there something you can do toward rescuing your three friends?" Mindoro asked Doc.

"I'm doing it now," Doc told him.

Mindoro was puzzled. "I don't understand."

"Come here and look." Doc indicated the disk on his wrist.

The others leaped to his side.

"Holy cow!" Renny shouted out. "Why, there's Long Tom, Monk, and Johnny!"

FLICKERING on the crystal-like lens of the telewatch was the somewhat vague image of a dingy office interior. The place held a pair of desks, filing cabinets, and worn chairs.

On three of the chairs sat Long Tom, Monk, and Johnny. They were bound hand and foot, tied to the chairs, and gagged.

"I know that place," Renny ejaculated. "It's the office of the Dragon Oriental Goods Company, across the street from the skyscraper under construction."

"Our friends were just brought in," said Doc.

Mindoro made bewildered gestures.

"That is a television instrument, of course," he muttered. "But I did not know they were made that small."

"They're not, usually," Doc explained. "But this one is not radically different from the larger sets. It is merely reduced in size. Being so small, it is effective for only a few miles."

"Where is the transmitter?" Renny questioned, "In the Dragon joint?"

"In the adjoining office. I installed it after leaving you and Mindoro in the taxi. Other transmitters, operating on slightly different wavelengths, are at the radio store and at the spot where Tom Too so nearly finished you. This one got results first."

Ham ran into the laboratory. He came out bearing several of the compact little machine guns which were Doc's own invention, gas masks, gas bombs, and bullet-proof vests.

Riding down in the high-speed elevator, Ham, Renny, and Mindoro donned the vests, belted on the machine guns, and stuffed their pockets with bombs.

Mindoro, who was unfamiliar with Doc's working methods, showed astonishment that the mighty bronze man did not follow their example.

"Aren't you going to carry at least one of these guns?" he queried.

Doc's bronze head shook a negative. "Rarely use them."

"But why?"

Doc was slow answering. He didn't like to talk about himself or his way of operating.

"The reasons I don't use a gun are largely psychological," he said. "Put a gun in a man's hand, and he will use it. Let him carry one and he comes to depend upon it. Take it away from him, and he is lost—seized with a feeling of helplessness. Therefore, since I carry no firearms, none can be taken from me to leave the resultant feeling of helplessness."

"But think of the handicap of not being armed!" Mindoro objected.

Doc shrugged and dropped the subject.

Ham and Renny grinned at this word play.

Doc handicapped? Not much! They had never seen the mighty bronze man in a spot yet where he didn't have a ready way out.

DOC rode the outside of the cab which whisked them down Broadway. He watched the diallike lens of his telewatch almost continuously.

Several Mongols were now in the Dragon concern office. They moved about, conversing. The image carried to Doc by television was too jittery and dim to permit him to read their lips. Indeed, he could not even identify the faces of the men in the room, beyond the fact that they were lemon-hued and slant-eyed.

Considering the compactness of Doc's tiny apparatus, however, the transmitted image was remarkably clear. An electrical engineer interested in television would have gone into raptures over the mechanism. It was constructed with the precision of a lady's costly wrist watch.

An interesting bit of drama was now enacted on the telewatch lens.

Monk, by squirming about in the chair in which he was bound, got his toes on the floor. Hopping like a grotesque, half-paralyzed frog, he suddenly reached the grimy window. He fell against the pane. It broke.

Some glass fell inside the room; some dropped down into the street.

A yellow man ran to Monk and delivered a terrific blow. Monk upset, chair and all, onto the floor. He landed on fragments of the window he had broken. Doc watched Monk's hands intently after the fall.

The Mongols peered anxiously out of the window. They drew back after a time, satisfied the falling glass had alarmed no one.

Doc's view was now interrupted.

A slant-eyed man came and stood directly before the eye of the hidden television transmitter. All the apparatus registered was a limited view of the fellow's back.

Doc waited, golden eyes never leaving the telewatch dial. None of his impatience showed on his bronze features. Three minutes passed. Four. Then the Mongol moved away from the television eye.

The situation in the Dragon concern office was exactly as it had been four minutes ago. The three forms bound to chairs were quiet.

Doc's head shook slowly.

"I don't like this," he told those inside the taxi. "Something strange is happening in that office."

Doc continued to watch the scanning lens. The three tied to the chairs were motionless as dead men. He could not see their faces.

"We're almost there, Doc," Renny said from the cab interior.

Doc directed the driver to stop the machine. They got out.

"Let's rush 'em!" Renny suggested, his voice a rumble like thunder in a barrel.

"That is probably what they're hoping we'll do," Doc told him dryly.

Renny started. "You think this is a trick?"

"Tom Too is clever enough to know you picked up the trail of his man at the Dragon concern office. He must surely know we are aware he has been using the office. Yet he chanced discovery in bringing our pals there, or having his men bring them. He would not do that without a reason."

"But what—"

"Wait here!"

Leaving them behind, Doc moved down a side street. Two or three pedestrians turned to stare after his striking figure, startled by sight of a physique such as they had not glimpsed before.

SOME distance down the side street, a street huckster stood beside a two-wheeled hand cart piled high with apples and oranges. This man had but recently arrived from his native land in the south of Europe, and he spoke little English.

He was surprised when a voice hailed him in his native tongue. He was impressed by the appearance of the bronze, golden-eyed man who had accosted him. A short conversation ensued. Some money changed hands.

The huckster wheeled his cart to a secluded spot. But he shortly reappeared, pushing his vehicle toward Broadway. He turned south on Broadway, and was soon before the Far East Building, on the tenth floor of which was the office of the Dragon Oriental Goods Company.

The door of the Far East Building was wide. The huckster calmly wheeled his car inside, an unheard-of thing.

The half-caste elevator operator dashed forward angrily. Another man was loitering in the lobby. His broad face, prominent cheek bones and almost entire absence of beard denoted, to an expert observer, Mongol blood. He joined the elevator operator.

They proceeded to throw the fruit vender out bodily. It took both of them. They wrestled the peddler clear to the sidewalk and dumped him into the gutter. Then they came back and shoved the cart out.

Neither man noticed the fruit in the cart was not heaped as high as it had been a moment before.

The huckster wheeled his vehicle away, barking excitedly in his native tongue. He disappeared.

Doc Savage had been hidden under the fruit. No one but the peddler knew Doc was now in the Far East Building—least of all the Mongol in the lobby, who was obviously one of Tom Too's pirate horde.

"Me think that velly stlange thing to happen," the Mongol told the elevator operator.

"Allee same lookee funny," agreed the operator. "Mebbe so that fella wolk alongside blonze man?"

The Mongol swore a cackling burst in his native tongue. "Me thinkee good thing follow fluit fella! Alee same cut thloat and play safe."

With this, he felt a knife inside his sleeve and started out. He reached the door.

Splat! The sound was dull, mushy. It came from the side of the door. Thin glass fragments of a hollow ball tinkled on the floor tiling.

The Mongol went to sleep on his feet—fell without a sound.

Doc had hurled one of his anaesthetic balls from the stairway. He had not intended to reveal his presence. But it was necessary that he protect the innocent huckster whom he had bribed to bring him here.

The elevator operator spun. He saw Doc. A screech of fright split past his lips. He charged wildly for the street door.

The cloud of invisible, odorless anaesthetic had not yet become ineffective. The man ran into it. He folded down, and momentum tumbled him head over heels across the walk.

Doc stepped to the door.

From two points—one up the street, one down it—machine guns brayed a loud stream of reports.

Doc had expected something like that. This was a trap, and Tom Too's men were hardly fools enough to wait for him on the upper floors of the building, where their retreat would be cut off.

He flashed backward in time to get in the clear.

Fistfuls of stone powdered off the building entrance as jacketed bullets stormed. Falling glass jangled loudly. Ricocheting lead squawled in the lobby.

Doc glided to the stairs, mounted to the second floor and tried the door of a front office. It chanced to be locked. He pulled—not overly hard, it seemed. The lock burst from its anchorage as though hitched to a tractor.

Entering the office, Doc crossed to a window and glanced down.

The machine guns had silenced. A gray sedan sped along the street, slowing to permit the Mongols to dive aboard. The car continued north. It reached the first corner.

Suddenly there was a series of sawing sounds, like the rasp of a gigantic bull fiddle.

Doc knew those noises instantly—the terrific fire of the compact little machine guns he had invented. Renny, Ham, and Mindoro had turned loose on the Orientals.

The gray sedan careened to the left. It hurdled the curb. There was a roar of rent wood and smashing glass as it hit a display window. The car passed entirely through the window. Wheels ripped off, fenders crumpled, top partially smashed in, it sledded across the floor of a furniture store.

Doc saw the attackers wade through the wreckage after the car. Several times their little machine guns made the awful bullfiddle sawings.

Then the three men came out and sped toward the Far East Building.

Doc met them downstairs.

"Three of the devils were in the car!" Renny grimaced. "They're all ready for the morgue."

"What about our pals?" Ham demanded. He seized Doc's wrist and stared at the telewatch dial. "Good! They're still tied to those chairs!"

Doc said nothing. His golden eyes showed no elation.

They rode up in the elevator. Renny raced down the tenth-floor corridor. He did not wait to see whether the Dragon concern office door was locked. His keg of a fist whipped a terrific blow. The stout panel jumped out of the frame like match wood.

Renny, continuing forward, tore the door from its hinges with his great weight.

Ham leaped to one of the bound figures, grasped it by the arm. Then he emitted a squawk of horror.

The arm of the form had come off in his hand!

"THEY'RE dummies," Doc said. "The clothes worn by Monk, Long Tom, and Johnny—stuffed with waste paper, and fitted with the faces of show-window dummies."

Ham shuddered violently. "But we saw Monk, Long Tom, and Johnny in here! They were moving about, or at least struggling against their bonds."

"They were here," Doc admitted. "But they were taken away and the dummies substituted while one of the Mongols stood in front of the television transmitter, unless I'm mistaken."

Renny's sober face was black with gloom. "Then they knew the television sender was installed here!"

"They were lucky enough to find it," Doc agreed. "So they brought the three prisoners here, hoping we would see them and come to the rescue. They had the machine-gun trap down in the street waiting for us. That explains the whole thing."

Ham made a slashing gesture with his sword cane. "Blast it! We haven't accomplished anything!"

Doc swung over to the fragments of broken window lying on the floor. One piece was about a foot square, the others smaller. He began gathering them.

"What possible value can that glass have?" Mindoro questioned curiously, still trembling a little from the excitement of the recent fight.

"Monk broke this window and his captors knocked him over," Doc replied. "He lay on top of the glass fragments for a time, while the Mongols looked down at the window to see if the breaking window had caused alarm. They did not watch Monk at all for a few seconds. During that time, I distinctly saw Monk work a crayon of the invisible-writing chalk out of his pocket and write something on the glass."

Renny lumbered for the door. "The ultraviolet apparatus is at the office. We'll have to take the glass there."

They left the Far East Building by a rear door, thus avoiding delay while explanations were being furnished the police.

In Doc's eighty-sixth-floor retreat, they put the glass fragments under the ultraviolet lamp.

Monk's message confronted them, an unearthly bluish scrawl. It was brief, but all-important.

> Tom Too is scared and taking a run-out powder. He is going to Frisco by plane and sailing for the Luzon Union on the liner *Malay Queen*. He's taking us three along as hostages to keep you off his neck. Give 'im hell, Doc!

"Good old Monk!" Ham grinned. "That homely ape does pull a fast one once in a while. He's heard the gang talking among themselves. Probably they figured he couldn't understand their lingo."

Mindoro had paled visibly. He strained his graying hair through palsied fingers.

"This means bloodshed!" he muttered thickly. "Tom Too has given up trying to get the roster of my political group. He will strike, and my associates will fight him. Many will die."

Doc Savage scooped up the phone. He gave a number—that of a Long Island airport.

"My plane!" he said crisply. "Have it ready in an hour."

"You think we can overhaul them from the air?" Ham demanded.

"Too risky for our three pals," Doc pointed out.

"Then what—"

"We're going to be on the liner *Malay Queen* when she sails from Frisco!"

Chapter X
THE LUZON TRAIL

THE liner *Malay Queen*, steaming out through the Golden Gate, was an impressive sight. No doubt many persons on the San Francisco waterfront paused to admire the majesty of the vessel. She was a bit over seven hundred feet long. In shipbuilding parlance, she displaced thirty thousand tons.

The hull was black, with a strip of red near the water line; the superstructure was a striking white. The craft had been built when everybody had plenty of money to spend. All the luxuries had been put into her—swimming pool, three dining saloons, two lounges, two smoking rooms, writing room, library, and two bars. She even carried a small bank.

Most of the passengers were on deck, getting their last look at the Golden Gate. At Fort Point and Fort Baker, the nearest points of land on either side, construction work on the new Golden Gate bridge was in evidence—a structure which would be nearly six and a half thousand feet in length when completed.

Among the passengers were some strange personages.

Of exotic appearance, and smacking of the mystery of the Orient, was the Hindu who stood on the boat deck. Voluminous white robes swathed this man from neck to ankles. Occasionally the breeze blew back his robes to disclose the brocaded sandals he wore. A jewel flamed in his ample turban.

Such of his hair as was visible had a jet-black color. His brown face was plump and well-fed. Under one ear, and reaching beneath his chin to his other ear, was a horrible scar. It looked as though somebody had once tried to cut the Hindu's throat. He wore dark glasses.

Even more striking was the Hindu's gigantic black servant. This fellow wore baggy pantaloons, a flamboyant silk sash, and sandals which had toes that curled up and over. On each turned-over toe was a tiny silver bell.

This black man wore no shirt, but made up for it with a barrel-sized turban. He had thick lips, and nostrils which flared like those of a hard-running horse.

Passengers on the *Malay Queen* had already noted that the Hindu and his black man were never far apart.

"A pair of bloomin' tough-lookin' blokes, if yer asks me," remarked a flashy cockney fellow, pointing at the Hindu and the black. "Hi'd bloody well 'ate to face 'em in a dark alley. Yer'd better lock up them glass marbles yer wearin', dearie."

The cockney had addressed a stiff-backed, very fat dowager in this familiar fashion. They were perfect strangers. The dowager gave the cockney a look that would have made an Eskimo shiver.

"Sir!" she said bitingly, then flounced off.

The cockney leered after her. He was dressed in the height of bad taste. The checks in his suit were big and loud; his tie and shirt were violently colored. He wore low-cut shoes that were neither tan nor black, but a bilious red hue. His hat was green. He smoked bad-smelling cigars, and was not in the least careful where he knocked his ashes. His face bore an unnatural paleness, as though he might have recently served a long prison term.

The cockney did not glance again at the Hindu and the black man.

The Hindu was Doc Savage. The black man was Renny. The cockney, he of the loud clothes and bad manners, was Ham—Ham, the one usually so immaculately clad and so debonair of manner. The disguises were perfect, a tribute to Doc's intensive study of the makeup art.

DOWN on the promenade deck, a steward was confronting one of the steerage passengers who had wandered into territory reserved for those traveling first class.

"You'll have to get back down where you belong!" growled the steward, showing scant politeness.

Courtesy did not seem to be due such a character as the steerage passenger. The man was shabby, disheveled. In age he seemed to be less than thirty. But he looked like a fever-ridden tropical tramp. His skin was light in hue, and he was a pronounced blond.

A close observer might have noted his eyes were unusually dark for one so fair-complected.

This man was Juan Mindoro.

Shortly afterward, Mindoro sought to reach the upper decks again. This time he succeeded. He made his way furtively to the royal suite, the finest aboard. This was occupied by Doc and Renny—otherwise the Hindu and his black servant.

Mindoro unlocked the royal suite with a key Doc had furnished, entered, and wrote briefly on the bathroom mirror with a bit of crayonlike substance he produced from a pocket. He wrote near the top.

No stewards encountered the blowsy-looking tropical tramp as he returned to the steerage.

Fifteen minutes after this incident, Ham also entered the royal suite and left a message—written near the bottom of the mirror.

The *Malay Queen* was some miles out to sea before the Hindu and his black man stalked with great dignity to their royal suite and locked themselves in.

Doc turned the ultraviolet lamp on the bathroom mirror.

Mindoro's message read:

The steerage is full of half-castes, Chinese, Japanese, Malays, and Mongols. But I have seen nothing to show Tom Too is aboard.

Ham's communication was:

No sign of Monk, Long Tom, or Johnny. And how I hate these clothes!

Renny snorted at the reflection of his own black face in the mirror. "Ham sure cuts a swath in his green hat and blood-colored shoes. I'll bet he breaks the mirror in his cabin so he can't see himself."

Doc took off his turban. He had dyed his hair an extreme black.

"Did you see any sign of Tom Too or his prisoners, Renny?"

"Not a hair." Renny drew funnel-like flaring tubes from his nostrils.

"They came from New York to San Francisco by plane, we know. We located the aircraft they had chartered. And the pilots told us they had three prisoners along."

"The big point is—did they sail on the *Malay Queen*?"

"We have no proof they did. But Monk's message indicated they intended to."

Renny scowled at his sepia reflection in the mirror, apparently trying to see how fierce he could look. The result was a countenance utterly villainous, especially when he replaced the tubes which enlarged his nostrils.

"Holy cow!" he grunted. "I wouldn't even know myself! I don't think Tom Too will recognize us, Doc. That gives us a few days in which to work. That's a long time."

"We may need it. This Tom Too is as clever a devil as we've ever gone up against."

They were not long in learning just how true Doc's statement was.

HAM gave Doc Savage news of the first development. This occurred the following day.

Ham furnished Doc his information in a rather curious fashion. He did it by smoking his vile cigar. He was seated at one end of the lounge. Doc was ostensibly reading a book at the other.

Ham released short and long puffs of smoke from his lips. The short puffs were dots, the long ones dashes. Using them, Ham spelled out a sentence.

Have you heard the talk going over the ship about the three maniacs confined to a stateroom on D deck?

Tom Too or any of his men, were they in the lounge, would hardly have dreamed the silly-looking cockney was transmitting a message. And Tom Too might very well be present—quite a few Orientals were numbered among the first-class passengers sitting in the lounge.

Doc shook a negative with his head, making it seem he was mentally disagreeing with something he had read in his book.

The three madmen are in Stateroom Sixty-six. Ham continued his smoke transmission. *Two Mongols are always on guard outside the cabin. That's all I've been able to find out.*

"And that's plenty," muttered Renny, who had also spelled out Ham's smoke words.

Shortly after this the Hindu and his giant black servant retired to their royal suite.

"That means they've got our buddies prisoners in the cabin!" Renny declared. "They've given out the word they're madmen to explain their keeping out of sight. Probably they're strapped in straitjackets, and gagged, too."

Doc nodded grimly. "You stay here, Renny. I'm going down and investigate—alone."

For the first time, passengers on the *Malay Queen* saw the exotic-looking Hindu moving about without his black man. Several eyes followed him as he entered the elevator.

"I wish to be let out on D deck," he told the elevator man, speaking the precise English of one to whom the tongue is not native.

D deck, being the lowest on the ship, held the cheapest accommodations. The staterooms were not perfectly ventilated, and it was necessary to keep the ports of the outside cabins closed much of the time lest waves slosh in and cause damage.

Cabin No. 66 was far forward.

Sure enough, two slant-eyed fellows lounged before the door. These were not half-castes, but of pure Mongol strain. Both of them looked fairly intelligent.

Blank-eyed, they watched the robed Hindu approach. With each step the Hindu's rich sandals appeared under his robes. He came to a stop within arm reach of the two Mongols.

What followed next was forever a mystery to the Mongol pair.

Two sharp cracks sounded. Each man dropped.

Doc had struck with both fists simultaneously, before either victim realized what he intended to do. Indeed, neither Mongol as much as saw Doc's white-swathed arms start their movement.

The stateroom door was locked. Doc exerted pressure. The door caved in. Doc glided warily through.

The stateroom was empty!

Doc was not given long to digest this disappointing discovery. Two shots crashed in the passage outside. They came close together, deafening roars.

Doc whipped over to a berth, scooped up a pillow, and flashed it briefly outside the door. More shots thundered. Bullets tore a cloud of feathers out of the pillow.

With a gesture too quick for watching eyes to catch, Doc flicked a glass ball of anaesthetic into the passage.

He held his breath a full four minutes—not a difficult task, considering Doc had practiced doing that very thing every day of his life since he had quitted the cradle.

In the interim he heard excited shouts. Men ran up. But their shouts ceased and they fell unconscious as the gas got them.

When he knew the anaesthetic vapor had become ineffective, Doc stepped out.

Only stewards and ship officers lay senseless in the passage. Of the man who had fired the shots there was no sign.

Both of the Mongols had bullet holes through their brains.

For the moment no other observers were in sight. Doc hurried past the unconscious sailors and returned to the royal suite.

Renny was disappointed when Doc appeared without their three friends.

"What did you find?" he demanded.

"That Tom Too is about as clever a snake as ever lived!" Doc replied grimly.

"What'd he do?"

"Spread a false story about three madmen being in the cabin just on the chance I was aboard. He figured that if I was, I'd investigate. Well, I accommodated him. And now he knows who I am."

"A bad break!" Renny growled.

"Tom Too is an utterly cold-blooded killer. He sacrificed two of his men, murdering them just so they would not fall into my hands. No doubt he feared they would be scared into betraying him."

Renny jerked a cast of dental composition out of his mouth. It was this which had thickened his lips.

"No need of us wearing these disguises any longer!" he declared.

"No," Doc agreed. "They'd just make us that much easier to find. Ham and Mindoro are safe for the time being in their disguises, though."

The two men busied themselves shedding their makeup. Remover used by theatrical players took the stain off their skin and hair. Doc peeled his throat scar off as though it were adhesive tape.

"This puts us in a tough spot," Renny rumbled as they returned themselves to normal appearance. "They'll spare no effort to put us out of the way. And no telling how many of them are aboard."

It was a vastly different-looking pair of men who stepped out of the royal suite. They were so changed an approaching deck steward did not recognize them.

"Is the Hindu in?" questioned the steward. "I got a note for him."

Doc plucked the note out of the startled steward's fingers.

It read:

There is an ancient saying about the straw that broke the back of the camel. Your next move will be the straw needed to break my patience.

Your three friends are alive and well—as long as my patience remains intact.

TOM TOO.

"The brass of the guy!" gritted Renny.

"Who gave you this?" Doc demanded of the steward.

"I dunno," muttered the flunky. "I was walkin' along, an it dropped at my feet. There was a five-dollar bill clipped to it, together with a note askin' me to deliver it. Somebody must 'a' throwed it."

Doc's golden eyes bored into those of the steward until he was convinced the man spoke the truth.

"On what deck did that happen?"

"On this one."

Chapter XI
PERIL LINER

MORE questioning revealed that no one had been in sight when the steward looked around after having the note drop at his feet.

The steward departed, perspiring a little. That night he didn't sleep well, what with dreaming of uncanny golden eyes which had seemed to suck the truth out of him like magnets pulling at steel bars.

In the royal suite, Renny made grim preparations. He donned a bullet-proof vest and harnessed two of Doc's compact machine guns under his arms, where they wouldn't bulge his coat too much.

"Tom Too is not gonna set back and wait to see if we intend to lay off him," he rumbled wrathfully. "We've got to watch our step."

"Not a bad idea," Doc agreed. "From now on we take no more meals in the dining saloon."

"I hope we ain't gonna fast," grunted Renny, who was a heavy eater.

"Concentrated rations are in our baggage."

"Any chance of a prowler poisoning the stuff?"

"Very little. It would be next to impossible to get into the containers without breaking the seals."

Renny completed his grim preparations. He straightened his coat, then surveyed himself in the mirror. His garments had been tailored to conceal guns worn in underarm holsters. The bullet-proof vest was inside, worn as an undergarment. Renny did not look like a walking fortress.

"What are we going to do about Tom Too?" he asked.

"We'll move slowly, for the time being. We don't want to get him excited enough to kill our pals," Doc said. "Our first move will be to consult the captain of the ship."

They found Captain Hickman, commander of the *Malay Queen*, on his bridge.

Captain Hickman was a short-legged man with a body that was nearly egg-shaped. Sea gales and blistering tropical suns had reddened his face until it looked as if it had been soaked in beet juice. His uniform was resplendent with gold braid and brass buttons.

Four nattily clad apprentice officers stood on the bridge, keeping watch over the instruments.

The first mate strode sprucely back and forth, supervising the apprentices and the general operation of the liner.

The first mate was somewhat of a fashion plate, his uniform being impeccable. He was a slender, pliant man with good shoulders and a thin-featured, not unhandsome face. His skin had a deeply tanned hue. His eyes were elevated a trifle at the outer corners, lending a suspicion some of his ancestors had been Orientals. This was not unusual, considering the *Malay Queen* plied the Orient trade.

Doc introduced himself to Captain Hickman.

"Savage—Savage—hm-m-m!" Captain Hickman murmured, stroking his red jaw. "Your name sounds very familiar, but I can't quite place it."

The first mate came over, saying: "No doubt you saw this man's name in the newspapers, Captain. Doc Savage conducted the mysterious submarine expedition to the Arctic regions. The papers were full of it."

"To be sure!" ejaculated Captain Hickman. Then he introduced the first mate. "This is Mr. Jong, my first officer."

The impeccable first mate bowed, his polite smile increasing the Oriental aspect of his features to a marked degree.

DOC SAVAGE and Renny went into consultation with Captain Hickman in the latter's private sitting room.

"We have reason to believe three of my friends are being held prisoner somewhere aboard this liner," Doc explained bluntly. "It is a human impossibility for two men, or even three or four, to search a boat this size. The captives could easily be shifted to a portion of the vessel which we had already searched, and we would be none the wiser.

We therefore wish the aid of your crew, such of them as you trust implicitly."

Captain Hickman rubbed his brow. He seemed too surprised for words.

"It is extremely important the search be conducted with the utmost secrecy," Doc continued. "Any alarm will mean the death of my friends."

"This is highly irregular!" the commander objected.

"Possibly."

"Have you any authority to command such a search?"

The flaky gold in Doc's eyes began to take on a molten aspect, an indication of anger.

"I had hoped you would cooperate freely in this matter." No wrath was apparent in his powerful voice.

At this point a radio operator entered the cabin, saluted briskly, and presented Captain Hickman a message.

The florid commander read it. His lips compressed; his eyes hardened.

"No search of this ship will be made!" he snapped. "And you two men are under arrest!"

Renny sprang to his feet, roaring: "What're you trying to pull on us?"

"Calm down," Doc told him mildly. Then he asked Captain Hickman: "May I see that radiogram?"

The skipper of the *Malay Queen* hesitated, then passed the wireless missive over. It read:

CAPTAIN HICKMAN
COMMANDER S S *MALAY QUEEN*
    SEARCH YOUR SHIP FOR MEN NAMED CLARK SAVAGE JR ALIAS DOC SAVAGE AND COLONEL JOHN RENWICK ALIAS RENNY RENWICK STOP ARREST BOTH AND HOLD STOP WANTED FOR MURDERING SEVERAL MONGOLIANS AND CHINESE IN NEW YORK CITY STOP
    SAN FRANCISCO POLICE DEPARTMENT

"Holy cow!" Renny thundered his pet expletive. "How did they know we were aboard?"

"They didn't," Doc said grimly. "This is Tom Too's work. Call that radio operator in here, Captain. We'll see if he really received such a message."

"I'll do nothing of the sort!" snapped Captain Hickman. "You two are under arrest."

With this statement the florid skipper wrenched open a drawer of his desk. He grasped a revolver reposing there.

Doc's bronze hand floated out and came to rest on Captain Hickman's right elbow. Tightening, the corded bronze digits seemed to bury themselves in the florid man's flesh.

Captain Hickman's fingers splayed open and let the gun drop. He spat a stifled cry of pain.

Renny scooped up the fallen weapon.

Jong, the first mate, pitched into the sitting room, drawn by his skipper's cry. Renny let Jong look into the noisy end of the revolver, saying: "I wouldn't start anything, mister!"

Doc released Captain Hickman's elbow. The skipper doubled over, whining with agony, nursing his hurt elbow against his egg of a stomach. At the same time he goggled at Doc's metallic hand, as though unable to believe human fingers could have hurt him so.

Jong stood with hands half uplifted, saying nothing.

"We'll go interview the radio operator," Doc declared.

THE radio installation on the *Malay Queen* consisted of a large lobby equipped with a counter, where messages were accepted, and two inner rooms holding enormous banks of apparatus.

"The message was genuine, all right!" insisted the radio operator. He gave the call letters of the San Francisco station which had transmitted the missive.

Seating himself at the semiautomatic "bug" which served in lieu of a sending key, Doc called the shore station and verified this fact.

"Let's see your file of sent messages!" Doc directed the operator.

A brief search turned up one which had been "marked off" as sent not more than twenty minutes ago. It was in code, the words meaningless.

"Who filed this?"

"I don't know," insisted the radio man. "I discovered it lying on the counter, together with the payment for transmission and a swell tip. Someone came in and left it without being observed."

"This Tom Too must be half ghost!" Renny muttered. He still held the captain's revolver, although neither the skipper of the *Malay Queen* nor First Mate Jong were offering resistance.

Doc studied the cipher message. It read:

JOHN DUCK
HOTEL KWANG SAN FRANCISCO
    DTOSS EARVR AAGSE IAHBR OOAFR ODIRDA

There was no signature. Radiograms are often unsigned, which made this fact nothing unusual.

"Whew!" Renny grunted. "Can you make heads or tails of that mess of letters, Doc? It seems to be a five-letter code of some kind."

"The last word has six letters," Doc pointed out. "Let's see what a little experimenting will do to it."

Seating himself before a sheet of blank paper, a pencil in hand, Doc went to work on the cipher. His pencil flew swiftly, trying different combinations of the letters.

Five minutes later he got it.

"The thing is simple, after all," he smiled.

"Yeah?" Renny grunted doubtfully.

"The first cipher letter is the first in the translated message," Doc said rapidly. "The second cipher letter is the last in the message. The third cipher letter is the second in the message; the fourth cipher letter is next to the last in the message, and so on. The letters are merely scrambled systematically!"

"Hey!" gasped Renny. "I'm dizzy already."

"It sounds complicated until you get it down on paper. Here, I'll show you."

Doc put down the cipher as it stood.

DTOSS EARVR AAGSE IAHBR OOAFR ODIRDA

Under that he wrote the translation.

DOCSAVAGEABOARDRADIOFORHIS ARREST

Renny scowled at this. Then its meaning became clear—the words were merely without spacing.

"Doc Savage aboard. Radio for his arrest!" he read aloud.

"The instructions Tom Too sent to a confederate in San Francisco," Doc explained. "Evidently they had agreed upon a course of action should we be discovered aboard."

POWERFUL radio-telephone equipment was a part of the installation aboard the *Malay Queen*. Using this, it was possible for passengers aboard to carry on a telephone conversation with anyone ashore, exactly as though there was a wire connection.

Using this, Doc now proceeded to do some detective work.

He called the Hotel Kwang in San Francisco.

"Have you a guest registered under the name of John Duck?" he asked.

"John Duck checked out only a few moments ago," the hotel clerk informed him.

Doc's second call was to the San Francisco police chief. He cut in a loudspeaker so everyone in the *Malay Queen* radio room could hear what the police chief had to say.

"Have you received any request to arrest Doc Savage?" Doc asked.

"Certainly not!" replied the San Francisco official. "We have a suggestion from the New York police that we offer Savage every possible cooperation."

Doc rested his golden eyes on Captain Hickman. "You satisfied?"

Captain Hickman's ruddy face glistened with perspiration. "I—er—yes, of course."

Doc severed his radio connection with San Francisco.

"I wish your cooperation," he told Captain Hickman. "Whether you give it or not is up to you. But if you refuse, you may rest assured you will lose your command of this ship within thirty minutes."

Captain Hickman mopped at his face. He was bewildered, angry, a little scared.

Doc noted his indecision. "Call your owners. Ask them about it."

The *Malay Queen* commander hurriedly complied. He secured a radio landline connection with the headquarters of his company in San Francisco. He gave a brief description of the situation.

"What about this man Savage?" he finished.

He was wearing earphones. The others did not hear what he was told.

But Captain Hickman turned about as pale as his ruddy face permitted. His hands shook as he placed the headset on the table. He stared at Doc as if wondering what manner of man the big bronze fellow was.

"I have been ordered to do anything you wish, even to turning my command over to you," he said briskly.

First Mate Jong stared as if this was hard to believe. Then he made a gesture of agreement. "I will start an immediate search of the ship. And I can promise you it will be done so smoothly no one will as much as know it is going on."

He hurried out.

Doc and Renny returned to the royal suite.

Renny eyed Doc curiously. "Just what kind of a pull have you got with the company that owns this boat, anyhow?"

"Some months ago, the concern got pinched for money," Doc said slowly, reluctantly. "Had it ceased operating, several thousand men would have been out of jobs. A loan of mine tided them over."

RENNY sank heavily into a chair. At times he felt a positive awe of the mighty bronze man. This was one of the occasions.

It was not the fact that Doc was wealthy enough to take an important hand in a commercial project such as this that took Renny's breath. It was the uncanny way such things as this turned up—the way the bronze man seemed to have a finger in affairs in every part of the world.

Renny knew Doc possessed fabulous wealth, a golden treasure trove alongside which the proverbial ransom of a king paled into insignificance. Doc had a fortune great enough to buy and sell some nations.

Renny had seen that treasure. The sight of it had left him dazed for weeks. It lay in the lost Valley of the Vanished, a chasm in the impenetrable mountains of the Central American republic of Hidalgo. This strange place was peopled by a golden-skinned folk, pure-blooded descendants of the ancient Mayan race. They guarded the wealth. And they sent burro trains of it to the outside world as Doc needed it.

There was one string attached to the wealth—Doc was to use it only in projects which would benefit humanity. The Mayans had insisted upon that. It was to be used for the cause of right.

Their insistence was hardly needed, for it would not have received any other disposition at Doc's hands. Doc's life was dedicated to that same creed—to go here and there, from one end of the world to the other, striving to help those who needed help, punishing those who were malefactors.

This was the one thing that motivated Doc's every act.

The same creed bound his five men to Doc. That, and their love of adventure, which was never satisfied.

Chapter XII
TREACHERY

THE search for Monk, Long Tom, and Johnny drew a blank.

"I can assure you we searched every stateroom aboard, and every box and bale of the cargo!" declared slant-eyed First Mate Jong. "There was no sign of three prisoners."

"I don't believe they're aboard!" Captain Hickman added.

Captain Hickman had taken to speaking in a low voice when in the presence of the big bronze man. He was completely in awe of Doc, and his manner showed it.

"I'm still betting they're aboard!" Renny grunted. "Unless—"

He wet his lips. His enormous fists became flinty blocks. It had just occurred to him that Tom Too might have become alarmed and slain the three captives, shoving their bodies overboard.

Renny's fears were dispelled by a plain white card they found under the door of the royal suite the next day. It said:

The straw did not break the back of the camel, you may be glad to learn. But it came very near.
                                        TOM TOO

"That snake is getting cocky!" Renny gritted. "How could the search have missed our three pals, granting they're aboard?"

"No telling how many of the crew have been bribed," Doc pointed out.

THE Malay Queen stopped at Honolulu for a few hours. Doc had gotten instructions to the flashy cockney and the disheveled tropical tramp, otherwise Ham and Mindoro, and they all kept close watch on such persons as went ashore.

No sign of Long Tom, Monk, or Johnny was discovered in the close inspection.

Immediately after the Malay Queen put to sea again, Doc Savage instituted a single-handed search for his three captive friends. Due to the great size of the liner, the task was a nearly impossible one.

A hundred of Tom Too's corsairs could conceivably have been aboard without Doc being able to identify one of them. Every Mongol, Jap, Chinaman and half-caste was a potential suspect.

Doc began in the hold. He opened barrels, boxes, and bales of cargo. He examined the fresh-water tanks. The Malay Queen was an oil burner, and he scrutinized the fuel tanks. Then he began on the D deck cabins and worked up.

It was on D deck, well toward the stern, that his hunt produced first results.

He found a stateroom which had been used, but which was now unoccupied.

The mirror was missing.

On the floor was a small smudge. Analyzing this, Doc learned it was the crayon he used for his invisible writing.

These discoveries told him a story. The prisoners were actually aboard. They had been kept here for a time. Monk had been caught trying to leave a secret message on the mirror. The mirror had been removed and thrown overboard. Either Monk or his captors had destroyed the crayon by stamping upon it. Probably that was Monk's work, since Tom Too's men would have wanted the crayon to learn its composition.

Doc continued his prowling. It was an interminable task. The Malay Queen had more than four hundred cabins. While Doc searched, Tom Too could easily move the prisoners to a stateroom Doc had already scrutinized.

DOC did not finish the hunting. Tom Too struck at their lives the second night out of Honolulu.

Doc and Renny had been ordering meals sent to their suite to keep Tom Too from getting the idea they were subsisting off rations carried in their baggage. The meals which were brought in to them they chucked overboard. This task usually fell to Renny, while Doc watched for enemies.

Gulls were following the Malay Queen. Swooping, the birds snatched anything edible which was tossed overside before the articles reached the water.

The birds bolted portions of the food Renny heaved over the rail.

Two of the feathered scavengers did not fly fifty yards before their wings collapsed and they plummeted into the sea, lifeless.

"Poison!" Renny grunted.

The cook and steward who had come in contact with the meal put in an uncomfortable half hour in front of Doc's probing golden eyes. They convinced the bronze giant they knew nothing of the poison.

Captain Hickman was perturbed when he heard of the attempt. He acted as scared as though his own life had been attempted.

First Mate Jong was also solicitous. "Do you wish me to make a second search of the ship?"

"It would be useless," Doc replied.

Jong stiffened perceptibly. "I hope, sir, you do not distrust the personnel of this craft!"

"Not necessarily."

Doc and Renny redoubled their caution.

The next night they found poisoned needles concealed in their pillows.

A few minutes later, when Doc turned on the water in the bathroom, a villainous, many-legged creature hurtled out of the hot-water faucet.

At this Renny's hair stood on end. He was in the habit of carelessly thrusting his big hands under the faucet when he washed.

"I've seen those things before!" he gulped, pointing at the hideous creature which someone had concealed in the faucet. "It's a species of jungle spider, the bite of which is fatal."

"Tom Too must have gone ashore in Honolulu and loaded up with death-dealing instruments," Doc suggested dryly. "It looks as if we're in for a brisk time."

Shortly after midnight, a bomb tore the royal suite almost completely from the liner. Partitions were reduced to kindling. The beds were demolished, the bed clothing torn to ribbons. Two passengers in nearby accommodations were slightly injured.

Doc's foresight saved him. He and Renny were bunking in with the cockney who showed such bad taste in clothes and manners—Ham.

Renny started to race to the scene of the explosion.

Doc stopped him. "Wait. Let Ham go and see how much damage was done."

Ham was not long on his mission.

"A frightful explosion," he reported. "The sides and roof of the royal suite were blown into the sea."

"Good!" Doc smiled.

"What's good about it?" Renny queried.

"We'll hibernate in here and make it look like we were blown overboard," Doc explained. "In the meantime, Ham and Mindoro will keep their eyes open."

HAM and Mindoro kept their eyes open enough, but it netted them exactly nothing.

The *Malay Queen* neared Mantilla, capital city of the Luzon Union. Arrival time was set for high noon.

Doc quitted Ham's cabin, descended to the lower deck, and approached Mindoro. The wealthy Luzon Union politician was more blowsy-looking than ever in his tropical-tramp disguise.

"How much influence have you with the police chief of Mantilla and the president of the Luzon Union?" Doc questioned.

"I made them!" Mindoro said proudly. "They're honest men, and my friends. I believe they would lay down their lives for me to a man."

"Then we will send some radio messages," Doc declared.

"You mean you want the liner searched upon arrival?"

"More than that. I want every person aboard questioned closely, and those who cannot prove they have been engaged in legitimate enterprises for the past few years are to be thrown in jail. Can you swing something that radical?"

"I can. And that should trap Tom Too."

"It'll at least put a crimp in his style," Doc smiled.

They repaired at once to the presence of Captain Hickman. The commander of the *Malay Queen* expressed vast astonishment at sight of Doc.

First Mate Jong, looking up from the binnacle, registered popeyed surprise.

"We wish to use the radio apparatus," Doc explained. "Perhaps you had better come along, Captain, in case the radio operator should object."

Captain Hickman had suddenly started perspiring. The mere sight of Doc seemed capable of making him break out in a sweat.

"Of course—of course!" he said jerkily.

First Mate Jong left the bridge at this juncture.

"Just a moment, please!" gulped Captain Hickman. "I must give an order. Then we shall go to the radio room."

Crossing to one of the apprentice seamen always on duty on the bridge, the commander spoke in a low voice. The words continued for fully a minute. Then Captain Hickman hurried back to Doc, apologizing for the delay.

They moved toward the radio cabin. The door of the apparatus room appeared before them.

Renny started violently—for he was suddenly hearing a vague, mellow, trilling sound that ran up and down the musical scale in a weirdly tuneless fashion. It was a melodious, inspiring sound that defied description. And it persisted for only an instant.

Renny knew what it was—Doc's tiny, unconscious sound, which he made in his moments of greatest concentration, or when he had come upon a startling discovery, or as danger threatened.

Instinctively, Renny looked around for the trouble. He saw it. Wisps of smoke, yellowish, vile, were crawling out of the wireless-room door.

Doc went ahead, a bronze flash of speed. He veered into the radio room. Two operators manned the instruments at this hour. Both sprawled in puddles of scarlet. They had been stabbed to death.

The wireless sets—both telephone and telegraph—had been expertly wrecked. They were out of commission.

Whoever had done the work was gone.

RENNY flung into the radio room. "Now if this ain't a fine mess!" he rasped hoarsely.

Captain Hickman had not entered.

Doc stepped to the door, looked out.

Captain Hickman's revolver blazed in his face.

Doc moved swiftly, as swiftly as he had ever moved before. Even his incredible speed and agility would not have gotten him in the clear had he tried to jump back. But he did duck enough that the bullet only scuffed through his bronze hair.

Before the treacherous skipper's gun could flame again, Doc was back in the wireless cabin.

Renny had whirled with the shot. "What is it, Doc?"

"It's Captain Hickman!" the giant bronze man said with a sort of blazing resonance in his voice. "He's on Tom Too's payroll!"

Renny sprang to the door. The snout of a machine gun bristled from either fist. He shoved one into the corridor and let it drum briefly.

A man shrieked, cursed—his profanity was singing Kwangtungese.

"That wasn't the captain!" Renny rumbled.

He listened. Speeding feet slippered in the corridor from both directions. They were coming nearer. Shots roared.

"They're closing in on us, Doc!"

Doc picked a glass globule of anaesthetic out of a pocket. But he did not use it. Renny could not hold his breath the three or four minutes necessary for the air to neutralize the stuff.

"Use the guns, Renny. Cut our way out of here!"

Renny sprang to the wall. Beyond lay the deck. He shoved one of the little machine guns out, tightened on the trigger, and waved the muzzle with a circular motion.

The terrific speed of the shots made a deafening moan. The bullets worked on the wall like a monster jig saw. A segment larger than the head of a barrel was cut almost completely out. Renny struck the section with his fist. It flew outward.

Renny and Doc pitched out on deck. Only a few startled passengers were in sight.

Doc sped to the nearest companionway. He reached the deck below in a single prodigious leap. Renny followed, waving the guns wildly for balance as he negotiated with three jumps and a near headlong fall the distance Doc had covered in one spring.

Passengers saw the guns and ran shrieking for cover.

HAM and Mindoro came up the grand staircase, shoulder to shoulder, guns in hand. Ham had his sword cane.

A bullet fired from the upper deck screamed past them. Somewhere in the dining saloon the slug shattered glassware. More lead followed.

"Watch it, Doc!" Ham yelled. "A herd of the devils are coming up from below!"

The words were hardly out his lips when snarling yellow faces topped the grand staircase.

Ham's gun hooted its awful song of death. The faces sank from view, several spraying crimson.

"I'm low on cartridges!" Renny boomed. "Ammunition goes through these guns like sand through a funnel!"

"My baggage is in the hold!" Doc said swiftly. "We'd better get to it There's two cases of cartridges in the stuff."

They raced forward along a passage, Doc in the lead.

Slant-eyed men suddenly blocked their way. Eight or ten of them! They corked the passage.

Hissing, one man struck at Doc with a short sword. But the blow missed as Doc weaved aside. The force of the swing spun the Oriental. His sword chopped into the passage bulkhead and stuck there.

Doc grasped the swordsman by the neck and one leg. Using the man as a ram, he shot forward like a projectile. Orientals upset, squawling, striking. Pistols flamed—nasty little spike-snouted automatics which could drive a bullet a mile.

Then Ham, Renny and Mindoro joined the fray. Their super-firing machine guns made frightful bullfiddle sawings. Before those terrific blasts of lead, men fell.

It was too much for the corsairs. Those able to do so, fled.

Continuing on, Doc and his men descended a companionway to the forward deck. Doc wrenched open a hatch which gave access to the hold. He descended.

The Orientals caught sight of them. They fired a coughing volley. Slivers jumped out of the deck. Slugs tapped the iron hatch. A bullet hit Ham's sword cane and sent it cartwheeling across the deck.

Ham howled angrily, risked almost certain death to dive over and retrieve his sword cane, then popped down the hatch. By a miracle, he was unscratched.

"You lucky cuss!" Renny told him.

"That's what comes of leading a righteous life!" Ham grinned.

They were in the luggage room of the hold. Trunks and valises were heaped about them. Doc dived into this stuff, hunting his own luggage, which had been put aboard in San Francisco.

At the same time, Doc kept a watch on the hatch.

Grimacing in aversion, Ham ripped off his flashy coat and vest. He had already lost the villainous green hat. He took off the blood-colored shoes and flung them out of the hatch.

"I'll go barefooted before I'll wear them another minute!" he snapped.

Renny snorted mirthfully as, an instant later, the

red shoes came flying back down the hatch, hurled by some Oriental.

Chapter XIII
WATER ESCAPE

SILENCE now fell. This was broken by singsonged orders. Ham and Renny listened to these with interest. The yellow men seemed to be speaking a half dozen tongues from Hindustani, Mongol dialects, and Mandarin, to Kwangtungese and pidgin English.

"There must be riffraff from every country in the

Doc stepped to the door ... Captain Hickman's revolver blazed.

Far East up there!" Renny boomed.

"I'm surprised at that," Ham clipped. "Tom Too's men in New York were all Mongols or half-castes with Mongol blood."

Mindoro explained this. "The rumors have it that Tom Too's most trusted men are of Mongol strain. Those were naturally the men he took to New York."

Doc Savage had found his trunks. He wrenched one open. Two cases of the high-powered little cartridges for the compact machine guns toppled out.

Doc grasped the edge of one box. He pulled. The wood tore away under his steel-thewed fingers as though it were so much rotten cork.

Mindoro, who was watching, drew in a gasp of wonder. He was still subject to dumbfoundment at the incredible strength in those huge bronze hands of Doc's.

"Keep your eye peeled, Renny!" Doc warned. "They're talking about throwing a hand grenade down that hatch!"

It was Renny's turn to be amazed. How Doc had managed to pick the information out of the unintelligible tumult overhead was beyond him.

Renny strained his eyes upward until they ached.

Sure enough, a hand grenade came sailing down the hatch.

Renny's machine gun blared. The burst of lead caught the grenade, exploded it. Renny was probably one of the most expert machine gunners ever to hold back a trigger. The noisy little weapons of Doc's invention, by no means easy to hold upon a target while operating, were steady as balanced pistols in his big paws.

There was quite a concussion as the grenade detonated. It harmed nobody, although a fragment hit Renny's bullet-proof vest so hard it set him coughing. Doc, Ham, and Mindoro had dived to cover in the baggage.

"We can play that game with them!" Doc said dryly. He opened a second trunk, took out iron grenades the size of turkey eggs, and flirted two up through the hatch.

The twin roars brought a yowling, agonized burst of Oriental yells. The attackers withdrew a short distance and began pouring a steady stream of bullets at the hatch.

This continued some minutes. Then the hatch suddenly flopped shut. Chains rattled. The links were being employed to make the cover fast.

A flashlight appeared in Doc's hand. It lanced the darkness which now saturated the hold. Rapidly he tried all the exits.

"They've locked us in!" he told the others grimly.

MINDORO, lapsing into Spanish in his excitement, babbled expletives. "This is incredible!" he fumbled. "Imagine such a thing as this happening on one of the finest liners plying the Pacific! It feels unnatural!"

"I'll bet it feels natural to the pirates on deck," Renny grunted. "This is the way they work it on the China coast. The devils ship aboard as passengers and in the crew, then take over the craft at a signal."

Comparative calm now settled upon the *Malay Queen*. The engines had not stopped; they continued to throb. They were modern and efficient, those engines. Up on deck they could not be heard. Down here in the hold they were barely audible.

"What are we going to do, Doc?" Ham wanted to know.

"Wait."

"What on? They've got us locked in."

"Which is probably fortunate for us," Doc pointed out. "We can hardly take over the ship, even if we whipped the whole gang. And they're slightly too many for us. We'll wait for—well, anything."

"But what about Monk, Long Tom, and Johnny?"

Fully a minute ticked away before Doc answered.

"We shall have to take the chance that they'll be kept alive as long as I'm living—provided they haven't been eliminated already."

"I don't think they have been killed," Ham said optimistically. "Tom Too is smart. He knows his three prisoners will be the price of his life should he fall into our hands. He won't throw away such a valuable prize."

"My thought, too," Doc admitted.

Mindoro was moved to put a delicate question. Perhaps the strain under which he was laboring made him blunt, for he ordinarily would have couched the query in the most diplomatic phraseology, or not have asked it at all.

"Would you turn Tom Too loose to save your friends?" he quizzed.

Doc's reply came with rapping swiftness.

"I'd turn the devil loose to save those three men!" He was silent the space of a dozen heartbeats, then added: "And you can be sure that when they joined me, they'd turn around and catch the devil again."

The others were silent. Mindoro wished he hadn't asked the question. There was something terrible about the depth of concern the big bronze man felt over the safety of his three friends—a concern which had hardly showed in his manner, but which was apparent here in the darkness of the hold, where they could not see him, but only hear his vibrant voice.

Minutes passed, swiftly at first, then slowly. They dragged into hours.

THE engines finally stopped. A rumble came from forward.

"The anchor dropping!" Doc declared.

"Any idea where we are?" Ham wanted to know.

"We've about had time to reach the harbor of Mantilla."

The four men listened. The great liner whispered with faint sound, noises too vague for Ham, Renny, and Mindoro to identify. But Doc's highly tuned ears, his greater powers of concentration, fathomed the meaning of the murmurings.

"They're lowering the boats."

"But this craft was supposed to tie up at the wharf in Mantilla," said Mindoro.

Silence fell. They continued to strain their eardrums until they crackled protest.

This continued fully half an hour.

"The liner anchored in about seventy feet of water," Doc stated.

"How can you tell?" Ham asked surprised.

"By the approximate number of anchor-chain links that went overboard. If you had listened carefully, you'd have noted each link made a jar as it went through the hawse hole."

Ham grinned. He had not thought of that. He gave their flashlight a fresh wind. This light used no battery, current being supplied by a spring-driven generator within the handle.

"Things have sort of quieted down," murmured Renny, who had been sitting with an ear pressed to a bulkhead.

Mounting the metal ladder to the hold hatch, he struck the lid fiercely with his fist. Bullets instantly rattled against it. A few, driven by rifles, came inside. Renny descended hastily.

"They haven't gone off and left us!" he grunted.

"What d'you reckon they're planning to do?" Ham questioned.

"Nothing pleasant, you may be assured," said Mindoro.

Mindoro's nerve was holding up. He showed none of the hysteria which comes of terror. His voice was not even unduly strained.

Faint sounds could now be heard on the deck immediately above. Wrack their ears as they might, Doc and his men could not tell what was happening.

"They're doing something!" Renny muttered, and that was as near as they came to solving the mystery.

The sounds ceased.

Mindoro's anxiety moved him to speak. "Hadn't we better do something?"

"Let them make the first move," Doc replied. "We're in a position down here to cope with any emergency."

Mindoro had his doubts; it looked to him as if they were merely trapped. But Ham and Renny understood what Doc meant—in Doc's baggage there was probably paraphernalia to meet any hostile gesture the pirates might make.

"This waiting gets in my hair!" Renny thumped. "I wish something would happen! Anything—"

Whur-r-room!

The hull of the liner jumped inward, shoved by a monster sheet of flame and expanding gases.

The Orientals had lowered dynamite overside and exploded it below the water line!

TRUNKS and valises were shoveled to the opposite side of the hold by the blast. Fortunately the liner hull absorbed much of the explosion force.

Doc and his three companions extricated themselves from the mess of baggage.

A wall of water poured through the rent in the hull. It scooted across the hold floor. A moaning, swirling flood, it rose rapidly.

Instinct sent Ham, Renny and Mindoro to the ladder that led to the deck hatch. They mounted.

"We can blow open the hatch with a grenade!" Ham clipped.

"Not so fast!" Doc called from below. "You can bet the pirates will be standing by with machine guns. They'll let you have a flock of lead the minute you show outside!"

A second explosion sounded, jarring the whole liner. This one occurred back near the stern.

"They're sinking the boat!" Mindoro shouted. "We'll be trapped in here!"

In his perturbation, he decided to ignore Doc's warning. He started on up the ladder to the hatch. But Renny flung up a big hand and held him back.

"Doc has got something up his sleeve!" Renny grunted, "so don't worry!"

Down in the hold, water sloshing to his waist, Doc was plucking out the contents of another of his trunks. He turned his flashlight on his three companions, then flung something up to them. He followed it with another—a third.

Renny caught the first, passed it up to Mindoro, and rumbled: "Put it on!"

The objects consisted of helmetlike hoods which fitted over the entire head and snugged with draw strings around the neck. They were equipped with gogglelike windows.

They were compact little diving hoods. Air for breathing was taken care of by artificial lungs carried in small back packs. Respiration was through a flexible hose and a mouthpiece noseclip contrivance inside the mask.

There were also lead bracelets fitting around their ankles, and heavy enough to keep their feet down.

Renny assisted Mindoro to don the diving hood, then put one on himself. Ham's sharply cut, hawklike face disappeared in another; he took a fresh grasp on his sword cane and waited.

Doc, his bronze head already enveloped in one of the hoods, was delving into other of his trunks, and making bundles of objects which he removed.

The generator-operated flashlights were waterproof. They furnished a pale luminance in the rushing, greasy floor that rapidly filled the hold.

THE liner sank. The boilers aft let go with hollow explosions. Water whirled a maelstrom in the hold, tumbling the four men and the numerous pieces of baggage about.

Water pressure increased as the vessel sought the depths. But at seventy feet it was not dangerous. With a surprisingly gentle jar, the *Malay Queen* settled on the bottom.

Locating each other by the glowing flashlights, the four men got together. Each carried a light.

Doc had four bundles ready—one for each man.

Thanks to the water-tight hoods, it was not necessary to keep the mouthpiece of the air hose between their lips at all times. By jamming their heads together, they could talk.

"Each of you carry one of these bundles," Doc directed. "We'll leave by the hole their dynamite opened—provided the ship is not resting so the sand has closed it."

The hole was open. They clambered through, using care that razor edges of the torn hull did not perforate the waterproof hoods.

The depths were chocolate-colored with mud raised by the sinking *Malay Queen*. The men joined hands to prevent being lost from each other. Doc leading, they churned through soft mud, away from the ill-fated liner. They were forced to lean far over, as though breasting a stiff gale, to make progress.

The water changed from chocolate hue to a straw tint, then to that of grapefruit juice, as the mud became less plentiful. Where the sea was clear, Doc halted the procession. They held conclave, heads rammed tightly together.

"Wait here," Doc directed. "If I'm not back in fifteen minutes, head for shore."

"How can we tell where shore is?" Mindoro demanded.

Doc produced a small, water-tight compass. He handed this to Ham.

"Granting that they sank the liner in Mantilla Bay, the town itself will be due east. Head that direction."

Doc now twisted a small valve on the "lung" apparatus of his diving hood. This puffed out the slack lower portion of the hood with air—gave him enough buoyancy to counteract the weight of the lead anklets. He lifted slowly, leaving his three companions behind on the bottom, an anxious group.

Nearing the surface—this was evidenced by the glow of sunlight—Doc adjusted another valve in the hood until his weight equaled that of the water he displaced, so that he neither rose or sank.

He paddled upward cautiously. If his guess was right, the pirates would be standing by in small boats, revolvers and machine guns in hand.

Doc wanted them to know he was alive.

This was of vital importance. As long as Tom Too knew he faced the menace of Doc Savage, he would not be liable to slay Doc's three friends, whom he held prisoner. Or were the three captives still alive?

They were. The instant Doc's head topped the surface, he saw Monk, Long Tom, and Johnny.

Chapter XIV
HUNTED MEN

MONK, big and furry, clothes practically torn off, crouched in the bow of a nearby lifeboat. He was shackled with heavy chains and metal bands.

The pale electrical wizard, Long Tom, and the bony, archaeologist, Johnny, were seated on a thwart in front of Monk. They were braceleted with ordinary handcuffs.

Other lifeboats and some launches swarmed the vicinity. Yellow men gorged them to the gunwales. Gun barrels bristled over the boats like naked brush.

Every slant eye was fixed on the spot where the *Malay Queen* had gone down. The sea still boiled there. Wreckage drifted in confusion, deck chairs, some lounge furniture, a hatch or two, and lesser objects such as shuffleboard cues and ping-pong balls. A pall of steam from the blown boilers hung above Mantilla Bay.

Doc sank and stroked toward the small craft which held his three friends.

He was hardly under the surface when a terrific explosion occurred in the water near by. It smashed the sea against his body with terrific force.

Swiftly he let all the air out of his diving hood. He scooted into the depths.

He knew what had happened. Some of the corsairs had glimpsed him and hurled a grenade.

Doc swam with grim, machinelike speed. Rifle bullets wouldn't reach him below the surface. But the grenades, detonating like depth bombs, were a grisly menace. He'd have to give up the rescue of his three men. He had no way of getting them ashore.

Chun-n-g!

Then a second grenade loosened. It couldn't have been many feet away. The goggles of Doc's diving hood were crushed inward. Gigantic fists seemed to smash every inch of his bronze frame.

Not missing a stroke in his swimming, Doc shook the glass goggle fragments out of his eyes. No serious damage had been done. He would merely have to keep the mouthpiece noseclip contrivance of the "lung" between his lips as long as he was beneath the surface.

His remarkable ability to maintain a sense of direction under all circumstances enabled him to find the three he had left beneath the waters.

Grenades were still exploding beneath the surface. But the blasts were so distant now as to be harmless.

Leaning far over against the water, the four men strode shoreward. Coming to a clear patch of sand, Doc halted, and, with a finger tip, wrote one word.

"Sharks!"

Doc had seen a pilot fish of a shark-following species.

After that warning they kept alert eyes roving the surrounding depths. Fortunately, however, they were not molested.

The bottom slanted upward; the water became translucent with sunlight. They were nearing shore. A roaring commotion passed over their heads, evidently a speed boat.

Upright wooden columns appeared suddenly, thick as a forest, shaggy with barnacles—the piling of a wharf.

Doc led his men into the forest. They rose cautiously to the top.

NO one observed them in the shadowy thicket of piling.

Out on the bay, boats scurried everywhere. Some were motor driven, some propelled by stringy yellow oarsmen.

Doc removed his diving hood. The other three followed his example.

"I know a spot ashore where we will be safe," Mindoro declared. "It is one of the rendezvous used by my secret political society."

"Let's go," said Doc.

Shoving themselves from pile to pile, they reached a hawser end which chanced to be dangling. Doc, tugging it, found the upper terminus solid.

He mounted with simian speed and ease. The wharf was piled with hemp bales. Nearby yawned a narrow street.

Now the others climbed up. They sprinted for the street—and stopped.

A squad of Mantilla police stood there. They held drawn guns.

"Bueno!" exploded Mindoro in Spanish. "We are safe!"

Ham and Renny scowled doubtfully. The police did not look friendly to them. Their doubts were justified an instant later.

"Fire!" shrieked the officer in command of the squad. "Kill the dogs!"

Police pistols flung up—targeted on the vital organs of Doc and his three companions.

Ham, Renny, Mindoro—all three suddenly found themselves scooped up and swept to one side by Doc's bronze right arm.

Simultaneously a small cylinder in Doc's left hand spouted a monster wad of black smoke. The cylinder, of metal, had come from the bundle Doc was carrying. The smoke pall spread with astonishing speed.

Police guns clapped thunderously in the black smudge. Bullets caromed off cobbles, off the building walls. The treacherous officers dashed about, searching savagely. Some had presence of mind to run up and down the street until clear of the umbrageous vapor. They waited there for the bronze giant and his companions to appear.

But they did not put in an appearance.

Not until the smoke was dissipated by a breeze, fully ten minutes later, did the would-be killers find an open door in one of the buildings walling the street. By that time Doc, Ham, Renny and Mindoro were many blocks away.

MINDORO was white with rage. From time to time he shook his fists in expressive Latin fashion.

"That group of police was composed of Tom Too's men!" he hissed wrathfully. "That explains their action. The devil must have enough of his followers, or men whom he has bribed, on the police force to take over the department when he decides to strike."

Doc replied nothing.

Ham and Renny exchanged doubtful glances. It looked as if they had stepped from the frying pan into the fire. Tom Too's plot was tremendous in scope. If the police were under the domination of the buccaneers, Doc would be in for some tough sailing.

They entered thickly crowded streets. The excitement in the bay seemed to be attracting virtually every inhabitant of Mantilla. Many, curious, were making for the bay at a dead run.

A tight group, Doc and his men breasted this tide of humanity. They avoided such of the Mantilla constabulary as they saw.

Mindoro soon led them into a small shop. The proprietor, a benign-looking Chinese gentleman, smiled widely at Mindoro. They exchanged words in Mandarin.

"To have you back is like seeing the sun rise after a long and dark and horrible night," murmured the Celestial. "This lowly person presumes you wish to use the secret way."

"Right," Mindoro told him.

In a rear room a large brass gong hung. It was shaped like a gigantic cymbal, such as drummers hammer. This was moved aside, a section of the wall behind opened, and Doc and his companions entered a concealed stairway.

This twisted and angled, became a passage even more crooked, and finally turned into another stair flight.

They stepped into a windowless room. The air was perfumed faintly with incense. Tapestries draped the walls; thick rugs matted the floor; comfortably upholstered furniture stood about. There was a cabinet laden with canned and preserved foods. A well-stocked bookcase stood against one wall.

A very modern radio set, equipped for long and shortwave reception, completed the fittings.

"This is one of several hidden retreats established by my secret society," Mindoro explained.

Ham had carried his sword cane throughout the excitement. He used it to punch the soft upholstery of a chair, as if estimating its comfort.

"How did you come to organize your political society in secrecy?" he asked. "That has been puzzling me all along. Did you expect a thing like this Tom Too menace to turn up?"

"Not exactly," replied Mindoro. "Secrecy is the way of the Orient. We do not come out in the open and settle things in a knock-down-and-drag-out fashion, as you Americans do. Of course, the secrecy was incorporated for our protection. The first move in seizing power is naturally to wipe out those who are running things. In the Orient, secret societies are not regarded as the insidious thing you Yanks consider them."

"Our first move is to find how things stand here," Doc put in.

"I shall secure that information," Mindoro declared. "I intend to depart at once."

"Can you move about in safety?"

"In perfect security. I will not go far—only to dispatch messengers to my associates."

Before departing, Mindoro showed Doc and the others three hidden exits from the room for use in emergency.

"These walls are impervious to sound," Mindoro explained. "You can play the radio. We have more than one broadcasting station here in Mantilla."

One of the concealed passages swallowed him.

DOC clicked on the radio. It was powerful. He picked up broadcasts from Australia, from China, from Japan, as he ran down the dial. He stopped on one of the local Mantilla stations. An announcer was speaking in English.

"We interrupt our musical program to read a news bulletin issued by the chief of police concerning the sinking of the liner *Malay Queen* in the Mantilla harbor not many minutes ago," said the radio announcer. "It seems that a group of four desperate criminals were trapped aboard the liner. They resisted arrest. Although many of the liner's passengers joined in the attempt to capture them, the four criminals took refuge in the hold. There they exploded a bomb which sank the vessel."

"Holy Cow!" Renny burst forth. "They've explained the whole thing with a slick bunch of lies!"

"This Tom Too is smooth!" clipped Ham, with the grudging admiration of one quick thinker for another. Ham himself was probably as mentally agile a lawyer as ever swayed a jury.

"Due to the foresight of brave Captain Hickman of the *Malay Queen*, the passengers were all taken ashore in safety before the four desperadoes exploded the bomb which sank the liner," continued the voice from the radio. "Several Mongols and half-castes among the passengers, who sought courageously to aid in subduing the four bad men, were slain."

"They're even making Tom Too's gang out as heroes!" Renny groaned.

"Flash!" suddenly exclaimed the radio announcer. "We have just been asked to broadcast a warning that the four killers reached shore from the sinking *Malay Queen*! They are now somewhere in Mantilla. Their names are not known, but their descriptions follow."

Next came an accurate delineation of how Doc, Ham, Renny, and Mindoro looked.

"These men are desperate characters," finished the radio announcer. "The police have orders to shoot them on sight. And Captain Hickman, skipper of the ill-fated *Malay Queen*, is offering a reward of ten thousand dollars for the capture of each of these men, dead or alive, preferably dead."

Music now came from the radio. Doc turned over to the short wave side and soon picked up the station of the Mantilla police. Mantilla seemed to have a very modern police department. The station was repeating descriptions of Doc and the others, with orders that they be shot on sight.

"It looks kinda tough," Renny suggested dryly.

"Tough!" snorted Ham. "It's the dangedest jam we were ever in!"

MINDORO was long-faced with worry when he returned.

"The situation is indeed serious," he informed them. "My associates succeeded in trapping one of Tom Too's Mongols. They scared the fellow into talking. The information they secured was most ominous. Tom Too is ready to seize power!"

"Exactly how is it to be managed?" Doc questioned.

"The physicians who attend the president have been bribed," Mindoro explained. "The president will be poisoned, and the physicians will say he died of heart failure. The moment this news gets out, rioting will start. The rioters will be Tom Too's men, working under his orders.

"Tom Too will step in and take charge of the police, many of whom are his men, or in his service because of bribes. They will put down the rioting with an iron hand—a simple matter since the rioting will be staged deliberately. Tom Too will be touted in newspapers and over the radio as the iron man who took charge in the crisis. He will ride into power on a wave of public good will."

"That is the sort of plan which will work in this day and age!" Ham declared savagely.

"It doesn't sound like pirate methods!" Renny grunted.

"Tom Too is a modern edition of a pirate," Doc pointed out dryly. "If he should sail into port with his warships, as buccaneers did in the old days, he wouldn't get to first base. For one thing, the Luzon Union army and navy would probably whip him. If they didn't, a few dozen foreign warships would arrive, and that would be his finish."

A messenger, a husky patrolman on the Mantilla police force, whom Mindoro trusted, arrived bearing a change of garments for all four of the refugees.

Doc studied the patrolman with interest. The officer's uniform consisted of khaki shorts which terminated above the knees, blouse and tunic of the same hue, and a white sun helmet. The man's brown feet and legs were bare of covering.

"Have Tom Too's men sought to bribe you?" Doc asked.

"All same many time," admitted the officer in beach English. "Me no likee. Me say so."

"They tell you who to see in case you changed your mind?"

"They give me name fella come alongside if I want some Tom Too's dolla'," was the reply.

"They told you who to see if you wanted on Tom Too's payroll, eh?" Doc murmured.

"Lightee."

Doc's golden eyes roved over his fellows.

"Brothers," he said softly, "I have an idea!"

Chapter XV
RESCUE TRAIL

SOME thirty minutes later, a husky Mantilla policeman could be seen leaving the vicinity of the secret room to which Juan Mindoro had led Doc Savage, Ham, and Renny.

The cop twiddled his long billy in indolent fashion, as though he had no cares. Yet he covered ground swiftly until he reached a sector of Mantilla given over almost entirely to Chinese shops and dwellings.

Here, he approached the driver of a small, horse-drawn conveyance known as a *caleso*. The driver was leaning sleepily against his mangy pony. The cop accosted him with an air of furtiveness.

"Alee same come by change of mind."

"No savvy," said the surly *caleso* driver.

"Me likee many pesos," continued the cop patiently. "Tom Too got. Me want. Me get idea come to you chop chop. You fixee."

The *caleso* driver's evil face did not change.

"Seat yourself in my lowly conveyance, oh lord," he said in flowery Mandarin.

The cop hopped into the vehicle with alacrity, crossed his bare brown legs and settled back.

The *caleso* clattered down many streets that would not pass as decent American alleys. These were swarming with people either coming from the excitement at the bay front, or going. The inhabitants of Mantilla were of every conceivable nationality, not a few of them a conglomerate of all the others. Mantilla seemed to be a caldron in which the bloods of all races were intermingled.

Several times, policemen or other individuals cast knowing leers at the big cop riding in the *caleso*. This was evidence the driver of the vehicle had corrupted more than one man. The mere fact that a cop was riding in this *caleso* was an indication he was en route to receive a bribe from Tom Too's paymaster.

The *caleso* halted before an ancient stone building.

"Will you consent to alight, oh mighty one," said the driver in Mandarin. The contempt in his beady, sloping eyes belied his flowery fashion of speech.

The big policeman got out. He was conducted into a filthy room where an old hag sat on the floor, cracking nuts with a hammer and a block of hardwood.

Only a close observer would have recognized the three irregularly spaced taps which the old crone gave a nut as a signal.

A door in the rear opened. The *caleso* driver herded the cop into a passage. The place smelled of rats, incense, and cooking opium.

They reached a low, smoky room. Perhaps a dozen Orientals were present, lounging about lazily.

Three men were manacled in a single pile upon the floor—handcuffed ankle to ankle and wrist to wrist.

They were Monk, Long Tom, and Johnny.

The *caleso* driver shoved the big cop.

"Step inside, oh resplendent one," he directed with a thinly veiled sneer. "Tom Too is not here, but his lieutenants are."

The next instant the *caleso* driver smashed backward to the stone wall. He was unconscious before he struck it.

Some terrible, unseen force had struck his jaw, breaking it and all but wiping it off his face.

THE Orientals in the low room cackled like chickens disturbed on a roost. The cackling became enraged howling.

Over the excited bedlam penetrated a sound more strange than any ever heard in that ill-omened room. A sound that defied description, it seemed to trill from everywhere, like the song of a jungle bird. It was musical, yet confined itself to no tune; it was inspiring, but not awesome.

The sound of Doc!

The human pile that was Monk, Long Tom, and Johnny went through an upheaval.

"Doc!" Monk squawled. "By golly, he's found us!"

The form in the airy garb of a Mantilla cop seemed to grow in size, to expand. A giant literally materialized before the eyes of those in the room—a giant who was Doc Savage.

Doc spat out bits of gum he had used to change the character of his face. He whipped forward, and there was such speed in his motion that he seemed but a shadow cast across the gloomy den.

The first Oriental in his path dodged wildly. The fellow apparently got clear—the tips of Doc's sinewy bronze fingers, now stained brown, barely touched the man. Yet the slant-eyed one dropped as though stricken through the heart.

A Mongol plucked a revolver from the waistband of his slack pantaloons. It tangled in the shirt tail which hung outside his trousers. He fought to free it. Then there was a sound like an ax hitting a hollow tree, and he fell.

The heavy hardwood stub of the cop's club had knocked him senseless.

Another man was touched by the tips of Doc's fingers. Then two more. The trio were hardly caressed before they became slack, senseless heaps upon the floor.

"His touch is death!" shrieked a Mongol.

That was exaggerated a little. Doc only wore metal thimbles upon his fingertips, in each of which was a needle containing a drug which put a man to sleep instantly. And kept him asleep for hours!

The thimbles were so cleverly constructed that only a close examination would disclose their presence.

Another Oriental went down before Doc's magic touch.

Gun muzzles began lapping flame. Lead shattered the oil lamp which furnished the only illumination.

Putting out the light was a mistake. With the darkness came terror. Yellow men imagined they felt the caress of those terrible fingers. They ducked madly, struck with fury, and sometimes hit each other. Two or three separate fights raged. Coughing guns continued to add to the bedlam.

Panic grew.

"The outer air is sweet, my brothers!" shrilled a voice in Mandarin.

No other impetus was needed. The Mongols headed for the door like skyrockets. Reaching the street, each vied with the other to be the first around the nearest corner.

The old hag lookout, who had made her nut-cracking a signal, had been bowled over in the rush. But now she legged after them.

MONK, Long Tom, and Johnny were scrambling about in their excitement.

"Hold still, you tramps!" Doc chuckled.

Doc's casehardened bronze hands closed over Johnny's handcuffs. They tightened, strained, wrenched—and the links snapped.

Johnny was not surprised. He had seen Doc do things like this on other occasions. Long Tom's bracelets succumbed to the bronze man's Herculean strength.

Monk's irons, however, were a different matter. Monk himself possessed strength far beyond the usual—sufficient to break ordinary handcuffs. His captors must have discovered that—the time he broke loose to write the message on the mirror—and decorated him with heavier cuffs. The links that joined them were like log chains.

"They moved you to various parts of the liner, so I couldn't find you, didn't they?" Doc asked.

"We were changed to different staterooms half a dozen times," Monk told him. "Doc, I don't see how you lived through that voyage. Practically every man of the crew was on Tom Too's payroll, to say nothing of the swarm of pirates that were among the passengers."

Doc went to work on the locks of Monk's enormous leg and arm irons. They were not difficult. Within thirty seconds, they fell away, expertly picked.

"This place isn't healthy for us!" he warned. "Tom Too's men will swarm around here in a few minutes."

Searching, they found a back exit.

"This place was a sort of headquarters for Tom Too's organization in Mantilla," said Johnny.

Johnny seemed little the worse for his period of captivity. His glasses, which had the magnifying lens on the left side, were missing, however. That was no hardship, since Johnny had nearly normal sight in his right eye.

The pale electrical wizard, Long Tom, had a black eye and a cut lip as souvenirs.

The furry Monk showed plenty of wear and tear. His clothes now amounted to little more than a loin cloth. His rusty red hide was cut, scratched, bruised; his reddish fur was crusted with dried blood.

"They pulled a slick one when they caught us in New York," Monk rumbled. "One of them came staggering into the skyscraper office with red ink spilled all over him, pretending he'd been stabbed nearly to death. He got us all looking down in the street to see his assailant. Then his pals walked in and covered us with guns."

Persons stared at the four men curiously. Thinking the cop had arrested the other three, some sought to follow. But they were soon outdistanced. Doc hurried the pace.

They returned to Mindoro's hideout by a circuitous route.

THERE was a hilarious reunion when they all met in the secret, soundproofed room. Renny cuffed Johnny and Long Tom about delightedly with his huge paws, rumbling, "I'll teach you two guys to go and get yourselves caught and cause us so much trouble!"

Monk leered at his old sparring mate, Ham, rubbed his hairy paws in anticipation, and started forward.

Ham flourished his sword cane menacingly. "I'll pick your teeth with this thing if you lay a hand on me, you ugly missing link!"

Mindoro stood to one side. He was smiling a little, the first time his face had registered anything but gloom for some days past. The fact that this remarkable group of fighting men were together again had heartened him.

"I had a lucky break in hunting them," Doc told Mindoro. "They were being held at the place where I was taken to be put on Tom Too's payroll. I expected a more difficult hunt."

The big policeman with whom Doc had changed clothes was still present. Doc gave him back his garments.

The boisterous greeting subsided. Doc put questions to the three he had rescued.

"Did you overhear anything concerning Tom Too's plans?" he asked.

It was Johnny, the bony archaeologist, who answered. "A little. For instance, we learned how he is going to take over the government of the Luzon Union."

Johnny's information jibed with that obtained by Mindoro, it developed as he talked.

"Tom Too's more villainous and ignorant followers are going to stage the rioting," Johnny continued. "They must be a mighty tough crew, because he hasn't dared to let them come into Mantilla. They're camped on a small island to the north, the whole lot of them, waiting for word which will bring them here."

"He hasn't let them come into Mantilla because he's afraid they'd start looting ahead of time," Long Tom put in. "I don't think he has any too strong a hold over the pirates camped on the island."

"I *know* he hasn't!" interposed Monk. "I heard talk which revealed the pirates on the island are tired of waiting, and are on the point of rebellion. They figure themselves as liable to get shot in the rioting, so they're not so hot about their part in the whole plot. There was talk that they intended to make a raid of their own on Mantilla, in the old-fashioned pirate way."

"They must be ignorant!" Ham snapped. "Otherwise, they'd know a thing like that won't work in this day and age."

"Of course they're dumb," Monk grinned. "Tom Too went up there the minute he landed. He knows he's got to calm them down, or his scheme to seize the Luzon Union is shot."

Mindoro put in a sharp query. "What does Tom Too look like?"

"We didn't see him," Monk said sorrowfully. "We've got no idea what he looks like."

"How did Tom Too go to the island?" Doc asked sharply.

"By boat."

"You sure?"

"I sure am!"

"That's swell."

"Huh?" Monk grunted wonderingly.

"We can get hold of a plane and beat him there," Doc said grimly. "Provided you heard the name of the island?"

"Shark Head Island."

"I can mark the spot on a map!" declared Mindoro eagerly. "The place is an all-night run up the coast by boat."

Chapter XVI
THE BUCCANEER MUTINY

THAT night, a ceiling of black cloud hung at ten thousand feet. Under this, darkness lurked, thick and damply foul as the breath of some carnivorous monster.

The hour was early. Lights glowed through the open walls of huts. Here and there a torch flared as some native went about night duties.

A mile high, just below the cloud ceiling, a plane boomed through the night. Exhaust stacks of its two big radial motors lipped blue flame occasionally. The tips of the single far-flung wing and the spidery rudder mechanism bore no distinguishing lights. The craft was an amphibian—the landing wheels cranking up into wells on the hull when it was desired to make a landing in water. In a pinch, the craft could carry sixteen passengers.

It carried only six now—Doc Savage and his five friends.

Mindoro had remained behind in Mantilla. He had been unwilling to be the stay-at-home, at first. But Doc had pointed out it was highly important that Mindoro assembled his loyal forces and prepare to resist Tom Too's *coup d'état*.

Mindoro's first move would be to throw a dependable guard around the president of the Luzon Union, so there would be no poisoning. The doctors who had been bribed by Tom Too's men to proclaim the poison death a case of heart failure, were to be disposed of. Doc hadn't inquired just what the disposal would be. It probably would not be pleasant.

It had been a simple matter for Mindoro to secure the plane for Doc's use.

Renny was navigating the plane. This was not an easy task, since they could not see the heavens, or the contour of the land below. Renny, thanks to his engineering training, was an expert at this sort of thing.

Doc handled the controls. Doc had studied flying just as intensively as he had worked upon other things. He had many thousands of hours of flying time behind him, and it was evidenced in his uncanny skill with the controls.

"No sign of a radio working on Tom Too's boat," Long Torn reported.

The scrawny-looking electrical wizard had hoped to locate Tom Too by radio compass.

"That's too bad," he added. "If we could find him, we'd make short work of him."

Due to the darkness of the night, there was no hope of sighting the craft bearing the pirate chief to such of his followers as were camped on Shark Head Island.

"We're getting near the place!" Renny warned, after studying a group of course figures he had scribbled.

"Any chance the presence of a plane will make them suspicious?" Ham wanted to know.

"The Mantilla to Hong Kong air mail route is not far from here," Doc pointed out. "Probably they're accustomed to hearing planes."

Several minutes passed, the miles dropping behind, two to the minute.

"There we are!" Renny boomed.

SCORES of camp fires had appeared a mile beneath the plane. Distance made them seem small as sparks.

Monk was using binoculars. "That's the layout, all right. I can see some of them."

"Take the controls," Doc directed Renny.

Renny complied. He was an accomplished pilot, as were all of Doc's companions.

"All you fellows understand what you're to do," Doc told them. "Fly on several miles, mounting into the clouds, until you're sure the motor sound has receded from the hearing of those below. Then you are to cut the motors, swing back, and land secretly in the little bay on the north end of the island."

"We got it straight," said Renny. "The pirates are camped on the larger bay at the south end."

"You sure you want us to stay away from them?" Monk grumbled.

"Until you hear from me," Doc replied.

Doc already had a parachute strapped on. As casually as if he were stepping out of the lobby of the New York skyscraper which held his headquarters, he lunged out of the plane. Safely clear, he plucked the ripcord.

With a swish like great wings unfolding, the silken 'chute folds squirted out. The slight shock as it opened completely bothered Doc not at all.

Grasping the shrouds of the 'chute, he pulled them down on one side, skidding the lobe in the direction he wished to take.

Marine charts of the thousands of large and small islands which made up the Luzon Union group had held a detailed map of Shark Head Island. The bit of land was low, swampy, about a mile long and half as wide. Its name came from the reef-studded bay at the lower end. This was shaped something like the snaggle-toothed head of a shark.

Doc landed on the rim of this bay, perhaps three hundred yards from the pirate camp.

The corsairs were making considerable noise. Tom-toms and wheezy wind instruments made a savage medley of sound. It was Chinese in character.

Doc got out of the 'chute harness and bundled it and the silk mushroom under an arm. Searching through the rank jungle growth in the direction of the buccaneer camp, his golden eyes discerned figures gliding about with the jittery motion common to action of the Oriental stage. From time to time, these persons made elaborate cutting motions at each other with swords.

They were entertaining themselves with some sort of a play.

Doc moved out to the sandy portion of the beach. He scooped several gallons of sand into the 'chute and tied it there. Then he entered the water, carrying the parachute and its burden.

Doc's bronze skin was still dyed with the brown stain he had applied when masquerading as the Mantilla policeman. The stain would not wash off.

He swam out into the bay. Where the water was deep, he let the 'chute sink. It would never be found here.

His mighty form cleaved forward with a speed that left a swirling wake. Near the middle of the bay, he headed directly for the grouped camp fires. They were near the shore.

A hundred yards from them, Doc lifted his voice in a shout. His voice had changed so as to be nearly unrecognizable. It was high, squeaky. It was the voice he intended to use in his new character.

"Hey, you fella!" he shrilled. "Me velly much all in! Bling help alongside!"

He got instant attention. The play acting stopped. Yellow men dived for their arms.

Simulating a man near exhaustion, Doc floundered toward the beach.

A villainous horde bristling with weapons, the pirates surged down to meet him.

Doc hauled himself onto the sand. With fierce cries, a score of men pounced upon him. They brandished knives, a crooked-bladed kris or two, swords, pistols, rifles, even very modern submachine guns.

DOC'S iron nerve control was never more evident than at that instant. He lay like a man so tired as to be incapable of another movement, although it seemed certain death was upon him.

"Allee same bling you fella big news!" he

whined in his piping voice. "Gimme dlink. Me one played-out fella."

They hauled Doc roughly to the fires. They surrounded him, row after row, those in front squatting so the men behind could see. There were Malays, Mongols, Japs, Chinese, white men, blacks—as conglomerate a racial collection as it would be possible to imagine. Turbaned Hindus mingled with them.

One thing they all had in common—lust and butchery, disease and filth, greed and treachery was stamped upon every countenance.

Doc's jaws were pried apart. He was fed a revolting concoction of *kaoliang* cooked with rice. It was a distinct effort to choke the stuff down. A spicy wine followed. Somebody went for more wine. Doc decided it was time to revive.

"Me stalt out in *chug-chug* boat," Doc explained. Strictly, this wasn't a lie. They had ridden out to the anchored seaplane in Mantilla in a motor boat.

"Him boat stop *chug-chug*. Me swim. Get this place by-by. Me plenty much play out."

"Do you speak Mandarin, oh friend who comes in the water?" asked a man in Mandarin.

"I do, oh mighty lord," Doc admitted in the same flamboyant lingo.

"How did you pass the tigers who watch at the mouth of the bay, our brothers who are upon guard?"

"I saw no tigers, illustrious one," said Doc. That was no lie. He hadn't seen the guards.

"The guardian tigers shall have their tails twisted!" roared the pirate. He whirled, snarling orders for some of his followers to hurry and relieve the guards.

"What brings you here?" the corsair asked Doc.

"It is said that man differs from sheep in that man knows when he is to be slaughtered," Doc said in long-winded fashion.

"You are one of Tom Too's sons?"

"I was. But no man wishes to be the son of a dog that would bite off its tail that it might walk upon its rear legs and be like a man."

The buccaneer was perplexed. "What is this talk of slaughtered sheep and dogs who wish to be men, oh puzzling one?"

DOC sat up. He did not lift his voice very much, for he was supposed to be a man suffering from exhaustion, a man who had come a long distance with important news. Nevertheless, his low and powerful tones carried far enough that several hundred slant-eyed and pasty-faced fiends heard his words.

"It is of Tom Too whom I speak, my brothers," he proclaimed. "The man who is your leader has told you that your share of his design upon the Luzon Union is to play the part of looters, that he may be the hero for subduing you.

"The real truth is that you will be shot down like wild ducks upon the hunting preserve of a rich merchant. Are you such fools as to believe many of you will not die? Tom Too will not hesitate to sacrifice you. He considers you rabble. You are the dog tail which he will cut off, and being rid of you, set himself up as a king.

"Are you without sense, that you think he will divide so rich a prize as you would the money box from a looted junk?

"Such money as Tom Too draws from the Luzon Union must be taken slowly, as a tapeworm sucks nourishment from the stomach of a fat money changer. There will not be great sums at one time. Do you think he will make you rich men, my brothers? If you do, you are but ostriches with your heads in the sand!"

"You have heard this is what Tom Too intends to do?" asked the spokesman of the pirate men, speaking furiously. "Does he intend to slay us while he is making himself a hero?"

"Why do you think I came here?"

"Truly, that puzzles me."

"I do not wish to see hundreds of our brotherhood meet death," Doc replied gravely. "I have warned you."

Doc had been speaking with all the firmness he could put into his powerful voice. This had the desired results. The pirates were virtually convinced Tom Too intended to double-cross them. No doubt they had harbored such suspicions before, as evidenced by the dissention which was bringing Tom Too here tonight.

"Even now, Tom Too comes to speak honeyed words into your ears," Doc added loudly. "If you are but flies, you will flock to the sweetness of his speech. If you are men, you will mount Tom Too's head upon a tall pole in your camp, that the buzzards may look closely at one of their kind."

This was a bold speech. It would either sway the pirates from their leader, or cause them to turn upon Doc.

"We have indeed considered the head on the pole," smirked the leader of the murderous horde, "and the thought finds favor."

Doc knew his propaganda had done its work.

"Tom Too will arrive by boat," he declared. "Then is the time to act—the instant he arrives."

"Wise words, oh brother," was the reply.

Excitement was mounting in the corsair encampment. Doc had spoken throughout in Mandarin, the principal tongue in China, and the one which most of the men understood. But now such of them as did not understand Mandarin, were getting a secondhand version of Doc's speech.

Doc listened, cold lights of humor in his golden eyes. The talk was making Tom Too out as the blackest of villains—which he certainly was.

"WHEN, oh one who brought important news, will Tom Too arrive?" a slant-eyed devil asked.

"Near the hour when the sun smiles over the eastern horizon," was Doc's wordy reply.

It speedily developed that there would be no sleep in the buccaneer encampment that night. From a score of matting tents and thatched huts came the steely rasp of swords and knives on whetstones.

The variety of weapons possessed by the cutthroats was astounding. Spears that were nothing but sharpened sticks were being prepared by having the points charred into hardness in the fires.

One yellow man with a face half removed by some sword slash in the past was carefully refurbishing a gun consisting of a bamboo tube mounted on a rough stock. This was charged with the crudest kind of black powder and a small fistful of round pebbles, and fired by applying a bit of glowing punk to a touchhole. It was such a gun as had been used by the Chinese thousands of years ago.

Contrasting greatly with these were a dozen or so late-model Maxims which could spew five hundred bullets a minute.

As their rage increased, the pirates snarled at each other like mongrel dogs. One man struck down another with a sword at some slight. The corpse was ignored, as though it were so much discarded meat.

Even Doc was appalled at the bloody savagery of these outcasts of the Orient.

Seven speedy launches were made ready. Doc gathered these were the only fast craft in the pirate flotilla, the other vessels being junks and sampans and a few old schooners and weatherbeaten sloops.

The corsair fleet was anchored in the bay. Due to the darkness, Doc had not yet seen the vessels. They would probably be a sight to remember.

The hours dragged. Doc mingled with the horde of butcherers, adding a judicious word here and there.

If he could get these human scourges to wipe out their leader, the rest would be simple. Mindoro could assemble a force able to deal with them, even should a large proportion of the Luzon Union army and navy be under Tom Too's domination.

Doc wondered briefly about his five men. He had not heard their plane land. That was a good sign. The pirates had been making a good deal of noise, enough to cover the silent arrival of the plane at the tiny bay which the map showed at the other end of Shark Head Island.

Dawn came up like a red fever in the east. It flushed the clouds which still lowered overhead. It set the jungle birds fluttering and whistling and screaming.

The yell of a lookout pealed, couched in pidgin English.

"Tom Too! Him boat come!"

Chapter XVII
THE SUNKEN YACHT

THE yellow horde surged for the boats. First arrivals got the seats, to the howling disgust of those behind. There followed a process of natural selection which resulted in the strongest fighters manning the boats. The weaker ones were simply hauled out by the more husky.

Every slant-eyed devil was madly anxious to go along. Tom Too was as famous a pirate as ever scourged the China coast. A hand in his slaying would be something to brag to one's grandchildren about when one was an old man and good for nothing but to sit in the shade of the village market and chew betel nut.

A toothless giant, great brass earrings banging against the corded muscles of his neck, grabbed Doc and sought to pluck him out of the largest and fastest launch. The pirate never was quite positive what then befell him. But he staggered back with both hands over a jaw that felt as though it had tried to chew a fistful of dynamite which exploded in the process.

Doc had no intention of being left behind. He wanted to see that Tom Too didn't talk the corsairs out of their murderous intention.

"Let us proceed, my sons!" shrieked one of the men.

The launches rushed across the bay, keeping in a close group.

Doc now had a chance to observe the remainder of the pirate fleet. The vessels were anchored in the bay by the score. The red flush of dawn painted them with a lurid, sinister crimson glow, making them seem craft bathed in blood.

Many were Chinese junks with bluff lines, high poops, and overhanging stems. These were made to appear top-heavy by the high pole masts and big sails with battens running entirely across. The steering rudders, sometimes nothing but a big oar, hung listless in the water.

Many sampans mingled in the fleet, so small as to be little more than skiffs. Some were propelled only with oars, others with sails. All had little matting-roofed cabins in the bows.

The rest of the armada was comprised of sloops and schooners of more prosaic description.

"Tom Too boat, him come in bay *chop-chop!*" sang a man in beach English.

Doc's golden eyes appraised Tom Too's craft.

The vessel was as pretty a thing as ever graced a millionaire's private wharf. It was a fifty-foot, bridge-deck yacht. Its hull shone with the whiteness of scrubbed ivory. The mahogany of the superstructure had a rich sheen. Brasswork glistened.

Several yellow men stood on the glass-enclosed bridge deck.

"We no waste time in talk-talk!" shouted a pirate furiously. "All same finish job damn quick!"

The group of launches spread out in a half moon. They held their fire until within less than two hundred feet of the pretty yacht.

THEN Maxim guns opened with a grisly roar. The weapons shook and smoked, sucked in ammo belts and spewed empty cartridges. A half dozen slant-eyed men clutched each weapon as though it were a mad dog, to keep recoil jar from throwing it off the target.

Automatic pistols popped; rifles spoke with loud smashes. Doc saw the ancient gun with a barrel of bamboo spit its fistful of pebbles at the yacht like a shower of rain.

Glass enclosing the bridge deck of the yacht literally vanished in the lead storm. The cutthroats inside, taken by surprise, were all but fused together in a bloody mass.

"Sinkum boat!" howled a corsair. "Shoot hole in hull!"

The guns were now turned at the yacht water line. The planking splintered, disintegrated. Water poured in. The yacht promptly listed.

Suddenly there was a terrific blast in the yacht entrails. The hull split wide. A bullet had reached explosive, probably dynamite, carried in the little hold.

The cruiser sank with magical speed. A single yellow head appeared, but the swimmer was callously murdered.

"Tom Too gone join his ancestors!" squawled the killers.

Doc Savage would have liked to inquire which of the men in the cruiser cabin had been Tom Too. But he couldn't do that, for he was supposed to have known the pirate king.

The launches now cruised about in hopes of picking up the body of Tom Too. Many a slant-eyed Jolly Roger expressed a profane desire to possess Tom Too's ears as a souvenir. Bandying ribald jokes as though the whole affair were a lark, the pirates reached an agreement to smoke Tom Too's head and mount it on a pole for all to observe. His body would be skinned, his hide tanned, and each man presented with a piece large enough for a memento. Human fiends, these!

There was much talk as to who had actually killed Tom Too. Many claimed he had not appeared on deck at all, but had remained below like the hiding dog that he was, and had been slain by the explosion.

They didn't find Tom Too's carcass. Disgusted somewhat, they headed for camp to celebrate.

Much strong Chinese wine would be consumed, pots of *kaoliang* cooked with rice prepared, and those who had opium would divide with those who had none. It would be a jamboree to remember.

Doc Savage ducked away from this uproar at the first opportunity. His work here was done. He would join his waiting friends. A quick flight back to Mantilla, and they would assist Mindoro in setting up machinery which would make short shift of the leaderless pirates.

Doc had not progressed fifty yards from camp when snarling, hissing yellow men set upon him.

THE slant-eyed fellows attacked in silence. Pistols were thrust in their belts. Pockets bulged with hand grenades. Yet they used only the crooked kris and short sword.

It was obvious the assailants wanted to finish Doc without attracting notice from the pirate camp.

Doc sprang backward, at the same time scooping up a wrist-thick bamboo pole which chanced to be underfoot. With this, he delivered a whack that bowled over the first swordsman.

Since they wanted no noise, he decided to make some.

"Help!" he piped in his shrill, assumed tone, "Help! Chop-chop!"

Instantly, pirates surged from the camp.

Doc's assailants abandoned their effort at quiet. They plucked out firearms.

Bounding aside, Doc put himself behind the bole of an enormous tree. Bullets jarred into the tree trunk. They did no harm—the attackers could not even see Doc behind the shelter. The tree was a good five feet thick, hiding Doc from view.

The yellow men rushed the tree, came around it from either side.

They stopped and goggled, eyes nearly hanging out.

Their quarry had vanished as though by magic. For two score feet up the tree trunk, no branches grew. The possibility that their human game had run up the tree, squirrel fashion, was slow occurring to them.

When they did look up, the foliage at the top of the tree had swallowed Doc.

One of the gang hurled a grenade at the approaching pirates. The explosion killed two men. A short, bloody fight followed. No quarter was given or expected. Four minutes later, not one of Doc's attackers remained alive.

Doc slid down the tree.

"These fella tly kill me," he explained. "Who these fella? How they get this place?"

He spoke in pidgin. The reply was couched in the same slattern tongue.

"These fella belong Tom Too's bodyguald!"

Cold lights came into Doc's strange golden eyes. "How they get this place?"

"We not know."

A short search was pushed in the immediately adjacent jungle, but no skulkers were found. The pirates repaired to their encampment. The preparations for the celebration went forward, although not as boisterously as before. The buccaneers were wondering how the members of Tom Too's personal bodyguard happened to be upon Shark Head Island.

Doc was doing some pondering also. The thoughts which came to him were not pleasant. He had an awful suspicion Tom Too was not dead, after all.

Within the hour, this suspicion crystallized into certainty.

A WEAZENED little yellow man appeared before Doc. No other corsairs were near.

The shriveled fellow extended a bamboo cylinder.

... scooping up a bamboo pole ... he delivered a whack that bowled over the first swordsman.

"This belong alongside you," he smirked.

Doc took the bamboo tube. Inside was a rolled sheet of thick, glossy Chinese paper. It bore writing:

The fox is not trapped so easily, bronze man. I had the foresight to come ashore during the night and send my boat into the bay with only the crew aboard, for I did not trust the rabble you have turned against me.

The gods were with me last night, for I came upon a plane in the bay at the north end of the island. Five men loitered near.

And now, bronze man, I have five prisoners instead of the three whom I held for so long.

Your life is the price which will buy theirs. But I do not want you to surrender. You are too dangerous a prisoner.

You will commit suicide, take your own life, in front of the assembled men of the camp. I will have observers present. When they bring me word of your death, your five men will be released.

No doubt you distrust my word. But I assure you it will be kept this once.

TOM TOO

Doc read this missive through with the cold expressionlessness of an image of chilled steel.

The shriveled messenger backed away. Doc let him go, apparently not even glancing toward the fellow.

The messenger mingled with the pirates, dodging about in the yellow horde with great frequency. It was apparent he was seeking to lose himself. Several times, he glanced furtively in the direction of the big brown man to whom he had delivered the message tube.

Doc seemed to be paying no attention. Finally, he entered a convenient tent of poles and matting.

The weazened messenger scuttled out of camp. He took to the jungle undergrowth and traveled with extreme caution. Each time he crossed a clearing, he waited on the opposite side a while, watching his back trail. He discerned nothing to alarm.

Nevertheless, the man was being followed. Doc Savage traveled much of the time in the upper lanes of the jungle, employing interlacing branches and creepers for footholds and handgrips. His tremendous strength, his amazing agility, made the treacherous and difficult way seem an easy one.

The shrunken messenger quickened his pace. He had been promised a reward for delivering the bamboo message tube. Tom Too had told him where it would be hidden, in a hollow tree not far ahead.

He reached the tree, thrust an arm into a cavity in the trunk, and brought out a packet. It was several inches square, very weighty.

"Him heavy like velly many pesos inside!" chortled the man.

Greedily, he tore off the wrappings.

There was a red-hot flash, a leviathan of flame that seemed to swallow the man's body. A mushroom of gray-black smoke spouted. Out of this flew segments of the unfortunate one's carcass, as though the fiery leviathan were spitting it out.

The package had contained a bomb.

Tom Too had planned that this man should never lead anyone who followed him to the hiding place of the master pirate.

Chapter XVIII
PAYMENT IN SUICIDE

DOC SAVAGE circled the spot where the weazened man had died. He sought the trail left by the one who had placed the bomb. His golden eyes missed nothing, for they had been trained through the years to pick out details such as went unnoticed to an ordinary observer.

A vine which hung unnaturally, a bush which had been carefully bent aside and then replaced, but which had a single leaf wrong side up—these vague signs showed Doc the course taken by the bomb depositor. The fellow had come and gone by the same route.

The trail turned out to be a blank. It terminated at the beach, where a boat had landed the man and taken him away.

Taking to the trees for greater speed, Doc hurried to the bay at the north end of the island. The plane was there, anchored a few yards offshore.

There was no sign of life about, except the jungle birds which twittered and screamed and fluttered the foliage.

Doc stood by a sluggish stream which emptied into the bay a few yards from the plane. He decided to try something.

Moving a little more than a rod down the shore, he suddenly sped into the open, crossed the narrow beach and shot like an arrow into the bay. He had appeared with blinding suddenness, and was in the water almost before an eye could bat.

Hence it was that a watching machine gunner got into action too late. A stream of bullets turned the water into a leaping suds where Doc had disappeared.

The gobble of the rapid firer galloped over the bay surface like satanic mirth. Then the noise stopped.

The gunner ran into the open, the better to see his quarry upon appearance. The man was stocky, broad, with a head like a ball of yellow cheese. He stood, gun ready perhaps a hundred yards from where Doc had entered the water.

Minute after minute, he waited. An evil grin began to wrinkle his moon of a face. He had killed the bronze devil!

He did not see the foliage part silently behind him. Nor did he hear the mighty form of a man who glided up to his back.

Awful agony suddenly paralyzed the fellow's arms. He dropped his machine gun. He groveled, struggled, kicked. He was flung to the sand. There he continued his fighting. But he might as well have tried to get out from under the Empire State Building.

He could hardly believe his eyes when he saw the giant who held him was the man he thought he had murdered.

Doc had simply swum underwater into the sluggish creek, crawled out and crept silently through the rank undergrowth to the attacker.

WITHOUT voicing a word, Doc continued to hold his victim helpless for the space of some minutes. Doc knew the psychology of fear. The longer the would-be murderer felt the terrible clutch of those metallic hands, the more terrified he would become. And the more frightened he was, the sooner he would tell Doc some things he wanted to know.

"Where is Tom Too?" Doc demanded. He spoke in his normal voice, couching the words in English.

"Me not know!" whined the captive in pidgin.

Doc carried the man into the jungle, found a small clearing, slammed the fellow on his back. The prisoner tried to scream, thinking he was to be slain.

But Doc merely stared steadily into the man's eyes. The gunner began to squirm. Doc's golden eyes had a weird quality; they seemed to burn into the soul of the captive, to reduce his brain to a beaten and helpless thing.

The man tried to shut his eyes to shut out the terrible power of those golden orbs. Doc held the man's eyelids apart.

Hypnotism was another art Doc had studied extensively. He had drained the resources of America on the subject, had studied under a surgeon in Paris who was so accomplished a hypnotist that he used it instead of an anaesthetic when he operated upon patients. A sojourn in mystic India had been added to Doc's perusal of the art. And he had conducted extensive experiments of his own. His knowledge was wide.

The gunner was not long succumbing. He went into sort of a living sleep.

"Where is Tom Too?" Doc repeated his earlier query.

"Me not know."

"Why don't you?"

"Me left at this place, watch canvas sky wagon. Tom Too no tell place him go."

Doc knew the man was telling the truth. The hypnotic spell was seeing to that.

"What about the five white men who were in the plane?" he demanded.

The reply was three words that froze Doc's great body.

"Him all dead."

FOR a long minute and a half, Doc neither moved, spoke, or breathed. The prisoner was not lying, not pulling a trick. The news was a ghastly shock.

"How did it happen?" Doc asked, and his voice was a low moan of a whisper that the gunner hardly heard.

"Tom Too, him use poison gas. Five white men, him sit on canvas sky wagon. Gas come. Five white men fall off, sinkee like log."

"Did you see this happen?"

"Too dalk see. Me hear. Men scleam, make big splash."

Doc was done. He dropped a hand into a pocket, brought it out with the needle-containing metal thimbles affixed to the fingertips. He touched the gunner. The fellow promptly slept.

Doc strode into the water and swam toward the plane. A few yards from it, he suddenly put on a terrific burst of speed. His corded arm shot up, grasped a wing strut. He swung aboard not an instant too soon—a great, slate-colored monster reached unsuccessfully for him, tooth-armored jaws gaping.

A shark! Other triangular fins cut the nearby surface.

Doc showed no perturbation over his narrow escape. But he felt slightly sick. No need to hunt for the bodies of his friends on the bottom of the bay, not with these hideous sea scavengers around.

Doc examined the fuel tanks of the plane, found them half full. He gave brief attention to the feed lines, up near the tanks.

The contents of the plane had not been disturbed. Doc got certain articles which he intended to use. They made a bundle a foot through, nearly four feet long.

He reached shore by the simple expedient of lifting the anchor and letting the breeze drift the amphibian to the beach.

Departing from the spot, he noted several birds lying dead in the jungle. The feathered bodies bore no marks. The gas released by Tom Too had undoubtedly killed them.

Doc did not attempt to search the island. It would have taken many hours to do a thorough job.

He headed for the pirate camp. He made speed, but he was careful of the bundle he carried.

The murderous horde were proceeding with their celebration over the death of Tom Too. They did not yet know he was not dead. The festivities consisted exclusively of drinking, gorging with food, smoking opium, to say nothing of frequent fights arising over disputes about whose bullet had actually slain Tom Too.

Doc singled out a husky half-caste who showed in the way he hogged wine and food that he was of a greedy nature. Several times, this fellow filched a jar of the celebration wine and carried it to his matting tent.

Doc was there to meet him when he arrived with one of the jars. In the seclusion of the tent, a lengthy conversation occurred. Once, when the half-caste learned some surprising news, it seemed certain a fight was imminent.

But a large roll of Luzon Union currency changed hands. After that, the half-caste became all smiles and nods of agreement.

The fellow belted on a big sword and went out to join the celebrants.

For upward of an hour, Doc worked furiously in the matting tent.

Stepping outside, he got a barrel of the gasoline used in the launches. This he placed, the bunghole open, near the matting tent.

His powerful voice pealed across the pirate camp.

"I would speak with all you fella!" he said in beach jargon. "All same come alongside plenty quick!"

Yellow men swarmed over, curious to hear what this giant had to say. They were puzzled about something else, too—the big man's voice had changed. It was no longer shrill, piping, but thunderous with latent power.

DOC surveyed the assemblage, standing just in front of the matting tent.

"I have made fools out of you!" he boomed in ordinary English, which most of the corsairs could probably understand. "I came here deliberately to persuade you to turn upon Tom Too!"

He went on, telling exactly what had happened. He informed them Tom Too was still alive. He flung out the note he had received, letting them read it, such as could read.

He carefully neglected any reference to his jaunt to the bay at the north end of the island, or his grisly discoveries there.

"Tom Too is holding my five friends!" he continued. "If I kill myself, he will release them. Therefore, I shall pay that price, so my friends may go free."

A remarkable change had swept the pirate horde. They glowered at Doc, muttering, fingering knives. The fact that the big man had stated he was going to kill himself to save his friends, made no good impression upon them. They were a callous lot.

"I shall now shoot myself!" Doc shouted. "You will all see my act. You can tell Tom Too."

The situation struck some of the corsairs as ridiculous, as indeed it was. The giant who had deceived them was crazy. Did he think Tom Too would release his five friends, once he was dead? Tom Too never kept his word, unless it was to his interest to do so.

Suddenly a husky half-caste sprang forward, waving his sword. It was the same fellow with whom Doc had conversed at length. The man's pants pockets bulged with Doc's money.

"Snake-dog!" he shrieked. "You stand in flont of my tent and befoul it! Fol that, I kill you!"

He rushed forward angrily.

Doc turned and dived into the tent, as though in flight. He seemed to stumble just inside the door, and fall flat.

Fully fifty pirates saw the half-caste's sword strike. The swordsman withdrew a blade that dripped red, and stepped to the tent door.

"My tent is luined!" he howled. "It shall be destloyed with flame!"

Whereupon, he kicked over the gasoline barrel. Fuel sloshed out. The half-caste struck a match and tossed it into the petrol. Flame instantly enveloped the tent.

The half-caste continued to dance around, as though in a great rage.

A close observer might have noticed three Mongols in the pirate crowd who swiftly planted themselves where they could watch all sides of the burning tent.

The flaming matting popped and cracked. Vile yellow smoke poured upward, mingling densely in the boughs of trees which overhung the spot.

The three watching Mongols squatted low, so there would be no chance of anyone running away from the blazing tent without being discovered in the act.

The fire raged fully thirty minutes. The tent had been erected upon a foundation of hardwood poles, and these gave off much heat.

LONG before the fire had burned out, the yellow cutthroats gathered in noisy groups to discuss the fact that Tom Too was still alive, and to ponder on what punishment would be theirs for turning against their master.

The three Mongols, however, took no part in this. They never removed the stares of their slant eyes from the conflagration.

When the remains of the tent had become glowing coals, the trio approached. With long poles, they knocked the embers apart.

They showed satisfaction at the sight of gray-white ash which was unmistakably burned bones. One of them raked out a partially consumed piece of bone and pocketed it.

To make certain, they dug into the earth upon which the tent had stood. There was no tunnel.

Throwing down the sticks, the three strode rapidly away. They did not take particular pains not to be seen. But they made sure none of the other pirates followed them.

The beach sand crunched softly under their bare feet. Birds twittered in the jungle. The clouds had cleared away overhead, and the sun was slamming down a hot glare.

"I did not think the bronze man would actually

kill himself, oh brothers," said one Mongol thoughtfully, speaking his native tongue. "But there is no doubt but that he did."

"He did not kill himself," another pointed out. "He was speared by the half-caste."

"And very well speared, too," chuckled the third. "And I have in my pocket a burned piece of the bronze man's bones. Tom Too should think highly of that souvenir."

"No doubt he will! Verily, this bronze devil has not been one thorn in our sides—he has been a whole thicket of them."

The three Mongols stepped into a small sampan, shoved off and paddled to the largest of the anchored junks.

The interior of this craft proved to be fitted in lavish fashion, with many tapestries, paintings done on silk and featuring dragons, rugs, and elaborately inlaid furniture.

Near the high stern, they entered a room which contained a modern-looking radio installation. One man threw the switch which started the motor generators, then seated himself at the key.

The other two Mongols stood beside him. Apparently they thought nothing of the incongruity of their surroundings, the commingling of the splendor of ancient China and the shiny copper wires, glistening tubes, and black insulation paneling of the radio transmitter.

The Mongol operator prepared to send.

There was a flash, a loud fizzing of blue flame from the upright instrument board.

The operator leaped up and made an examination. He found a short length of wire. This had short-circuited two important double-pole switches. The man cursed in the Mongol dialect.

"The apparatus is ruined!" he snarled. "It is strange the wire should fall upon the switches! Where did it come from?"

"Where from, indeed?" muttered another. "It is not electrical wire. It looks like a part of a small iron wire cable."

They discussed the mystery profanely for some minutes.

"We cannot send our news to Tom Too by radio," one complained. "We must now go to him in person."

They quitted the pirate junk.

Chapter XIX
TOM TOO'S LAIR

THE Mongol trio now took considerably more pains to see that none of the pirates had followed them. Plunging into the jungle, they turned northward. Occasionally they swore softly at noisy tropical birds; the feathered songsters insisted on following them with many shrill outcries.

Midway up the island, on the east shore, was a tiny inlet. It was not over a dozen feet wide and fifty deep. Branches interlaced a mat above it; creepers hung down into the water like drinking serpents.

A sampan was concealed in this. The boat was about thirty feet long, rather wide, and fitted with a mast. The matting sail was down and hanging carelessly over the little cabin in the bows.

The sampan had a modern touch in a powerful outboard motor.

The Mongol trio were about to step aboard when a startling development occurred.

A kris, sixteen inches of crooked, razor-sharp steel, came hissing out of the jungle. It missed one of the Mongols by inches, and embedded in a tree.

"Some dog has followed us!" rasped one man.

Drawing their own knives, as well as a spike-snouted pistol apiece, they charged the spot from which the kris had been thrown. Their stocky bodies crashed noisily in the tangled plant growth. Birds fled with an outburst of noise fit to wake the dead.

The knife thrower could not be found. There was no sign, not even a track.

"We will not waste more time, my sons," said a Mongol.

They entered the sampan. The outboard motor was twisted into life. The sampan went scooting out of the inlet.

The Mongols in their strange craft looked like a trio of innocent fishermen, for the waters of the Luzon Union swarmed with vessels such as this.

The tropical sun slanted down upon the waves with a glittering splendor. Spray tossed from the bows of the flying sampan scintillated like jewel dust. The air was sweet with salt tang. A hideous slate triangle of a shark fin cut across the bows.

Some four or five miles distant was another island, smaller than Shark Head. Tall palms crowned it. Sand of the beach was very white. The whole islet was like a salad of luxurious green set upon a snowy platter. It fascinated the eyes with its beauty. As the sampan swished close, the stench of the overripe vegetation of the island was like the sickening breath of a slaughterhouse.

The sampan curved around the island, made directly for a part of the beach which seemed a solid wall of plant life, hit it—and shot through into a pond of a harbor.

With a belligerent bang or two, the outboard died. Momentum sent the sampan gently aground.

The three Mongols scrambled over the sail piled atop the little bow cabin and leaped ashore.

MORE flowering plants flourished upon this islet than upon Shark Head. Their blooms were a carnival of color. But the place smelled like a swamp; foul, poisonous.

The Mongols gained higher ground. Here stood a house. It was built of hardwood, with the sides of shutterlike panels which could be opened to furnish relief from the heat.

Some half dozen evil-looking men sat in the main room of the house. A strange tension was noticeable in their attitude. They hardly moved a muscle. And when they did stir, it was done slowly and carefully, as if they were afraid of breaking something. They were like men in mortal fear of an impending fate.

The Mongols dashed in upon this solemn assemblage with loudly boisterous cries of elation.

"Where is Tom Too, oh brothers?" they demanded. "We have news for the master. Great news!"

In their excitement, the trio failed to note the air of terror about those in the room.

"Tom Too is not here," said one of the frightened men shrilly.

"Where did he go?"

"He did not say. He merely go."

The three Mongols could not hold back their news.

"The bronze devil is dead," one chortled. "The man did not have great wisdom, as we had thought. He was a fool. He thought he was saving his five friends. He did not know that the five were dead from the gas we released. So he got up before the dogs who would turn against Tom Too and made a speech, telling them who he was, and saying he was going to shoot himself. But one of the dogs cut off his head with a sword and burned his body in a tent. We watched flames consume the body. And I carry in my pocket a bit of the bronze man's bones, which was not consumed. Tom Too will want that souvenir. Where is the master?"

"He go away!" insisted one of the listeners shrilly.

The three Mongols suddenly perceived the tension in the room. They were surprised.

"What is wrong with you, oh trembling ones?"

The reply to that came from a totally unexpected source.

"They're afraid of gettin' pasted with lead!" boomed a slangy Yank voice.

A curtain across the end of the room suddenly snapped down. Five men lounged there. Each held a terrible little implement of death, a compact machine gun that looked like an overgrown automatic.

The five were Doc's friends—Monk, Renny, Long Tom, Ham, and Johnny.

THE three Mongols had been reared amid violence and death. They knew these five men, knew them for mortal enemies of their kind. They tried to make a fight of it.

Yellow hands sped for knives and pistols.

The half dozen others, who had been sitting so fearfully because they were covered by the guns of Doc's men, decided to aid the Mongols. They had been disarmed, but they dived for anything handy. Three got chairs. Two tore legs off a rickety table. Another seized a wine bottle, broke it, and rushed with the jagged end held like a dagger.

The room went into pandemonium. Knives flashed. Fists swung. Shillelahs whacked at heads. Guns bawled thunder.

The five white men concentrated on the three armed Mongols. Two dropped before the bullfiddle roars of the frightsome little machine guns. Monk closed with the third. A slap of his hairy hand sent the gun flying from the man's hand.

The Mongol struck with his knife. Monk evaded the blade with an ease astounding for one of his bulk, then pasted the yellow man with a hirsute fist. So terrific was the blow that the Mongol dropped his knife and staggered like a drunk, then fell.

Ham closed with a slant-eyed man who wielded a table leg. He fenced briskly, warding off terrific blows with deft parries of his bared sword cane. An instant later the yellow man sprang back, the ligaments in his wrist severed. Squawling for mercy, he shrank into a corner.

Renny pulped a nose with one of his monster fists. Long Tom and Johnny closed with respective opponents. They did not use their guns again. Barehanded, they were more than a match for the pirates.

The fray ended as suddenly as it had started. The corsairs lost their nerve, shoved their arms in the air, and joined Ham's victim in screeching for quarter.

"A fine gang of yallerhammers!" Monk complained. "Can't even fight enough to get a man warmed up!"

He picked up the Mongol he had struck. The fellow was the only one of the three messengers now alive.

"So you thought the gas got us, eh?" Monk growled. "Well, it didn't! You turned the stuff loose in the jungle so the wind would blow it toward us. We heard birds dropping dead. That warned us. So we dived overboard. It was dark enough so that we didn't have no trouble gettin' away! Then we hung around listenin' to you guys talk."

The Mongol only rolled his slitty eyes.

"We heard enough talk to learn Tom Too was gonna hole up here!" Monk continued fiercely. "So we made a raft out of two logs and paddled over. We been holdin' your pals here, hopin' Tom Too would turn up."

Ham swung over, sword cane poised ominously.

"This is the bird who bragged he was carrying a piece of Doc's burned skeleton!" he said grimly. "Let's see it!"

Monk searched the prisoner and soon brought the charred bit of bone to light.

Johnny, the gaunt archaeologist, took one look at

it—and laughed loudly as he turned the bone in his hand.

"That's a hunk of ordinary soup bone—off the leg of a cow!"

Knowing bones was part of Johnny's business. He could look at a skeleton from a prehistoric ruin and tell some remarkable things about the ancient to whom it originally belonged.

"Then Doc ain't dead, after all!" Monk grinned.

"That's fair guesswork," said Doc Savage from the doorway.

A ROAR of pleasure greeted Doc's appearance.

"How'd you work it?" Monk wanted to know.

"Used the old magician's stunt with mirrors to make it seem that I had been stabbed," Doc told him. "One of the pirates was in on the trick and swung the sword. I paid him plenty. The sword blade ran through a wad of cloth soaked with red ink instead of my body."

"Hey!" Monk interrupted. "How'd you get out of the tent?"

"The tent was set on fire. I had sprinkled chemicals on it so there would be a great deal of smoke. Overhead was a large tree branch. I had previously rigged a silk cord, small enough not to be noticeable, over the limb so a stout wire could be drawn up. I climbed that, concealed by the smoke, taking my mirrors along. It was not hard to get to other trees and away."

Doc nodded at the survivor of the Mongol trio. "This chap and his two companions went to a junk and prepared to communicate with Tom Too by radio. I broke off a bit of the wire cable with which I had climbed the tree limb, tossed it onto a couple of switches without being noticed, and put the apparatus out of commission. I figured they'd go to Tom Too in person.

"It was necessary to throw a knife at them to decoy them away from their sampan long enough for me to get aboard and find a place to hide under the sail."

Doc fell silent and let his eyes rove over the room. It was not often that he went into such detail in describing his methods. But finding his five friends alive had made him a bit talkative.

Long Tom whipped aside the curtain behind which he and the others had been concealed for a time. This disclosed an army type portable radio transmitter and receiver.

"This is undoubtedly the set the Mongols intended to communicate with from the junk," he declared. "But where's Tom Too?"

"Did he have a chance to dodge you?" Doc asked.

Ham tapped his sword cane thoughtfully. "He might have. We met two of the pirates on the bay shore, had a little fight, and the others came to see what it was about. Tom Too might have remained behind, seen we had cleaned up on his gang, then skipped out."

"He hasn't had a chance to leave the island!" Monk grunted. "We searched the shore line. There wasn't a boat around. And one man couldn't navigate by himself the log raft we came over on."

Countless times Doc's ability to observe any movement about him, however slight, had proved invaluable. It served again now.

His mighty form whipped aside and down, flaky golden eyes fixed on the door.

Lead shrieked through the space he had vacated. A pistol, firing from the jungle, made stuttering clamor.

"Tom Too!" Renny boomed.

Chapter XX
THE TIGHTENING NET

THE shot echoes were still bumping around over the island when Doc's five men turned loose with the little machine guns. The weapons poured bullet streams that were like rods of living metal. The slugs razored off leaves, twigs, branches the thickness of Monk's furry wrist.

After one volley they ceased firing.

Loud crashings reached their ears over the caterwauling of disturbed birds.

"He's beating it!" Renny shouted.

Doc and his men dived out of the room, leaving the cowering prisoners to their own devices. They weren't important game, anyway.

"Did you get a look at Tom Too's face, Doc?" Ham demanded.

"No. Only his gun shoving out through the leaves. I didn't even get the color of his skin. He was wearing gloves."

They spread out in a line, in the order of their running ability. Doc was far in the lead. Next was Johnny, gaunt and bony, but a first-class foot racer. Monk and Renny, the two giants, trod Johnny's heels. Ham and Long Tom were last, pretty evenly matched, with Ham the hindermost because he was trying to keep thorns from tearing his clothes. Ham was always jealous of his appearance.

"He's heading for the sampan!" Doc called.

An instant later they heard the outboard motor on the sampan start.

Doc reached the pondlike bay just in time to glimpse the stern of the sampan vanishing beyond the curtain of vines which screened the tiny harbor from the sea.

His men came up. They drove a few rasping volleys of lead at the drapery of creepers. Then they ran around the bay. This consumed much precious time.

The sampan was nearly three hundred yards distant, traveling like a scared duck.

If they had hoped to glimpse Tom Too's features,

they were disappointed. The pirate leader was not in sight.

"Lying in the bottom of the boat to be out of the way of bullets!" Renny said grimly, and took a careful bead on the distant sampan.

His gun moaned deafeningly. The others joined him. Their bullets tore splinters off the sampan stern and scraped the sea all about the craft. But the range was long, even for a rifle, and they did not stop the fleeing boat.

"Where is the raft you fellows came over on?" Doc demanded.

"Up the beach!" rapped Ham, and led the way.

The furry Monk lumbered alongside Ham. They came to a spot where mud was underfoot, slimy and malodorous. In the middle of this Ham suddenly fell headlong. He floundered, then bounced up, smeared with the smelly goo from head to foot. He waved his sword cane wrathfully.

"You tripped me, you hairy missing link!" he howled at Monk.

"Bugs to you!" leered Monk. "Can I help it if you fall over your own feet?"

However, Monk was careful to keep out of Ham's reach for the next few minutes.

Nobody had seen Monk do the tripping, but there was no doubt about his guilt. He had done worse things to Ham. And it was also certain that Ham would return the favor with interest. The going seldom got so hot that these two forgot to carry on their good-natured feud.

They reached the raft.

"IT'S a wonder the sharks didn't get you birds, riding that thing," said Doc, surveying the raft.

Monk snorted. He was in high good humor, now that he was one up on Ham.

"This shyster lawyer here wanted to feed me to 'em, claimin' they'd die of indigestion from eatin' me," he chuckled with a sidelong look at Ham. "Fallin' in the mud serves him right for makin' cracks like that."

Ham only scowled through the mud on his face.

The raft consisted of a pair of long logs, crumbling with rot, secured in catamaran form with crosspieces and flexible vines.

Doc eyed the sticks which had served as oars. They were highly inefficient.

"Put it in the water!" he directed. Then he vanished into the jungle.

The raft was hardly in the sea before Doc came back. He was carrying an armload of planks ripped from the house. These were much more suitable as paddles.

"What about the prisoners we left in the shack?" Renny demanded.

"They were still there." Doc exhibited one of the fingertip thimbles containing the drug-laden needles—thimbles which produced long-lasting unconsciousness. "They'll be there quite a while, too."

They shoved off, taking positions on the shaky raft like a trained rowing crew. In a moment the paddles were dipping with machinelike regularity, shoving the crude craft forward at a fair clip.

Their eyes now sought the sampan bearing Tom Too.

Doc had expected Tom Too to head for the pirate encampment on the south end of the island. But the sampan was skipping for the northern extremity, where the plane lay.

"We're in luck!" Doc said softly. "Tom Too doesn't know the temper of his cutthroats. He could dominate them easily and send the whole horde out to finish us. But he's afraid to go near them."

"Yeah, but he's headin' for our plane!" Monk grunted. "And there's bombs aboard it."

"Oh, no, there's not!" Ham clipped. "I stayed behind a little while last night after we heard the birds falling off their roosts and knew there was a gas cloud coming, long enough to chuck the bombs overboard."

The sampan swerved around the north end of Shark Head Island, entered the little bay, and was lost to sight.

Johnny spat a couple of words that would have shocked the natural science class he used to teach, and chopped at a cruising shark with his paddle. After that every one was careful that his feet did not drag in the water.

"Will they jump out of the water and grab a man?" Monk asked doubtfully.

"Probably not," said Johnny.

They kept their eyes on the little bay at the north end of Shark Head Island. The rattle of the outboard motor, made wispy by distance, had stopped.

Suddenly a shower of what looked like sparks shot into the air around the bay. The sparks were gaudily colored tropical birds. A moment later the froggy moan of plane motors wafted over the sea. It was their starting which had flushed up the birds.

"Why didn't you think to take something off the motors so they wouldn't run, wiseheimer?" Monk asked Ham.

Ham glared through his mud, said nothing. He did not dare dip up water to wash his face, due to the sharks.

Soon the plane skidded up into the sunlight. It wobbled, pitched, in the bumpy air. It flew like a duck carrying a load of buckshot.

"He's a rotten flyer!" Johnny declared.

"A *kiwi!*" Monk agreed.

The plane headed directly for the laboring raft.

Monk reached up and clawed his hair down over his eyes to keep the sun out. "I don't like this! That bird is going to crawl up. He may be the world's worst flyer, but I don't like it!"

RENNY followed Monk's example in getting his hair down on his forehead to shade his eyes from the sun. It was the next best thing to colored goggles. They'd have to look up to fight the plane. And gazing into the tropical sky was like looking into a white-hot bowl.

"We left machine guns on the plane!" he muttered. "It's gonna be tough on us!"

Johnny poked another shark in its blunt, tooth-pegged snout.

Doc Savage seemed unworried. He sat well forward, driving his paddle with a force that made the stout wood grunt and bend. So that his mighty strokes would not throw the raft off course, he distributed them on either side with scarcely an interruption in their machinelike precision.

Renny shucked out his pistollike machine gun and rapped a fresh cartridge clip in place.

"You won't need it," Doc told him.

"No?" Renny was surprised.

"Watch the plane!"

The amphibian came howling toward them. Tom Too was not trying for altitude; he wanted to be low enough to use his machine gun with effect—for no doubt he had found the rapid firers in the plane. His altitude was no more than five hundred feet.

"It's about time it happened!" Doc said grimly.

Doc's prediction was accurate.

Both motors of the amphibian suddenly stopped.

Tom Too acted swiftly. He kicked the plane around and headed it back for Shark Head Island. His banking about was sloppy; the ship side-slipped as though the air were greased.

"He can just fly, and that's all!" Monk grinned. "What stopped the motors, Doc?"

"I plugged the fuel lines close to the tanks," Doc replied. "The carburetor and fuel pipes held enough gas to take the craft upstairs, but no more."

The big bronze man neglected to add that it would have been simpler to cut off the fuel at the carburetors, but that this would not have left enough gas available to get the plane off should circumstances have sent them to the craft in such a hurry that they would not have had time to unplug the fuel lines.

Tom Too was gliding the dead-motored plane at a very flat angle, getting the maximum distance out of his altitude. Probably this was by accident rather than flying ability.

"Holy cow!" groaned Renny. "Is he gonna get back to Shark Head?"

"He will come down about a hundred yards offshore," said Doc after a glance of expert appraisal.

The estimate was close. With a sudsy splash, the amphibian plunked into the sea. It pushed ahead for a time under its own weight. It stopped a bit less than three hundred feet offshore.

Then the ship began to move backward—blown by the offshore breeze.

"He'll be blown right into our hands!" Ham ejaculated.

"Or he'll find the plugged fuel lines!" Monk pointed out.

TOM TOO wasted no time hunting for what had silenced the motors, however. Probably he was no mechanic. He appeared atop the amphibian cabin.

He was too distant for much to be told about his appearance. Even Doc's sharp vision could not distinguish the fellow's features.

One thing they did note—Tom Too carried a large brief case.

The pirate leader reached up and struck savagely at the plane wing. There was a knife in his fist.

"Hey!" squawled Monk. "He's lettin' the gas out of the tanks!"

It was worse than that. Tom Too backed up, struck a match, and flung the flame into the petrol drooling from the punctured tanks.

Flame gushed. It wrapped the amphibian until the craft was like a toy done in red tissue paper. Yellow smoke tossed away downwind, convulsing and boiling in the breeze.

Tom Too sprang into the sea. He swam madly for the shore of Shark Head Island.

Johnny gazed at the sharks cruising about the makeshift raft, then at the distant splashes that marked Tom Too's progress.

"That guy has got nerve!" grunted Johnny.

"Fooey!" said Monk. "A rat will fight a lion if he's cornered."

Doc Savage was standing up, still paddling, the better to watch Tom Too's progress.

Renny also watched. His eyes were second in sharpness to Doc's.

"There goes a shark for him!" Renny bawled suddenly.

They all saw the triangle of lead-hued shark fin cutting toward Tom Too.

"There ain't nothin' I like less than sharks!" Monk chuckled. "But I'm gonna find it hard to begrudge that one his meal!"

Tom Too had seen his danger. He swam desperately. But he did not lose his head. He kept his eyes on the approaching fin. It disappeared.

Tom Too promptly stopped. Doc caught the faint glitter of a knife in the pirate king's hand.

"He's going to handle the shark native fashion!" Renny grunted.

Distance hampered their view of what happened next. But they knew enough shark lore to guess. Sharks do not have to turn over to bite an object in the depths, but commonly do so to seize a man swimming on the surface. The pale bellies offer a warning flash.

Tom Too disappeared from sight momentarily. There was a splashing turmoil in the water. Tom Too's knife struck repeatedly.

The pirate leader appeared. He swam for shore with renewed energy.

"He got the shark—daggone it!" Monk wailed.

TOM TOO reached the beach without further incident. He sprinted for the jungle.

Doc's sharp eyes noted something the others missed—Tom Too no longer carried his briefcase. Evidently he had dropped it in his short fight with the shark.

The plane was burning briskly. Flame ate into the fuselage. A Fourth of July uproar came as heat exploded machine-gun bullets in the craft.

The ship sank suddenly.

Tom Too vanished into the jungle.

Doc and his men continued to bend their paddles.

They reached the spot where the plane had gone down. A score of yards beyond, the shark Tom Too had slain floated near the surface. The water lashed in turmoil about the carcass—half a dozen other sharks were devouring it.

"Whoa!" said Doc.

Monk wore in his belt a knife he had picked up somewhere. It was a serpentine-bladed kris.

Doc grasped the knife, clipped the blade between his strong teeth, and dropped off the shaky raft. He disappeared in the depths.

"Jimmy!" Monk gulped. "With all these sharks around, Daniel in the lions' den was a piker!"

They waited anxiously. Bubbles gurgled up from the sunken plane. A minute passed. Sixty feet away, cannibal sharks fought with horrible splashings. Another minute groped into eternity.

Doc did not appear.

On the shore, coarse-voiced tropical birds cried like hideous harpies.

Three clapping shots interrupted the birds. Monk ducked as a bullet made cold air kiss his furry neck, nearly lost his balance on the ramshackle raft, but recovered himself.

Tom Too had fired at them—water does not wet the powder in modern pistol cartridges.

Doc's five men sprayed lead at the jungle. There was nothing to show they hit Tom Too. But they kept him from shooting again.

Renny glanced at a waterproof wrist watch. He nearly screamed.

Doc had been beneath the surface a full four minutes!

Ten seconds later, Doc's bronze head split the water beside the raft. Doc's bronze hair and metallic skin had a strange quality; it seemed to shed water like the back of a duck; he could immerse himself, and his skin and hair would not seem wet when he reappeared.

Doc's shirt front bulged more than his chest should have made it.

Doc's five men wiped cold sweat off their foreheads. The fact that Doc had remained underwater so long was not in itself alarming. They had seen the giant bronze man stay below for incredible intervals. But the sharks made these waters reek death.

"Have any trouble?" Monk asked.

Doc shrugged. "Not much."

At this point a second shark carcass appeared beside the first. The hideous creature had been slain with a single expert knife rip. Monk and the others recognized Doc's handiwork. He had battled the monster underwater and dismissed it as "not much."

"Huh!" ejaculated Monk. "What were you doin' way over there? The sunken plane is under us."

"Tom Too had a briefcase with him, but dropped it when the shark tackled him," Doc replied. "I dived for it from here, not wanting him to know I was after it."

"You get it?"

The bulge in Doc's shirt front gave answer.

THEY now paddled the raft to shore. Tom Too did not fire at them again—a wise move on his part.

"Make for the sampan!" Doc directed.

They sped northward along the beach.

Monk glanced over his shoulder. "Hey—lookit!"

Wheeling, the rest saw Tom Too. The master pirate had come out on the beach half a mile to the south. He was running for dear life, headed for the encampment of his yellow cutthroat horde.

"I'm in favor of going after him!" Renny boomed. Apparently it did not occur to him that they might not be able to whip several hundred slant-eyed pirates who had been fighters all their lives.

"The sampan!" Doc said impatiently. "We'd better get it and clear out of here."

They resumed their sprint for the sampan, smashing their way through the jungle growth in a short cut across a little headland and reached the beach in short order.

"Good!" rapped Ham, catching sight of the sampan where Tom Too had beached it. "I was afraid he might have jabbed a hole in the bottom, or something."

Renny pointed at the outboard motor.

"Look!" he roared. "The gasoline has been let out!"

The valve of the fuel tank was located in such a position as to spill the emptying fuel upon the sand, where it was hopelessly lost.

"This puts us in a swell mess!" Monk groaned.

Four hardwood paddles reposed on the sampan floorboards. Doc indicated them. "Grab 'em!"

"We can't escape by paddling," Monk pointed

out. "The pirates have speed boats. Tom Too will send them after us."

With a mighty shove, Doc sent the sampan into the water.

"We'll get back to the other island!" he declared.

There was no more argument. The sampan surged away from the beach, propelled by lusty paddle strokes.

Ham, between sweeps of his paddle, nodded at the bulging front of Doc's shirt, which held the contents of Tom Too's briefcase.

"Do you suppose there's anything worthwhile in there?" he asked.

"We'll let that slip for a while and examine it later," Doc said, then leveled an arm. "Tom Too didn't lose much time!"

They all followed Doc's gesture. Around the other end of the island, a pair of junks appeared, together with several speed boats. More craft followed—junks, sampans, launches, and other boats.

The hardwood paddles bent and creaked as Doc's men increased their pace. Water split away from the sampan bows with a steady, sobbing noise. They were making good speed for the palm-crowned smaller island.

"We'll beat them to the island!" Ham decided aloud.

"Yes—and then what?" snorted Monk.

Doc's five men exchanged bleak looks. They were perfectly aware they had never faced greater odds. They were experienced fighting men, and they knew a fight against these hundreds of pirates could be nothing but hopeless.

A corsair machine gun dropped a shower of slugs some hundreds of yards short. The spent bullets continued to drop in the water, coming closer and closer. But the little island was now but a few fathoms distant away from the men.

The rasp of the sampan keel on the beach was a welcome sound.

Chapter XXI
SEA CHASE

DOC and his men piled out. A few rifle slugs made chopping noises in the tangled jungle growth. Doc eyed the belts and bulging pockets of his men.

"Got plenty of ammunition?" he questioned.

Monk grinned wryly. "Not as much as I'd like to have. We've got a couple or three hundred rounds apiece. That was about all we could swim with when we left the plane last night."

"Latch the guns into single-shot fire," Doc directed.

Each man flipped a small lever on his compact little machine gun. The weapons now discharged only a single bullet for each pull of the trigger.

Using a sampan paddle as a spade, Doc set to work digging a shallow rifle pit. He located it slightly within the jungle, so he could quit it without being observed.

The others followed his example, saying no word.

Straight toward the beach plunged the pirate boats. The launches, being more speedy, were far in the lead. The pirates had erected small shields of sheet steel in the craft—their usual precaution, no doubt, when going into battle.

Prows scooping foam, they approached to within two hundred yards. Then a hundred! Their speed did not slacken. A machine gun in the bow of one began to cough bullets through a slit in a metal shield. The lead hissed and screamed and tore in the jungle about Doc and his men.

"Let the first one land!" Doc commanded.

An instant later the leading speed boat hit the beach. It was traveling fast enough to skid high and dry out of the water. The slant-eyed killers, braced for the impact though they were, nevertheless slammed against thwarts and bulkheads.

"Now!" Doc clipped. "Get 'em in the legs and arms!"

His gun spat. The weapons of his men rapped a multiplied echo. They were crack marksmen, these men. They took their time and planted bullets accurately.

Two yellow men fell out of the launch almost together, hit in the legs. Pain made them squall noisily. Others cackled in agony as slugs, placed with uncanny precision, took them in the hands and arms.

There was psychology behind Doc's command not to kill. One wounded Oriental, yelling bloody murder, could do more to spread fear among his fellows than three or four killed instantly.

Bedlam seized the launch occupants. They could not even see Doc and his men. A tight group, they sought to charge. Those in the lead went down, legs drilled.

Howling, the gang ran back and tried to shove the launch into the water. They were not sufficient in number for the job. In remorseless succession, these also fell.

"Now—the other launches!" Doc ordered.

The volley he and his men fired sounded ragged, scattered. But hardly a bullet went wild.

The nearer launches, four in number, could not hold up before shooting like this. One careened about madly, the helmsman pawing a drilled shoulder, and barely missed crashing another craft. Then all four sheered off, the occupants expressing their opinion of Doc and his men in assorted tongues.

They were going to await the arrival of the heavier junks and sampans.

Monk, flattened in the pit he had scooped, asked Doc: "What now?"

Doc's pit was in the jungle to the right. No

answer came from the spot. Puzzled, Monk squirmed up to look.

Doc was gone. He had vanished silently the instant the fight was over.

NO more than a minute passed before Doc returned. He bore a bulky object—the army-type portable radio transmitter and receiver which Tom Too had left in the island cabin.

Doc gave a short gesture of command. The men plunged out of the jungle and leaped for the speed boat stranded on the beach.

A wounded pirate shot at them, but he was wounded in the arm, and missed. Doc fired a single bullet, and the corsair shrieked as the lead mangled his hand. The other yellow men fled, dragging themselves along or running furiously, depending on where they were hit.

Doc and his five aides laid hands on the launch, strained, and ran it back into the surf.

Out to sea, the pirates suddenly saw the purpose of Doc's strategy in permitting the most speedy craft to land. He was seizing the fast little vessel!

The slant-eyed buccaneers headed for the island again. Machine guns cackled from their boats, rifles whacked spitefully.

Doc shoved the nose of their own launch around while his men sprang aboard. Renny worked over the motor. The propellers had not been damaged by the forcible beaching.

Lead clanged on the sheet-steel shield, chewed splinters off the gunwales, and, hitting in the water nearby, dashed spray over them.

Doc and the others returned the fire with slow precision while Renny fought the motor. The engine caught with a blubbery roar. The light hull surged forward, the propellers flinging water up behind the stern.

At the tiller, Doc sent the boat parallel to the beach. In a moment they were stern-on to their enemies, rendering the steel bullet shield useless.

Doc wrenched the shield from its mounting. "Put it up in the stern."

Monk did that job. He howled wrathfully as lead hit the metal plate, transferring a sting to his hands. Renny lunged to help him, then grunted loudly and clapped a hand to the upper part of his left arm. He had been hit. He tore off the sleeve of his shirt with a single wrench.

"Missed the bone an inch!" he decided.

"We're going to make it!" Ham yelled. He was using the tip of his sword cane to jam a wadded handkerchief into a bullet hole in the launch hull near the water line.

Doc put the rudder hard over. The launch veered to the right—and was suddenly sheltered by the tip of the island. Bullets no longer came near them.

Setting a course toward the distant coast of one of the larger islands of the Luzon Union, Doc held the throttle wide. The boat, traveling at tremendous speed, jarred violently as it slammed across the tops of the choppy waves.

The corsair craft heaved around the end of the island. Once more bullets whistled about them. But they had gained considerably. Doc's men did not waste lead returning the fire.

Fifteen minutes of flight put them out of rifle shot. Doc cut their speed.

"Hey!" Monk grunted. "We low on gas or somethin'? Those birds aren't giving up the chase!"

"Plenty of gas," Doc told him, and fell to watching their pursuers.

IT was a weird-looking flotilla which followed them. Behind the fast launches were the sampans. Then came the junks, such of them as were fitted with engines in addition to sail power. They strung out for miles. The most sluggish of the sailboats were hardly outside the corsair bay on Shark Head Island.

One launch began to draw ahead of the others.

Doc opened the throttle, spun their speed boat about, and raced for the boat which had left the others behind. But not a single bullet was exchanged. Their quarry dropped back with the other pirates.

Continuing their flight, Doc turned the controls over to Monk.

Working swiftly, Doc tugged bundle after bundle of soggy papers, loose-leaf notebooks and cards from his shirt front—the stuff Tom Too's briefcase had held! He studied it with much interest.

"Anything worthwhile there?" Ham asked.

Elated little lights glowed in Doc's flaky golden eyes.

"Tom Too's organization was too large to keep track of without written records," he explained. "These are the records."

"A break, gettin' 'em, huh?" Monk grinned.

Not answering, Doc bent over the portable radio apparatus. He adjusted the dials. The tiny key was of the variety known as a sideswiper, requiring experience to manipulate. Doc fingered dots and dashes out of it with machinelike precision, then twirled the receiver dials, the headset pressed over his ears.

The noise of the launch motor prevented the others hearing what Doc was sending and receiving, although they were all expert operators. However, Doc began to consult notebooks and papers which had come from Tom Too's briefcase. That explained what he was doing.

"He's gotten hold of a Mantilla station and is giving them the names of Tom Too's men in the city," Ham decided. "That should enable Juan Mindoro, with a handful of reliable police, to clean the pirates out of town."

After a time Doc laid Tom Too's records aside. But he continued to send and receive over the radio instruments, evidently carrying on a conversation with the distant station. Finally he ceased, and studied his men quietly.

"Want to take a big risk on the chance of destroying this pirate fleet?" he demanded.

"Sure!" Monk said promptly.

"Should the motor of this boat fail, it'd mean our finish!" Doc warned the men.

Monk made a gesture of patting the throbbing engine. "I'm willing to take that chance."

The others seemed of a like mind.

Doc resumed transmitting over the radio, and sent rapidly for some minutes. Then he deserted the apparatus and took over the launch controls.

Their boat now dawdled along just out of rifle range of the pursuers. Twice during the next two hours Doc swerved back as though to attack the leading launches of the yellow men. These retreated warily.

The hazy bulk of one of the larger islands of the Luzon Union heaved up ahead. Doc worked over the radio set. He seemed satisfied with the coded information which he had plucked out of the ether.

Swinging a wide circle, Doc and his men turned back for Shark Head Island. Like the tail on a slow comet, the pirate fleet followed.

DOC'S boat was at least a dozen miles an hour faster than the swiftest of their pursuers. Several times bullets danced on the water near them, but the yellow men did not get close enough for accurate shooting.

The sun, which had blazed upon them with a heat that almost cooked, balanced like a red-hot stove lid above the evening horizon.

The corsair bay of Shark Head Island opened before the launch. The entire fleet manned by the slant-eyed men had been left behind.

Renny, standing erect to get the first glimpse into the bay, groaned: "Aw—blazes!"

On the shore of the little harbor stood a number of yellow cutthroats. These were ill or wounded pirates who had been left behind.

"They won't give us much trouble!" Doc decided.

Nor did they. Doc beached the launch some hundreds of yards from the Orientals. He sent a few long-range shots at the fellows to stop their charge, then plunged, along with his men, into the jungle.

With all sails set and engines laboring, the corsair vessels began reentering the bay. Howling, brandishing weapons, yellow men dived into the jungle. They were highly elated. They couldn't understand why the big bronze man and his five aides had deliberately put themselves in a trap, but they did not give that much thought.

There was one exception—the buccaneers aboard the largest of the junks, the vessel which was fitted lavishly with tapestries, paintings, rich rugs, and inlaid furniture. In the hold of this craft was a powerful engine.

It bore Tom Too himself. The master pirate did not land. Instead, after directing his men to pursue Doc, he ordered his junk to stand out to sea.

The Oriental craft was plowing through the mouth of the bay when a pair of speedy planes dropped out of the evening sky. Without the slightest hesitation, the aircraft loosened machine guns upon Tom Too's vessel.

Matting sails of the junk acquired great ragged rips. Splinters flew from the decks and hulls. Several of the crew dropped. Others replied to the machine-gun fire of the planes. A bomb, dropped by one of the aircraft, narrowly missed the junk, but made it roll sickeningly. The junk put back into the bay.

Out of the twilight haze that mantled the sea plunged several slender, gray, grim vessels. These were destroyers, little larger than submarine chasers, of the type that served the Luzon Union as a navy. Other planes appeared—giant tri-motored bombers and fast, single-engined pursuit ships.

The truth dawned on the yellow pirates. Instead of the bronze man being trapped, they were themselves cornered.

Doc had summoned aid by radio!

Chapter XXII
RED BLADE

FROM the concealment of the jungle, Doc and his men watched developments.

"Juan Mindoro is aboard one of the planes," Doc declared. "At least, he should be, according to the information he gave me by radio."

"Can he depend on the men manning the planes and destroyers?" Ham questioned uneasily. "Tom Too may have some of them on his payroll."

"He did have," Doc admitted. "But the records I got out of that briefcase gave their names, and I passed the dope on to Mindoro. Tom Too's hirelings are under arrest."

Monk kneaded his enormous, furry hands. "How about us getting in this scrape?"

"We'll tackle that big junk," Doc agreed. "Tom Too is probably aboard."

The junk in question had hove to close to the beach. Yellow men were dropping a light boat overside, evidently to be used in ferrying Tom Too ashore. A bomb exploded in the bay, and the wall of water it flung out smashed the small boat against the junk hull.

Doc and his men ran for a sampan beached nearby. They were fired upon, and returned the lead. A plane dived upon them, unable to distinguish them from foes in the increasing darkness. Doc led the others back into the jungle to evade the searching machine-gun metal. There they encountered a gang of a dozen desperate pirates. They fought, skulking in the jungle, each party shooting at the gun flashes of the other.

Plane motors bawled overhead. The planes flew so low that prop streams thrashed palm fronds. Detonating bombs made such concussions that the very island jumped and shuddered. Men yelled, cursed in an assorted score of dialects. Machine guns gobbled continuously.

"Kinda like old times!" Renny rumbled in the gloom.

Doc and his fellows rushed the yellow gang with whom they skirmished. Doc used only his hands in the scrap that followed. He moved like a bronze phantom. Man after man fell before his fists, or was rendered helpless with wrenched and broken limbs. The pirate group broke and fled.

"To the sampan!" Doc's powerful voice commanded. "We'll make another try at reaching that big junk!"

They ran out on the beach, found the sampan, and shoved off.

Overhead, a plane dropped a parachute flare, then another. The calcium glare whitened the entire island.

The illumination showed Tom Too's junk trying to work out of the bay. Destroyers, however, blocked its escape. The hulking vessel turned back.

The flares sank fizzing into the sea and were extinguished. Bending to the sampan paddles, Doc's party headed for the junk.

"They won't expect to be boarded from a small boat," Renny boomed softly.

Doc guided the sampan expertly. They came alongside the junk in the gloom. A pirate saw them, hailed. Doc answered in a disguised tone, speaking the same dialect, telling the corsairs to hold their fire.

The sampan gunwale rasped along the junk hull. All six leaping at once, Doc's gang gained the deck of the larger vessel.

ANOTHER bomb, exploding harmlessly on the distant beach, threw a flash like pale lightning. It disclosed Doc's identity.

A yellow man howled and leaped, swinging a short sword. Doc twisted from under the descending blade. His darting fist seemed a part of the same movement. The Oriental collapsed, his jaw hanging awry.

Fighting spread swiftly from end to end of the junk as Doc's men scattered. In the darkness, they could fight best when separated.

Doc himself made for the high, after part of the vessel, seeking Tom Too.

Below decks, the Orientals manning the engines became excited and threw the craft into full speed ahead. It plowed about aimlessly, no hand at the tiller.

Doc found a long bamboo pole, evidently a makeshift boat hook. He converted it to a weapon of offense, jabbing and swinging it in club fashion. A corsair bounced off the pole end as if he were a billiard ball, and tangled with one of his fellows.

The little machine guns had been latched back into rapid-fire. Once more they tore off series of reports so rapid they resembled the sound of coarse cloth tearing.

"One!" Doc barked.

"Two!" echoed Renny's strong voice. "Three!" said Long Tom. The others called off in rapid succession—four, five, six!

This was a procedure they followed often when fighting in the darkness. It not only showed the entire gang was still up and going, but also advised each man where the others were located.

Doc descended a carved companionway. He wanted to get the engines stopped before the junk crashed into some other craft.

He found the engine room without difficulty. Only two Orientals were there, huddling nervously under the pale glow of an electric lantern. They offered no fight at all, but threw down their weapons at Doc's sharp command. Doc shut off the motors.

"Where is Tom Too?" Doc asked.

The yellow men squirmed. They were scared. They had seen this giant bronze man slain by the sword and his body burned. Was he a devil, that he could come to life again?

One pointed toward the stern. "Maybe Tom Too, he go that dilection," he singsonged.

Doc made for the spot—the richly fitted quarters which were no doubt Tom Too's private rooms. Two Orientals barred his way. He was almost touching them before they were aware of his presence, so dark was the junk interior.

Doc shoved them both violently, and while they stumbled about and slashed viciously at black, empty air, he eased past them. There was movement ahead, and the glow of a flashlight.

A faint rasping sounded—a windowlike porthole of the junk being opened! It must be Tom Too, Doc knew. And the man was in the act of escaping from the junk into the waters of the bay.

Doc flung for the port—and had one of his narrowest escapes from death. Tom Too was easing through the porthole feet first. He turned his flashlight on Doc and threw a knife.

Doc saw the blade only when it glinted in the flash beam. He dodged, got partially clear. The blade lodged like a big steel thorn in his side, outside the ribs.

Tom Too dropped through the port. His madly splashing strokes headed for shore. Suddenly the splashing increased. A terrified scream pealed out.

Doc leaned from the porthole.

Overhead, a plane dropped another aerial flare.

been more timely, for the swimming figure of Tom Too was plainly disclosed.

A small shark had seized the pirate leader. Tom Too had no knife with which to defend himself this time—he had expended that on Doc. The corsair chief screeched and beat at the grisly monster which had fastened upon his leg.

The shark was but little longer than Tom Too. For a moment it seemed the pirate king would escape. Then a larger sea killer closed upon the human morsel.

Tom Too's distorted face showed plainly before he was submerged to his death.

The features were those of slender, dapper First Mate Jong of the ill-fated liner, *Malay Queen*.

IT was dawn, and the sun blazed a flame of victory in the east. The fighting was over. A cowed, frightened cluster, the surviving pirates had been herded upon the beach and were under heavy guard, awaiting consignment to a penal colony.

The planes had managed to land on a level portion of the beach. Juan Mindoro had boarded the big junk. He was striving to express his gratitude to Doc Savage and the other five adventurers who had done so much for his native land.

"I have just received a radio message from Mantilla," he said, addressing Doc. "Thanks to the information in Tom Too's records, which you gave us, the pirates in Mantilla have been captured, almost to a man. They even got Captain Hickman, of the *Malay Queen*. There is only one thing bothering me—are you certain Jong was Tom Too?"

"Positive," Doc told him. "The records disclosed that Jong, or Tom Too, undoubtedly bribed Captain Hickman to sign him on the *Malay Queen* as first mate."

Mindoro ran a finger inside his collar and squirmed. "Words seem very flat when I try to express my thanks to you. I shall ask the Luzon Union government to appropriate a reward for—"

"Nix," Doc said.

Mindoro smiled, went on: "—a reward which I think you will accept."

Mindoro was right, for the reward was one Doc found entirely satisfactory. It consisted of a simple bronze plate bearing the plain words: "The Savage Memorial Hospital."

The plate was embedded in the cornerstone of a structure that cost millions. Other millions were placed in trust to insure operation of the hospital for years. The institution was to operate always under one inflexible rule—payment from no one but those who could afford it.

The laying of the cornerstone was accomplished with ceremony before Doc and his men left the Luzon Union.

Monk, uncouth in high hat and swallowtail coat, perspired under the derisive gaze of the dapper Ham throughout the ceremony. He was glad when it was over and they got out of the admiring crowd.

"Fooey!" snorted Monk, and made a present of his high silk hat to a brown-skinned, half-naked street urchin. "It'll take a good fight to get me feelin' like a human being again!"

MONK was destined not to wait long for his fight. The fame of Doc Savage and his five men was spreading, and it was that fame which was to plunge them into the thick of a labyrinth of death, violence, and deceit. It was a slice of hell itself which the future held, a slice carved from the heat-blistered deserts and rugged canyons of the Western United States. A great dam was under construction, and even now a mysterious terror had dropped its clutch upon the humans laboring there.

Monk was going to get his fight, even if he didn't know it.

THE END

Somewhere in the fastness of the African jungle is a tremendous reward—a prize in wealth and the lives of human beings. From within

THE LOST OASIS

comes a call for help to Doc Savage, the only man who can overcome the evil forces that rule this dread spot from which there is no escape! Then, lost in the Sargasso Sea, unwary ships great and small fall prey to

THE SARGASSO OGRE

in a thrilling adventure with all the glamour of the sea, the mystery of nature's inexplicable wonders and the marvels of Doc Savage's abilities.

Don't miss these two action-packed thrillers in *DOC SAVAGE* #7!